Darken
the
Stars

The Kri

&v&

Darken the Stars

The Kricket Series
Volume 3

AMY A. BARTOL

47N●RTH

Published by 47North, Seattle

www.apub.com

Amazon, the Amazon logo, and 47North are trademarks of Amazon.com, Inc., or its affiliates.

ISBN-13: 9781503947429
ISBN-10: 1503947424

Cover design by Mae I Design

Printed in the United States of America

For Tommy, Max, and Jack: for when things became dark

Contents

Darken the

Stars

PROLOGUE

Archive: The Order of the Tempest

Are you sure we're in knob-knocking Amster, Jax?" Wayra Waters whispers as he stands watch by the door. It's dark in the command center control room they've just broken into. He rubs a scrap of cloth over his throat, wiping the sweat from the black tribal tattoos that mark him as a Rafe soldier.

"We're in the north corridor of the abandoned city." Jax Roule's deft fingers conduct the virtual keypad of the holographic screen with military precision. As he sifts through hundreds of holographic image files, a sliver of light falls on his violet eyes. "This place is a decaying skeleton with modern innovation wired into it."

Wayra ignores the crumbling Gothic architecture. His focus is on his job as watch. "I bet you can't even get venish here," he mumbles. His lips twist with scorn. "How long will it take you to infiltrate their technology?"

"I'm in," Jax replies. "How are we?"

"We're clear. Their patrol is at midcycle. Did you locate Kricket?"

"No."

Wayra's fierce stare turns sharply to Jax. "Stop messing around. We have to find and extract her."

Jax's grim expression is half in shadow. "She's not here—"

"It's true then? That band of Alameeda half-breeds who raided us gave her to Kyon Ensin?"

Jax nods. "They traded her to him for her sister, Astrid Hollowell."

"That's messed up—I didn't even know Kricket had a sister."

"I don't think Kricket knew either. You want to hear something worse? I think I just found her father."

"You're lying!" Wayra accuses, his nostrils flaring in anger.

"No, I'm not. It's Pan Hollowell. He's alive."

"Where has he been all her life?"

"Here."

"On Ethar?"

"In Amster."

"What's he been doing here?"

"It looks like he's been building an army of rebels." Jax searches some more. "I found something." he hisses. Wayra takes another long look outside before joining Jax by the hologram projector.

"What is it?"

"It's a training tape—it's for these half-breed soldiers who run this city—they call themselves the Order of the Tempest."

"What a bunch of nims!" Wayra scoffs and comes closer to the virtual image.

"Here, watch this hologram. It's Pan in Amster before they rebuilt this fortress several floans ago. He's explaining the Order of the Tempest—and Black Math!" Jax tugs the earpiece from his ear and hands it to Wayra, who puts it in his ear as Jax replays the message.

Pan Hollowell's larger-than-life image walks on air in the holographic channel. Filmed amid the ancient ruins of the city of Amster, Pan looks every bit like a military officer in his black uniform.

"He's one of us!" Wayra whispers. "He could've been in our unit!"

"He's ex-Cavar, you can tell by his tat—he was a Rafe Triclone in the war before this one." Jax points to the concentric triangle tattoos that cover the side of Pan's throat.

"How old is this recording?" Wayra asks.

"Almost as old as Kricket. Shh! This is the part I want you to hear!" Jax says.

In the recording, Pan's piercing eyes scan the devastation surrounding him. "Black Math had its origins here," he says, "in the once-thriving metropolis of Amster. This plague destroyed most of Ethar a thousand floans ago." He walks among the desolate shells of buildings. "Many people believe that it was a naturally occurring epidemic, begun by chance. They're wrong. Black Math was inflicted on masses of Etharian citizens by a man named Excelsior Ensin, to seize power from established nations and to form the five Houses of Ethar: Rafe, Comantre, Peney, Wurthem, and Alameeda.

"For centuries, Excelsior Ensin has been creating an enhanced race of female Etharians known as the Priestesses of Alameeda. Through genetic manipulation, these females are all born with extrasensory gifts. These gifts range from telekinesis, to soothsaying, to mind control and more. My consort, Arissa Hollowell, inherited one such gift: the gift of prophecy.

"The Alameeda Brotherhood has made it illegal for males with the same abilities to exist. They hunt them because they fear them. It's why we've formed our secret society here in the abandoned city of Amster. We will save them because they are the future of Ethar.

"This is the origin of the Order of the Tempest. Our mission is to protect the true priestess of the prophecy: the priestess, born of two worlds and two Houses. She will become our Empress of Ethar."

CHAPTER 1
PULLED UNDER

Kyon's lips against mine are coaxing. With aching gentleness, he attempts to ease the resistance he finds in my tight-lipped response to his kiss. "Kricket," he whispers. *His lips should be cold,* I think, *a mirror of his ice-blue stare.* I try to turn my head and escape the curves of his mouth. My lips skim lightly over the stone rigidness of his jaw, tasting the saltiness of the sea air that settles there. His lips hunt mine, finding them again— claiming ownership by covering them once more.

The pleasure he finds at having me in his arms is unmistakable. His heartbeat drums against my hand on his chest. I gasp as my fingertips feel the small, raised scar on his skin—the only indication that I'd stabbed him. Kyon wastes no time in seizing the opportunity my parted lips present. His tongue delves into my mouth, stroking against mine. A shiver trembles through me. He feels it. It prompts him to pull me tighter to his body.

My thin nightgown is no protection from the heat of his bare chest. It seeps through the cloud of white fabric. I'm dwarfed by the size of him. He holds me with his hand against my lower back while his other hand traces a delicate path to my shoulder. Continuing on, his warm fingers splay against the nape of my neck. *He can snap it without even trying,* my mind whispers.

The warmth from Kyon's hand causes goose bumps to spread over my flesh. His kisses turn demanding—restless against my lips. I listen to the soft, lapping water pushing its way onto the white sand near us. The sea breeze lifts my hair from around my shoulders, scattering long blond strands of it across Kyon's masculine cheek. He moves his grasp to my jaw. His thumb caresses my earlobe as strong fingers entwine in my hair.

While Kyon's lips continue their assault, I'm a ghost in the darkness, waiting while my mind works out what to do. My knuckles must be white and bloodless—my fingernails pierce my palms. He won't allow me to pull away.

With a growl, I bite down hard on Kyon's bottom lip, tasting his blood. My knee comes up in an attempt to connect with his groin. I miss.

He seizes my wrist, twisting it behind my back, forcing me to let go of his lip before he breaks my arm. I'm pinned to him. My cheek presses against the brutal solidness of his chest. It's no haven from pain. His huge fist twists in my hair at the base of my skull. He jerks it and makes me look up until our eyes meet.

He's furious. Blood seeps from his bottom lip. I match his stare with a defiant one of my own.

Seeing enough, he lets go of my wrist and lifts me off my feet, hoisting me over his shoulder. He crosses the stone patio to a wrought-iron gate. He unlatches the ornate catch. It doesn't squeak as it swings wide. His bare feet sink into white sand. I pound on his back with my fist, trying to kick my legs, but they're trapped in the vise of his forearm. "Let go!" I demand.

I lurch up and make a grab for his hair, but he drops me down so far that I can't gain enough leverage to get to it. Reaching the water, he pulls me off his shoulder and secures me in his arms. He keeps my wrists pinned so I can't hit him. When the first cold wave splashes me, soaking my white nightgown, I begin to panic in earnest.

"Don't!" I yell. It comes out in a high-pitched screech. I look up at his handsome profile, seeing his jaw clench. He doesn't reply, he just continues to take me farther out into the water. "No, no, no, *nooo!*" Waist deep, he stops. Violently, he grips me by the front of my nightgown and plunges me into the water, holding me under. My hair waves in my face, floating in the current. With eyes wide open, I see the phosphorescent glow of coral. Its shine causes my skin to take on a greenish-blue tint. I hold my breath. My heart wants to break out through my chest. Gripping Kyon's brutal forearm, I dig my nails into him, scratching so that he'll let go of me. It does nothing. I beat on his arm with my fist. He pulls me up out of the surf. My nose and throat burn, and I choke and gasp for air. I can feel the heavy blond tendrils of my hair plastered to my face.

Kyon's fist tightens again. I'm thrust under the water and held down. The lack of oxygen makes my lungs feel like they'll explode at any second. I panic. Every cell of my body fights for life, except for a small part of me, which is tempted to succumb to the madness of the moment. Kyon expects me to struggle, but he doesn't want me dead. He went through so much trouble to have me—too much to kill me now. He wants my compliance—acceptance of the fact that he and the Alameeda Brotherhood own me. I have to gain the upper hand. I have to figure out a way to control a control freak.

I stop struggling against him, allowing my fingernails that are dug into his wrist to ease. I let go of him. My hands slip into the water, beneath the surf. My limbs wave in the current washing over me, lost within its embrace.

Kyon pulls me up once more. I break through the surface of the water. The starlight is just a blur. The glow from the Sea of Stars is reflected on Kyon's angry face, highlighting the tight muscles of his neck and his cold stare. "Give up?" he asks me quietly.

"Never," I croak.

"I can kill you right now."

"You won't."

"How do you know?" he asks in a sinister tone.

"I'm your *little savage*. You want me too much."

It's there on his face. I'm right. We both know it. "I do want you too much," he admits, "but I won't tolerate defiance."

"You're sadistic. You enjoy defiance. It's what makes me different from everyone else. I won't blindly obey you."

"I like it when you use your mind. But you're wrong," he says with a gentle voice as his fingers brush my wet hair from my cheek. "Right now I insist upon your obedience."

A wave crashes into my back, pushing me against his chest. I clutch his shoulders and try to steady myself in the water. His hands move from the front of my nightgown to my waist. When the next wave pushes me forward, my breasts press against his chest, and his expression changes from anger to desire. He leans near; his rough cheek rubs against my much softer skin.

"I brought you here to hurt you," Kyon murmurs, the timbre of his voice rumbles through his chest into mine. His words make my heart squeeze tight.

"Do your worst," I retort with bravado, but inside I quake.

"Nothing's in your control. When I hurt you—or how," he replies, summing up my problem in a nutshell. "Submit to me. I own you."

"You sound like owning me is something remarkable—an accomplishment. You don't know what you have, do you?" I ask with an insincere smile. "I'm just a collection of sad stories, Kyon."

"I want to know every one of those stories. Don't fight me. We can make our story perfect."

My blood is as thin as the seawater surrounding me. It courses through my veins too quickly, making me dizzy. "Where would be the fun in that?"

The deep rumble of his laughter vibrates through my chest as he holds me closer. "Our story will never end, Kricket. I'll never let you go—not when we fit so well together. You're my darker half."

My eyes widen in surprise. "You've gotta be kidding, Kyon. If anyone is dark, it's you."

"A star will shine brighter than all the other stars just before it goes dark forever," he murmurs, as if it's a secret he's imparting to me.

"You mean as it explodes and extinguishes forever?"

"I mean right before it transforms into something infinitely more powerful. And once your heart turns black, there will be no escaping it."

"If I'm the dark one between us, why am I afraid of you?" I ask.

"Because you should be."

My trembling becomes more pronounced under his intense gaze. I have to hide everything from him—keep everything I'm thinking a secret. His assault on me will be brutal—mentally as well as physically.

I have no place to hide, not the way the stars have aligned against me. I'm in this with Kyon until I find a way out. That realization makes me do something that I never thought I'd do in a million years: I pull Kyon to me and rest my cheek against his shoulder. Our feet touch beneath the water; toe-to-toe we stand. "I don't want to be dark."

Kyon's arms tighten around me before he slides his hand up my back to the nape of my neck. "You make me want to beat the life out of you one moment, and in the next I ache to drag you to the beach and make love to you in the sand."

"Is there an option C?"

His touch is restless; the same as the sea that swirls around us. "No. No option C."

He lifts me up in his arms and brings me to the shore. My blood drains away from my face. He lays me on the sand and covers me with his body. I expect to be crushed, but I'm not. He holds his weight on his elbows. Still, I'm trapped, unable to move from beneath the cage he's created with his enormous frame. Waves pour over our feet and thighs. The glow from the two moons above us is enough to see every line of his sharp jaw as he studies me.

"I want this." His nose skims up my throat in an intimate caress.

"I don't," I growl between my teeth.

"You need someone you can't control. Someone who will protect you and advise you."

I point a finger at his face. "You're wrong. I need to be in control. Without it, I'm desperate. Knob knockers like you have tried to control me my entire life!"

"You seem to be out of options," he says, but he doesn't make any move to kiss me again. He just studies me as if I'm a mermaid washed up on the shore.

My mind whispers, *Don't stay* . . . I hope for the Sea of Stars to swallow me up. "There's one option you haven't thought of, Kyon," I reply. I concentrate, wishing for sweet oblivion. Escape. A tear slips from my eye as I whisper, "Trey."

CHAPTER 2
LISTEN TO YOU BREATHING

I'm violently ripped away from myself. My consciousness leaves my body. Hovering above me for a moment, I see Kyon holding my cold, lifeless form. He notices the change in me immediately. He knows I'm no longer there. Shaking me in anger, he growls when I don't open my eyes. "Kricket," he snarls, knowing somehow that I'm still here. He pulls my lifeless body up from the sand, gripping my shoulders; he shelters my wet body from the pull of the sea.

My attention wanes from Kyon because I'm everywhere and nowhere; woven in the air with only one thought: Trey. I become a compass needle searching for north. In no time, I'm miles high, scorched by heat even when I'm bathed in darkness that only the light of the Etharian moons relieves.

I travel over the water. It glows beneath me with an ancient, iridescent fire. A galaxy of stars burn beneath its surface, but the Sea of Stars doesn't last. I flash forward, crossing over cities I've never been to before, past mountains and wilderness that harbor herds of creatures for which I have no names. In the moonlight, the abandoned husk of the City of Amster slouches. I recognize it from the time that I had traveled through the restricted area with Trey on my way to Rafe. It sits in a valley and grows haphazardly into the horizon. Waves of decrepit buildings crest the landscape in currents.

What I know of this city is that a plague called Black Math deci-mated it more than a thousand years ago. Ancient walls that were built up to the clouds are crumbling now. The wind whistles through their broken windows, echoing low, sorrowful moans.

I arrive at a dust-covered junction where buildings meet to form a triangle. Abandoned vehicles line the streets. Weathered by time, they resemble the skeletons of decaying beasts. No one stirs to disturb the quiet of the rusting boneyard.

I lurch sideways, being tugged to marble steps in front of a gothic, gray stone structure. I move like a ghost through the tangle of vine and vegetation that clings to the twisted stone railings. I don't use the entry-way ahead, but instead surge through the solid wall as lightning into a metal rod. Dust-covered marble floors inlaid with gold greet me on the other side. Above me, cathedral ceilings with fresco paintings of elaborate detail spreads out as if they were tattoos on an aging sailor. Their fading colors still portray the beauty of a bygone era.

Movement draws my attention. Around me, soldiers like matchstick men with fiery eyes and thin, well-honed bodies keep watch at strategic points. They're ready to take fire and give it. Clad in feather-light high-polymer vests, they're heavily armed with sophisticated weaponry. Their sharp eyes look right through me, invisible as I am, not being of their time but, rather, days behind them.

This building is a gateway, *I think.* They're defending something.

I don't remain with them, but lurch through grand cathedral-like chambers until I pass through the outer wall onto a raised stone terrace. Outside once more, my whole perspective changes in an instant. It's an oasis in a wasteland of decay. Gone are the dilapidated shell buildings; they're replaced by a small, sparsely lit city. It's concealed under an iri-descent dome, which rises into the night sky.

I'm drawn down the stone steps with a swift yank. Lamps hover on either side of the walkways near grassy thoroughfares. I ghost-move by the floating lights that resemble elaborate Aries' heads. Its wrought-iron horns coil around its ears. Passing beneath one, I see that light shines out from the bleating ram's mouth.

My attention shifts to the buildings. They've been patched up with repurposed items. One of the majestic gothic-style edifices has an awning made from the blade of huge turbine windmills that used to generate power for the ancient city. Sturdy, herringbone-etched columns, bearded by leafy vines, holds it up. Another building clearly had a domed capital at one time, but now it has a flat metal roof with wicked-looking aircraft crouching on its brow.

A pair of hovercycles power up and take off. Quiet and stealthy, the cycles draw closer. I note the riders are the same type of matchstick men whom I saw when I first entered this city. They drive slowly, patrolling the empty thoroughfare with just the low hum of their vehicles to mark their progression.

I hurry forward and pass through an archway. It's guarded on either side by gigantic statues of sword-wielding strongmen. I spare only a brief glance at the statues' maniacal expressions, their laurel crowns of blue-green patina, and their general nakedness—only enough time to make sure the statues remain inanimate.

I pass over a thick concrete slab bridge that was added over a dry moat. A courtyard greets me on the other side. This must've been the residence of the mayor or some other figurehead of the city. It's a head-quarters now, inhabited by more matchstick men built for war, if the dull fire in their eyes is any indication.

The cavernous old building houses a flurry of activity. Sophisticated control rooms make up most of the ground floor. Monitoring stations wrap around central holograms amid the backdrop of the ornate, gothic chambers. The holograms map out and scrutinize sections of Amster, but others monitor a variety of places on Ethar. I recognize the Isle of Sky—or what's left of it. In the war-torn streets of Rafe's city, just out-side the courthouse where I was made Manus's ward, the wounded and dead lie in piles in the streets while Alameeda Strikers, wearing eerie, snake-coiled gas masks with owlish eyeholes, point flamethrowers at them and turn them into billowing-embered bonfires.

The Amster soldier nearest me watches the carnage playing out on the holographic screen. His expression changes from stoic to fearful. It unnerves me as much as the scene in the holographic image. I don't want to see more. I keep moving, skirting another hologram—this one of a pristine city where fireworks of every color burst and shatter the skyline with brilliant-colored letters spelling out the Etharian word for V I C T O R Y in the darkness. The scene draws a crowd of soldiers. Their passionate eyes are made shiny by the colorful light before them, painting their faces burning red, gold, and umber.

Time won't wait for me to figure out what's going on. The invisible chain I'm dangling on tugs me toward the wide stairs in the corner of the room. The black uniformed Amster soldiers on the staircase don't know I'm there. I pass through them uncontested and rise up the uneven flagstone. It winds around inside the walls like a spiraling seashell. I reach a landing. A commissary encompasses this floor. I don't stop, but continue to climb, following the urgent tug.

Behind me there's a loud clatter. Giffen stands in front of an overturned chair amid a roomful of soldiers who continue to move and talk around him. His handsome features bear the expression of someone who has had all the hairs on the back of his neck stick straight up. His long, sandy-colored dreadlocks fall behind his shoulders and away from his face as he turns his head. His eyes, as they dart in my direction, are unexpectedly intimate. For a moment I think he sees me. He flexes his hands in an animalistic way as he straightens his broad shoulders, but his green eyes leave me and scan the area, searching for the source of the change of energy in the air. I'm glad he can't see me. I'm not here to talk to him. I hope he thinks I'm a demon rising from the dead.

Without pause, I'm dragged to the top of the building. I pass through a large carved-stone threshold into a high-ceilinged room with dormers that lead to the rooftop outside. Unoccupied, hovering cots line the walls *in rows. The lighting is so dim that anyone could hide in the crevices of the room undetected. A low hum of a distant machine captures my attention. In the last hoverbed in the corner I find Trey. My nonexistent stone heart squeezes tight like a phantom limb.*

Unconscious on a hovering cot, Trey is surrounded by odds and ends of wires and tubes. They appear to be some sort of monitoring system, checking his vital signs. A thick metal band clamps his brow and wraps around the circumference of his head. The band has readouts made of flashing lights.

I eliminate the space between us, if not the time, by crawling in bed beside him, cuddling my phantom form up to his real one. "I'm here," I say the words, but I don't know if he can hear me. Maybe they're just thoughts.

From around the corner comes the thump of running feet. Astrid skitters into the room with a startled expression on her face. She reaches out and grasps the back of a chair to steady her tall frame. She bends a bit at the waist, trying to catch her breath. She clearly ran up the stairs outside to get here. Tossing her long black hair back over her shoulder, she straightens and glances behind her as Raspin tumbles into view. His large form fills the doorway. He sweeps the bangs of his copper-colored hair away from his face as he watches Astrid.

Giffen taps Raspin on the shoulder, getting his attention so that he can squeeze by his friend and enter the room. Giffen looks around in confusion and says, "I thought I felt—"

"Shh!" Astrid shushes him. She looks away from her two companions. "Kricket," she whispers breathlessly, and as she says my name, it's as if the sound emanates from within me even as she speaks. Her blue eyes—so like our mother's—scan the room. Giffen watches her. He isn't breathing heavily at all, even though I know he must've run up a ton of stairs to be here.

Astrid takes tentative steps to the middle of the room. "Kricket," she says again as she turns in a circle. It's a vibration in my mind—a thought.

Her special talent of communicating nonverbally works even without my body being present.

Raspin extends his hand to Astrid protectively. "Astrid—"

"Hush!" she admonishes him with her finger to her lips. "She's here! I know it."

"How do you know?" Raspin asks while moving closer to Astrid. He peers warily into the dark corners of the room.

Astrid raises her hand and turns around again slowly, holding it out in front of her. She stops turning when she faces me again. She takes a step in my direction. "I feel her."

From behind her, Giffen says, "I feel her too."

I ignore them. "Trey," I try to speak to him. I see him breathing, but his normally vibrant skin is pale and drawn.

Astrid's head snaps in our direction. "It is you! I knew I felt you!" She turns to Raspin and says, "It's her! She's here!" Raspin's tall Frankenstein-like frame inches closer to Astrid. He hovers indecisively, as if I pose a threat to her in my astral state. He clearly can't hear me. Scratching his long, copper-colored head, he adopts a vacant stare, trying to puzzle out why he can't see or hear me.

Astrid nears Trey and me. "He's responding well," she says gently. "He woke for a few moments earlier. He asked for you."

"He did?" I hate the way that sounds—weak.

"Yes," Astrid says, nodding.

"What's wrong with him?" I demand.

"His brain swelled. We were able to decrease the inflammation, though."

Fear infects me. "Will he be okay?"

"Yes," she says.

"Does he know I'm . . . gone?"

"That you've been handed over to the Alameeda?"

"Yes."

"That was never supposed to happen!" The words tumble out of her in a rush. "When I figured out what they did—"

"Does he know?"

She raises her hand in a helpless gesture toward Trey. "No. We haven't told him yet. There hasn't been time. He only just woke up and it was brief—I'm so sorry, Kricket! I didn't—"

"Don't! Don't talk to me! Just go away. Leave us alone!" I warn.

Astrid flinches. She wrings her hands and glances at Giffen. His jaw ticks. Giffen growls. "Where is she?" he asks Astrid.

Astrid gestures lamely to where Trey is lying with me curled up to his side. "Over there by him."

Giffen frowns. "How long has she been here?"

Astrid shrugs, the frown lines on her face deepen. "I don't know. How long have you been here, Kricket?" Astrid asks. I ignore her question, mulishly trying everything I can to keep her out of my mind. "She won't talk to me!" The forlorn twist of her lips causes Giffen to scowl.

Giffen raises his hands in my direction. He uses his power of telekinesis to connect to me in the most intimate of ways, infiltrating my spirit. Energy as thick as muddy water swirls within me. Giffen's power spreads through me like a fever. It's as if I've swallowed the light of the sun. His essence mingles with mine, and the sensation is nothing less than euphoric. I hate him for it. I shimmer and become a golden silhouette of billowing stardust and light—apparently visible to them, if Astrid's gasp is any indication.

Giffen walks forward until he stands just next to me. Crouching down by my side, he murmurs, "Kricket, you can't stay here. You have to go back." He can definitely see me.

I'm not leaving! I think. I don't need the ability to speak with him. He's a part of me now. He's interfering with my time with Trey. I have so little left.

"If you stay much longer, your body that you left behind will die."

I know he's right. The pull to leave is so strong.

"Your body needs whatever this is—" he waves his hand in my direction "—to survive."

"Why do you care?" I snarl.

"You're my—" he hesitates "—you're frightening your sister." His response is as lame as he is.

Even without a body, my response sounds like a snort. "I don't care."

"You're no good to us dead! We need information, and you're the only one in a position to provide it. You're the only one who can get close to them. Stop being a selfish child!"

I want to lash out at him—hurt him. I want his heart to ache like mine does. "I'm not helping you."

"Then help yourself! You should learn when to go! Your gift will kill you!"

"Good!" I retort.

"Your life is failing." He pushes more of his own life force into me, strengthening the silhouette of me that is beginning to fade. "You have to go back! Now!"

"I'm never going back," I reply. I look away from him. The shiny, gold stardust of my hair runs in shimmering waves over Trey's chest as I rest my cheek against him.

"Then you'll die!" Giffen roars as he swipes his hand across the side table, knocking vials of liquid and scattering them across the floor with a loud racket.

"You're going to have to find another way in with the Alameeda. I'm done."

"Why? What's wrong? What's going on there?"

"You know," I accuse him.

"If I knew, I wouldn't ask."

"Please go back, Kricket," Astrid pleads.

I stab her with my golden stardust stare. "He's going to make me sleep with him."

She looks as if I punched her in the stomach. "Who's going to make you?"

"Kyon—your Alameeda friend who traded you for me. He owns me now. They gave me to him."

Her face loses most of its color. "He's not my friend."

"He's not mine, either," *I reply.*

She looks at Raspin, whose face contorts in shame. She points her finger at him. "I'm never speaking to you again!" *Her venom turns on Giffen next.* "You have to get her out of there!"

Giffen shakes his head. "There's no way right now, but even if there were, I wouldn't do it. You think she'd be safe here?" *He gestures to me while he snarls at Astrid.* "She's in the only place where she won't be under the constant threat of death every single rotation. Ruthless or not, Kyon will protect her. He can't help himself. I saw the look on his face when he saw her—when I ransomed her. It was relief. He'd never have negotiated with us for you if she weren't the trade. He would've brought his army and crushed us instead. He needs her, and we need her there. She's going back! The Alameeda Strikers are annihilating Rafe. It's only a matter of time before they turn their attention to us. We have to find a way to take them out now, and your sister is the only one we have on the inside."

"So I'm expendable," *I say to Giffen.* "I think that's the theme of my life with you guys."

"You're an asset! Start acting like one!" *Giffen refuses to be cowed. He paces in front of me with a withering look upon his face.* "I used to think you were so strong."

"When did you think that?" *I ask.*

"Never mind. Where has he taken you?"

"I can't go back. You don't know Kyon! He's all bite. There's no bark. He just strikes and keeps on striking!"

"You're smarter than him. Make him yours," *Giffen retorts.*

"There's no making him mine! Anyway, it doesn't matter anymore. I told you. I'd rather die than go back."

"I can't let you do that," Giffen replies.

"You have no choice."

"I haven't watched you all this time to let you kill yourself now! You'll return to him and find a way to take down the Alameeda, or so help me I'll kill you myself!"

"You've watched me? When did you watch me?"

Giffen doesn't answer as he stands in front of me breathing heavily in an attempt to rein in his anger.

Astrid answers instead. "You were given to him to protect. He's been your keeper."

"My keeper?"

"He's a member of the Order of the Tempest—it's the society of mostly male Alameeda offspring who survived with the EVS819 gene."

"Is that what you call our freak gene—EVS819?" When she nods, I say, "And your band of lost boys are the Tempest?"

Astrid gestures to Giffen and then to Raspin. "They're the ones who swore an oath to protect the priestesses of the prophecy—that's us." She indicates herself and me with a gesture of her hand.

"I think you mean protect you because, so far, I've been on my own."

Astrid steps toward me. "That's not true! Giffen has been there for you when—"

"Quiet, Astrid!" Giffen yells as he points at Astrid, who clamps her lips shut, startled by the tone he's taken with her.

"When what, Astrid?" I demand.

Astrid turns pleading eyes to Giffen. He shakes his head. Turning to me with a determined look, he states, "Where have they taken you?"

"Screw you!" I retort, barely holding on now. I can't argue further. I want to, but I'm a flickering light—no longer made of star fire but merely gypsy dust in the pale moonlight.

Giffen hovers above me, a new moon whose silhouette is the only thing I can see. "I'll find you. Watch for me. I'm sending you back before you kill yourself!" He raises his hands to me again, and the force *of energy he sends into me knocks me back into the current of time—into a celestial flood. I spin backward, following the path that had led me to Trey.*

✦

I land to a cacophony of sounds in my head. I feel an anvil on my chest. Someone is trying to squeeze my heart out and shove it up into my throat by administering chest compressions. I hear myself gasp in soughs that rattle around in agony in my chest. I cough in choking breaths. The anvil ceases to fall. Steady pressure over my heart replaces it. Reaching my hands up, my fingers entangle in Kyon's hair as he presses his ear to me. He listens to my heart. Waves lap against my toes. The water feels hot—so much warmer than me.

Kyon lifts his head from my chest and gets up on his knees. His strong hand grips my chin, forcing me to look into his eyes. I blink a few times, wondering at the shadows of fear that I see in his stare. The panic in his features abates as he takes deep breaths with me. He gathers my limp form to him, nearly crushing me. My wet night-gown sticks to us both. The coldness of my wintry skin against his causes goose bumps to break out on his flesh. "Kricket"—his hushed voice is urgent—"I have to get you warm."

Kyon stands, bringing me with him. I'm shivering so hard that it vibrates through me in racking quakes. The heat of his skin beneath my cheek almost burns as I lie against his neck. My core temperature is deathly low.

He hurries toward the house. It rises before us, a giant ghost ship. Its pale frame of bone-colored concrete and wood looks like sails of white in the light of the blue and silver moons. Night birds fly overhead, silently stalking prey. Kyon takes me straightaway to the patio and over it. We pass by the gaping maw of the bedroom entryway. Soft, white curtains wave at us in surrender.

Rounding the bend of the wraparound terrace, Kyon takes me to a large outdoor enclosure. Three of the walls are weathered—made of wood with small cracks between the slats. The fourth wall is an enormous fireplace made from the smooth, gray breaker rocks that surround the shoreline. Without a roof, the glow of stars shines on us. I can make out the sea between the gaps in the wide-plank boards.

Kyon walks to a raised black control panel and passes his hand over the surface. It triggers the fireplace—flames leap to life in the hearth. At the same time, small white tapers ignite from low wicks around the enclosure. The soft light doesn't diminish the shine of the stars and moons above us.

We move near the wooden slats of the wall that faces the sea. He makes a gesture with his arm reminiscent of a conductor signaling to his musicians to prepare to play. Five black orbs uncoil from the floor. Startled, I gasp as they spring up like snakes from a charmer's basket, hissing and arching above our heads. Water pumps through long tail hoses attached to their diamond-shaped heads as they surround us.

Flinching away from the scalding heat, I wrap my arms around Kyon's nape and turn my trembling lips against his neck trying to find shelter from the hot water. The inky, round circles that mark his throat stare back at me. Kyon holds me tighter, murmuring unintelligible words to me in a low voice. Steam rises around us, and for several moments, neither of us moves. The only sound from me is the chattering of my teeth.

Slowly, I warm and relax against Kyon. Water slithers over me in a pelting rhythm.

"Why did you come back?" Kyon asks. His lips are near mine. "When you sent yourself into the future, I waited, but then your heart stopped and I knew—you weren't coming back. I tried to keep you alive anyway, but I didn't really think you'd return." His tone is thoughtful. "I know how stubborn you are."

My eyes drift to his. He's watching my mouth. The water tastes of a thousand tears on my lips when I speak. "The better question is: Why would you work so hard to bring me back? I'll kill you before I let you control me. You should've just let me go."

He laughs low. "You've already tried to kill me. It didn't work."

"So why bring me back?"

"I look at you and I see the loneliest girl in the world."

My chin ticks up. "I have a stone heart, Kyon. Nothing touches it." *It's a lie that I need to make true again.*

He watches me for a moment. I somehow feel like he knows all there is to know about me. "Maybe it's your tragic innocence that made me keep you alive. Maybe I want to see it die screaming my name." He leans his lips closer to mine. My hand grasps his wet hair. I tug on it with enough pressure to get his attention. His eyes shift from my mouth to my eyes.

"You have to earn me."

Water streams over the sharp angle of his cheek to drip from his chin onto me. His black tattoos rope around his corded muscles and run down his neck. The thick lines bunch, forming a coiling side-winder at my words. He lets go of my legs, allowing me to slide over his tattoo where it winds down his abdomen until my toes touch the hard stone floor.

"I don't have to earn you, Kricket. You're already mine." He waves his hand in a dismissive gesture. The hovering shower heads turn off and descend to resting positions on the ground. He leaves me where I am for a moment as he walks to a recessed alcove. Pulling a sheetlike towel from a pile of them, he strips off his wet clothes. I turn away, blushing. My fingertips grip the rough, wooden slat that separates me from the sea beyond. I peer through the gap. How do I escape from here?

Kyon moves behind me; he's so quiet that I don't know he's there until I feel him grasp the edge of my sopping nightgown. I shy

23

away from him, bumping into the splintered wood. "What are you doing?" I gasp.

He has a dry towel draped over his arm. The other towel is wrapped low on his hips. "I'm taking care of you," he replies, holding fast to my hem.

I try to swat his hand from it. "I don't need you to take care of me."

"It's my duty," he replies, not letting go.

"I absolve you of it," I say through my teeth.

"It's my right."

I struggle to get away, but as I turn my back to him, he presses his hand flat against my shoulder, holding me against the wooden slats while he lifts my nightgown. He moves his hand to pull it over my head. I shiver again in the cool breeze as my back rounds away from his touch. Kyon's fingers skim down my back—a caress. I don't look at him. I can't.

He wraps the length of thin fabric around me, covering my bare skin. Tucking the end into the top, his hand reaches for mine. I pull my fingers back, but he latches on and holds them fast until I look up at him. His expression is stoic. He waits for me to figure out that he's not going to let my hand go. I relent. He turns and takes me back toward his house.

We enter the bedroom through the wide opening in the wall. He leads me directly to the large bed. The bed is still unmade from where I'd climbed from it earlier. He straightens the sheets and holds them back with a gesture for me to get in. When I don't immediately comply he says, "Do you want me to make you get in?"

I sigh and climb into the bed wordlessly. Lying on my side I pull the blanket up to my chin while I turn and face away from him. Moving around the other side of the bed, Kyon gets in too. I immediately turn away from him again and move to the edge of the bed. His arms wrap around me. He pulls me to him and tucks me close to his body. My muscles go rigid. Kyon kisses my hair and snuggles tight against me. I begin to struggle and try to pull away from him.

"Don't move."

"I don't want you to touch me."

"I don't care what you want. This is what I want. You need to know that I'm the only person to whom you can turn."

"I don't need you."

"You will."

Realizing that struggling only makes him hold me tighter, I relax and try to pretend his body isn't molded against mine. I can't reason with him. At the moment, the only thing he's capable of grasping is me. The warmth radiating from him is not unpleasant though. The stress and the struggle to survive are catching up to me. My eyes grow heavy—I fight to keep them open.

Kyon says, "Sleep." It's as if he reads my mind.

"I can't. Who'll protect me from you if I do?" I murmur wearily.

"No one."

I struggle to stay awake, but it has been such a brutal night that I eventually drift off to sleep in the arms of my enemy.

CHAPTER 3

HOLLOW WELL

My cheek presses against bare skin. I shift to see the broad expanse of his chest. Moving my fingertips, I notice they're resting against a sliver of a silver scar. I trace it, not knowing what it is right away. *When did Trey get this?* I gasp. My fingers curl on his flesh and I quickly look up. "Kyon!"

His deep voice murmurs, "I like to hear you wake with my name on your lips." With his shoulders resting against plump, white pillows, Kyon's blue eyes hood as he continues to stare at me. He moves his hand along my hair, stroking me like a favorite pet. "You slept," he adds, as if letting me in on a secret. It all comes rushing back to me in a flood. My head jerks off of him as I cover my face with my hands and sit up. "How do you feel?"

I can't tell if his concern is genuine. I peek at him through my fingers, shooting him a sidelong scowl. "My chest hurts like someone tried to drown me."

"It's still bruised. I compressed your heart after it stopped beating last night." Stone-faced, he watches my reaction. "I'll cut your hair now so that you'll heal more quickly." He gathers some of my hair away from my face. I blanch. It still troubles me that I'm genetically engineered to regenerate cells when my hair is cut. It makes me feel like I'm somehow less than real, and being in Ethar is already enough of a dose of unreality.

Dropping my hands, I sweep my hair away from him. "No. Don't. I'm fine." *I don't want you touching me, chester,* I think, using the Etharian term for "pervert."

"You'll feel better instantly when I cut it. Your bruises will disappear." He reaches for me again and I shy away.

My arm rises defensively. "I don't want to feel better." He reaches under the pillow behind him and extracts a wicked-looking knife with an ivory handle. My eyes widen and I stiffen as my breath catches in my throat. "What are you doing? Why do you have a knife under your pillow?" I'm proud of the way my voice doesn't quiver, even when my blood is roaring through my veins.

Kyon holds the handle of the knife while he lazily fondles the steely blade with his finger. "Tell me, when you were remanded to that institution on Earth, after you ran away from your foster home, did you ever feel the need to hide a weapon near you while you slept?"

My heart pounds in my chest, as I think about the time I spent in a juvenile facility in Chicago. The streets had been safer than that place. "Yes," I answer honestly.

His eyes pierce mine as they shift from the knife to me. "Why?"

I'm held by his intense stare, unable to look away. "Because I had enemies."

"You still do," he replies.

Reaching forward, his huge hand grasps a fistful of my hair. Angling the sharp blade of the knife, Kyon slices off my hair near the nape of my neck. The severed hair in his fist turns black and shrivels up until it's no more than dust in his palm. Billowing shafts of new hairs rapidly regrow from my scalp. Pale blond, it falls over my shoulders in waves, resuming its former length. Kyon weaves his fingers in it, feeling its corn-silk softness against his skin. The oppressive ache and tightness in my chest eases, allowing me to take the first full breath I've had since last night. He plays with my hair for a moment, completely mesmerized by it. "Who are *you* afraid of?" I ask.

His stare turns cold. His hand tightens uncomfortably in my hair, but I don't flinch. "No one," he replies. "They're afraid of *me*." I wonder for the first time what he has gone through in his life to make him so ruthless and unbending.

"Who's afraid of you?" I can imagine, looking at the psychopathic killer next to me, that there aren't many people who aren't afraid of Kyon.

"Anyone who's smart enough to see us as a threat." The truthful resonance of his voice is as frightening as his words.

I want to shudder, but I don't give into it. "I need a weapon."

He doesn't hesitate. Opening his palm, he holds out the wicked knife for me to take. I pause, not sure if his offer is a trap. He waits patiently for me to come to a decision. Cautiously, I reach out, touching the ivory handle. As fast as the snap of a snake's bite, Kyon's hand closes over mine so that we each hold the knife with the blade pointed toward the mattress. "Use this on me, Kricket, and I'll make you regret it."

Refusing to retreat, I reply, "You haven't made me regret stabbing you the first time."

A slow smile develops on his lips. It spreads over his face. His eyes crinkle with humor. "That's because you only served to convince me that you're perfect for me. My little savage—the darkest star."

He's a psychopath. "Who's coming after us, Kyon?"

He's stony once more. He lets go of the knife, relinquishing it to me. It's heavy in my hand. "No one I can't handle. Are you hungry?"

I exhale deeply. I shove the knife under my pillow, hiding it from view once more. "Yes."

Light dances off his face from the open doorway that leads to the sea. He's a golden god—one at home in his surroundings. "What do you like?" he asks.

"Anything that won't make me sick."

His leans toward me, his nose nearing mine. With his eyebrows crashing together, he asks, "What do you mean by that?"

"I mean don't make me sick."

His frown deepens. "You think I'd poison you?"

I shrug. "You just tried to drown me last night."

He points his finger in my face. "You'd be dead if I truly wanted to drown you. I was establishing who is in charge here. It's not you."

I shiver, but don't look away. "Is that what we were establishing? That's not what I got from it."

His eyebrow rises in question. "What did you glean from the encounter?"

"It's a good year for hunters."

His eyes sharpen, becoming a deeper blue. "Remember that. I'll find you, no matter where you go." His fingers touch my cheek, brushing my hair away from it.

I lean away from his hand. "Why do you always threaten me?"

"That was a promise."

"It was a threat."

"You belong to me. I won't let you go—not ever." Something in his eyes changes, making his face attractive in its austerity. He's in control, and he knows it. He needs me to know it too.

"Maybe if you asked me to stay and if you were nice, I'd *want* to be here."

His pupils sharpen, as if what I've said makes me more interesting prey. Gripping my chin, he makes it so I can't look away. "I'm never nice."

"You could try." I know what I'm suggesting is ludicrous.

"You crave strength."

"I crave pancakes." Lifting my chin, I pull it from his hand. "With syrup."

"Then you shall have them," he purrs.

"Are you going to make them for me?" In truth, I can't picture him in a kitchen cooking—not that I can picture any Etharians cooking, since they rely on automation to do most of their domestic tasks. I've yet to see another living soul around here. It worries me.

"I don't know what pancakes are. It sounds as if you'd like to eat metal." His look is discerning. He's trying to figure me out. "This isn't Rafe—there's technology that will sort it all out for us." He speaks in a louder tone, "Oscil?"

A holographic screen materializes in front of us. It's the size of one of the flat-screen televisions that used to hang behind the bar in Lumin, the nightclub where I worked in Chicago. "Requirement?" the sexy fem-bot voice asks.

"I require pancakes."

Hundreds of different types of pancake recipes stream in front of us. I lean nearer to Kyon to scan the colorful pictures, my brow wrinkling at the selection. "These?" he asks, pointing to something that looks like crepes.

"No," I murmur in concentration. "These." I point to a picture of a stack dripping with syrup. "Buttermilk."

Kyon takes my hand in his large one, and stretching my finger toward the picture of the pancakes I want, the image ripples like I touched water. The image fades, and then disappears. Items that pair with pancakes appear in its place: syrup, fruit, juice, whipped cream. Kyon selects all of them for me, sending the pictures rippling away.

My stomach growls loudly. "How long until they're ready?" I ask.

"It will be here shortly. You can ask Oscil for anything you require. Just say its name and it will assist you, but only when you're in or near the residence or onboard one of my airships. It doesn't have the ability to respond to requests beyond a certain proximity to a receiver."

"What is Oscil?"

"It's a prototype intelligence technology that I developed and use throughout my estates. It only responds to a few select voices. Yours is one of them."

"What does it do?"

"It controls all the automation and sensors throughout my residences. It is also meant to be a personal assistant."

"Where is it? How does it work?"

"You remember being on my satellite?"

I think for a moment, recalling seeing Kyon in his medical stasis capsule onboard an elaborate space station. "That place is yours?"

"Yes. I designed it. I own it."

"Technically, I was never there, not physically anyway—and it looked more like a space station to me." I had projected there from the past in order to spy on Kyon. I don't know how smart it is of me to admit that to him, but he seems not to be too worried about it now. He'd known I was there at the time.

"Oscil is primarily housed on the satellite, near the moon of Inium, but I have backup facilities in several locations throughout Ethar. They can all run simultaneously or autonomously."

I don't pretend to know how this all works, but the fact that he does makes me shiver at his extreme intelligence. The chill causes me to look down at myself. I have only a sheet wrapped around me. It has slipped low, but it isn't indecent. "Do you have something that I can wear?" I ask.

Kyon is busy making a selection from the menu in front of him. When he finishes, he waves his hand in a dismissive gesture and the hologram evaporates into the air. His eyes skim over me slowly, lingering on my breasts in a way that makes me pull the sheet closer. "You don't have to wear anything. We're alone here."

I don't know what's more frightening: the fact that we're alone here or the fact that he might make me walk around naked. "I'm not really a clothing-optional kind of girl."

"That's a shame."

"Do you have clothes for me or not?" I ask with forced calm.

"I do. Everything you need is in your dressing room." He looks past me to the set of white doors on the far wall opposite the ocean. I slide over to that side of the mattress. When my feet touch the floor, I hold the sheet to me and walk in that direction. I'm halted by a firm tug on the tail of my sheet. Looking over my shoulder, I glare at Kyon, seeing him wrap the end of my sheet around his hand.

"You didn't ask me what you should wear," he says in a stern tone.

My eyes narrow at him. "I'm a big girl. I don't need your help dressing myself."

He looks me over from head to toe again. "You're tiny."

I'm irritated by that comment. "Whatever." I turn back around and try to take another step, but Kyon doesn't let go of the sheet. I exhale a breath and pivot to face him. The sheet twists awkwardly around me. I glare at him. Kyon's eyebrows pull together as his expression turns malignant. He jerks the sheet. I try to hold my ground but I end up being reeled back to his side.

Nose to nose with me, he growls, "Tell Oscil that you want to select garment number three thirty-three."

His warm breath is on my cheek as I stare into his chilly eyes. "Where I come from," I say slowly, so that my voice won't quiver, "that number means half evil."

His lips twitch, and then curl into a genuine smile. "On you, it'll be the same thing." He lets go of the sheet. I inch back from him. My sweaty palms clutch the soft material as I retreat. He watches me go, his expression unreadable. When my feet touch the floor again, I take a few backward steps away from the psycho freak. Gaining some distance, I turn from him and hurry to the dressing room.

Opening the doors, I find a large round room that can probably fit twenty people or more. High, round windows look out over sea-grass-covered sand dunes. An elaborate driftwood chandelier hangs in the center of the room, glowing brilliantly. I close the doors behind me and slump against them, letting out a deep exhale.

It takes a few seconds for me to pull myself together, but once I do I rush over to the windows, looking for an exit. My chin is flush with the bottom of the sill. Outside there are stone paths through the dunes. Benches line the paths and in the distance copses of tropical trees sway in the breeze. But that's it. I see no other living creatures about and no mode of transportation. I didn't really expect to though. Kyon was telling the truth when he said we're alone here—wherever here is.

I turn around and look at the room. There's a chaise lounge and several elegant, high-backed chairs covered in sea-foam-colored silk. There aren't any clothes in sight. "What am I supposed to wear?" I ask in frustration. I think for a second. "Oscil."

"Requirement?"

"I need to dress for the rotation."

"Please step into the channel and make a selection," a fem-bot voice says. In the middle of the room, a dark cylindrical enclosure rises from the floor. I eye it warily. Approaching it, I take a deep breath and enter the shadowy area through its open panel. "Please make a selection," the voice restates. The panel closes, shutting me inside.

"Three thirty-three?"

A blue light descends from the top of the cylinder, scanning my body. When it drops into the floor, four steely, sharp scissor blades lift up out of round holes that open up in the floor. The blades spin around on steel robotic arms, whirling in helicopter-rotor swipes. I clutch and scratch the walls of the tube, clawing to get out, as the machine sheers the sheet from my body. The pieces of material fall to the ground. The fibers shred and are inhaled into lung-shaped holes in the floor by my feet. I bang on the tube, looking for a way out.

"Stop!" I cry. *"Stop! Halt! Cease! Shut the hell off!"* Nothing happens. The machine keeps cutting and shredding. It has the same attitude as its creator.

When the scissors reach the top of my head, the blades retract into the arms of the machine. I pant and gasp as I try to calm myself. Next, aerosol cans emerge on the ends of the robotic arms. "Lift arms . . . lift arms . . . lift arms," the fem-bot voice chants.

"Stop, you piece of junk!"

"Lift arms . . . Lift arms . . . Lift arms . . ."

Tentatively, I raise my hands a little. The voice continues to chant, "Lift arms . . . lift arms . . ." I keep raising them until they're over my head.

The aerosol cans whirl around me, spraying every area on my body except my head. All my unwanted body hair disappears in an instant.

When the robotic arms reach the floor, the aerosol cans retract inside the automated arms. In their place, long slender knitting needles emerge on the ends of two of the arms while smaller needles present themselves on the other two. Threads spool out between the needles, weaving and sewing golden fabric around me as they rise up from the floor. When the robotic arms reach the top of my head, I'm attired in a flimsy gold-colored two-piece bathing suit. The whirling, deadly-sharp chopstick fingers descend again, this time spinning a web of see-through golden fabric around me. A golden tullelike wrap skirt circles my waist to my toes.

The mechanical arms rise to my head again. As they descend once more, the same shimmery golden fabric is woven around my shoulders and arms. When the arms slip away back into the floor, the dark cylinder surrounding me becomes a reflective mirror. I stare at my image. I'm attired in a golden cover-up with a long train that flows out behind me. Beneath it, a bathing suit is my only other cover.

"Do you require grooming?" the fem-bot voice asks.

"Ur . . . okay?" I murmur with a bit of apprehension.

"Shall I pair your grooming with your attire?" the automated voice inquires.

"Ahh, sure."

The robotic hands come up from the floor again, but this time they're not scissors or needles; they're brushes and combs. In less than a minute, my hair is brushed and swept up in a high ponytail with intricate braids throughout.

After the arms disappear once more into the floor, the voice asks, "Do you require further assistance?"

"No," I reply. The cylinder drops back down into small slats in the floor, and I'm left again in the middle of the room. My hands slide over the soft material of my outfit. I look down at myself. Golden sandals lie near my feet. I slip them on—a perfect fit.

Facing the doors that lead back to the bedroom, I tiptoe to them. I nudge the lever, opening the door a crack. Peering out, I don't see Kyon anywhere. He's not on the bed where I left him. Squaring my shoulders, I open one door wider, taking a tentative step outside the dressing room. My skin prickles, and I sense Kyon before I feel his hand come to rest firmly on the back of my neck. Every cell in my body reacts when I look up to see him beside me. He must've been leaning against the wall, waiting for me to open the door. He traded the white sheet around his hips for midnight blue swim shorts that show the obscene V-shape of his abdomen. His bare chest is disgustingly perfect and covered only by his black tattoo.

Hiding my fear of him within an annoyed expression, I continue to walk in the direction I was going. I try to outpace him so that his hand will drop from the nape of my neck, but he slows me with a warning squeeze.

"Breakfast is ready on the terrace," he says in a satisfied murmur near my ear. I wonder at his tone for a moment until he says, "Number three thirty-three looks even better on you than I imagined."

I don't reply. Passing through the room out onto the terrace, I approach the round stone table. A kitelike awning extends over the table, shielding us from the glare of the tropical sun. Kyon pulls out a cushioned chair for me. It's so big and tall that my feet barely reach the stone patio.

A levitating service cart is waiting near us. Kyon retrieves pewter-covered dishes from its surface. He places a platter in front of me. The lid lifts from it on its own, resting on a hinge. The aroma of pancakes rises. I inhale, my mouth watering. My eyes shift to Kyon's plate as he sits next to me. He has something that looks like boiled squid on his plate. I shudder and make a face at it. Then, I stab a pancake from the towering stack on my plate, thrusting one onto the side of his plate.

"Eat that," I say in challenge.

Blue eyes the color of the sky cast down upon me. "Why?" he asks.

"Because I don't eat my pancakes until you do," I reply with a lift of my chin.

He tries to hide his smile behind a sigh. "I have no need to drug you, Kricket. I can overpower you whenever I desire."

"That's nice—you already drugged me, so your point is moot. Here, have some syrup too." I lift the heavy pewter dispenser in front of me and pour a generous amount of syrup over his pancake.

He looks at me like I'm being dumb, but he doesn't balk. Instead he lifts his cutlery and slices into the pancake. He mops up the syrup with the pancake on his fork. With more elegance than anyone should have, he takes a bite and chews it demonstratively. With a smug smile, he reaches over and lifts my glass of water. Saluting me with it, he takes a large sip. He puts it down along with his cutlery and holds his hands palm up in an *are you satisfied* gesture.

I sniff and lift my cutlery, beginning to eat. As soon as the morsel crosses my lips, I have to stifle the urge to groan with pleasure. It's divine. "So," I ask between bites. "What are we doing here?"

"We're having breakfast," Kyon replies. The ocean breeze stirs his hair. The sunshine makes his skin look golden.

"Okay. What are we doing after breakfast?" I ask.

"I thought I'd show you around your new home."

"You actually live here?"

"*We* live here."

"Alone?"

"I don't like people."

"You don't like them or they don't like you?" I ask.

"Does it matter?"

"Not really," I say with a shrug. His presence dominates my entire being. He invades my senses with his nearness. I can't ignore him and the silence is suddenly heavy. "Have you lived here long?"

"Long enough."

"Long enough to fall in love with it?"

"You could say that," he agrees. I try to hide a smile, but he sees it. "What's funny?"

"You. The idea that you'd be in love with anything."

"Why would that surprise you?"

"You strike me as someone who's accustomed to extreme wealth—something like this must be like camping for you," I reply. The house is amazing, but it's obviously meant to function with no staff. When Kyon was at the palace, he was constantly with an entourage of Alameeda underlings, all waiting on his every whim.

He lifts his glass, takes a small sip. Replacing it on the table, he casts me a quick glance. "How do you know to what I'm accustomed?"

"You think that I simply ignored you while I was the Regent's ward? I had to sort through and find the truth among the lies that your people kept feeding me, but I managed to learn a few things about you."

His eyes narrow dangerously. "Such as?"

"Such as your position within the Brotherhood. You have the

most coveted seat in Alameeda. The prestige of controlling the Loch of Cerulean is unequaled—as are the trappings that it brings. An ambassador of Wurthem suggested that you were not originally in line for it."

"Did he?"

"Mmm. He implied that you gained it through other means."

"What other means?"

"Intimidation. Assassination."

"Do you always listen to gossip?" he asks.

"Always," I say between bites of pancake.

"What else do you think you know?"

"You're a shrewd investor. A source said you own some highly lucrative ventures in Wurthem—a fact that annoyed my source, since he believes that only the social elite in House Wurthem should be able to hold its wealth. He said your connections in Alameeda make you untouchable, but he refused to say which connections. Which made me think that he feared your connections more than he feared you."

Kyon frowns. "*I* make me untouchable," he says with more force than I expect. I've touched on something here. His loner-ish persona has roots that run deep.

I decide to push on despite the icy reception my words are garnering. "My source indicated that your business prowess was underestimated at first. He didn't initially believe that a soldier such as yourself would understand the intricacies related to high finance."

"What do you think?"

I shrug. "Strategy is strategy. Learn the game and play it. From what I know of you, I would think that you'd be better than most at that."

"Why is that?"

"Because when someone like you gets outmaneuvered, he can usually push through it by using force."

"Is there a point to this?" Kyon asks as he leans back in his chair. I lean back in mine as well. I wipe my mouth with my napkin before resting it by my plate. "No. No point. Just making conversation."

Kyon rises from his seat and extends his hand to me. "You want to talk? I'll show you around and you can talk."

I eye his hand for a moment. I don't take it, but stand on my own and push my chair away from the table. "Oscil," he says in an even tone. "Clear the table." He indicates that I should follow him back into the house.

On the way, I look over my shoulder. A large hole opens in the center of the table. The dirty plates are magnetically pulled into it and swallowed up, then the hole disappears and the table resumes its solid form. A floating tray passes over the top of the table, spraying it with a cleaner and using a robotic arm to clean the surface. I watch it all with fascination before I feel Kyon's hand on the small of my back guiding me away.

We enter through the bedroom archway, and he walks me through the elegant room to the doorway on the left. Once through it, we enter a high glass-ceilinged room. It's a solarium of sorts that looks like an upside-down Viking ship. Wooden ribs jut out from the long spine and frame the glass panels of the ceiling. Glass walls facing the sea automatically lower and recess into the floor as we walk through the space, allowing the ocean breeze to touch my skin. A small river of water runs down the center of the room from one fountain into another at the opposite end. There are deck chairs and low tables arranged here and there for sitting and enjoying the view of the water outside.

A spiral staircase at the end of the room winds up through the ceiling to the next level. Taking the stairs up, we arrive at the next floor. Another gallery greets us. This one has wood-plank floors. Sconce lighting lines the walls. We pass doors to closed rooms. "What's in them?" I ask.

"They're guest rooms," Kyon replies. We pause at one, and Kyon opens it. It's a beautiful space with a view overlooking the floral garden on the other side of the house, but there are no furnishings. It's empty inside. I glance out the window; garden-bots hover about on the grounds below, trimming shrubbery into perfect angles.

"So . . . no one stays here with you?"

"You're the first."

Lucky me! I think sarcastically. Turning away from the window, we quietly leave the room. We cross a gallery without opening any more doors. Finding another spiral staircase that climbs up into the ceiling, I grasp the trident-shaped wrought-iron newel. These stairs take us to the third floor, where a large office sits at the end of a short hallway.

The office is a command center. Every aspect of the island is visible by way of the virtual screens that encompass the circumference of the room. The island isn't very big, maybe three or four miles. It's shaped like a star, and from what the satellite imagery reveals, there are only a few other smaller buildings on the island.

"What are these?" I ask, pointing to a screen that shows a couple of thatched roofs fit between clusters of palm trees on the other side of the island.

"Small cottages. No one lives in them. They're for our use."

"And this?" I point to a huge building on the top of a mesa near a rapidly flowing waterfall.

"Hangar. It's where I store all the skiffs and airships. Have you learned to operate any of them?" he asks.

"No."

"Would you like to?"

I peek at him suspiciously. "Yes."

"I'll teach you."

"Why would you?" I ask.

"It's a skill you need to know, don't you agree?"

"I heard that priestesses aren't taught those kinds of skills," I say with a frown. They're treated like pretty idiots until someone wants to use whatever extrasensory gift they possess, then they're tapped and used for their expertise—whether they agree to it or not.

"They're not, but you and I will hold ourselves to a higher standard." I look away from him as I process his answer. "And this building?" I ask, pointing to the largest building other than the house.

"Boathouse."

I look around his office. There's a solid wooden desk that is something only a pirate would own. I go to it and run my fingers over its smooth surface. A grid of light illuminates on the surface of the desk—it's a keyboard of sorts to access the control center. I walk around the desk and sit in the massive chair behind it. It's made to fit Kyon's broad shoulders. I ease back, feeling like a child in an adult world. My fingers round on the ends of the armrests. I rub them, trying to get a feel for the person who owns it.

Kyon slowly takes a seat in a chair facing his desk—his hands temple as he watches me watch him.

"This place is so different from the places I've been to on Ethar," I observe.

"It is."

"Everything is minimalistic."

"I thought it would be less confusing for you."

"For me?" I scoff.

"You spend much of your time observing the surface of things, and you hardly ever take time to assess what's underneath." He holds up his hand, staving off my angry retort. "It's not an insult," he barks threateningly.

I hesitate, and then say in a calm tone, "Alright." I realize abruptly that he's reacting to the anger he sees on my face, and the fact that I was just about to yell at him. It affects him—he doesn't know how to talk to me. I lean back in the chair once more. "So that was not meant as an insult—please explain."

He takes a breath, trying to regain calm. "You've been thrown into a world filled with an overabundance of technology and wealth and excess. I've observed you peel away the layers a bit at a time, processing everything quickly—as is your way. I thought that it would be easier for you to see me without all those distractions. I could've brought you aboard one of my yachts, but I've observed you on the boats in the little lake at the Rafe palace. You hid your panic well, but I knew you hated every moment that you were afloat. It made you feel helpless. I also could've taken you to one of my estates, where you would've found ways to hide yourself away in so many of the distractions they provide. No. I wanted you here. I want us to see each other."

"You think you know me?" I ask.

"No. I don't think anyone really knows you. We have that in common."

"How long do you think it will take for us to know each other?"

He shrugs and is about to say something when a cacophony of beeping interrupts him. His jaw tight, he rises from his seat. "Oscil, report."

"Incoming Vindercrafts, seven series."

"Image." A holographic landscape image appears over the surface of the desk between us. A stunning aircraft that resembles a matte black boomerang flies low over the glassy water, but leaves no shadow on the surface. Behind it, there is a fleet of similar airships, a score at least, following it in a V formation.

Kyon frowns. "Are they armed?"

"Fully armed."

"Occupants?"

"Twenty-seven life forms in the lead ship."

"Approach?"

"Quadrant two."

"Time?"

"One fleat," the fem-bot replies, indicating that in a minute that ship will be here.

"Have they been warned not to attempt to land here?"

"Affirmative. Shall I initiate termination protocols?" the computer asks dispassionately.

"Hold termination," Kyon murmurs. "Allow the lead ship through. Bar the rest of the formation."

"Who is it?" I ask, watching him. I can't tell if he's happy or unhappy about the visitor.

"Alameeda Strikers."

"Why are they coming here?"

"They intend to return you to the Brotherhood."

"And you're going to say no?"

"That's right."

"Why?"

"Because you're mine," he replies.

The hologram between Kyon and I shows the armada of aircraft behind the lead ship suddenly veer off in several different directions, avoiding an iridescent, bubblelike dome that exists between them and their lead ship. As they scramble in the air, realigning in a clump behind the shield, the lead boomerang-shaped ship halts abruptly at the edge of the beach. It shifts its shape and draws in its wings; it soon resembles a black salamander. Four legs form from the body, anchoring it to the beach. Black armor-clad soldiers slither around inside the mouth of the ship when it opens onto the shore. Kyon doesn't look at all concerned. Finding it hard to breathe, I swallow the bile that rises in my mouth.

"Oscil," Kyon says calmly.

"Requirement?"

"Enemy infiltration. Is Excelsior among them?"

"Scanning for Excelsior Ensin," the dispassionate voice replies. "Negative. Excelsior Ensin is not detected."

Kyon looks disappointed as he says, "Exterminate all foreign entities."

"Authorization code?"

"Formulate Infinity."

"Who is Excelsior?" I demand.

Kyon is distracted, watching the hologram between us as he says, "He's the Supreme Chancellor of the Alameeda Brotherhood—my father."

"Your father is the Supreme Chancellor!" I say in shock.

"What? Your source never mentioned that?" Kyon asks sarcastically. He gives me a derisive look. "Maybe he assumed you knew."

"Maybe I should start paying my sources," I mutter.

On the desk between us, light flickers from the holographic images projected there. Crystal-blue water and a golden sun become the backdrop to the monstrous black stage formed by the mouth of the open aircraft. A troop of miniature soldiers acts out a strange scene as they spill out into the water on the edge of the beach, igniting smoke canisters that act as heavy, red-roiling smoky curtains on the peripherals of the stage.

The soldiers quickly divide into two units. Armed with wicked weaponry, mainly riflelike guns called frestons that can be set to project electro-pulses, laser projectiles, or bulletlike ammunition, the first unit moves forward. They have black utility belts that hold spare battery cartridges, clipped around their combat armor. The belts have heat seekers and silver cylinders known as sanctum amps that Hollis once told me explode when they're thrown. "I take it you're not close to your dad."

"We don't enjoy each other's company," Kyon replies. My stomach is in knots. I want to run to the door of his office and bar it, but a closed door won't stop them, not with the guns they have.

I look past the scene playing out in front of me, to Kyon. The images from the hologram form light patterns on his face. "I need another weapon," I say urgently. "I left my knife in the bedroom."

Kyon smiles at me as if I've just said something funny. "You'll be fine, Kricket." He points at the hologram. My eyes pan back to it, catching sight of a ripple appearing beneath the sand near the house. A shock wave moves outward so fast that the sand swallows the first unit before they can take another step.

I blink in disbelief. "Where'd they go?" I whisper.

Kyon glances up at me from the hologram. "They've been buried alive. The defensive systems on the island are following protection protocols."

The second unit of soldiers near the water scream out names of the missing. Nothing stirs beneath the white waves of sand, though. A tall, blond soldier becomes frantic; he runs to where the first unit was last seen, jackknifes into the quicksand, and disappears from sight. Kyon shakes his head and murmurs, "There's always someone who loses his mind and does that. You can't train that out of them."

The soldier Kyon referred to doesn't resurface. The others retreat back into the shadowy recesses of their dark ship. "Are they leaving?" I ask hopefully. My sweaty hands clutch the edge of the desk.

Kyon shakes his head. "They're under orders to retrieve you. Should they return without you, they'll be executed. Better to die here."

Kyon is right. The Strikers soon reappear in the doorway of their aircraft. Clad in Riker Paks, blue flames kindle from beneath the two fuselage-shaped canisters on each soldier's jet pack. They lift off from the shore one by one and fly toward the house.

The house's defenses react. A scorching wave of fiery light rolls out in concentric circles from spouts on the eaves. The fire ignites the airborne Strikers, shorting out their jet packs while it burns them. They fall from the sky, and the hungry sand greets them, extinguishing the flames as it pulls their charred carcasses under.

Oscil's silky fem-bot voice startles me. "All foreign life-forms have been terminated," it states.

I shiver. Kyon looks away from the hologram on the desk and over to the bank of screens that show different aspects of the island and the interior of the house. He's tense; his jaw is rigid. He studies the other ships that can come no closer to the shore.

"Can they get past your shield?"

"No."

"How long do you think they'll sit out there?" I ask, while worrying a piece of my hair between my fingers.

"It's intimidation. They're letting me know that although they can't get in, we will not be allowed to leave without detection." He glances at my face. "I hadn't planned on leaving anytime soon, but when I do, it won't matter who's out there to greet us."

Oscil breaks in again. "Incoming transmission from Excelsior Ensin."

Kyon leans back in his seat. I wait for him to answer the message, but he makes no move to do so. I raise my eyebrow. "Are you going to answer that?" I ask.

"I just said everything I needed to say to Excelsior."

"Should I answer it?" I ask.

"I don't know, should you?" he returns my question. His expression is unreadable. "Do you want to hide behind me, or do you want to stand up for yourself?"

"I'm not going to rely on you for anything, Kyon."

"Then, by all means, you should answer it. Tell Oscil to accept the transmission." He temples his hands again, looking at me in challenge.

I lean back in Kyon's enormous chair and try to adopt a serene mien. Lifting my chin, I murmur, "Oscil, accept the transmission."

Like some retro mission control, Oscil responds, "Transmission accepted."

CHAPTER 4
NO SHADE IN THE SHADOWS

Between Kyon and me, a holographic image of a handsome blond man takes shape. Excelsior's resemblance to Kyon is, in a word, ridiculous. Although Kyon's forty-something-looking father has a different hairstyle, which is short, blond, and severe, there's no doubt in my mind what Kyon will look like when he's that age—that is, if Excelsior somehow lets him live that long. The leader's shiny eyes, made from blue light, hood in reaction to his seeing me in the seat behind Kyon's desk.

"Where is my son?" His stern voice has a similar resonance to Kyon's.

I try to play it cool. "Greetings, Excelsior. Lovely day. Are you enjoying the warm sea air?"

Excelsior barks, "I will ask you again, where is he?"

I shrug, trying not to seem afraid. "I think he went to get a snack." I gesture with my thumb. "Is there something I can do for you instead?" I ask innocently. Glancing at Kyon, I see a grudging smile developing on his lips.

Excelsior growls, "Kricket."

I raise my eyebrows. "Excelsior."

"So you know who I am?"

"I've heard of you."

"From Kyon?"

"No. He has hardly spoken of you. I don't think he likes you very much," I whisper conspiratorially.

"Get him. *Now!*" he roars.

"No. I don't think I will," I state calmly. I hold out my hand, studying my fingernails, as if I don't have a care in the world.

The silence stretches on for a few long breaths, before Excelsior says, "You do look exactly like your mother . . . except for your eyes. Violet."

My eyes shift back to his once more. "And you look like Kyon."

He frowns. "He looks like me. It's why he isn't dead."

"He was saved by your narcissism then? I'm sure he'll be happy to hear that."

"He was saved by the fact that I know he's mine," he replies. What he says is true, but at the same time it isn't. His answer makes me pause in confusion.

"There's always a paternity test," I mutter. "No need for doubt."

"One can't always believe those. Too many bleeding-heart technicians who are eager to save a child." I understand what he's referring to because, unbeknown to him, I have met a few of the gifted "lost boys" whom he's failed to destroy—the males born to priestesses who exhibit the kind of freak gene I have.

"I'd suspect that after meeting you, anyone would go *way* out of her way to deny your paternity."

"They go out of their way to claim that the males born to priestesses, like you, are declared ungifted . . . even when they're not."

I think of Giffen. He's one of those. "Sounds as if no one wants you to slaughter innocent children."

"I'm saving the people who count. Should those males survive, they'd rise up and kill us all."

"Or maybe just you. I think I'd like to see that."

He scowls. "I know you would. That's why I'm here."

"So I can watch you die? Aww, that's sort of thoughtful of you. I'll enjoy that."

He ignores me. "Kyon must be made to understand that you're not worth his demise."

"You're right—I'm really not. Maybe we should convince him to take me back to Earth? I promise I won't return to Ethar."

"You'll never leave Ethar. You have something that belongs to me."

"I don't think I do, but what is it that you think I owe you, Excelsior?"

"The future."

"Do you expect me to read your palm or something? Could you really trust me if I did?"

"I have all the predictions I need. Your mother saw to that. She gave us her prophecies. No, I'm speaking of your other future."

"Which would be?"

"Your offspring, Kricket. They belong to me."

My mouth hangs wide. I glance at Kyon. He's watching me. My eyes travel back to the image of Excelsior. "I don't have any children."

"Nor will you."

"Then how do you intend to take ownership of my offspring?"

"Your organs will be harvested. I'll have everything I need to create my own daughters from your bloodline."

I feel myself growing pale. "You're a sick psychopath, Excelsior. I'm going to make it my mission to mess you up in ways you can't even imagine!" I'm bluffing. Inside, my blood turns cold with dread.

"I hope you prove to be more of an adversary than your mother. She was so trusting until it was almost too late."

"She was a child."

"You're a child."

"You're wrong. I haven't been a child for a long time."

"When I come for you, I'll divide you up into so many pieces that you—"

"Oscil, end transmission," Kyon interrupts. The image of Excelsior evaporates, leaving me face-to-face with Kyon instead. I don't say anything. My mind is buzzing with the knowledge that my plight just went from completely awful to extremely wretched in a matter of a few moments. I don't know how long I stare at Kyon, unseeing, but I flinch when he speaks. "You scare him, Kricket. He isn't one to verbally threaten his enemies. He usually never lets them know they're his enemies until after he strikes them with a death blow."

"I don't know if I like that distinction."

"I don't mind it. It gives us something in common."

"How long until Excelsior gets through your defenses, Kyon?"

"You'll have to let me know the answer to that question."

His response scares me. "I'd like to be alone."

Kyon shrugs. "The airships will be kept at bay—that makes the island open to you." He indicates the aircraft on the bank of screens that surround the office. They're moving away. "We're safe while they formulate another strategy. If you'd like, you can take a walk through the gardens and paths behind the house."

I rise to my feet, desperate to get away from here. I move around the edge of the desk. When I near him, he reaches out and grasps my wrist gently. "Stay off the beach until I say otherwise," he orders. I nod numbly. "And don't go too far. It's easy to get lost."

"Fine." I shake off his hand.

"I expect you back before it grows dark."

"I'll keep that in mind," I murmur. It takes everything I have not to run from the room. When I reach the doorway, I pause. Without looking at Kyon, I ask, "Why is Excelsior afraid of me?"

"He knows you're here to kill him."

It's not voluntary, the way I react to what Kyon says. I don't remember crossing the threshold of the room or getting to the staircase, but somewhere on the second floor, I realize I'm running. Retracing my steps back to the main floor, I rush around until I find a foyer made of thousands of panes of glass. It leads outside. The glare of the sun meets me, blinding me for a moment as I stumble around, looking for a direction to run. Finding a stone-covered path, I follow it away from the house.

Passing garden-bots, whose metallic bodies glimmer in the harsh sunshine, I shield my eyes from the glare. The path leads through manicured hedgerows. As I dart around them, I scrape my arms on their sharp angles. I glance over my shoulder to make sure Kyon isn't following me, but all I see is the house. It's a fairy boat of timber and glass.

I hurry farther away from it toward the high sea grass and a forest of palm trees in the distance. Moss-covered stones mark the path I travel. When I make it to the trees, I instantly feel relief from the sun within their shade. A gentle breeze drifts against my face. Panting, I slow my pace a bit, following the grassy path that winds ahead of me.

Unable to think clearly, I'm capable only of putting one foot in front of the other at the moment. The impulse to hide is so strong. I don't know how far I am from the house, but I pause when I spy a slate roofline deep in the woods. It's a small, stone gazebo built on a knoll to overlook the sea in the distance. Beside it, a small brook babbles and flows over smooth stones on its way to the side of the hill in a trickling waterfall. I go to the ledge of the shelter, sitting on it. In the distance, the Sea of Stars sparkles like the glimmers of a thousand searchlights. Watching it, I try to get my head together, but I can't brush off the events of my nightmarish morning.

Excelsior Ensin is insane. People like me don't win against people like Excelsior. I know that from growing up in Chicago. If I stand up to him, I die. The huge obstacle I face is that Kyon refuses to let me go. I have to find a way to escape them both. This has never been my fight, not really. I'd been discarded on Earth. Ethar means almost nothing to me, or at least, it never used to—now I'm not so sure. It's Trey's home and he's my home.

"I need you to come and find me," I whisper, as if my words could change time and space and bring me my heart's desire.

The snap of a stick nearby makes me bolt to my feet. I reach for a stone on the ground, picking it up in my fist. I glance around, scanning the area for anything that moves. I hear a deep, male rumble of laughter. Winding back, I throw the stone in the direction of it. The rock changes course and veers away as soon as it reaches the entrance of the gazebo. It falls to the ground in the middle of the pavilion. My eyes widen in surprise as a voice says, "You almost hit me."

"Giffen!" I whisper accusingly, still unable to see him.

"Your intuition is uncanny. Good throw, by the way."

"Knob knocker!" I spit. "Where are you? Get me out of here!"

"You just got here."

"Come out of hiding so I can murder you!" I growl.

He instantly appears under the archway of the gazebo. His hand falls away from a small, silver box clipped to the waistband of his black belt. He's attired in the same type of uniform that I saw the matchstick soldiers of Amster wearing when I projected into their compound last night. He sweeps his light-brown dreadlocks back from his face, then rests his hand on the hilt of a knife holstered on his side. It makes him look dangerous, even when he doesn't make a move to draw it. I take a step back from him. He notices. His eyes follow mine to his hand on the knife. He moves his hand away from the blade and strokes his beard instead, smoothing the hair that is the darkest side of blond. His green eyes pass over me as if he's assessing my well-being.

"I'm not here to hurt you, Kricket."

"Good, because I'll kill you if you try."

"You can't kill me." It's not said in a derogatory way—it's just a statement of fact.

"All I'd need to do is tell Kyon you're here and you're a dead man."

His face contorts in anger. The muscles bulge around his rolled-up shirtsleeves. "Is he your man now?"

"Screw you! How did you even know I was here?"

"The Brotherhood deployed an armada of aircraft. They weren't hard to detect. I've been watching the action on the beach. When it ended, I hung around and watched the house. Then . . . you came out, so I followed you."

"You knew I was here."

He shrugs. "I had an idea. You're our ghost. I told you I'd find you and make contact."

"You're wasting your time—I'm not telling you anything until you get me out of here."

He shakes his head. "That's not how this works."

"That's how it works for me unless you'd like me to let Kyon know you're here." I make a move toward the entrance of the gazebo.

He takes a step in front of me to block my way. His jaw clenches as he points at me. "I'd be gone by the time you could make it back to the house."

I want to scare him. "Don't forget I know where you live—" No sooner are the words out of my mouth than I am lifted up off the ground and slammed into the stone pillar behind me. He keeps me pinned to the pillar using his telekinetic power. I cough and wheeze, trying to catch my breath as I dangle above the ground.

"Careful, Kricket," Giffen warns. "The moment I actually believe that you'll flip on us is the moment you're truly dead."

"How did you get past Oscil? The security on this island is extensive; there are sensors everywhere."

"I'm unique, Kricket. I've been using my abilities to obstruct the sensors. They won't pick up on me unless I allow them to."

"What do you want?" I gasp. I must have bitten my lip because it throbs and I taste blood in my mouth.

"Information. What can you tell us about the ships we saw amassed around the island?" he asks.

I don't reply; I just stare at him, hoping somehow it'll kill him. Why didn't I get that ability? Death-ray eyes. Seeing the future is completely useless compared to that.

He sighs. "You do know we have Trey? You were just there. His welfare depends on how well you do here."

"Astrid won't let you hurt him."

"Astrid won't have any say in what happens to him. He's my prisoner. If you want to keep him alive, you'll cooperate."

Giffen underestimates Trey. He'll have Trey only as long as Trey is hurt. After that, Giffen won't have crap. I only have to hold on until then. All we need is time. I relent, saying, "The ships were sent by the Alameeda Brotherhood, led by Excelsior Ensin. He intended to swing by and pick me up."

Giffen shows little emotion. "Kyon refused to relinquish you to his father?"

"That's right."

Giffen glances up at me, his green eyes narrow. "How long does Kyon plan to stay here—on this island?" He walks closer to me, coming to stand beneath where I'm pinned to the wall. The shadow of the pillar on him hides the golden streaks in his hair.

I study the handsome contours of his face before I reply, "I don't know. Kyon said he wants us to get to know each other. He thinks it'll be too hard to do that with other people around."

Giffen's lips twist. He almost looks jealous. "Why? What does he want to know about you?"

I shrug. "I don't know. Given our history, the only thing I expect from Kyon is pain." Giffen's frown deepens, causing me to say, "You don't think I'm right."

"He didn't hand you over to Excelsior. He kept you instead."

"Maybe Kyon wants something from Excelsior in exchange for me and is just waiting to raise the stakes."

"Or maybe *you're* what he wants," Giffen retorts.

"You believe that," I whisper softly.

"He could've demanded anything in exchange for you and it would've been granted by his father. He didn't do that."

"I think you're wrong. They hate each other with the kind of loathing I've only seen in bad foster homes," I murmur thoughtfully. "Kyon may not have given me up just *because* it's Excelsior who wants me."

He shakes his head again. "It's more than bad blood, Kricket. Kyon has a plan in place. I need you to find out what it is."

"You're not taking me back with you?" Something inside me squeezes tight. I think it's my bloodless heart, but I'm not sure because my entire chest aches.

"You're valuable to us here—with Kyon. You can get close to him; find out what he knows about what the Brotherhood is planning. Win his trust. Stay valuable to us and you stay alive. Should that change . . ."

"What? You'll kill me?" I ask, even knowing that his threat was implicit. "My father would let you do that?"

"This is bigger than any of us. This is the fate of Ethar. I know you don't care about that—how could you—deep down, you still think you're from Earth."

"Whose fault is that?" I ask.

Giffen comes to stand just beneath me. "Be our eyes, Kricket, and you'll survive this." He lets me fall from the pillar, catching me in his arms. As my feet slide to the ground, he pulls me against his strong chest, holding me steady. My cheek rests briefly against the soft fabric of his uniform. I inhale his scent. A memory flashes in my mind—Chicago in autumn—my face resting against fallen leaves—an unbelievable ache in my chest—that smell—his smell—his voice saying, *"You'll be okay. I'm going to make you okay, just hang on—"*

Giffen disrupts the images by saying, "I have to go. Your father wanted me to give you a message when I saw you."

"Don't. I don't want to hear it." I try to push away from him, but he won't let me.

Giffen strokes his hand over my hair. "He told me to tell you, 'The future is what you make it.'" I let go of Giffen entirely, but he continues to hold me to him.

"Did he steal that from a cat poster or something?" I ask scornfully.

Giffen grasps my upper arms and pulls me away from his chest so he can look into my eyes. "What? No! It was heartfelt."

"Okay, you've delivered your message. Now let go of me." He immediately turns me loose. Distancing myself from him, I stare out over the far away Sea of Stars. "You can go now."

"Is there something you want me to tell Pan in return?" Giffen asks in a strained voice.

"No."

"This is not how your father wants things—"

"But this is how things are," I reply bitterly. I turn around sharply, glaring at him. "Just go! I want you to leave!"

He reaches out to me, gathering my hair in his fist. "I hurt you." His other hand clutches my chin. He rubs his thumb over my bottom lip. A smear of blood shows on his skin. "Let me cut your hair so it stops bleeding."

"You're so bad at this!" I try to brush his hand away from my hair, but he holds it tighter.

"What do you mean?" he asks defensively. His eyebrows come together in a scowl.

"You can't threaten to kill me, and then care about my bloody lip—and you honestly mean both! Which is totally schizo!"

He pulls out a knife and cuts my hair without a word. Letting the ashes of it fall from his fingers, he turns away from me and says over his shoulder, "Find out what Kyon is planning. I'll be in touch." His hand reaches for the silver box on his belt. An instant after that, he disappears from my sight, becoming invisible.

I don't move right away. Even after the sound of his footfalls die away, I just stand where I am like a complete idiot. Finally, I take a step to leave, but I stop. I look around. I don't know where I'm going—back to Kyon's house? Why would I do that? I should be trying to find a way off this island . . . but then what? Where would I go? Amster? I'm not welcome there—and that's if I made it, which I probably wouldn't.

My knees tremble. I sink to the ground, sitting down and leaning my back against one of the stone pillars. Drawing my knees up to my chest, I rest my head on them. I need a plan. The only one I can come up with right now involves hanging on long enough for Trey to get well enough to come find me, but I hate that plan. It's weak.

I lift my head from my knees. Looking around, I'm unsure if I'm alone. The technology here is ridiculous. I decide I don't care. I may not be able to physically leave here, but I can still leave, at least for a little while. I rub my hands together, leaning back against the pillar, but then I think better of it. Instead, I stretch out on the floor of the gazebo so I don't accidentally hit my head when I leave my body. My skin prickles with fear. The last time I did this I almost died, and there are oceans between me and where I want to be, but I have to go anyway.

"Trey," I whisper. "I wish I was with you still." I chase my dreams of him, trying to concentrate on where I want to go and when.

As I exhale, I see smoky curls of my frigid breath float away from between my parted lips. Nothing can really prepare me for the separation of my being from my skin. It's always brutal.

As I ascend away from my body at an incredible rate, I endure the torture. I'd writhe in the burning heat of it if I had a body to writhe in. The searing pain fades quickly to only slight discomfort, though, as I move in a flash-forward. Taking a rail spur in time, it leads me to where I'd gone last night—the long room at the top of the recently renovated Gothic-style governor's mansion in Amster.

Moving by the line of empty hoverbeds, I see the backs of Raspin and four other uniformed Amster soldiers. They're cautiously moving toward a bare-chested Trey. He's attired in thin cotton trousers that are cinched at his waist by a drawstring. He seems disoriented, as if he's trying to piece together where he is and what's happening to him. He holds his hand to the side of his face, touching a large, black bruise with his fingertips. He winces, and then looks at his hand. He studies the small, time-release, drug-dispensing cylinder fastened to it.

Between the Amster soldiers and Trey, Astrid is holding out both of her hands, pleading with Trey, "You need to get back into bed. You've been very sick." She touches his chest where his tribal tattoo swirls and weaves a path over his skin to his chiseled abdomen. She tries to redirect him back to the vacant hovercot behind him. He shakes off her hand, inadvertently disconnecting a couple of wires that had been attached to him.

"Where is she? I want to see her!" Trey demands with a half-panicked, half-bewildered look in his violet eyes. In the distance, doors slam, feet are running. More grim-faced soldiers crowd around in the hallway outside, watching, waiting.

Sunlight shines into the room from the high dormer-style windows above, putting Astrid and Trey in a golden spotlight. Their hair is a similar color: raven's wings in this light, blue-black with the hint of night. Raspin prowls closer to Astrid. He touches her arm, intending to guide her away from Trey, but she won't let him. She shakes him off. Her focus is on my Rafe soldier. "Do you know who I am?" she asks.

Trey grasps his forehead as if he has a massive headache. "No—but you're part Rafian."

"And I'm part Alameedan. You probably noticed my blue eyes already," Astrid replies gently.

"Should I know you?"

"Yes . . . and no," Astrid stammers, "that is to say, we've met—briefly—you were barely conscious, though."

"Are you the medic?" Trey asks, straightening and dropping his hand from his forehead.

"I've been assisting with your care, Trey," Astrid replies, using his name.

Trey touches her upper arm, and says in a rush, "There's a girl. Her name is Kricket. She—"

"You should get back in bed so I can tell you—"

"—she was with me at my house in Rafe territory—we were attacked—" He tries to get closer to Astrid, but the wires attached to his chest get in his way, snapping him back. He grabs them all with his other hand and tears them off his chest without flinching. A myriad of beeping and alarms ring out on the hovercot. Astrid goes to the hovercot and turns off the offending noise by pressing buttons on its console. Trey faces her, ignoring the men behind him. "She's short"—he holds up his hand, measuring my height on his chest—"blonde, looks like a priestess, but she's not one of them, she's one of us. Do you know where she is? Was she brought here too?"

Astrid straightens to face Trey again, but she has deflated a bit from her statuesque posture. She tucks her long, black hair behind her ear. "My name is Astrid. Do you know who I am?"

"No . . . I . . ." Trey pauses. "Did you say Astrid?"

She nods, "I did."

He looks at her then—really looks at her. "Who are you?"

"I'm Kricket's sister—her younger sister."

He's hardly fazed by her answer, which attests to either his brain injury or the fact that he's singularly focused on me. "Kricket's here?" He nods his head as if to make it so.

She shakes her head. "No. It's complicated. Sit down and I'll explain it to you."

"I don't need to sit down. Where is she? Is she alive?"

"She's alive," Astrid replies, "we think—"

"You think? You don't know if she's alive?"

"We believe she's alive. We think we may know where she is now, but it's unconfirmed. Giffen hasn't reported back yet—"

"Giffen? Is he a Comantre soldier—was he on the Ship of Skye before it was destroyed?"

"He was there," Astrid affirms. "He's one of us, though, not Comantre."

"He's part of this?" Trey waves his hand around, indicating the other soldiers.

"He's part of the reconstruction of New Amster."

"Does he have Kricket?" Trey asks.

"No. He believes he has located her. We're waiting for his confirmation—"

"Where?"

"The Sea of Stars." She all but chokes on the words.

"The Sea of—that's Alameeda—" His face contorts as if she's thrown ice water on him. "That's Kyon's family seat. Does he have her?"

"We're trying to locate her."

Frustration makes him snarl, "Does Kyon have her?"

Astrid makes a slow retreat from him. Backing away, she answers, "Yes."

Wayra's voice interrupts them then. "Giffen and that tall, dopey-looking one over there"—he points to Raspin—"gave Kricket to Kyon in exchange for her sister, Astrid." Wayra's contemptuous words resound in the room as he shoves his way in past soldiers who are almost as big as *he is. Someone has given him a coal-black Amster uniform, but he has modified it. It no longer sports a collar, having been ripped off so that more of the swirling, black military tattoos on the side of his throat are visible. Jax is behind him, sidestepping the other soldiers with a bit more tact than Wayra displayed.*

"You're her sister?" Trey asks Astrid in confusion, like she hadn't already told him that.

"That's correct," she replies as she wrings her hands.

"Why would you do that? Why would you give her to him?" Trey can't understand that kind of disloyalty. It's not in him.

Wayra doesn't let her answer the question. "Kyon had Astrid. It was an even exchange."

"Why didn't you stop it?" Trey retorts, turning on Wayra in anger.

Wayra doesn't back down. "I had my head beaten in too." He points to the side of his head. His ear is cut up and looks as if it might have been sewn back on with knitting needles. "I didn't find out about it until I came to, here in knob-knocking Amster!" He sneers, but it's not directed at Trey. His taunting words are for the soldier near Astrid. One of them growls and makes a move toward Wayra. Astrid stays the soldier with a gesture of her hand. Wayra's lip curls in contempt. He wants a fight. He's begging for one.

"We can fix your scars," Astrid says to Wayra.

He rounds on her. "Why would I let you do that? You're a blood traitor! You gave up your own sister!"

Astrid becomes emotional as well. "I didn't give her up! I was trying to save her!"

"Wayra," Jax says behind him. "Let me give Trey an update on what we've learned."

Jax moves around Wayra, getting closer to Astrid. He gives my sister a brief nod, saying, "If I may?"

Astrid responds immediately with a smile to his innate kindness. Jax has that effect on almost everyone. "Of course," she replies, raising her hand to usher him nearer to Trey.

"Sir," Jax says, facing Trey, "we were just down in one of the ops rooms. They have positive confirmation that Kricket is alive. She's on a small island in the Sea of Stars."

"Is she okay?" Trey asks.

"She's well, by all accounts."

"When is her extraction?" Trey asks. "I want all the details."

Jax hesitates, and then says, "There's no extraction, sir."

"Why not? Is it still in the planning stages?"

"Negative. She's embedded."

"Embedded? Kricket is spying?"

"No," Jax says, grimacing. "I wouldn't term it quite that way."

"Explain," Trey growls.

"She started off as a ransom, an exchange given for Astrid, who was caught and held by Strikers near the Isle of Skye. New Amster has no intention of rescuing Kricket, though. A plan was formulated early on, but it's been scrapped."

"Why?"

"Kricket is shaping up to be something of a distraction to the Alameeda—something for them to fight over. If she can provide information to New Amster then that's a bonus, but given her intelligence, they've found that simply inserting her in the fray has sent the Brotherhood into chaos mode . . . and New Amster is rather enjoying it."

"Why would they use her like that?"

Jax glances at Astrid before looking back at Trey. "If the Brotherhood is fixated on Kricket, they aren't looking anywhere else. New Amster is a rebel base. They plan to fight the Alameeda and all its allies."

Whatever Jax is saying gets through to Trey and it acts as a tolling bell to a sleeping giant. Trey turns away from Jax and grasps the tabletop by his bedside, hunching over it. He lifts it up and bashes it against the floor a couple of times before he throws it clear across the room. The soldiers near the door duck out of its way. It crashes into the wall, *splintering into a thousand pieces. He rounds on the other New Amster soldiers, the closest being Raspin.*

Jax catches him before he can attack Raspin. "Wayra," *Jax says imploringly,* "a little help?"

"Why?" *Wayra retorts, but he grips Trey's shoulders anyway.* "We should kill all these wackers!"

Jax grunts, not faring well against Trey, even in his weakened state. "Because then . . . we leave her alone in a fight she can't possibly win!" *he snarls.*

Wayra and Jax struggle to keep Trey away from Raspin, until Wayra forces Trey back against the wall. "Brother," *Wayra pants,* "we've got this." *He looks into Trey's eyes as if they're the only two here.*

"She's all alone, Wayra." *Trey's voice sounds sinister.*

"So we do what we do. We find her on our own and we get her back." *Releasing his arms, Wayra grasps Trey by the shoulder and he hugs him to him, saying,* "Baw-da-baw, Trey."

Trey's hand clenches, but his arm around Wayra's shoulder hugs him back. "Baw-da-baw," *Trey replies as he stares coldly at Astrid over Wayra's shoulder.*

I can't stay any longer. An ice-water wind blows mercilessly through me. The pull on me to return to my body is undefeatable, and it has me fading into the darkness like a colorless star. I give in to it and snap backward faster than a Jetstream to return to my body.

Taking possession of myself once more, I struggle to inhale a full breath. My lungs are deflated, like a bagpipe with no wind. I open my eyes to a prism of bleeding colors in the bright sunlight, and I close them again. I'm conscious enough to understand that someone is carrying me—Kyon. I'm jostled and bumped against his chest as he runs with me in his arms. The light that shows red through my eyelids suddenly dims, and I hear his shoes clap against the stone floor.

He lays me on a soft mattress. We're now in our bedroom. The next thing I feel is a hard slap to my cheek. I open my eyes and see him above me. Lifting my hand to my swelling face, I groan, "Yeah, I felt that."

"You're back," he says. He exhales in relief. He gazes down at me like he's glad to see me.

"Worried, were you?" My voice is gravelly as I quake with cold. I feel frozen from the inside out.

"You have to gain some control over your ability, Kricket, or it will kill you." *He's sort of handsome when he's concerned*, I think begrudgingly. He gathers the blanket on the bed and tosses it over me, covering my trembling limbs.

"I'll work on it if you agree to stop hitting me," I say, rubbing my stinging cheek. My skin is freezing and I have vanilla ice cream breath. There is something in my mouth. I spit it out into my hand. Looking in my palm, I find a sliver of a vanilla bean, only it must be the Etharian version because it's the size of a coffee bean. I let it fall into the folds of the blanket.

"I was told that the taste of vanilla would sometimes bring your mother back from the future," Kyon explains. He picks it up and throws it outside onto the patio.

"So you shoved a bean in my mouth?"

"I've been carrying them with me since last night. I thought it might help bring you back. Did it?" he asks.

"I don't know," I reply honestly. I'm starting to thaw. "I liked it better than the slap."

He flops on the bed next to me, and we both lie shoulder to shoulder looking up as the waning sunlight moves across the ceiling. My teeth stop chattering. I glance at him; his shirt is wet with sweat.

"Did you carry me all the way back from the gazebo in the woods?"

"Yes, and you weigh a ton," he lies. "I'll have to stop feeding you pancakes."

I study his cameo-perfect profile. His blond hair covers mine. "What happened?"

"You're asking me? I'm not the one who just came back from the future."

"You found me on the ground in the gazebo?"

"Yes. It will be dark soon. You should've been back sooner. I went looking for you."

"Were you worried?" I ask with a frown. "I thought you said we're safe here from attack."

"A lot of things can happen here. There are other ways to get hurt."

"Oh." I shrug that off. "I can take care of myself."

"Clearly," he scoffs, gesturing in my direction.

"I'm all right," I murmur.

"A few more moments away from your body and you wouldn't have been. I tried everything I knew to get you to come back."

"Clearly. The bean was genius," I tease him.

"You were gone a long time. You must have seen something very important."

"I didn't see anything," I lie.

"And I didn't just hit you."

I need to change the subject. I turn toward him, drawing my legs up. "Why do you hate your dad?"

He shows no emotion as he says, "You didn't seem to like him much, either."

My laughter is hollow. "I tend not to like people who want to kill me. It's this rule I have."

"He wants to kill me too. He wants to kill anything he can't control."

"He can't control you?" I ask.

"Not anymore. Not for a very long time."

"So we're allies in that."

"In what? In staying alive?" he asks with a small smile.

"Yes," I say softly.

"If you'd like," he replies.

"I'd much rather go home."

"You *are* home."

I turn away from him and look up at the ceiling once more. "That's funny—this doesn't look anything like my apartment in Chicago."

"You've outgrown Chicago," Kyon replies. He leans over and kisses me quickly on the cheek. He rolls to the edge of the bed and stands. Peeling off his damp shirt, he tosses it on a nearby chair. He turns to me, and I get an eyeful of his ridiculous physique. He looks fake—someone had to have airbrushed his abdomen or something because it's too perfect. I can feel myself blushing. I look back at the ceiling again.

"I'm going for a swim. Do you need anything before I go?"

I shake my head no.

"You're sure you're feeling better?" he asks.

"I'm good."

"I'll be back, and then we can dine together."

"Fine."

He leaves then, and I crawl up to the pillows on the bed. Resting my head against one, I stretch out beneath the blanket, bringing it up to my neck. While Kyon is distracted, I should probably check out the house for weapons and places to hide, but I'm beat. I feel like I've been run over and my head is achy. I reach under my pillow, finding that the knife I'd stashed there this morning is still there. I shove it back under the pillow and close my eyes.

⁂

"Kricket." Kyon's deep voice penetrates my groggy mind.

"What?" I groan, trying to cling to sleep. I squint at him and see that it's dark outside.

"Are you hungry?" he asks, stroking my hair.

"You're waking me up to see if I'm hungry?" I ask soporifically.

"Yes," Kyon murmurs.

"You're so mean," I grumble. "I was sleeping! I never get to sleep on this stupid planet!" I sigh. "Someone is always chasing me, or hitting me, or waking me up. This planet is so rude."

Kyon laughs. "So you're not hungry?"

I turn away from him and bury my head beneath another pillow. Kyon stretches out next to me and slides me to his chest. I would pull away, but I don't have the energy to fight him. I feel like I've been awake for days. "Go to sleep then," he whispers near my ear.

I try to ignore him.

"You're safe here."

I sigh heavily and turn over to face him, saying "Shh!" as I cover his mouth with my hand. I can feel him laughing beneath it. He pulls my hand away from his mouth and threads his fingers through mine. He rests his chin against the top of my head and doesn't say another word.

CHAPTER 5

DAWN GOLDEN

My eyes open to brilliant sunlight streaming into the bedroom. The white curtains beside the archway that leads to the sea billow in the late morning sun.

"Are you awake now?" Kyon asks. He's lying beside me with his head on a couple of ivory-colored pillows. I panic for a second when I see him, but then I remember where I am.

"Yes," I say, stretching. I'm still in the same clothes as yesterday, which makes me feel better. He didn't try anything criminal last night.

"Do you feel well? You slept a long time." He turns away and sets a tablet on the table beside him, giving me a view of his back. My eyes skim over his bare skin. *Do I feel well? No, I don't. I hate the disturbing feelings he inspires in me: fear, hatred, attraction . . .*

I rub my eyes. "I usually don't sleep as long as most Etharians. I'm used to shorter days and nights. I get tired more often."

"That will change over time. Are you hungry now?" he asks.

"I'm starving," I reply, sitting up against my pillow.

He frowns, and right away I can tell that he's taking me way too seriously. "Do you feel faint? I've already ordered you some pancakes. You should've eaten last night!"

I hold up my hand to stave off a bigger freak-out. "I'm not really starving, Kyon. It's just an expression. I'm moderately hungry."

He pauses, considering what I just told him. "Your idioms are confusing," he replies.

"I know," I murmur, "but they're a habit. It's hard to change them. So when I tell you I'm starving, I just mean I'd like to eat soon."

"How did you survive on Earth? No one there says what they mean."

I scoff. "Like it's any different here."

"I say what I mean."

"And you mean what you say."

"Is that wrong?"

"It is when it's in direct opposition to me," I reply.

"You don't know what you don't know, Kricket."

"Does anyone really know what they don't know, Kyon? And you'd be surprised what I know."

"Would I?'

"Mmm."

"What do you know?" he asks.

I lean near him and whisper secretively, "It's very dark in Pretty Town." I straighten again. "You can quote me."

"I don't know what that means."

"It means you're dark," I reply.

"And you think I'm pretty?" he asks. He doesn't know if he should be offended or flattered, but I think he's leaning toward the former.

"Are those the pancakes?" I ask, avoiding the question as a gleaming hovercart glides into our room and comes to rest at the side of the bed. "Are we eating in bed?"

"You showed such a propensity for it last night that I thought you might enjoy dining here. Afterward, I can show you the rest of the island."

The cart opens up, jettisoning two silver-colored, floating trays. One stops in front of me. When I touch it, the lid opens, revealing a huge stack of pancakes. I glance at Kyon. He has an equal stack of pancakes on his plate. He picks up his fork and says, "You know these aren't very good for Pretty Town."

I nearly choke. When I can speak once more, I murmur, "I think Pretty Town can handle it."

When we're finished eating, Kyon shows me how to nudge the tray away. It glides to the hovercart and inserts itself inside. The hovercart floats away then, probably headed for the dishery. I head for the Commodus, and then into the shower in the lavare. From there I get made over in the dressing room. I emerge from behind the white doors wearing a black two-piece bathing suit with a matching, flowy wrap skirt and an ivory scoop neck top.

Kyon has his back to me as he stands in the archway, watching the sea. He must have showered outside or went for a swim because his hair is wet, but it's pulled back from his face. He has changed into loose-fitting dove-gray swim shorts and a soft white shirt. Turning to face me when he hears me approach, his eyes fall on my hair. It was braided by the robotic beauty-bots.

Kyon touches the small of my back and guides me outside onto to patio. "The boathouse is this way," he says.

Before I step onto the sand, I ask, "Is it safe?"

"For you." He waits for me to step down on the white sand. When I do, he takes me down to the beach. I slip off my sandals and we walk along the shore together. The sand is hot, so I wade into the water and splash around to cool off.

"I'll teach you," he says, gesturing to the water.

"Teach me what?"

"To swim," he says in a low tone.

I look out at the water and then back at him. "You mean you can teach me to swim in the water that you tried to drown me in?"

"Yes."

I shiver involuntarily. "No thanks. I'm good," I say and take a few steps.

He grips my arm. "You will learn to swim. It's not a request. You can't have any weaknesses."

I can't square him or what's happening here. *Is he serious?* He's been hunting me for months, preying on all my weaknesses. Now he wants to teach me to swim so I won't be weak? He's as mercurial as they come. I shrug, noncommittal.

He continues the tour of the island, taking me to the boathouse. It's constructed of huge timber logs and steel joints. Inside, there are four boats suspended in the air on hydraulic lifts. Two of them can probably carry forty people or more, and the other two are smaller, made to be fast, judging by their aerodynamic designs. Each has the capacity to carry only three or four people. He owns two black, bullet-shaped hydrocycles that resemble hovercycles, but they travel on the surface of the water. He also has a berth where a submarine floats on the lapping waves. It resembles a stingray with undulating wings and a slippery skin with marine mammal markings on it.

"Which one do you like the most?" I ask, gesturing to the menagerie of toys before me.

"Which boat?" he asks. "This one." He points to the long rowboat with oars that's shelved on the wall beside us. It's silver with black rally stripes on the hull.

"Why?" I move closer to the sleek rowboat. It's archaic in terms of Etharian standards, a kind of boat that someone who's well versed in rowing would use to train. There are no automated parts to it. I run my fingertips over an oarlock. It feels like steel.

"Because it requires strength," Kyon says behind me. "It can hurt you, but it can also set you free."

For some reason, I wonder if we're still talking about the boat. "What would someone like you need to be free of?" I wonder.

"Questions, for one," Kyon replies.

"What's wrong with questions?"

"You like questions? I have one. What did you see our first night here?"

"Excuse me?"

"You left me with just your body on the beach. You projected into the future. I want to know what you saw there." His arms form a cage around me, resting on the hull of his favorite boat.

I stare up into his blue eyes. I find it hard to swallow all of a sudden. There's no way I can tell him any of it. If I do, it would be as if I put a gun to the head of each person in Amster and fired. Kyon will slaughter them all with impunity.

"I didn't see much," I lie.

"You were gone a very long time. I think you saw plenty."

"I saw your Alameeda Strikers stack wounded civilians in the streets of Rafe and burn them alive." I hurl the statement at him. It's my only weapon.

His eyebrows draw together as he scowls. "They're not my soldiers. If they were mine, I'd be leading them out of Rafe."

"What are you talking about?"

"They're your soldiers."

"How can you say that?"

"You have but to claim them as your own. By not doing so, every day you're allowing Rafe to die. Only you." He believes what he's saying.

"I don't understand what you're telling me."

"You will." He turns away from me, toward the entrance. "I've had enough of you for now. You can see yourself back to the house," he says over his shoulder.

"You think you have me tamed, Kyon?"

Kyon turns with a cold look in his eyes. "I plan to bring you to your knees again, Kricket."

"I hate you!" I rasp. "I wish someone would just kill you!" Icy air exhales from my mouth like smoke from dry ice. I try to stay in my body. "Why is this happening?" I whisper as my spirit involuntarily leaves my body.

My consciousness rises up into the air as my body collapses onto the wide planks of the boathouse floor. My head bounces off the floor with a dull thud. Kyon runs to my side, kneels down next to me. I float above him, bewildered and silent, unable to stay in this moment.

Even separated as I am from my physical self, I feel fiery heat in my nonexistent bones. Thunderous air rolls under my feet, propelling me into the future. In less than one second, I'm on the other side of the island by the small thatched-roof cottages that crouch in the tree line just off the white-sand beach. Darkness falls like it would if viewed in time-lapse photography. The waves crash against the shore until they cough up dozens upon dozens of black wetsuit-clad swimmers. These men emerge from the surf and form a small huddle on the shore.

Stripping off their masks and black, sealskin headgear, they each reveal short, platinum-colored hair. They're Alameeda. Spitting out breathing devices, they leave them on the beach. One digs weapons out of a waterproof bag and hands them out to the others.

Without a sound, they spread out over the beach. They're hunting. I move with them, a gazelle following lions. Soundlessly, they surround Kyon's main house. Just as one almost makes it to our bedroom doorway, a squelch tracker emerges from it. It locks onto him, and a long spike projection ejects from its silver body. The metallic assassin device jets forward. A high-pitched scream comes from it as it impales the wetsuited soldier in the abdomen. He screams too, but it doesn't sound like a seal's wail when lasers flail out of the squelch tracker and cut him to ribbons.

An explosion on the far side of the house indicates that another soldier has found a trap set by Kyon. Two more squelch trackers find the Alameeda soldiers, reducing them to piles of flesh and bone.

Kyon silently emerges from beneath the white sand. He cuts the throats of two soldiers before they can even set foot on the stone patio. Kyon moves off the beach. He's near our bedroom when a projectile tears through his side. Swinging around, he fires his automatic freston at the Alameeda soldier who shot him. They both unload hollow-pointed ammunition into each other. The enemy soldier falls to the sand without half of his face, but Kyon is a bloody mess too. He drops to his knees. His nostrils flare as he tries to gulp in air. Holding his hand to his side, he looks down at his abdomen and finds a large chunk of it missing. Unable to walk now, he crawls to the door of our bedroom.

Screams of pain come from inside—my screams. The pale moons shine on the bed where I'm fighting and clawing to get away from a soldier who is holding me down. At the same time, I kick my legs and struggle against another vicious soldier as he cuts my clothes from me. "The Brotherhood sends its love," the one with the knife snarls. Kyon lifts his freston and shoots the soldier in the head. The soldier's brains explode all over the bed. Before the other soldier can react, Kyon is able to get off a few more shots, killing the one holding me down.

Kyon collapses onto the ground. I see my future self sit up on the bed and crawl onto the floor to Kyon's side. Placing a hand over his wounds, the future me tries to stem his bleeding, but it's futile. Kyon's injuries are far too serious.

More soldiers enter the room. They don't attempt to take me hostage. Two shots ring out: One tears through my heart, and the other goes through my head. My corpse falls next to Kyon's on the floor.

What happens next is chilling. One of the soldiers kneels down next to my body. He injects a tube into my vein and extracts my blood. While he does that, another soldier slices open my abdomen and extracts my ovaries from my corpse. Horrified, I can't stay any longer. I escape from the house through the starlit rush of time.

CHAPTER 6
HAUNTING IDLE

Pain greets me as I fall into my body, reclaiming it. My back arches as I grasp my chest where I'm shot. I gulp in frantic breaths of air, trying to alleviate the pain in my aching heart. The tightness in my chest is strange, though. My fingers search for the massive, gaping wound, but I find nothing wrong with me. In a few more breaths, the pain eases and begins to fade away.

Kyon's eyes are a soft blue as I look up at him. My head is on his lap. His hand is gentle as he strokes my hair in a slow, rhythmic way. My teeth chatter, not just from the pain and fear I just experienced, but also because I'm so cold. My whole body quakes.

"Easy," he murmurs. "Breathe slowly."

We're still in the boathouse. Water laps against the support beams below us, making soft sounds.

"They're—" I wheeze "—coming!" I take a few more straining breaths. "Soldiers—"

"Shh, I need to get you warm. You're freezing." He gently lifts my head from his lap and rests it on the wooden floor. He lies next to me, takes me in his arms, and holds me against his chest to share his body heat. My cheek rests against his shoulder as he rubs my arm, dispelling some of the goose bumps. It takes a few minutes for my breathing to slow and my teeth to stop chattering.

Kyon's lips brush my hair before he murmurs, "When do they come?"

Fear is the unmistakable quality in my shaky voice when I whisper, "Tonight." I try to sit up, but Kyon tightens his arms, not allowing me to move.

"How many?" he asks in a calm tone.

"At least a hundred—maybe more—"

"How do they come?"

"What?" I close my eyes, feeling his hand gently rub my back. It eases some of my anxiety.

"How do they gain access to the island? Is it an air strike?"

"No," I shake my head. "They come by water—they swim to shore—that's how they get in undetected."

"On what part of the island do they stage their arrival?" he asks.

"The beach in front of your cottages."

"Is that their only access point?" I think for a moment, and then I nod my head. Kyon pulls me closer to him, resting his chin on my head. "Good girl," he whispers.

"You don't get it!" I try to pull away from him. He lets me go enough so that I can look into his eyes. "We have to leave! They're going to kill us!"

His eyes soften. There's no fear in them whatsoever. "No, they're not—"

I clutch his arm, trying to make him understand. "Yes! They *are*! They're coming and you can't stop them all—"

"They can't do anything to us now, Kricket, because you're going to tell me everything you know that will happen and I'm going to take care of the rest."

Panic overwhelms me. *He still doesn't get it!* "There are too many of them! They're sent by the Brotherhood—by Excelsior!"

"I know. You scare them."

"*I* scare *them*?" I laugh humorlessly.

My incredulous response is met by unflagging stoicism. "More than anything in this world," he replies.

"Why haven't you handed me over to him?"

His expression turns angry. What I just said to him is something he finds completely offensive. "I told you—you're mine."

I shiver. "They want me dead."

"They want to kill anything they can't control."

"Well, they're gonna do it tonight," I promise as I look up at the exposed beams of the boathouse ceiling. The water makes diamond patterns on the wood. Normally it's hypnotic and beautiful, but now I find no pleasure in it.

Kyon's hand reaches over and cups my cheek. Turning my face toward his again, he says, "If we're to die tonight, then I want one last kiss."

Before I can react, he covers my lips with his own. It's not a last kiss—there's no desperation in it. Instead, his body grows closer to mine, as if magnetically pulled to me. As his lips move over mine, my skin erupts with fresh goose bumps. I want to fight him, but there's something in his kiss that I desperately need at the moment—an assurance that we'll live. My traitorous body reacts to his, to the safety he offers in this moment. The moment passes, though, and I wrench my lips away from his. My heart pounds hard against the cage of my chest. His breathing is heavy against my neck.

"We're going to live, aren't we?" I ask with a shaky voice, touching my fingers to my swollen lips, which still feel his against them.

He smiles against my skin. "That I can promise you," he says softly, "at least for tonight." He lifts his head to look at me. His blue eyes make me think he can see inside my soul. He lets go of me and gets up from the boathouse floor, then extends his hand. "I need you to show me exactly where they come ashore."

I grasp his hand and he helps me to my feet. I feel dizzy. He holds me close, but I push away from him. "I'm fine now," I grumble. I feel awkward. I just want to put some space between us.

"You need me, Kricket." He reaches for my hand again.

I snatch it back from him. "No, I don't."

He frowns, but he doesn't try to take my hand again. Instead, he gestures toward the door. I precede him to it. Outside in the sunlight, everything feels more unreal. *How can anything be wrong in this place—this tropical paradise?*

"It's this way to the beach cottages." He walks along a small, sandy path through the palm trees. I follow him, and he slows until we walk beside each other on the path. I wrap my arms around myself in a protective way. My thoughts are consumed with the imminent attack. When we reach the other side of the island, I show him the precise point where the soldiers will make it onto the beach. We discuss the type of weaponry they'll possess. I tell him about the squelch trackers.

Kyon listens to every detail, making me go over things several times. Then he says, "I'll set more squelch trackers to accommodate their numbers."

"I hate squelch trackers," I mutter, remembering the one that almost killed me.

"None of the squelch trackers I'll set will hunt you, Kricket. If one comes across you here, it will ignore you. They're programmed for specific targets. They'll be unable to hurt you."

"One was set for me at the palace."

"Two were set for you at the palace. I found and destroyed the second one."

"Who set them?"

"I suspect it was Em Nark," he replies honestly.

I remember him. I called him "the Narc." He hated me. He was the pudgy-faced ambassador from Alameeda who tried to negotiate my release from Manus's custody on behalf of the Alameeda Brotherhood.

"Did you kill him? His trift blew up before he left Rafe territory."

Kyon shakes his head. "I planned to." He smiles wickedly. "He would've been dead the moment he landed at his estate in Alameeda. I had my people on it, but he never made it there."

"Then who killed him?"

"Manus," he says matter-of-factly.

"Manus? Why?" I wonder.

"He didn't want Em Nark relaying to anyone your specific gift as a soothsayer—a diviner of truth. If others knew you could tell when they were lying, it would make your gift somewhat moot. They would simply refuse to speak in your presence. Manus killed Em Nark so your secret would remain intact. It made your gift valuable. We had a conversation about it—the Regent and I. We both agreed that it was in our best interests that the Brothers knew nothing about it."

"You spoke to Manus about me?" The information makes my heart lurch in my throat for some reason.

"I spent every single rotation that you were a captive in Rafe trying to negotiate your release from Manus's custody. That is, until he arrested me and nearly executed me. But, we both know how that turned out for him. Manus was not nearly strong enough to protect you from the Brotherhood."

"And you are?"

"I'm your only hope. You realize that the Brotherhood is trying to kill you during your claiming? They're required to respect this time between us as part of the contract that I made with them."

"My claiming? What are you talking about?"

"It's the time we are to spend together after a commitment is made," he struggles to explain, looking at me like I should know what he's talking about.

I think for a second, my nose wrinkles like I just smelled something bad. "You don't mean honeymoon, do you?" I look sidelong at him while I frown. That thought is unsettling.

"Honeymoon?" he says the word like he has no idea what it means. "We're supposed to spend time together—alone—in order to get to know each other as a couple."

I narrow my eyes at him. "We're not a couple."

He frowns. "We *are* a couple."

"I don't want to be claimed."

"You have no say in the matter."

He's primed for a fight. He looks very muscly all of a sudden. I ignore his insanity for a moment, because we can fight about that later if we live. Instead, I ask, "So the Brotherhood didn't approve of this?" I move my pointed finger back and forth between us.

He frowns. "The Brotherhood promised you to me. We have a contract. They want to void the contract. They always secretly planned to rescind it."

"Aren't you part of the Brotherhood?"

"I am," he says, nodding.

"Then don't you have a say it what happens?"

"I have a vote. I have some influence, but I can't always control what they do. They're a vicious, snarling group of politicians who'll smile to your face while they're plotting your death."

"Super. Nice club you're in. Why don't they want you to claim me?"

"Together you and I are exceptionally powerful. They knew I was their best chance of finding and killing you if I was unable to secure you for Alameeda. If you remain with me, they can't control you."

"And you knew all of this beforehand?"

"Of course."

"All their little plots and schemes are going awry. How do you think they feel about that?"

"I'm sure it's all rather upsetting for them. One might say they feel murderous."

I blink. *Did he just make a joke?* I can't tell. He's so straight-faced. I rub my forehead. I don't feel well. It's as if I died earlier today and have been resurrected. "Okay." I look around me for a way to help. "So what should I do? Dig holes for land mines? Carve stakes out of bamboo? Make coconut-shell bombs? What?" I'm only half kidding. I don't want to die tonight, especially not in the way they have planned for me. I'd also like to keep all of my organs, so I'd rather turn this around on them, if I can. "Or we could just leave. We could hide you know—somewhere they'll never find us. Do you know how to get to Chicago? Because if we could get there, I could hide us—"

Kyon gathers me up in his arms and kisses me hard on the mouth. I push against his chest, but he's caveman strong. He lets me go on his own. "You're so adorable sometimes. I almost don't regret not killing you."

I wipe my mouth with the back of my hand. "You're insane. You know that, right?"

"I am the sanest person you know," he says honestly.

"Or the most delusional. I'm leaning toward the latter." I sigh. "What do you want me to do to help?"

"Here, I'll show you." He puts his arm around my shoulder and leads me to the cottage just off the beach. It's only small by the standards of the bigger house on the island. Made of teak, it looks like a bunch of huts connected by brown, wooden bridges with polished driftwood railings. Thatched roofs blow and rustle in the sea breeze, making the same sound as the palm trees on the shore.

We climb the wooden steps and come to a deck. It's lined with legless, hovering chaise lounges for lying in the sun. Plump cream-colored mats cover the hovering chairs. Up a few more stairs and we face a series of interconnected teak structures. To our left is a thatched-roof gazebo with a hammock strung from its wooden pillars. A deck connects it to the structure directly in front of us. It's also made of teak with thatched roofs, wooden floors, and open-wall archways. Under the shelter of a peaked roof, a few elegant, moss-green-covered chairs cluster around the rustic hearth and driftwood mantel. A small bar and commissary are behind the sitting area. Beyond the bar, there are two rooms: One appears to be a bathroom—or, as they call it, a lavare, because it has a glass shower that opens on one side with a view of the sea. The other room is a lovely bedroom with a dreamy froth of white netting over it and an open wall to access a wooden bridge that leads to more thatched-hut structures behind this one.

We enter the hut straight ahead of us through an open wall that has lush green potted palms on either side of it. "Would you like some water?" Kyon asks. I nod to him. He passes the sitting area and goes to the bar. I follow him and lean against the sandstone counter-top while he rounds it to the other side. "Oscil, two glasses of water."

From the center of the sandstone, a hole opens up in the counter, and beautiful goblets of water emerge from beneath its surface. Reaching for a glass, I take a sip of it as Kyon says, "Oscil, prepare the cottages for setting three."

"There is no inclement weather detected in this area. The likelihood of a hurricane making landfall here is point zero zero zero zero—"

"Override hurricane probability. Secure the cottages to setting three. Access to emergency settings restricted to Kyon Ensin."

The gazebo to our left changes. Glass-panel walls emerge from the wood floor, blocking access to the hammock within. Once the transparent barriers are in place, metal hurricane shutters roll down over the glass.

I glance at Kyon for a moment as he drinks his water and watches me. I look away and see most of the open walls to this teak structure begin to close, leaving all but one wall to the outside open—it's the way we came in. The outside walls of the bedroom close off access to the bridge that connects it to the other teak huts as glass partitions emerge from the floor. Steel shutters come down over the glass in this area too, darkening the room. The same thing happens in the lavare—it's shrouded in darkness within seconds by hurricane shutters.

"What are we going to do here?" I ask as I turn toward Kyon again in confusion and find him gone. Looking around, I see him nearing the only exit left open to the cottage.

"You're going to wait here. You'll be safe," Kyon says as he leaves. I hurry toward the exit too, but a glass panel comes up from the floor between us, blocking my way out.

"*No, no, no, no, no!*" I whine as I put my hands on the glass and try to stop it from closing completely. It's no good; I'm not strong enough. The hurricane shutters begin to come down over the outside of the transparent wall. I bang on the glass. "Kyon!" I yell at him, as he smiles at me from the other side.

"Take a nap," he calls back. "You're still exhausted."

The shutters close over all the glass walls and windows, leaving me in total darkness inside. "Oh, no he did *not* just lock me in here and tell me to take a nap! What a *total* knob knocker!" I try to cross the room, stumble into a chair, bruise my knee, walk a step farther, bump into a small table, flail my arms, and stub my toe. "Oww!" I lift my foot and rub it. "Oscil!" I yell in frustration.

"May I be of assistance?" The fem-bot voice asks from above.

"I need some light." Every single light in the place turns on at once. "Let me out of here," I order.

"You are not authorized for a change in command mode."

"Oh, he's such a *wacker*!" I fume. "Oscil, open shutters."

"You are not authorized for that command."

"Override setting three!"

"You are not authorized for that command."

"What can I do?" I growl.

"You may utilize the commissary functions. May I suggest a cup of kafcan?"

"No. What other functions are available to me?" I cross my arms.

"You have access to climate control."

I look around the room. "Do I have access to the fireplace?"

"Yes," Oscil responds. "Do you require a fire?"

I smile. "Why, yes, Oscil. I do require a fire."

The fake logs stacked in the fireplace ignite from a gas starter. A pleasant fire snaps in the hearth. Going to a chair, I pull off one of the fluffy moss-colored throw pillows. Taking it to the fire, I shove it in the flames until it catches. Pulling it out, I toss the pillow onto the chair. In moments, the elegant seat is a raging, burning ball of revenge with black smoke curling from it.

"Fire detected, fire detected," Oscil repeats the statement in a mantra.

"Oh, no. Help," I say in a bored tone. "I must get out. Open the door."

"You are not authorized for that command," Oscil states.

Adrenaline courses through me as I feel a moment of panic. It's short-lived, however, because in the next moment, the sprinklers overhead turn on and douse the sitting area with a high-powered spray of water. It doesn't take more than a few moments for the fire to go out and for me to be completely soaked.

"Dammit!" I mutter. The smoke cycles out of the small room through an air-filtration system. Cleaner-bots emerge from small slots in a wall. A robot trundles around, sucking up the puddles of water on the floor. Another one hovers over the furniture, sucking the water from the upholstery. A third bot strips away the burned material from the elegant frame of the chair and laboriously begins the task of reupholstering it. "You have *got* to be kidding me!" I fume in disgust at the efficiency of the place. I look up at the ceiling, but it's not thatched on the inside—it's solid wood.

I strip off my wet shirt and wrap skirt, balling them up, intending to shove them in the trash in anger until I look at how pretty they are. Instead, I shake them both out and lay each of them on a chair by the commissary to dry. In my black, two-piece bathing suit, I walk out of that room in frustration and move into the bedroom. I find a closet and look inside. It has a couple of wetsuits and some male beach attire—a few shirts. I choose a sky-blue shirt that was definitely made for Kyon, because when I put it on, it looks like a dress on me. I don't care, though. It's soft and perfect at the moment.

Closing the closet, I go to the huge bed. It has a white silk coverlet. I climb onto the bed and wrap the blanket around me. I pull one of the fluffy pillows into my arms and hug it for comfort. I close my eyes. I'm exhausted, but I can't let myself sleep now. I need to plan my escape—our escape—Trey's and mine. Squandering this time alone would be stupid. I try to concentrate on the future. I just need to go a few minutes ahead of now, but it's not just "the when" that I need to control, it's also "the where" and "the what" I want to see that's important. I need to control the randomness of my gift. Getting lost in time is not going to help me, so I focus on "the who." Trey.

My body temperature drops, bringing with it an icy exhale of breath. I lie still on the bed and the conscious part of me lifts out of my body.

Instead of resisting the force being exerted on me, I obey the sky as it pulls me up into it. Flashing forward over a blur of terrain, I'm not at all surprised when Amster materializes before me. I'm outside of the governor's mansion once more. The massive statues of brawny warriors tower above me. Matchstick men are converging here—something major is happening for them to amass this many soldiers in Amster.

I ghost-move up the stairs to their headquarters. The entire first floor is packed with men. They crowd around in one of the cavernous rooms. The Gothic architecture is at odds with the sophisticated graphics and imaging set up to display a small section of a city—one that I've never been to before.

It's extremely quiet in the room, except for the deep voice of a tall soldier with short, auburn hair and brown eyes. He addresses the crowd of soldiers, pointing out buildings in an unfamiliar three-dimensional cityscape grid. "The optimal positioning is to place the charges here . . . here . . . and here." *He uses his laser pointer to indicate the places he's discussing on the holographic model. My attention wanes from him—I'm not interested in what they're planning. I'm only interested in finding Trey. I pass through the bodies of soldiers who are packed close together.*

Someone asks, "How do you propose we get the packages to those positions? Their security is impossible to breach. We've been studying it for a few specks and we haven't found a way in." *A low murmur of discussion passes through the crowd.*

A voice I recognize responds, "You don't need a way in. In fact, you don't have to be there at all before it happens."

I feel like I might melt into the floor. Trey's voice has the same effect on me as playing my favorite song: I want to turn it up, get closer, and feel the vibration of it.

"Who said that?" *the redheaded soldier asks as he scans the crowd. The crowd parts and if I had a real heart, it would stop beating.*

Trey comes into view. He doesn't look good—I mean, he's still incredibly handsome, but he looks as if he might fall down at any moment. Dark circles haunt his eyes. He still has deep bruises on his left temple and jaw.

"Trey Allairis," *Trey introduces himself.*

"Rossi Latener," *the redhead replies.* "You're Rafian."

"I am," *Trey replies.*

"Welcome. You were saying?"

"You can deliver the packages with drones."

The room erupts in laughter. Wayra pushes soldiers aside to stand next to Trey. He looks like he hasn't slept in a few days, either. His expression is murderous as his violet-colored eyes glare at the laughing faces of the Amster soldiers. "You hear something funny?" he fumes. The soldiers closest to him stop laughing. It's probably because he's huge and menacing, towering over them like an avenging angel. The dark warrior tattoo on his neck makes him look scarier than he really is, or maybe he is scary and I just forgot that because we're friends.

Rossi tries to be somewhat diplomatic as he says, "We were just discussing Kalafin's heightened security. We haven't been able to get our men past their interlocking matrix here or here"—he points to places on the three-dimensional hologram with a laser pointer—"let alone our drones."

"I'm not suggesting you get your men or your drones past their security matrix. I'm saying you won't need to because we'll use their drones."

Jax comes to stand on the other side of Trey. "Gennet Trey has been hacking into Alameeda drones and taking control of them since the war started. He can infiltrate any mother ship and get you as many of her baby drones as you require."

Wayra gets nose to nose with the Amster soldier next to him as he sneers, "Are we funny now?" As the soldier backs away from him, the room explodes with a rumble of voices.

Trey waits for them to quiet a little before he raises his voice and says, "We're talking about fully armed drones." The room falls silent. "The kind of arms that can erase a city from Ethar."

Rossi glances to his right. I look in that direction too, and see a dark-haired soldier leaning against the ledge of the console that houses a hologram. He's so familiar, and yet I can't remember where I might have met him until he asks, "How soon can you get us those drones?"

The resonance of his voice cleaves me in two. My whole world shifts on its axis. Right is left and left is wrong. Trey recognizes him too. "You're Pan Hollowell."

"Yes, I am," my father says. He's the tallest person in the room. He doesn't have a single gray hair—he looks as young as Trey does. In fact, they're strikingly similar. Short dark hair, violet-colored eyes, a military bearing. Although the tattoos on their throats are different shapes, Trey's are interlocking swirls and Pan's resemble concentric triangles; they're both inky-black and intimidating. Pan looks amazingly well for someone who has been dead since I was five.

Trey straightens to his full height, ignoring the obvious ache it causes to do so. "I can get you the drones as soon as you provide us with a ship and some weapons so we can get your daughter back."

"You know my daughter well?"

"Yes. I love your daughter."

"Then you should have left her where I hid her."

Cringing, my vision blurs. There's an aching pull within me to return to my body. I try with all my might to resist it. I don't want to leave Trey; I want to be his shadow, but something is very wrong. Have I been gone from my body too long today? *I wonder.*

Trey explains, "When I found her, Chicago had become a hostile environment for her—she was hunted."

Pan crosses his arms over his chest. "We had eyes on the Alameeda in Chicago—Kyon, Forester, Lecto—they wouldn't have gotten off Earth alive with her. We didn't anticipate you. Once we put together what happened—your abduction of Kricket—we nearly had you at Naren Falls. If it weren't for the Comantre Syndics there, you would've been in Amster sooner than now."

"You had eyes on her on Earth? Whose eyes?"

Pan looks in my direction. "Giffen has been Kricket's keeper since her last keeper was killed. How long has it been, Giffen?"

From behind me, Giffen says, "Almost six floans." I turn around. Giffen's eyes are rooted on me—on the spot that I occupy. He knows I'm here. He can sense me.

Trey glowers at Pan. "How could you leave Kricket behind on Earth? She was a child. She was defenseless. Your keepers were worthless—none of them sheltered her."

"They were ordered not to shelter her. She's stronger for it. Kricket has a destiny. What she learned on Earth will determine how she acts here. Now."

"Do you realize that she didn't even know that she had a sister? She thought Astrid was a doll or toy that she lost when her parents died— when you died, Pan! It didn't stop her from looking for Astrid. She just didn't know what she was looking for."

Pan glances away, unsettled by the information. "The nepenthe assured us that all of her memories of Astrid would be expunged."

"The nepenthe?" Trey asks in confusion.

"Sanham. He's the first Alameeda male offspring with the EVS819 gene that I rescued from being exterminated. After I met Arissa, Kricket's mother, we began our mission to find and shelter as many enhanced males that we could smuggle out of Alameeda alive. Sanham's gift is instilling forgetfulness. He wipes away memories. He attempted to make Kricket forget us. Unlike with most Etharians, it didn't work very well on her. She repelled it. She's always been exceptional."

"Why would you do that to her? Why would you try to make her forget everyone she loved?"

A part of me hopes that he'll say that he didn't want me to suffer with my memories of them. "I have two daughters," Pan says. "I had to protect Astrid in case Kricket was discovered and interrogated. Sanham's gift worked well enough. She forgot Astrid and Astrid was safe."

I feel as if I've been stabbed. His betrayal is almost more than I can take.

Trey's expression turns ugly. "Do you care about her at all?" he asks with resentment in his voice.

"Do you?" Pan tosses the question back at him.

"More than anything," Trey replies without having to think about it.

"Then help us deliver the packages to Kalafin. That might help her. The Brotherhood has to have a reason to keep her alive. They have to need her."

Darkness is caressing me. My vision is tunneling and I'm losing everything on the periphery. I'm overwhelmed by it—fighting myself to remain. Everything about me wants to return to my body, but my will—my will wants desperately to stay. The only people I care about now are my Cavars: Trey, Jax, and Wayra. Everyone else here can rot for all I care. I need to stay long enough to figure out how to communicate with Trey. I need to make him see me.

"Time for you to go, fighter," Giffen whispers to me, as if he doesn't want anyone else to know that I'm here. "Go back and run with the wolves. Don't lose. I'm counting on you." Whatever it is that he can do with the energy of his gift—his telekinesis—he uses it on me. The instant he pushes it in my direction, I'm banished from their presence.

Returning to my body in this time, I cannot move right away. I'm paralyzed. I breathe in shallow breaths; the first of which are characterized by icy air from my lungs. My skin is a bluish tone and frigid.

Something explodes outside on the beach. The cottage rattles. Decorative green glass bottles containing sand and shells clatter and fall off the teak shelves. Broken shards and sand settle on the wide-plank teak floors. It grows silent. Kyon is fighting the Strikers already. I haven't been gone that long, but it must already be dark here. I must've come back to a later time. Staying away too long has cost me time.

Jerking my limbs, I crawl to the side of the bed, but I can't rise from it. I slip to the floor and crawl on my belly to the bathroom, dragging my legs. Beside the shower, there's an enormous bathtub made of dark wood that resembles a huge salad bowl. I crawl past it to a vanity made of the same dark wood. Looking up, I pull myself up against the countertop. Using my fingers, I scratch them over the surface. A group of small shelves rise from the teak surface. Among the bottles of lotions, oils and perfumes, combs and brushes, I find what I need. I grasp a pair of tortoiseshell-handled scissors in my fist.

Sinking down to the floor once more, I roll over on my back, hearing a familiar sound. It's coming from outside. It sounds like gunfire—the automatic kind. I gather my hair in my fist and put the scissors to it. I cut off huge, blond chunks of it, and it grows back instantly. The circulation returns to my useless legs, my knees no longer ache as much, and I'm able to get to my feet. Panting, I place my hands on the surface of the vanity and gaze at my pale reflection in the round mirror. One thing is clear, if I'd stayed away from my body for much longer, I wouldn't have survived it.

A horrendously loud, garbage-can-lid-banging noise pierces the air beside me. I let out an involuntary scream, jumping and shying away from it. Something car-fender-big rams against the storm shutter. Each time it crashes into the metal, I jump. As I back away, another hard jolt pummels the shutter, this time shattering the glass too. Shards of it spew all over the floor.

Reacting out of fear, I stab the air with the scissors, cutting nothing. Fear bleeds in watercolors through my veins. In the bathroom, someone outside yanks on the metal storm shutter, rattling it like it's a vending machine that refuses to spit out chips. "Oscil!" I hiss. "Kill intruders!"

"You are not authorized for that command," Oscil replies.

My teeth clench and I growl. I try to weigh my options. If I leap into the future now, I'll leave my body too vulnerable to whoever is breaking in. I dash to the front room, looking for a place to hide, but another shriek tumbles from me when some kind of explosion fractures the metal and glass in the front of the hut.

I turn to run back to the bedroom, but an Alameeda Striker is standing in the doorway to it. His nightmare-blue eyes roam over me. I wish that I had more on than a bathing suit and Kyon's T-shirt. Another soldier joins him in the bedroom doorway. He's in a seal-skin black aquatic combat uniform. It looks like its made more for swimming than for protection. The soldier who just arrived nudges the first one hard from behind with his shoulder. "She's not going to hurt you, Valko. Didn't you read her bio? The only gift she has is a fortune-teller stare."

"You go first then, Cree," Valko offers.

Cree punches his friend playfully before he strides toward me. Grabbing me by the throat, he picks me up off my feet and raises me up with beastlike strength. He smirks, "See, she's weak and—"

I plunge my scissors into his eye. Cree drops me and starts screaming. Blood gushes everywhere as he wrenches the scissors from his head.

I dash toward the lavare, but Valko lifts me and throws me against the commissary bar. I fall against the countertop. "You're not weak, are you?" Valko snarls.

"Oscil! Kafcan!"

A pot of kafcan rises from the hole in the countertop near me. I grab the urn and smash it into the side of Valko's head hard enough to knock his brain sideways. Wax-melting-hot, coffee-colored kafcan scalds his skin. Valko groans as his flesh turns bright red. Straightening, he takes a step in my direction. Kyon comes up behind him, clasps his hand to Valko's forehead, and twists. Valko's neck breaks in one smooth jerk.

As the Striker's body falls on the floor, Kyon moves on to Cree, who won't stop screaming, and slits his throat. Cree makes a gurgling sound and then falls silent.

Kyon isn't breathing hard at all, while I can't seem to catch mine. He picks up the scissors that I used on Cree. My knees weaken. I can't move. Trembling with full-body quakes, I watch numbly as Kyon goes to the sink beside me. He runs the scissors under water, washing away the blood. Drying them off, he brings them back to me. I take them from his palm. Clutching them in my fist, I hold them to me.

"Are you hurt?" Kyon asks, stroking my cheek and patting it softly.

"No."

Gathering me up in his arms, Kyon takes me to the chair by the fireplace that is completely restored from having been burned. He sets me down on it. "Oscil, light a fire," he commands.

A cheerful fire roars to life and snaps in the grate. I watch it for a long time while Kyon moves around the hut, hauling out dead bodies and ordering robots to undertake the massive cleanup. At some point I stop shaking. Resting my head against the arm of the chair, I close my eyes, but I keep my scissors close.

CHAPTER 7
THE MARK IS MADE

Soft raindrops patter on the deck and thatched roof outside. The hurricane shutters are open in the bedroom. There's unfettered access to the teak bridge as well as the deck that leads to the beach. Becoming more awake, I try to move but I'm tucked beneath Kyon's arm. We're entwined on the soft bed, beneath the lovely, sheer mosquito netting.

My back is molded to Kyon's front. The scent of spent shell casings clings to his large hand, which rests on my hip. Looking at him over my shoulder, I see Kyon's nose close to my cheek. He's asleep. I turn my face back to rest against the pillow, watching the rain, wondering if I should move. I might wake him if I do, and I don't think that's something I want to deal with right now. I notice the scissors lying on the mattress near my hand. I grasp them, holding them tight once more.

"You won't need those," Kyon murmurs. His mouth is by my ear. His deep voice causes me to tense. I fear him—his ultraviolence—it scares me. My heart drums in my ears because he's crazy, maybe even a little crazy for me. His ruthlessness is attracted to my savagery.

"How do you know I won't need them?" I clutch the scissors tighter, afraid that he'll try to take them from me, and right now, I need them.

His fingertips slowly trace a path from my shoulder down my arm toward the scissors in my hand. "We killed everyone that the Brotherhood sent last night—some I tortured first, but in they end, they all perished."

"You tortured some?" I shiver as his fingers change directions and move back up my arm to sweep my hair off of my shoulder and neck.

"I broke them for you, Kricket," he whispers like it's a secret. A fire ignites beneath my skin, and I'm too warm all of a sudden.

"Won't the Brotherhood send more of them?" I ask, as he snuggles me closer. It's disturbing how well I fit in his arms.

"Right now, they're more than likely calling a meeting of the High Council. Some Brothers will take their time to get there—most of them can't be bothered to attend to business before the sun's zenith, and not all of them will come. Once the ones who do show up finally assemble in the forum, there will be dissenting opinions regarding what action to take against me, and by default, you.

"It will be divisive. Some will want to mount another attack against us, even though this one failed and they already used their best-trained soldiers. They know that I have an advanced missile defense system here. They know that because I designed *their* missile defense system. They'll scramble to get their technicians on the task of creating a new system that will lock me out. But that will take a significant amount of time and they won't find all the hidden doors I have woven into the one they now use. When they come to this conclusion, they will see that assassination cannot be achieved while we're here on the island."

"So we're safe here?" I exhale. My fingers loosen on the scissors.

"For now. In a few rotations, they'll send a delegate to speak to me. He'll be someone who I count as a friend. He'll try to convince me to speak to the High Council and come to a resolution."

"A diplomatic solution?" I ask.

"Yes."

"Do you believe there can be such a solution?"

"No."

"Why not?

"I don't want one."

"What do you want?"

"I want to know why you're wearing my shirt."

"Huh?"

"My shirt. Why are you wearing it?" He runs his hand down my side, grasping the hem of the sky-blue shirt in question as he inches it up to my hip.

I squeak, "Kyon! Don't!" and put my hand over his and attempt to stop him from raising it more.

"Tell me why you're wearing it," he demands, keeping tension on the hem in a threatening way.

I'm just barely keeping him in check. In a rush, I explain, "I sort of set your cottage on fire."

His hand stills. "You did what?"

"I torched your chair."

"Why?"

"I thought the doors would open if I started a fire."

"They didn't, did they?"

"No. The sprinklers went on," I reply.

"So you got wet."

"Soaked."

"And instead of having something made for you by Oscil, you chose to wear something of mine?" he asks, as if I've done something harebrained.

"This is comfortable. What is this, Egyptian cotton? It's so soft."

"No one has ever worn my clothes before."

"No one would dare," I murmur. "You're a scary beast."

"You dared."

"I did, but I have a problem with authority."

He smoothes the shirt back down over my hip and rests his hand there possessively. "What would you like to do today?"

"Not die," I reply.

"Other than that?"

I would say *go home to Earth*, but I don't want to make him mad, so instead, I reply, "I don't want you to be scary today."

"That's entirely in your hands. If you obey me, I won't have a reason to scare you."

"I don't obey. It's not something I do well."

"You'll have to learn . . . quickly."

I want to hit him. He's so arrogant. I sigh instead and try again. "You said you want to know who I am. Is that true?"

"Yes."

"Well, then, let's *try* to act normal. Why don't we do what you normally do when you're here alone so that I can see who you are?"

"You mean do something I like?"

"Yes."

"The two of us."

"Yes."

"I want to teach you to swim."

"I don't think that's a—"

"It's not a request," he snarls. His body is rigid against mine.

I ignore his snarl. "What if I'm really bad at swimming?"

"Then it will be a long day."

"This should be fun," I say under my breath. "Okay . . . so you'll give me a swim lesson today, and then you can teach me to use a jet pack or a flipcart—something I want to learn."

Kyon relaxes against me once more. "You don't know how to operate a flipcart?"

"I don't even know what a flipcart is, but I've heard that it's fun."

"You don't know what a flipcart is? How is that possible?"

I point to myself. "Raised on Earth, remember?"

"It would be hard to forget it. You remind me of it every time you open your mouth."

"It's that bad, huh?" It's a rhetorical question. I know that my upbringing, or in my case, lack of a proper upbringing, makes me look like pond scum to most people from Alameeda, not to mention the fact that I'm half Rafian. That doesn't help with their perception of me at all.

He surprises me as he says, "It's not as bad as you think. You don't cower, even when I frighten you. I attribute that to Earth. Someone there must have taught you not to back down."

Did someone teach me not to back down? Was it my father? I don't know. He tried to have my memory erased, so I can't be sure what I learned from him or my mother. Without thinking, I blurt out, "Would you hide someone on Earth? Someone you loved?" I bite my bottom lip and wait for his answer.

"No. I don't hide. I fight."

"But if you did have to hide? Would Earth be a good place?"

Kyon is quiet for a moment and then he says, "No."

"Why?"

"I would probably hide someone I loved in the Forest of Omnicron, but I would make it look like we had gone to Earth."

"Why would you do that?"

"Because it would be easy to convince my enemies that I'd gone there. Earth is the obvious place to hide. But Earth is hostile with primitive customs and medical care. There are so many ways to die on Earth. The probability that my enemy would succumb to one of those ways while tracking me there would be high."

So if Pan could convince the Alameeda Brotherhood to search for us on Earth, maybe even leave something unimportant there for them to find, he could keep safe the person whom he holds most dear—someone who's more important. He could hide her on Ethar, right under their noses. He could better protect Astrid if he left me behind as bait. I don't say this aloud. I'd be killing them if I did. I've already said too much. Kyon isn't stupid. He could figure it all out quite easily if he knew Pan was alive or that I have a sister named Astrid—one that he had in his hands and gave away.

I grip the scissors in my fist as tight as I can until the metal cuts into my palm. Even with that pain to distract me, I still can't hold back the angry tears that cloud my eyes. I'm a con, a pigeon—I'm a mark. That's all I am to them—someone they can throw away to mislead their enemies from finding the true treasure: Astrid.

"I'm ready for that swim lesson now," I murmur as I slide out from under Kyon's arm, taking the scissors with me.

"Right now?" he asks, sounding surprised. "Don't you want to have breakfast first?"

I don't turn around to look at him—I can't let him see me cry. I just shake my head no and reply over my shoulder, "I'm not hungry. I'll meet you on the beach."

I rush outside to the wet deck and around the front of the teak hut. Soft rain falls gently on my face. It mixes with my tears as I take the stairs down to the sand. The tide has come up higher, so whatever happened here last night has been washed away. I slow when I reach the edge of the water. There isn't much wind; it's just overcast and gray with a light drizzle. With the scissors still in my hand, I reach up and cut my hair again. In a few moments, the palm of my hand stops bleeding. Walking into the surf, I rinse the blood from my hand.

Tossing the scissors onto the beach, I pull strands of my newly regrown hair between my fingers, weaving it into a thick braid. The action helps to settle my raw emotions. But the bitterness I feel runs deep, and just when I think I can stop crying, another tear rolls down my cheek to shame me some more.

I knot the end of my braid and pull Kyon's shirt off over my head. The black bathing suit I've had on since yesterday is very skimpy—not something I'd choose to learn to swim in. I wipe my face on his shirt before balling it up and tossing it in the sand behind me, far enough away so that the tide doesn't get it. Wading into the water again, I go as deep as I dare, up to my chest. Using my good hand, I splash water on my face, erasing the evidence of my emotion.

Pan wants to protect Astrid? Fine. But the minute I can get the hell off Ethar, I'm gone. He'll never see me again. The thing that I'm most angry about in this moment is that I've given him the power to hurt me. *I'm stone. I'm stone. I'm stone*, I repeat to myself.

"Are you ready?" Kyon asks from behind me.

Looking out over the horizon, I nod.

"Then let's begin."

I hate swim lessons right away. Everything Kyon wants me to do is designed to drown me. I have a problem even floating on my back or putting my face in the water, but as the hours drag on, I realize that Kyon isn't going to let up on me until I master the skill—whichever one he's teaching me from moment to moment.

As I stand up and listen to what Kyon wants me to do next, a small wave crashes into me, nearly knocking me over. I don't have much strength left. I can hardly lift my arms up past my chest. Another wave comes and it knocks me against him. I clutch his waist so that I don't get taken under the water. "What's wrong with you? Are you tired?" Kyon asks with a frown.

"No," I lie. "But if you need to take a break, I'll understand."

His arm goes around my waist to steady me. "You're exhausted. You can't even stand up."

"I can stand up," I say mulishly.

"No, you can't," he replies. He refuses to let go of me, which is sort of a good thing, because I don't know if I'll make it out of the water without his help. My limbs tremble as we get to shore. Without the buoyancy of the water to support me, it's much worse. My muscles quiver. I'm surprised I'm so destroyed by one stupid swim lesson. The months that I'd spent at Rafe's palace as Manus's ward have made me weak. I was never allowed to do anything too strenuous there, and as a result I'm a creampuff.

"You can't even walk." He lifts me in his arms. His body is rigid. He takes me up the stairs to the deck and lays me on a soft-cushioned, legless lounge chair. From a nearby recessed shelf, he grasps a big, white towel, which he lays over me. I'm grateful for it and the fact that it has stopped raining.

Closing my eyes, I intend to rest for just a second. When I open them again, the sun is out. There's a vermillion-colored, kitelike umbrella flying over me. It's blocking the worst of the sun's powerful midday rays. Kyon lounges on another legless deck chair with a whole command center of electronics surrounding him on hovering modules. He's watching something on one screen and making lists on another at the same time. I can't hear what he's listening to, though, because he's using an earpiece.

My deck chair is all the way reclined, but when I sit up, the back of it comes up to support me. Kyon looks my way. "Your lunch is ready." He gestures to the floating tray beside me.

"Thank you," I reply before I begin to eat.

Kyon watches me for a moment, and then he glances back at his screens. "You've been monitoring the future—often, haven't you?"

I don't see a point in lying, so I reply, "I see things."

"Did you see anything else last night?"

"And if I did?"

"Then I want to know about it."

"Because we've established a circle of trust?" I reply sarcastically.

He shakes his head. "Your loyalty is so misplaced, Kricket." He turns one of the hovering monitors to face me. It shows surveillance footage with a time stamp running at the bottom of the screen. My pulse quickens when I see myself on it. I'm strapped to a metal chair in a desolate cell, being brutally beaten by a Rafian soldier— a Brigadet. He punches me in the stomach, and then he follows it with an uppercut. It's clear that he has knocked me unconscious, but it doesn't stop him from hitting me until another soldier forcefully pulls him away from me. He spits on me as I sag motionless in the chair, dripping blood from a multitude of open wounds.

Adrenaline surges into my bloodstream and I'm no longer hungry. I have to turn away. "I don't want to see anymore."

"It's footage from the Ship of Skye," Kyon says with anger he can't hide. "This is what happened to you before I found you shackled to a pole."

"I know where it's from," I murmur. It's the interrogation that Trey told me about—it happened. Even if I can't remember it, it was real.

"Nice friends you had, Kricket. *They* did this to you," he says with contempt.

Looking at the monitor again, I watch as I'm struck again and again. "It wasn't my friends."

"They're all part of Skye. They brought you there and allowed this to happen to you."

I turn away from the gruesome scene playing out on the monitor. Swinging my legs off the lounger, I get up from the chair. The towel on my lap slips to the ground as I bump into the hovering tray, knocking my plate off of it. It shatters on the deck as I hurry down the stairs to the sand. I turn up the beach and run blindly away from him. I don't know where I'm going and I don't care, as long as I can get as far from Kyon and the interrogation on his monitor as possible.

When I'm no longer able to run, I slow and walk along the shore, panting and clutching at the stitch in my side. To my left, a wide, grassy path comes into view. Wanting to get off the beach and out of the blistering sun, I turn onto it. It takes me into a grove of palm trees. The trail is lined with conch shells and tropical flowers, which I avoid, because one never knows about the flowers on this ridiculous planet. The path becomes steeper as it wraps around a hill. The trees become thinner. I notice I'm above the beach. There's a waterfall coming off the cliff face in the distance; it pours into the sea below. Nestled on the cliff near the waterfall is the hangar that I saw on the satellite maps in Kyon's office.

Continuing to follow the grassy path, I eventually come to the hanger. It's made almost entirely of glass, with enormous wood beams supporting a metal roof. It reminds me of a longhouse, but on a much grander scale. I walk up to the glass-paneled wall, and it opens for me, granting me access. Inside, there is every kind of airship imaginable and some that are, to me, unimaginable. It feels like a museum with shiny vehicles all polished to the hilt of perfection.

I wander to the airship nearest to me. Etharians call it a trift—it's a kind of plane, but there are so many different types that "plane" isn't an adequate description. I don't know what this type of trift is called; it's so different from the ones I've seen up close, which are only a handful, really. The outside of this one has scales, like dragon skin—muted brown with freckles of green and gold. I run my hand over the hull, and it feels like hardened leather. It's shaped like a bat. I'd look inside it, but I don't even know how to get into it.

In the center of the building, a group of hovercycles is arranged in a star pattern, with the rear of each cycle meeting in the center. I walk around them. They're mean looking. Powerful. One appeals to me more than the others. "Unlace compartment," I murmur next to it. The hood lifts up, exposing the interior. I slide onto the wide, ice-blue seat, placing my hands on the grips.

"You chose the Ensin hovercycle," Kyon says from across the room, by the entrance to the hangar. I refuse to look at him.

"No, I didn't. I chose the blue one."

He comes closer to me, his footsteps echoing in the cavernous room. "They're each made from the best manufacturers from the five houses of Ethar. This one is from a company I own in Alameeda."

It's hard not to be impressed, but I try anyway. "You design hoverbikes?"

"No. I pay people to design hoverbikes."

"Oh. What's this one called?"

"The Empress." There's something in his tone that makes me look up at him.

"I had no idea it was female," I murmur.

"Would you like to pilot her?" he asks.

"You'll teach me?" I ask breathlessly. I want so badly to learn to drive this. It can get me out of here—be the thing that helps me escape.

"Only if you don't waste my time. You want to learn, correct?"

"Doesn't everyone?" I ask rhetorically, running my hands reverently over the curves of the bike.

"No," he frowns at me. "Especially not priestesses."

"Why not?" I ask. They'd have to be out of their minds not to want to learn how to do this.

"It's not seen as feminine," he says. "It's beneath them. And dangerous."

"That's silly," I snort. "I want to learn how to pilot every single vehicle in your garage."

"Hangar." He moves past me to the hoverbike I just vacated. I go to Kyon. He sits on the hovercycle and lifts his arm, indicating that I should sit in front of him. I hesitate for a second. I should've picked a different kind of vehicle, but it's too late, and I want to learn how to fly this one. I climb onto the seat in front of him.

Being this close to Kyon always scares me. I expect him to hurt me. It's like being near an exotic animal, like a lion. Even if the lion has been somewhat domesticated, in the end, it's a ferocious beast and it'll probably wind up tearing your head off.

Kyon's thighs nuzzle mine as he leans forward. He adjusts the deck where our feet rest. "You're so little," he says close to my ear. "I have to bring the pedals forward." He does, and my feet finally fit into the slots on either side. He rests his hand on my left thigh. "This foot controls altitude. Press down on the pedal, the bike rises—ease up on the pedal, the bike will drop."

"Got it," I say, pressing down to feel the resistance. The hoverbike doesn't move, because he hasn't started the engine yet.

Kyon places his hand on my right thigh. "This foot controls your acceleration. Steering is on the handles. When you twist the left handle, you turn in that direction. Same goes for the right side." His hands are heavy on me. The heat of them permeates my clothing.

"Is that it?" I ask.

"Squeeze the handsets hard and the hoverbike will brake." His hands squeeze my thighs lightly.

"Like this?" I grip the handsets, leaning forward.

"Yes," Kyon replies. He speaks to the hoverbike: "Lace compartment. Ignite engine."

The hood of the hovercycle closes, securing us inside. The engine revs up; it vibrates beneath me just enough to let me know it's on.

"Press the white button on the control panel to open the ceiling access," Kyon murmurs in my ear. I do. Above us, a spiral opening forms in the ceiling as pieces of it retract, leaving a hole.

"Let me put my feet beneath yours on the pedals so that you can feel what I'm doing," Kyon says. He moves his feet under mine. He leans forward so that he blankets my back with his chest as he places his hands over mine on the handlebars. The contact is extremely intimate. He makes me feel afraid and at the same time alive in ways that I feel only when I'm with him. He's like waking up to fire. I know I can't stay too long or he'll burn me.

Gently, he maneuvers the hoverbike so that we rise up. Glancing down at the tops of his other aircraft as they grow smaller beneath us is another kind of awakening to life—it makes me somehow larger. As we emerge outside, the sun blinds me for a moment, until Kyon says, "Deepen tint." The lid of the hoverbike darkens and the glare is cut. "Do you want to see the island?" Kyon asks.

"Yes."

His cheek brushes against mine as he says, "Hold on." Diving down, he drives the hovercycle in a death spiral toward the ground. I have the sensation of losing my stomach, but I resist the urge to close my eyes. He levels off the hoverbike just before we crash into a bed of wildflowers. We take the grass path that led me up to the hangar. At face-melting speed we move through the trees, twisting on the shell-lined path. My blood is violent in my veins.

When we reach the beach, he flies us on a cushion of air above the sand and out over the water. The sea beneath us is fire blue and siltless. Kyon makes a sharp turn; the hoverbike rears up like a nervous stallion. I suck in air. My rigid arms force me against Kyon's chest. The back end of the bike drops into the water and causes a rooster tail arc to splash out of it until he brings the front of the vehicle down to level us off again. I breathe heavy in fear; my heart thumps in fleeing-rabbit beats.

"I like you like this," Kyon says softly in my ear, as he drives at breakneck speed over the water.

"Like what," I whisper breathlessly.

"At my mercy." Nuzzling my neck with his firm lips, his left hand relinquishes mine on the handset. He wraps his arm around my waist.

My flesh tingles where the bristles of his skin touch me. An assault of shivers racks my body, not all of them unpleasant. "If you don't stop kissing me, I'm gone and I won't come back."

With a frustrated growl, he continues to caress my neck with his lips. "You're forever running away from me, Kricket. Don't you wonder what it would be like if you were brave enough to face me?"

"No," I reply.

His foot beneath mine lifts up a little on the accelerator. We slow. "Do you want to try it now?" he asks as he eases away from me a bit.

"Yes," I reply. Anything would be better than his driving. We've traveled around one side of the island, but I hardly saw any of it because he was going so fast. He allows me to take control of the hovercycle by moving his hands from mine to my waist.

For the next few hours we cruise at a much slower pace around the perimeter of the island. Kyon shows me all the basics to piloting the vehicle. I almost can't help myself when I begin daydreaming ways in which I can use this hovercycle to escape from Ethar. Kyon leans near my ear and says. "Take us to the house."

I nod, continuing to assess the approximate distance of every point on the island. I'll need to map out how far it is from the main house to the hangar—know to the second how long it will take on foot to get there and retrieve the hoverbike.

Rounding the large cliffs on the side of the island, the cove where the main house rests comes into view. It resembles an elegant pirate ship that only awaits the tide to take it back out to sea. I maneuver the hovercycle to the shore, bringing it to rest on the sand by the wide stone patio. From behind me, Kyon says, "Unlace compartment." The lid of the hovercycle opens. Kyon rises and extends his hand to me. I ignore it and stand on my own. My legs are stiff from riding for so long.

"I need to go over the security sensors. I will be in my office, should you need me. We'll dine on the beach in two parts."

"Do you want me to take the hoverbike back to the hangar?" I ask, trying to hide my surprise at the freedom he's allowing me. I may just have to seize the moment and leave now, even if I don't know where I am or how to get to where I need to be.

"No. I'll send it back." He lifts his wrist, displaying a silver watchlike band. Tapping it with his finger, a lighted grid projects from his wrist. He touches the light on his skin, scrolling through menus before entering a coded sequence of lighted numbers. Next to me, the hood to the hovercycle closes. It lifts from the ground and travels unpiloted in the direction of the hangar.

I must have a look of despair in my eyes, because Kyon says, "If your plan is to use one of my vehicles to escape, you should truly rethink that strategy. I can easily override the manual controls and call any of them back without much effort."

"It's kind of you to point that out," I mutter.

"The shield is up as well. You'd have a problem getting through it."

"Noted," I say, nodding.

"And the defensive systems would activate to alert me the moment you're no longer detected by them."

My smile is grim. "I'm not leaving, am I?"

"Not without me," he replies. "I will meet you here in two parts. Don't make me come look for you."

CHAPTER 8
FUTURE TRIP AND VIKING SHIP

The fire is hypnotic. I lean back in one of the large chairs Kyon had dragged out here to the beach. The campfire wavers beneath a metal grill placed over it. Smoke curls around the crustaceans Kyon is cooking for our dinner. After Kyon checked on the sensors today, we collected shellfish from traps in the sea. First he showed me how to set the snares, then showed me the best spots to catch the ugly creatures. They look a little bit like lobsters, but their shells are bright pink and they each have three heads and two tails. I, quite frankly, find them disgusting to look at, but my stomach growls every time their aroma floats in my direction.

The seawater is continually exhaled onto the shore nearby. It breathes something into me with every wave that crashes onto shore. I had no idea that water could make me feel this way: small and vast, and ancient and new, all at the same time.

The sun has almost disappeared into the horizon, and the breeze has turned cool. I shiver and rub my hands over my arms. Kyon walks up with an armload of firewood. He stacks the wood in the sand. Straightening, he glances in my direction and frowns. "Are you cold?" he asks.

"A little," I admit, "but I don't feel like moving right now to get a jacket."

He dusts the stray pieces of bark from his dark, long-sleeved shirt before he pulls it off over his head and hands it to me. "Here, this is warm." He straightens the short-sleeved shirt he still has on before flopping down in the sand at my feet and using a long stick to stir the fire. He leans back against the leg of my chair.

I hold his shirt in my hands for a moment before I straighten it out and pull it over my head. As it falls over my shoulders, I'm hit again by how much bigger he is than me. He's a freaking giant. I'm swimming in his shirt. His scent is all over it too. It's the scent that I've associated with fear. It's at war with the warmth enveloping me.

Kyon cooks our dinner on the grill over the fire. I watch him in fascination, since I never expected any of this from him. From his seat on the ground in front of me, he hands me a plate over his shoulder. He glances back and asks, "Do you need me to taste it for you?"

I hold the plate in my lap and shake my head. "No," I reply. "I think we're past that now."

We eat using our hands. It's so good I find myself licking my fingertips. "Where did you learn to cook like this?" I ask.

Kyon smiles. "I was a soldier. I learned basic survival: hunting fishing, trapping. Part of that entails preparing food."

"I think this is my favorite thing about you," I say, eating another delicious morsel from my plate.

He laughs. "You're so easily bribed. I had no idea I could score points with food."

I laugh too. "Food has always been a priority. There were days when I was younger that I made a meal by just smelling something like this."

Kyon sobers. "What do you mean?"

I shrug as I continue to eat. "Oh, you know—I just know what it's like to be hungry. Sometimes I didn't have any money, so I used to sit in this alley outside my favorite pizza place in Chicago and inhale the aroma coming from the oven vents. I got really good at pretending to eat."

"How often did you do that?" he asks. I glance up from my plate to see that he has stopped eating.

I try to minimize what I just said. I don't even know why I told him that. I shrug again, "Not that often." No one really wants to know things like this. They think they do, but poverty is seen as a failing—a weakness. He turns to me and puts more food on my plate. "I'm good!" I laugh. "I can't possibly eat all this!"

"You'll tell me when you're hungry," he orders sternly.

"Okay," I reply, bewildered.

He rises from the ground and brushes the sand from his clothing. When I'm finished, he takes my plate. I let him. He walks away with it to the house and disappears inside. Absently rubbing my hands on my napkin, I watch the fire and wonder at Kyon's demeanor. I don't know what to make of any of it. He's being decent, for a psychopathic kidnapper. Friendly. I don't like it. It's confusing.

Returning to the beach, Kyon carries with him a silver salver and a couple of long skewer sticks. He sets down the silver tray on the low table by the fire; it has a short, fat porcelain carafe with two porcelain shot glasses. Pouring a splash of the white liquid into them, Kyon looks over the rim of one at me as he takes a sip. He extends the other cup for me to take. I stand and walk to where he is by the fire. Taking the cup from him, I'm not at all sure that I'll drink it. "What is this?" I ask. I sniff it. It smells like pears.

"It's a mild alcohol." I try to hand it back to him, but he puts up his hand and says, "It won't hurt you. It goes with this." He bends and picks up a little red bead of goo from the silver tray. Taking one of the skewer sticks, he impales the red bead on it and hands the stick to me. Holding the implement in one hand and the cup in the other, I watch him pick up another bead of goo from the tray and impale it on the other stick. "You'll need both hands for this," he remarks, eyeing the cup in my hand.

Reluctantly, I drink the pear alcohol; it burns my throat. I try not to cough as I set the porcelain cup back on the silver tray. "Mild," I gasp ruefully.

Kyon chuckles. "You don't really think that was strong, do you?" he teases.

"You see my eyes watering?" I reply as I wipe the mist from my eyes.

"You're small—maybe you can't tolerate it like I can."

"I'm not small," I sigh.

He snorts. "One only needs to see you in my shirt to see the truth in my statement."

I shake my head. "Just because you're all giant freaks does not make me small."

He grins. "Perspective is everything. Now, do you want to see this or not?" he asks.

I shrug. "See what?"

"Dessert."

He walks closer to the fire and places the end of the skewer with the red bead on it in the flames. He rolls the skewer between his palms. The sugar paste activates with a sizzling sound and begins to puff out like cotton candy does. Whirling it around the stick, it hisses as Kyon creates a lovely red flower within the flames. He pulls it out, and the delicate petals open and bloom before my eyes. Plucking a petal, he extends it to me. I try to take it from him, but he pulls it back. Instead, he dangles the petal near my lips. I relent, allowing him to place the dessert on my tongue. The warm sugar melts in my mouth.

"Mmm." I savor the taste. When I glance at Kyon, he's watching me with fascination. It unnerves me enough to turn away from him.

I push my long sleeves up to my elbows and thrust the cherry-red sugar bead on the end of my stick into the fire. Trying to copy what Kyon had done, I roll the skewer between my palms, but I lack his technique. Mine quickly becomes a lopsided cobra weaving chaos on the end of the stick, and then all of a sudden, it explodes with a loud pop and falls into the fire. I laugh as I make a face. I pull the empty stick from the flames. Smoke wafts up, spreading the odor of burning sugar. "Aww! I'm so bad at this! I broke mine!" I feign a forlorn expression, and then laugh.

"Do you want to try again?" Kyon asks.

I nod vigorously and hold my stick out to him. He expertly impales another cherry-colored sugar bead to the end of it and then helps me with my technique as we cook it together. When we pull the stick out of the flames, the corners of some of the petals are a little singed, but it's not too bad. "You did well," Kyon says as he bends his face nearer to mine.

"Thanks," I say breathlessly. Turning away from him, I take it back to my seat and pull it apart slowly, eating it as I watch the fire flicker. Kyon sits by my feet, eating the other sugar flower.

When we're finished, I help Kyon clean up. Then we sit again in front of the fire and Kyon feeds it huge logs, making it leap and dance. It feels good, staving off the chill of the night air. Kyon sits in the large seat next to mine. He lifts a guitarlike instrument from where it was propped against his chair.

"Do you know how to play that?" I ask as he tightens some of the steely strings. He doesn't answer, but begins to run his fingers over the instrument. The sound is poignant and sweet. Strings of paper hearts are cut from the sound to float up to the stars. Shivers move down my shoulders. It doesn't take long for the hypnotic strains of the music, the haze from the alcohol, and the dancing heat of the fire to conspire and make me drowsy.

My breathing slows. I exhale a curl of cold air from my lungs as my fingers turn arctic and clutch the arms of the chair. Unwillingly, my consciousness leaves my body.

I don't know where I am when I come to rest from my flash-forward through time. I don't even know what I'm seeing right away. Looking around, I'm in the middle of a beautiful park at dusk. A wild group of unaccompanied young boys about twelve or thirteen floans old fly by me on boards that resemble snowboards. The decks of these devices hover above the walkway while flame-blue light shines beneath them. Rounding a tall lamppost at the end of the path, they shoot back around, as if they've turned on a berm. It's really the force of air beneath the board that flips them back in my direction.

The baby-faced one in front has shoulder-length brown hair and wears a tall, licorice-black hat. His canary-yellow jacket flaps in the wind as he nears me. He has the best smile—infectious. As he passes, I'm able to see the word flipcart embossed on the deck of his board. My mouth drops open. It's such an "aha" moment for me that I turn and follow them along the park path that cuts through the trees.

Ahead, there's a lake where a few people have gathered with their children to race authentic-looking toy boats. I pause here while the flip-cart riders keep going. An older gentleman stands over a leather bag for a long moment. The boy beside him is maybe five or six floans old. The child waits with shining anticipation. "Are you going to let me steer it this time, Grandsire?" he asks.

The older man hefts the object from the bag, revealing a Viking-like ship with a carved wooden dragon figurehead. He shakes the dragon's fangs at the boy as he roars at him. The boy squeals in delight. The older man laughs and straightens. "Do you think you can keep it from crashing into the shore?" he asks his companion.

"Yes!" The exuberance of the answer brings a smile to the man's face.

Together, they place the boat in the water. The canvases of the sails billow, looking lavender instead of white in the dusk-colored twilight. The older man crouches down and holds out the boat's controller for the boy to take. Two sandy-brown heads lean close together as the boy guides the vengeful dragonhead away from the shore. I watch it, captivated by the rippling wake that turns the black surface of the water white.

The low hum of aircraft causes the water to tremble. Usually, the noise is not this pronounced—it must be a low-flying craft. First one black-winged drone, and then two more come into view, casting predatory shadows over the boats floating on the surface of the water. They move toward the horizon, where the city lights have the appearance of a carnival's midway.

The drones frighten the boy; he drops the controller and turns to the shelter of the older man's arms. "Tut, there's nothing to be afraid of! Those are our sentinels. They patrol the sky to make sure we're safe."

"Why do they do that?"

"So no one can hurt us."

"Why would someone want to hurt us?"

"Remember when I taught you about the five Houses of Ethar?" he asks the boy with a cautious smile.

"Yes."

He straightens the boy's green surge jacket. "Well, it has been decided that we only need four Houses."

The boy's brow wrinkles. "Who decided that?"

"Well, we did. Along with our allies in Alameeda."

The boy frowns. "What House doesn't get to stay?"

"The House of Rafe," the man replies with no hint of remorse.

"What's going to happen to it?" the boy asks as he rubs his nose with the back of his hand.

"You don't have to be concerned about that—they're way over in Rafe and we're here in Wurthem. They probably don't even know where Kalafin is."

The boy's eyes lift to the man's. "But won't they be sad?"

"Not for long," the man says as he picks up the controller from the ground and hands it back to the boy with a smile.

The drones continue over the water until they disappear into the lights of the city. Then the wind pulls forward in a strange way, but only for a moment. The sky lights up. A bright light changes dusk to day. Two more brilliant flashes follow it. The older man makes a choking sound as he tries to shield the boy from the light by turning them away from it. His terror-filled eyes are nearly white as he holds the boy's face against his chest. From the horizon, a tremendous rattle and roar shakes everyone nearby to the ground. Behind them, out across the water near the city, a fireball rolls outward, taking on the shape of a ring of stampeding flame-horses. The dust they kick up mushrooms into the sky. Fire sweeps over the water with a thunderous hissing sound. The man and the boy ignite, but the fire is so hot that it quickly reduces them to ash. Flames strike me, but instead of catching fire, I tumble backward in a rush of time.

I can't seem to take a breath at first after I catapult back into my body. My lungs feel burned, and I wheeze. The fire near me snaps. Kyon has stopped playing music. I'm on his lap and he's holding me. He strokes my hair while my forehead rests against his neck. His skin is warm against mine. I shiver and my teeth chatter a little. Kyon rubs my arm, trying to warm me up. I lift my head for a second, looking around. Everything else is the same. The fire still burns brightly and it's still dark.

"You're back," Kyon says gently.

"How long was I away?" My voice is feeble and thick, as if I've been screaming for hours. I'm disoriented.

"Not long. You never stopped breathing, which is an improvement."

I rest my forehead against his neck once more. It's less awkward than looking into his eyes. "Everything is so broken," I mutter. I feel like sobbing, but there's no way I'll ever cry in front of Kyon.

"What's broken?" Kyon asks in a soothing tone.

"Me. Us. Everyone on this sucky planet!"

"Broken things can be fixed," he replies.

"There's a reason that everything I'm seeing is broken."

"Is the future that upsetting? What happens?" When I don't answer him, he sighs. "I can't fix anything if you won't tell me what happens."

"You can't fix this! It's beyond your control."

"Nothing is beyond my control," he replies arrogantly.

"You can stop bombs?"

"Where?"

"Kalafin."

"House of Wurthem," we say in unison.

Kyon's tone takes on a thoughtful air. "When?"

"Now," I whisper.

"How bad?"

"Kalafin is gone."

"The Brothers didn't order it," he says assuredly. "They wouldn't try to bring down Wurthem yet. They still need them to tame the other Houses, especially Comantre."

I know he's right. It wasn't the Brotherhood; it was Pan and the members of the Tempest—and Trey—his stolen drones. This is war. Alameeda and Wurthem are the monsters that declared it. Rafe has been devastated by it. Now Wurthem is suffering its first casualties. From what I saw, they'll be shocked by it. I think they were under the impression that they'd all get through this unscathed. This adds a new layer of chaos to the conflict. Wurthem won't know from where this attack originated. They may suspect their allies, Alameeda. It's a really smart strategic move by the rebels in Amster, pitting the two forces against each other.

It's clear to me that Trey has joined Amster and the resistance they're mounting there. It makes sense. He's an outlaw to Rafe— they think he's a traitor because of me. The rebels in Amster know differently. But deep down I know that Trey did this for me. Pan told him it might help me survive the Brotherhood, so he didn't hesitate to hack into the Wurthem drones and use its own weapons against it. I don't know why something like this would make the Brotherhood need me. And in truth, I don't want them to need me; I want them to leave me alone.

"Tell me everything that happened in your foray into the future," Kyon orders.

I know I can't mention the drones. Anything that connects Trey to this would be reason for Kyon to suspect that he may still be alive. I can't have that. As I tell Kyon the story, I omit how the bombs were delivered in Kalafin, which doesn't leave me much to tell, other than what it looked like when the explosions occurred.

Kyon's military acumen surprises me as he murmurs, "It was more than likely a drone strike. They're the only devices that would deliver that kind of weaponry undetected by Kalafin's security matrix. We had something similar occur in the Isle of Skye while I was searching for you—not of this magnitude, but our drones were infiltrated."

I pretend not to know what he's talking about and simply remain silent, but I can name the programs that commandeered their drones and made them assets to Rafe. I attempt to change the subject. "Where are we sleeping tonight?" I ask.

"Your choice," Kyon says.

"Okay. You sleep in the teak hut and I'll sleep in this one," I point to the main house behind us.

Kyon ignores my suggestion. "You don't really want me to leave you alone. You'd be afraid. I'd find you sleeping in a closet. We can both sleep in the main house if it's more to your liking. Is it?"

I shrug. I hate that he's right. I hate that I need him, at least for now until I can either escape or the Brotherhood becomes less of a threat. Since I don't think either of those things will be easily accomplished, I have to accept him remaining close. I don't, however, have to like it.

CHAPTER 9
LIFT THE VEIL

Kyon is a presence in my life that I can't compartmentalize. My skin is slowly growing accustomed to his skin. Lying beside him at night, he's the well-worn mitt that fits without effort. His hand when it rests on my hip, or his cheek when it brushes my neck, is seduction itself. It's my darkly held secret that's sharply felt. I'm not in love with him. I would never call it that. It's more of a growing fascination with him. He's unlike anyone I've ever known, but he's maladjusted and broken—unpredictable and frightening.

In a way, I'm almost an apprentice to him. Everything he does, he brings me along and shows me how to do it. It doesn't matter what it is. It could be setting traps to catch sea creatures, or dismantling and cleaning weapons, or programing garden-bots. He teaches me what he knows. I feel less of a stranger in this world for it. It only takes him a few rotations to teach me to swim. Something that has plagued me since I've been here is now a skill . . . because of him.

I realize what he's doing, though. He's occupying and monopolizing my time. I have little of it to myself, so I cannot secretly project into the future and explore ways in which I can outmaneuver him. He is nothing if not a keen strategist. I may have met my match with him in that regard.

So I'm surprised one afternoon, when I'm strolling along the beach, to hear the hum of an engine overhead. I shield my eyes from the glare of the sun to locate the aircraft in the sky. Wisps of my blond hair dance in the ocean breeze. Gazing in the direction of the main house, a small, silver, hawk-shaped airship flies over it, idling for a moment above the hoverpad on the rooftop. It floats down in a spiral, like a lost feather, to rest on the two talonlike claws that piston down from its belly. The airship powers down while the side of the craft melts to form a doorway with levitating steps. A tall, brawny blond man appears in the doorway of the craft, descending the stairs. He's not dressed for the beach. He's attired from head to toe in a military uniform. Squaring his broad shoulders, he walks purposefully into the spire that resembles a crow's nest at the top of the house.

I stuff the shells I have in my hand into the burlap satchel that rests on my hip. My eyes stray to Kyon, who has also seen him. He emerges from the surf at an unhurried pace and moves toward the house. I know him well enough now to understand that he has been expecting this visitor, or the aircraft wouldn't be here.

I feign disinterest in our visitor, continuing to collect shells while Kyon rinses off in the outdoor shower. He wraps a towel around his hips and enters the house through our bedroom. I cautiously make my way there too. I press against the adjacent wall before I peek around the corner. The room is empty. I wait. I pull back from the opening and press flat against the wall when Kyon emerges from his dressing room attired in a black Striker uniform.

He moves through the bedroom. I follow him at a slower pace, making sure he doesn't see me trailing him. He takes the stairs at the end of the gallery. I follow him up to the top of the house in the direction of his office. My feet make no noise but I leave a sandy trail on the floorboards that I have no hope of hiding. Clutching the burlap satchel on my hip so the shells don't clink together, I reach in and grasp the knife that Kyon gave me. When I come to the top of the stairs I pause. Looking down the short hallway that leads to his office, I don't have to strain my ears to hear the raised voice coming from it.

"You're being summoned! This isn't a request!" the angry voice of our visitor states. I watch as Kyon leans against the front of his wooden desk. His arms cross over his broad chest.

Goose bumps break out on my arms. I know our visitor—at least, I've seen him before. He's my half sister Nezra's consort—or whatever they are to each other. When I spoke to her, she claimed that he owns her. She was given to him by the Brotherhood, a fact that she despises. She wanted to be claimed by Kyon. For a moment, I wonder if I should pity our visitor.

Nezra's consort continues to pace, saying, "You cannot ignore a summons from the Brothers. They want to compromise. They see they were wrong in seeking extermination."

"What has happened to bring about their change in attitude?" Kyon asks.

"We need her. The war is not over as everyone would like to claim. There's a rebellion being mounted against us as we speak. A counterattack was implemented on a scale that we didn't anticipate."

"What do you mean?" Kyon feigns surprise.

"Wurthem was targeted—a sophisticated strike."

"Targeted by whom—Rafe?"

Our guest shakes his head. "No. Rafe is broken and scattered. We don't know who it is, but they're smart. Whoever they are, they made it look as if the attack came from us. Kalafin was completely decimated—everything within seventy clicks of Wurthem's capital is annihilated. Their communication satellites were taken out as well. They've gone black. Our allies are turning against us. Brother Excelsior himself has sent me here to bring you back. I can assure you that he wants the priestess alive. Her protection is of the utmost priority." It's true, or at least he believes that.

"She knows nothing of the attack, Chandrum," Kyon lies.

"Does she not? Really? She's a self-taught precognitive who has been living with the enemy for as long as she has been on Ethar. I'm sure she knows something—or she can find out. He wants her with him. Now. No excuses."

"She's with me or she doesn't come. She's not ready to operate in our society. She's a savage," Kyon says in a low growl.

"You think he cares if she's ready? You know him. She comes now or she dies. She cooperates with us or he kills her."

"I'll never allow that to happen," Kyon says in a sinister tone. It makes a shiver tear through me.

A soft chuckle comes from the room. "You're serious, aren't you?" Another laugh bubbles from Chandrum, louder this time. "Have you bonded to her?" he asks in disbelief. "You have, haven't you?" He's one big smug smile, as his eyes crinkle in amusement. "I never thought I'd see the day when you'd bond to a priestess!"

A hand encircling my upper arm startles me. A Teflon-coated soldier with big blue eyes and shiny blond hair sneers down at me as he increases his bruising grip on me. "Well, hello, hello, hello! Listening, were you?" he asks with a lisp as he smiles at me, revealing a gap between his two front teeth. He tugs me off the top step and into the short corridor. Another soldier that was behind the gap-toothed one seizes my other elbow with equal fervor. He looks as though he broke his nose recently. A thick red welt spans the bridge of it. I wonder about it briefly while he takes a position next to me, trapping me between them.

The gap-toothed soldier wrenches my arm, yanking my hand from inside the burlap bag. I grip the knife I'm holding tighter, ready to stab him. He doesn't give me a chance. Plucking the handle of it from my grasp with his other hand, he holds it up. He *tsk-tsk*s me in a scolding way. "Now what were you going to do with this?" he asks. Releasing my hand, he holds my knife up to my cheek. I tense, waiting for him to cut me, smelling his breath as he leans near.

We both hear the racking sound of a weapon being armed from the other end of the hallway. Kyon has a very large shotgun pointed at the soldier holding the knife to me. Its nose is wide, and it looks suspiciously like the Mossberg that Luther always kept behind the bar at Lumin when I worked there—the one he threatened Kyon with on Earth.

My eyes go to Kyon's. I pale. He's well beyond angry—he's livid. My knees are weak and begin to tremble. I want to say something in my defense, but my mouth is suddenly very dry. The gap-toothed soldier pressing my knife to me says, "We caught her hiding on the stairs—she was listening to your conversation."

"You caught her?" Kyon asks. His voice is outwardly calm, but he still looks as if he's ready to murder me. I swallow hard. His eyes go to the soldier's hand on me.

The bad-breathed soldier at my side is smug. His face erupts in a carefree grin. "She was sneaking around."

Kyon's jaw is tight as he says, "This is her home—she lives here. She's free to go anywhere in it—there's no need for her to sneak."

The soldier's gap-toothed smile fades when it becomes apparent to both of us that Kyon isn't aiming his weapon at me; he's aiming it at the soldier next to me. Abruptly, the soldier pulls the knife away from me. He holds it up in front of him with a nervous laugh. "She had this in her bag."

"I gave that to her," Kyon retorts.

"Priestesses aren't allowed to possess weapons."

"She uses it to dig for clams," he lies. "Check her bag. It's full of shells."

Anxiety replaces the bravado that was there—the soldier begins to sweat. "We didn't know—we've heard stories—she's been a fugitive for so long—it's been said that she has enchanted you with her powers."

Kyon shifts the gun in his hand. It passes from the soldier he's speaking to, over to me once more. I'm rooted to the floor as I stare at the dark eye of the muzzle. I can't breathe. Abruptly the weapon passes over me again—to the soldier holding my elbow.

Boom! The gun barrel smokes. I'm violently jerked as the second soldier beside me is hit in the face. His hand tugs briefly on my elbow, but his grip goes slack as he's ripped off his feet. The shell sprays the wall to the side of him, but miraculously, not one piece of shot hits me.

I listen as a squeal of pain comes from the soldier on the ground behind me. *Rock salt. It's loaded with rock salt*, I think.

"*Kyon!*" Chandrum yells. He moves closer to Kyon, but Kyon fends him off with one hand, shoving Chandrum away. When Chandrum comes at him again, Kyon swings the muzzle of the Mossberg in his direction. Racking the weapon, a red shell casing pops out of it. Chandrum stops and backs up.

Kyon's voice is controlled and deadly calm, "They touched her. No one has a right to touch her but me."

Chandrum holds out his hand cautiously. "Has there been a Claiming Ceremony?"

Kyon doesn't lower the Mossberg. "She belongs to *me!*"

Chandrum tries a placating tone. "We haven't had the Claiming Ceremony yet. They're Excelsior's men!" Chandrum waves his hand in our direction. "They're here on official business. Technically, the Brotherhood still owns her."

"Technically," Kyon says, "I shoot anyone who touches her without my permission." Extending his arm straight out, he swings the barrel of the gun away from Chandrum, aiming at the soldier who now looks as if he's seeing the devil before him.

The blond-headed soldier puts up both his hands, but it does no good. *Boom!* The soldier is lifted off his feet, thrown backward from the force of the shot. My hair stirs and my ears ring. Even though I knew it was coming—could see the intent on Kyon's face—the noise still makes me jump. The smell of blood and spent shells assaults me, but I can't move. I stare straight ahead at Kyon. It's like I'm not here, though. For a moment, I'm back in the ballroom of the Palace in Rafe, and I'm helpless to stop anything happening to me.

Kyon lowers the gun and walks to me. I still can't move. He's gentle when he takes me in his arms and hugs me. My breath comes out in hacks from my tight chest. I can't think. I feel numb, like I got shot, but I didn't.

Tucking me to his side, Kyon leads me away from the carnage at my feet. I refuse to look at the wounded soldiers. I don't want to know if they'll live or not. I don't want to know about them at all. Over his shoulder, Kyon orders, "Take care of them, Chandrum, and then meet us on the beach."

"I'm not a curer—"

"Do it!" Kyon barks. "Call your people. I know they're stationed all around here. There's no stealth in any of them. I allowed them to get close so they could witness something for me. I've been watching them since before you landed."

Chandrum swears under his breath, and then says, "I'm under orders to protect the priestess." It's the truth. They want me alive for now.

"I'll remember that the next time I'm asked to intervene with Nezra." I don't get to assess the impact my half sister's name has on Chandrum, because Kyon points me at the stairs and ushers me down them.

It seems as if it's only ten steps later and I'm in the bedroom I share with Kyon. *Am I in shock?* He leads me to my dressing room. Opening the doors for me, he guides me to the automated seamstress. The cylinder rises up from the floor, trapping me inside.

"Please make a selection," Oscil requests.

He speaks to the seamstress program. "Number one."

My clothing is cut from me and shredded at my feet. The softest fabric I've ever felt touches my skin, weaving around me in silvery tat patterns of lace and cloud. The collar forms a high, stiff arc behind my neck, forcing my hair to fall over my shoulders and rest on each of my breasts. A deep V forms in front of the intricate, long-flowing gown. The bare skin between my breasts is exposed. Seeing it, my heart beats a misbegotten rhythm.

The sleeves of the gown come to a point over my hands and loop around my index fingers to hold them in place. I hardly blink when a shimmering silver veil falls over my eyes, clouding my vision. The walls of the automated cylinder disappear. A warm hand takes mine. Gently, Kyon guides me toward the doors.

"My shoes," I murmur, trying to pull away from Kyon to retrieve them.

"We'll come back for them later. You won't need them now."

Kyon takes me out through the bedroom to the beach. The warm air catches the thin veil covering my hair and face, making it dance around me in shimmering folds. Nearing the water, Kyon stops close to Chandrum, who looks on with mild annoyance. "*He* is not going to like this," Chandrum says in a warning tone.

"*He* doesn't have to like it. He just has to respect the claim." Chandrum still looks irritated, but he gives a curt nod to Kyon. Kyon takes something from the pocket of his uniform as he turns to me. He's no longer angry—at least I don't think he is. He wears a calm expression that has my numb brain tumbling over itself to decipher what is happening.

Seabirds fly overhead. Kyon's eyes, the bluest of blue, stare down at me. He reaches for the nape of my neck and ties a red flower around my throat. It's a black-ribboned choker. His elegant black dress uniform seems out of place in the fading light of the setting sun upon the water. With sand between my toes, I stare at the lapping waves on the beach. Gold and silver shines in the tide along the shoreline, a seaside with all the stars of the heavens captured within it. The thin veil covering my eyes parts. His eyes lean to me, bringing with them havoc within my bones. I stifle my instinct to recoil. "With this flower," Kyon says, smiling down upon me, "I keep thee to me . . . always. Welcome home, Kricket."

CHAPTER 10
DELEGATION

Chandrum slaps Kyon on the back, unaware of Kyon's distinct scowl at being touched by him. "I never thought I'd see the day that Kyon Ensin would claim anyone. If I hadn't just witnessed it for myself, I would call it a ridiculous rumor."

Kyon doesn't respond. He's watching me—gauging my reaction. I continue to stare back at him, giving him nothing. The air around us is tense.

Chandrum doesn't notice the silent war going on between Kyon and me. "I will ready the trift. We're to be there by nightfall."

"I have arranged for an escort for us," Kyon replies. "Excelsior's wounded men can ride with them. They'll be tended to on board."

"I will see to it," Chandrum replies. One more clasp on the back to Kyon and he leaves us.

"This changes nothing!" I say with a hollow voice. I pull the veil off of my head, tossing it away from me. It's caught in the wind and blows away down the beach.

Kyon narrows his eyes at me. "You're right. You were mine already. This just unites us in the eyes of the Brotherhood. You belong to me."

"*I* belong to *me*." I point at my own chest.

He points at his chest. "The only way you survive is with me. Your right to exist will not go unchallenged. Your blood is impure. You need me by your by side."

"Because I have Rafe blood?"

"Yes."

"That just means I dodged the insanity gene that seems to run so strong in your kind."

His jaw tenses. "Blood is an issue, especially since you've displayed strong precognitive abilities. It makes the science look wrong."

"What science?"

"The genetic science they're going to want to study using you as a baseline."

"They want me as a lab rat?"

"Some do. Some want you for what you can do—to tell them the future—to manipulate it to their favor. But some don't want you at all."

"What do you want?" I ask.

"I want you to obey me," he replies.

He can't be serious, even though I know he is. "I thought you were going to shoot me—in the hallway outside your office." My hand gestures in the direction of the house.

"Did I scare you?"

I place my hands on my hips. "You know you did."

"Would you rather I smother you in false security like everyone else?"

"I would rather you were not a monster."

"What I did is send a message to the ones who sent the soldiers. No one disrespects you in front of me. Neither of us should permit any dissension from others. Like it or not, we're together—a unit. You're only as strong as me, and I, you. I won't tolerate weakness or disloyalty. Think about that—your survival relies on it."

He takes my elbow none too lightly and escorts me from the beach to the house. We stop briefly to gather the exquisite shoes that go along with my gown. I slip them on, and he ushers me through the house. When we reach the stairs, he places his hand on the small of my back as we climb them together.

Rounding the landing near the second floor, I ask, "You were supposed to kill me, weren't you?" He pauses. Glancing at me, he loses some of his scowl. "At the palace," I continue, "and again when you found me aboard the Ship of Skye. They wanted me dead from the beginning and they told you to do it."

His hand grips the wrought-iron balustrade tight. "I was to kill you if I couldn't claim you for Alameeda. Your potential to rule frightens many, especially Excelsior."

A disbelieving laugh trickles from me. "You're not serious?" Kyon takes my hand in exasperation and continues climbing the stairs. I tug on it, trying to get him to stop again. "Wait! You *are* serious!"

"When have you ever known me not to be serious?" he growls.

"When you say rule, you mean rule Alameeda?"

"I mean rule Ethar."

"Your ambition scares me, Kyon."

"Your lack of it angers me, Kricket," he retorts honestly.

"Why would I want to rule Ethar?"

"It's not a matter of want. It's a matter of need."

"You think I need to rule Ethar?"

"You'd like to live, correct?"

"It's sort of a priority for me," I say with a nod.

"We only live if we rule. It's as simple and as hard as that, Kricket. Kill Excelsior and the Brotherhood or eventually they kill us."

"Those can't be the only options," I breathe. "Someone else can rule once they're gone."

His grip on my arm becomes painful as he pulls me along. At the top of the stairs, we exit the house onto the rooftop. Chandrum waits for us in his silver airship. Once inside, Kyon shows me to a large, comfortable seat by a long window in the back away from the cockpit. He takes the seat next to me. The airship lifts straight up into the sky. Several ships that resemble silver hawks fall in with ours. They form a V-shaped line, like geese in flight, when we rocket away from Kyon's small island.

"Who are they?" I point to the other fowl-like airships.

"Armed escorts."

"Protecting us or making sure we don't leave?"

"They're my people. They work for me. We'll be safe until we get to Urbenoster."

"What's in Urbenoster?"

"It's the capital of the House of Alameeda."

"Are you worried about our reception?" I ask.

"I never worry. I handle whatever comes." He's not lying. He's someone who doesn't waste much time on an emotion like worry. I envy that in him.

When I spy Urbenoster ahead of us through a pass in the mountains, it takes my breath away. Rocky snow-capped peaks encircle the glimmering city like a stony tiara. Two mountain-sized griffins have been carved from the rock where a gap resides in the mountain range. The fierce sentinels stand on either side of the opening to the city. The carved griffins have eaglelike heads attached to the bodies of lions. Gray, stone wings flourish from the backs of the statues. As we approach, the sun is behind the stone images, casting shadows that give the eagle faces a more sinister mien.

If there were ever a city made of the tail end of a rainbow, it's this one. Gone is the Viking enclave that I've been living in for the past few rotations. Everything here is shiny and new. There's nothing misshapen or occurring by happenstance. Every line of every building has the appearance of being meticulously planned in advance, giving it the feeling of completeness in thought and form. The buildings soar above the mountaintops. Blue silken flags wave in the breeze on every eave and rooftop. Glittering, golden confetti pours out of windows to float on the wind as we fly at a sedate pace through channels of airspace between the skyscrapers.

"They're celebrating," Kyon murmurs to me.

"What are they celebrating?" I ask.

"The end of Rafe."

My throat grows tight and I no longer find any of it beautiful.

Not long after entering Urbenoster, we're met by vehicles that resemble silver wheel-less chariots, manned by men in blue uniforms with blue helmets with griffin wings on the sides. They escort us into an empty traffic channel. No other airship traffic is about on this route. We pass by streaming blue flags that each have a white emblem of a griffin in its center.

My head begins to hurt. My breathing slows and my hands turn to ice. Kyon glances over at me. His hand reaches out and covers my frigid fingers. He whispers, "Don't fight it, Kricket. Let it come."

"Let what come?' I ask in misery, fighting desperately to maintain consciousness within my body.

"Let the future come to you. Let it show us of the danger that lies ahead," he whispers. He lifts my cold finger to his lips, kissing them. "Tell me why we shouldn't be here, Kricket." With those words, I'm ripped from my body, leaving it behind.

⚬⚬⚬

"Stop!" I scream, just as I did when I was in the future. Spilling back into my deflated body, my eyes fly open and I arch in pain. I paw at my chest, because my fingers don't work like they should. I groan, my mouth opening in agony. A hand sweeps my fingers from my chest, covering my erratic heart as it beats out of control.

"I've got you, Kricket," Kyon murmurs.

Wild-eyed, I pant and strain against his hand. He holds me in my seat as I thrash against it. I have the strongest urge to get up and run, but there's nowhere to run. *I need to leave.* Slowly, the deep stabbing pain in my chest turns into phantom pain and recedes. My breathing begins to slow.

"How are they going to kill us?"' Kyon asks me.

I wince. "How do you know they're going to kill us?" I ask.

"I expect nothing else from the Brotherhood. It's a test. If you can read it, you get to live . . . for now. Do they succeed?"

"Yeah—they definitely get us."

"How?"

"It's our welcoming committee—they're not so . . . welcoming. Four assassins. Two snipers on the eaves of the buildings at one o'clock and fifteen o'clock and two soldiers at close range—the ones in Peney diplomatic uniforms who will be on either side of Em Sam. You remember Em Sam, right?"

"Em Sam—his title 'Em' means 'preeminent'—he's an ambassador."

"He's an ambassador from Wurthem," I tell him. "We both met him at the palace when I was Manus's ward. We had several dinners together."

Kyon's eyes narrow in contempt. "I remember him. He's the ambassador from Wurthem who spent a lot of time trying to seduce you right under Manus's nose."

"He never tried to seduce me!" I reply in confusion.

"He did. You're just naïve. If he had gotten you alone, he planned to smuggle you out of the palace to his home in Oxfortshire." Kyon pulls out his harbinger from the holster on the thigh of his uniform. He checks the side arm's power level. Absently, he asks, "Did you die?" My eyes move from the gun to his face. My brow wrinkles. He nods his head to the side. "In the future, did you die?"

"Yes," I reply, "but not before you. You stepped in front of me." I swallow hard, remembering how Kyon's head exploded with blue sparks that pushed his teeth out the back of his head, spattering blood all over me.

"Did that surprise you?"

"Yes."

"Why?"

"Given our history, I didn't think you cared for anyone but your-self."

"For someone who can see the future, you're blind. At least your precognition is clear."

He glances at me. I must look scared, because his eyes soften. Reaching over, he cups my cheek. "You did well." I find his touch oddly comforting for a moment, until he adds, "We might survive tonight after all."

The airship lands and he gets to his feet. Chandrum joins us from the front of the aircraft. "I need your harbinger," Kyon says as if he's asking to use Chandrum's communicator.

Chandrum doesn't hesitate at all before handing Kyon his side-arm. Kyon then goes to a compartment near us. Opening it, I see it's loaded with ferocious-looking weapons. "Should she wait here?" Chandrum asks as he indicates me. From the rack, Kyon takes down a long-barreled, riflelike weapon that Strikers usually carry.

"Yes." Kyon replies. To me he orders, "Stay here."

"Seriously?" I ask him in exasperation. He doesn't wait for me to voice my objection, but moves toward the front of the airship. I call to his back as he reaches the open doorway. "I'm the one who knows who they are!" I remind him.

"And you've already told me," he replies. "So your job is done." He puts the high-powered rifle to his shoulder. The barrel of the weapon breaks the plane of the door as Kyon looks through the rifle's digital sight. He snaps off several quick shots, and then exits the aircraft.

I jump up from my seat and follow him as he disappears down the steps. Racing to the doorway, I'm in time to see Kyon make it off the bottom step where he drops his rifle. I shield my eyes from the sun and look to the two buildings. On the eaves of both, I see dead snipers slumped over rifle barrels.

My feet are made of lead, but I force them to move away. I follow Kyon as he walks toward the delegation of statesmen. There are thirteen of them in all, six on either side of Em Sam. Most of them are hunched in confusion, like they don't know whether to keep pretending to be a welcoming party there to greet us with open arms or if they should drop their ruse and run away from the crazed gunman.

Kyon's arms extend, forming a V as he raises his two harbingers and shoots the two delegates on either side of Em Sam—the ones who were sent to kill us. The ambassador of Wurthem holds up both of his hands in front of him with a barely suppressed smile on his face. He seems pleased with this outcome as he looks past Kyon to me on the stairs. It confirms what they'd heard of me: I can read the future—I can change the future.

Kyon keeps walking forward. His arms spread wide again. I cringe as he aims at the so-called diplomats on either side of the line of men in front of him. They react, scrambling to take cover as they pull out concealed weapons of their own, but there isn't anywhere for them to hide here in the open; having selected this spot for their ambush, it has now turned on them. Kyon's rapid-fire precision shots are unavoidable. The assembled men fall bleeding to the ground, each shot in the head by Kyon until every single one of them is dead in a pool of his own blood—all of them except for Em Sam.

When Kyon reaches him, Em Sam is on his knees. Kyon holds both barrels of his guns to the ambassador's forehead. "Did I get them all?" Kyon asks Em Sam.

The ambassador doesn't speak; he just closes his eyes and fervently nods his head. Sweat slides down the side of his face and a little bit of drool falls from his mouth.

I hurry to Kyon's side and lay my hand on his arm. "Kyon. You got them. There were only four who were charged with killing us. The rest were just backup," I murmur in a placating tone.

He continues to stare at Em Sam. He lifts the harbinger in his left hand, waving it negligently around at the dead bodies on the ground. "They were all complicit. Especially him." Kyon presses the barrel of the harbinger in his right hand harder into Em Sam's forehead, making the ambassador wince and whimper.

"They said I had to," Em Sam whines. "They said you wouldn't kill me if you lived."

Kyon squats down in front of Em Sam, leaning closer to his ear. "They don't know what I'll do, Sam," he says in a conspiratorial way. "They can't see the future." Kyon pulls back and smiles into Em Sam's eyes before, *boom!* The gun in Kyon's hand goes off, blowing a hole in Em Sam's forehead.

I jump in response to the noise. The shot jerks Em Sam back and he falls with his eyes wide open staring up at the sky. I should be used to this by now, but I'm not. I can only stand there looking down at Sam, shaking at the knees. "You didn't have to kill him," I say in a voice that doesn't sound like mine.

"Yes, I did," he replies. He wraps his arm around my shoulder and pulls me to his side. "Brother Excelsior will know that you read the future, because I killed the snipers, but he'll also know that I won't allow you to be tested without them paying a price for it."

He shoves one of his harbingers back in his holster. Turning us around, he walks me back to the hawk-shaped ship. Entering it, he tells Chandrum, "You can get out here. I will have your ship returned to you."

"I will stay with you. You need my help," Chandrum replies. "I didn't know he would test her like this—he has been keeping me out of their circle when there is talk of you or Kricket," he says. "The Brotherhood knows we're friends as well as Brothers. Do you plan to go back the Sea of Stars now?" He's worried. It's like he's our handler or something.

"No," Kyon replies, showing no emotion. "Kricket and I will remain in Urbenoster. I have plans to show her around her new city." He says that like I own the place or something. "I plan to introduce her to her people."

"Her people?" Chandrum asks, looking startled.

"The citizens of Urbenoster," Kyon says this like it's the most natural thing in the world.

"But . . . she's a priestess. The Brotherhood doesn't allow them to mingle with common citizens." Chandrum smiles like Kyon just said something completely ridiculous. "She should be with her own kind—with her sister Nezra. They've made a place for her at Freming House—for both of you. I understand that now that you've bonded to her, you won't want to be apart from her, but you have to compromise. You know that the Brothers have rights to her gifts as well."

"No one has any rights to her but me. I tracked her. I found her. I fought for her. I claimed her. If it were not for me, she'd be dead to us. Those same Brothers who think they have a claim to her were also the ones who planned to assassinate her while she was in Rafe. When they did that, they forfeited any rights to her. Kricket and I won't be staying at Freming House. We'll be staying at my estate in Urbenoster. Should any of the Brothers want to meet her, they'll have to do so at my leisure and only with my permission."

"You know that you will always have my loyalty," Chandrum lies.

"I know it," Kyon lies as well.

"Should I bring Nezra to you to greet Kricket?"

Kyon looks at me and I stiffen at the mention of my half sister's name.

"No. Not just yet. I think Kricket needs time to adjust to her new life before we try to make them play nice together."

Chandrum ventures to smile. "You know Nezra."

"I do," he agrees.

"I'll leave you here then." Chandrum nods then turns to me, smiling. "It's been a great pleasure to greet you, Kricket. Congratulations on your Pairing to Kyon. It was an honor to have been a witness to it."

I want to kick him off his ship. I doubt he would lift a finger to help us if things go bad for us. My smile is as bright as his as I say, "Yes, such a pleasure to meet you, Chandrum. Please give my regards to my sweet sister Nezra."

Chandrum doesn't know if I'm being serious or sarcastic. Kyon knows, though. He sees that I'm brittle beneath my smiling veneer. Chandrum turns away and disembarks from his aircraft.

I raise a shaky hand to my forehead, rubbing it. "He's not loyal to you, but you know that."

"Yes, I know it," Kyon agrees. "I don't blame him. He's weak. He has always been weak."

"You're sure that they don't know that I can tell when they're lying?"

"Who would tell them?" Kyon asks. "The only other person from Alameeda who knew about your ability to decipher lies was Em Nark, but he blew up somewhere over Rafe territory before he had the chance to reveal it, and I don't tell your secrets to anyone."

"How do they know that I can see the future, then?" I ask him.

"They knew your mother. They were sure you would inherit her gene."

"Why are they so sure?" I know that neither my older half sister, Nezra, nor my younger sister, Astrid, seem to have the trait.

"When your mother was very young, she was unguarded. She gave Excelsior her predictions without thought. She was a naïve child. She didn't understand the ramifications of what she saw. When Arissa was asked if any of her own children would inherit her ability to see the future she said, 'I will bequeath it to my strongest daughter.'"

"How did you know she meant me?"

"How could she not?" he replies. "You survived Earth alone. Come, do you want to learn how to fly Chandrum's Hallafast? If you crash it, it won't cost me a thing."

I drop my hand as I stare at Kyon. "Did you just make a joke? Now? After what just happened out there?" I point outside where corpses are littering the hoverpad.

He smiles. "Too soon?"

"Yes."

"You cannot feel bad for them. They were going to kill us." He takes my hand, leading me toward the front of the Hallafast. He hands me into one of the two seats. Leaning over me, he presses a button that activates the seat belts. They crisscross my body. He selects a small marble from several on the console and hands it to me. "Put this in your ear," he advises. He takes the seat next to mine.

"Will it eat my brain?" I ask.

He looks confused. "No."

"Mind control?" I ask.

"I wish."

I place the marble in my ear, and a microphone grows out of the earpiece to hover near my mouth.

He takes the seat next to mine. "I'm going to engage the manual controls." He presses some buttons, and two joysticks emerge from the console, one for each of us. Each joystick has a rollerball on top. "This aircraft has more advanced controls, but this is how most of us learn how to fly. Once you get the basics down, we'll move on."

"You can't be serious? You're going to teach me to fly? Now?"

"Why not?"

"You just killed some people," I reply.

"People who were going to kill us," he corrects. He gestures to the console in front of us. "This should take your mind off of it."

Indicating the joystick in front of me, he says, "Pull back on the stick—we rise. Push forward on the stick—we dive." Using his thumb, he spins the rollerball on the top of the stick. "This controls direction." He points to two buttons on the grip of the stick. "These control speed. Acceleration is the top button, deceleration is the bottom one."

"So the bottom one is the brake?"

"Yes."

"If I stop us in midair, will we fall?"

"No. We'll hover, but someone will probably crash into us and then we'll all fall in a fiery ball of death." I frown at him and he shrugs. "It's true. Here, I'll start us off."

Kyon skillfully lifts the Hallafast up from the ground with the grace of a blooming flower. Through the side window, I observe the silver wings of the ship ripple and spread out wider. We hover in the air. I look at Kyon who I find is watching me. He nods toward the stick in front of me.

"What? Now?" I ask him in panic.

"Yes. Now."

"What if I crash?"

"Then I'll be really angry with you."

"You're not going to let us crash, right?" I ask.

"I might let us crash. It's not my Hallafast." He's telling the truth.

"You're so mean," I say as I exhale.

I grip the stick and press the top button. We jerk forward with neck-snapping force, which makes me grip the stick harder, which makes us rocket faster.

"Ease off on the acceleration," Kyon says calmly.

I shift my finger to the bottom button and squeeze it hard. Both of our heads lurch forward and I hear loud crashes like plates shattering coming from the back of the airship. I shift my finger off the brake and gently accelerate once more. I swallow hard.

"Chandrum is going to be mad at you," Kyon teases me.

"Good," I reply.

We're heading straight for traffic—it's moving from right to left in front of us. Beyond that, there's a very tall building. "Ease into the flow," Kyon instructs.

"How?" I growl.

"Use your thumb, slide the rollerball left and merge in between the other ships."

I use the pad of my thumb to roll the controller. We shift in the air, banking in the direction we need to go.

"You're going too slow. This isn't a spix," he admonishes.

"You think?" I retort with a scowl.

"Speed up," he barks.

I squeeze the top button—the ship goes faster, but my seat begins to shake. "Why is my seat rumbling?" I ask with wide eyes.

"Because you're dangerously close to that Terraglide next to you," he says calmly. "Don't worry about it. They'll move." I look to my right and see the oval airship next to us veer away. The seat stops rumbling. "Just follow the traffic. That's right," Kyon says. "How are you feeling?"

"Sweaty," I reply. He laughs.

We fly around the city. I don't see any of it except for the tail end of the aircraft that merge in and out in front of me. After a while, I relax enough to enjoy myself. I listen to Kyon explain how to merge into traffic above us and how to descend into traffic below us.

"Have you had enough?" Kyon finally asks. I glance at him. He's smiling.

"Do they hire people to fly here?" I ask.

"Are you looking for a job?" he chuckles.

"This wouldn't be a bad job. You take people where they need to be and if you do it right, everyone gets home safe."

"The job you just described would kill a person like you."

"Why would you say that?"

"Courage is a value that you hold dear. Without danger, there is no courage. You live for danger."

"I can't avoid danger. There's a difference."

"No. You slap danger in the face and wait for it to react."

"So I should just start calling you danger?"

"If you like," he says.

"I've had enough danger for one day."

"There is never enough danger," he replies. He takes hold of the stick on the console in front of him. "Let go of your control." When I do, he says, "Come here and sit on my lap. I want to show you how to program a route and a destination."

"Can you show me from here?" I ask reluctantly.

"No," he replies.

I resist for a moment, but I really want to learn how to program a route. It's a skill that can help me escape one day, and I'd be stupid to turn down the opportunity to learn. I disengage the seat belt and move to his side. Kyon reaches over and pulls me onto his lap. As he flies the Hallafast, he explains the way to input coordinates and determine the best possible route. The control panel is intricate, but I begin to understand it as I ask him questions. I relax against his chest. His deep voice is engaging. It's confusing, this dance he's doing with me—I'm his enemy, I'm his possession, I'm his lifeline to the future, I'm his slave, I'm his confidante, I'm his pupil.

Once Kyon finishes his explanation, the route and destination are logged in. He switches the Hallafast to autopilot. The console in front of us retracts and the manual joysticks shift back and disappear into the dashboard. It leaves just readouts in front of us, but little else to distract me from the view. I try to stand, to move back to my seat, but Kyon's arms wrap around me and hold me in place on his lap.

"We're almost home," he explains. "There." He points to where the buildings fall away. In the middle of this elaborate metropolis, where the skyscrapers reach into the clouds, there's a large chunk of dead air. It's called dead air because the elaborate, sprawling estate buildings on the site below it are only about twenty stories high.

On Ethar, where most of the land is annexed, being close to the ground level—to terra firma—is afforded only to the very wealthy. It is an extreme extravagance to have unoccupied airspace. To have this much of it is borderline vulgar.

The city of Urbenoster is surrounded by mountains—a ring. The beautifully constructed skyscrapers wreathing the inside form another circle—a second ring. Kyon's estate is in the middle of it all—a third ring—or the pupil of the eye, whichever way you want to look at it. A river cuts through the city from the mountains. It comes from a waterfall off a mountain peak. It flows directly to Kyon's estate, then splits into two rivers that flow around the estate on either side and merge again on the far end. Thus, it acts as a wide moat separating the estate from the rest of the city.

"All roads lead to Rome," I murmur. "I don't understand *at all*."

Kyon frowns. "What don't you understand?"

"You!" I cover my face with both my hands and rub it. "Who *are* you?"

"You seem upset," he observes. His cheek brushes the back of my hand. It feels a little like fine sandpaper.

"I *am* upset," I reply. I take my hands away from my face and glare at him. "No wonder you're insane! This kind of wealth makes people crazy! I bet you never relax! I bet you're always obsessing about something—how you can beat something, or do something, or kill something, or win something!"

"Sometimes I sleep."

"I'm serious!" I growl. I try to get up off of his lap again, but he pulls me back down.

"Don't let this scare you. You'll stay by my side until you adjust."

"Staying by your side doesn't help that—at all—in fact, it exacerbates the problem."

"That wasn't a request," he says.

We fly over the moat; the landscape is so stunning that it leaves me breathless. The grounds are laid out to resemble a flower, but not just any flower. I recognize the intricate pattern—the perfection of it. "What do you see?" Kyon asks.

I study it. It's not really a circle, it's a hexagon composed of evenly spaced overlapping circles. Every tree line, hedgerow, and garden path conspires to form the flowerlike pattern with a symmetrical structure of the hexagon. "I see a Flower of Life."

Kyon exhales against my throat; it makes goose bumps rise on me. "What else do you see?" he whispers, his lips finding my pulse.

My heart hammers in my chest. In the dead center of the Flower of Life pattern is a majestic palace of epic proportions. "Your house is a castle. It has thirteen round spires—it resembles a snowflake."

"That is its two-dimensional shape. What else do you see?" he asks me.

I see a few possible shapes: icosahedron, dodecahedron, octahedron, hexahedron, and star tetrahedron. "Your house is the shape of Metatron's Cube—seventy-eight possible lines connecting the thirteen circular spires."

"I knew there was so much about you to like," he murmurs.

The structure is gorgeous, made from the gray stone that appears to be quarried from the mountains surrounding the city. The architecture is a mix of glass and stone walls with multiple roofs of slate. The height is only about twenty stories at its highest point, but it's massive in breadth and depth. It makes the palace in the Isle of Skye look quaint.

The Hallafast descends like a bird of prey to a hoverpad in the middle of an intricate garden. Topiary mazes continue the Flower of Life patterns over the lawns. We touch down in the middle of one; it shrouds the hawk-shaped airship from the house. I pull the earpiece from my ear, placing it on the console.

Kyon allows me to rise from his lap as he places his earpiece back on the console. He stands too, looping his arm around my waist and holding me to him when I would've walked away. The feelings he provokes in me are confusing—fear and desire. I need to get away from him, but I can't. I hold my breath and wait to see what he'll do as his hand sweeps my hair away from my neck in a caress. "I'm going to miss having you all to myself."

"You've never struck me as someone who enjoys sharing."

"I don't share—" his fingers gently caress my nape "—not you, not ever."

"Let's make sure the Brotherhood knows that. I have no intention of being their toy."

I push away from his embrace without looking at him and walk to the door. He follows me. I wait as he opens it. Kyon's arm goes up, barring the doorway. "You never go first, Kricket. It's not safe. You always allow me go first so that I can take whatever fire is meant for you."

"That's not a good plan for you. What makes you think I won't shoot you in the back?"

His lips twitch as he suppresses a smile. "You're right. Together then?" he asks.

"If you insist."

"I do."

Kyon takes my hand as we disembark. Once on the ground, the privacy we shared for the last few rotations is gone. Armed security is everywhere, stationing themselves along our route to the house and by every door and every stair that I see. People stream from every direction to gawk at us.

I look straight ahead, keeping my eyes on the impressive entryway. It's at the top of wide stone steps. The wooden doors are enormous, making it appear as if giants live here instead of just really tall Etharians. The edifice itself with all of its cathedral-like detail makes me feel like a munchkin. The lintel is made from marble and contains carvings of Ethar's two moons: Inium and Sinder.

Before we reach the massive entrance of the castle, a tall soldier approaches us. I lose color when I recognize him. He's the soldier who I tricked into trusting me right before I shot him in the neck with my stolen tranquilizer gun and escaped from the doomed Ship of Skye. It makes me shudder, remembering my feeling of desperation as I tried to leave then—the raw fear. *What was his name?* I wonder with dread. His blond hair is cut shorter than it was—it doesn't touch his ears anymore. The change makes his massive shoulders look even broader.

"Keenan," Kyon says as he greets the soldier.

The soldier nods to him. "Brother Kyon."

Kyon gestures to me. "You remember Kricket, I'm sure."

Keenan doesn't smile when he looks at me. "I do, cousin. Greetings, Elle Kricket." He uses the title of "Elle" to denote my priestess status. It's also very formal. *We're not going to be friends.*

"Greetings," I mutter. His jaw is rigid. I have no luck at all.

Kyon keeps walking, holding my hand so that I move with him. He says, "Keenan will take the lead on your security. He'll be with you when I cannot. I chose him for you because he has an appreciation for how resourceful you can be."

I look over my shoulder at Keenan as he falls in step behind us. His gun faces away from us in a safe position as he narrows his blue eyes at me. I turn back around and face the house once more. *Dammit!* I think.

A very calm older man waits for us at the top of the stairs. He has the military build that I'm used to seeing in all the fair-haired men on this cursed planet, but his eyes are brown. Streaks of gray hairs mix with his long blond ones. It's rare to see it. They all live so long—thousands of years—it's insane to think about how old he must be. Two thousand? Three? He fascinates me right away. He's extremely amused with this situation, if the humor in his eyes is any indication. "So you found her," he says by way of greeting to Kyon.

"I found her. I lost her. I found her. I lost her." He gestures to me. "I found her."

"If I'm lucky, he'll lose me again," I say absently.

This elicits a delighted bark of laughter from the older gentleman. "I wouldn't call that luck."

"Oh no?" I respond.

"No." He sobers a bit. "I would call that tragic—for you both." His eyes shift to Kyon. "You have visitors."

"Do I?"

"Curious fools," he replies.

"Ah," Kyon says. "Thank you for entertaining them for me, Fulton."

"Would you like to meet some of the Brothers, Kricket?" Kyon asks me.

"Not really," I reply.

"Smart girl." Fulton smiles at me in delight.

"Too smart," Kyon agrees.

"Is there such a thing?" Fulton asks with an admiring grin.

Kyon addresses me. "Fulton is my mentor. He has been with me since my childhood."

"I think of him as my son," Fulton says with an affectionate glance at Kyon.

"Did you foster the ruthless spirit in him?" I ask point-blank.

"I cannot take credit for his iron will. It's a trait he inherited from his real father and . . . from circumstance—"

"*Kricket!*" My name is screamed with a desperate fervor. Startled by it, we all turn to look behind us. Across the lawn, a young woman is running toward us. She's soaking wet, having obviously climbed out of the river moat. She's got a fanatical, frenzied look on her face. Armed men are chasing her. With her arms spread wide, she shouts, "Kricket! I love you!"

She's tackled to the ground. One soldier knees her in the back while another secures her hands behind her with handcuff spray.

She struggles, continuing to call my name. She's brought back up to her feet where she has to be lifted off them to get her to move in the other direction away from us. She screeches at the top of her lungs, "I just want to greet her! You don't understand! I love her! She's the one! She's the one!" The soldier uses a tranquilizer gun on her and she becomes unconscious.

"Your security has holes," Kyon states as he turns to scowl at Keenan.

"I'll make sure we find the breach in security and report it to you by tonight," Keenan replies.

"Who was that?" I ask, startled. I stare at them. There was reverence in that girl's tone when she shouted my name. She was desperate to get to me.

"You are beloved here, Kricket," Fulton replies. "Some citizens have been waiting for you for a long time."

"What do you mean?"

"She doesn't know?" Fulton asks Kyon.

"No. And here is not the place to discuss it." Kyon points to the yellow bird perched on the lintel above us.

Fulton nods. "Falla Kirk."

"Go home, Falla," Kyon calls to the yellow bird.

"Auden will be angry with me if I don't tell him something useful," the yellow bird says in a melodic feminine voice. The round shape of my eyes shows my surprise.

"Tell him to bathe more. That's useful," Kyon replies to the beautiful canary.

Kyon takes me by the elbow and escorts me through the doors. Inside we enter the first spire of the castle. The reception room is an enormous circle. The floors are made of blue glass with the Flower of Life pattern etched into them and repeated over and over. Silver pillars shaped like ancient trees grow up from the floor to a vaulted ceiling. The ceiling itself resembles a cosmic nebula of galaxies and stars—the same stars that reside in the sky above Ethar. Below the ceilings, there is a gallery with white archways overlooking us on the floor beneath.

As I walk the room, all of the exquisite panels on the walls project holographic landscapes of Ethar. They're like altarpieces in the way they hang and take up large areas of space. Some of the landscapes are familiar to me because I've been to them in the Forest of Omnicron and seen them firsthand. I shiver when I come upon the waterfall where I waded with Trey before the Comantre Syndic soldiers found us.

I move on. There are glass doors that lead out to the grounds and some that lead to private, walled courtyards built into the interior of the castle. I pass archways with curtains that can be drawn to hide small niches. What interests me most is that there appears to be no stairs that lead to the gallery above and no way to access the rest of the house through this entrance. I make a complete circle and end up where I started, at the entrance.

"Are you lost?" Kyon asks with his cunning smile—the one that tells me he has a secret.

I'm drawn back to the portrait of the waterfall that Trey and I slept near. I remember what it was like to lay next to Trey—to have his arms around me, protecting me. An exquisite ache squeezes my chest. I want that back.

I gaze at the landscape. It's so clear that I feel as if I could step into it and be transported there. My hand reaches out to test the theory, but Kyon stays it at the last possible moment with his hand on mine. "You don't want to do that," he says as he puts my hand to his lips, kissing the back of it.

"Would this take me there?" I ask. My hand trembles in his giant one.

"Nothing gets by you, does it, my little savage? This is a portal of a kind. I have yet to perfect it, however. It still has complications that make it . . . unsafe."

"Complications?" I ask. I glance back at the landscape. The air feels misty, stirred up by the impact of water hitting water.

"Keenan," Kyon says over his shoulder to my bodyguard who has been trailing us around the room. "I need a volunteer."

Keenan goes to the entrance and hails a guard from outside. I glance at Fulton, who winks at me conspiratorially. A brawny soldier enters through the large doors. He angles his automatic weapon— a freston, which is actually three weapons in one—downward in a safe position.

"Come here, please," Kyon requests as he continues to look at the landscape of the waterfall in front of us.

The soldier looks at us and decides that he was the one Kyon meant. He does as he's ordered and stands next to Kyon.

"What do you think of my landscape?" Kyon asks the soldier.

"It's very nice," the soldier replies.

"Nice! It's nice?" Kyon laughs, seemingly amused. He lets go of my hand and clamps his arm around the soldier's shoulder. "Why don't you have a closer look?" Kyon pushes the man into the landscape. The soldier disappears from the room and reappears on the bank of the waterfall in the portrait where he falls to his knees, blood dripping out of his mouth, ears, nose, and eyes. He collapses on the ground in the grass.

I take a step back from the portrait. Kyon glances at me. "You see? It has a few problems."

"Why didn't you just tell me the problems? You didn't have to kill him!"

"I made it easy for you to understand that you can never use this to leave here. I could've told you, but you don't trust me. This way, I can be assured that you believe me."

"Why do you need it?" I ask, turning away from the dead man on the other side of the portal. I hold my hands behind my back so no one will see them shaking.

"Think of the ramifications that something like this can have for us. We could move troops—be everywhere and nowhere in a matter of seconds. It is a very useful tool—if I can get it to exert less pressure on the soft tissue of the body, it will be perfect. I have to find a way to protect the brain and internal organs," he says absently.

"The funny thing about weapons like this, Kyon, is that the door works both ways. Someone could find it and come to us as well," I reply.

Kyon turns and faces me. "I did not have you pegged as a 'glass half empty' person."

"I'm not. I'm just being practical," I reply to cover up my gut-wrenching fear of his intellect. He's so smart. He won't need priestesses or me soon. He's a force all his own. I take another step back from him. I rest my hand against the nearby tree pillar for support. Instantly the glass floor becomes a platform and lifts me to the gallery level.

Kyon laughs below me. He comes to stand next to the tree pillar on the opposite side. "You figured out my puzzle," he says. He puts his hand on the pillar, and another glass platform raises him up to me. "Now what?" His eyebrow arches in question. I glance across the open airspace to the gallery railing across the room.

I have no idea what will happen if I move forward off the glass step, but I know that something will, because Kyon is watching me with an air of expectation. I take a deep breath, hold it, and take a step forward toward the railing. My foot connects solidly with another glass step in the shape of a clear river stone.

"Did you know it was there? Or were you just being brave?" Kyon asks.

"I was being hopeful."

From below, it must look as if we're walking on air as we cross the room to the gallery railing, which turns out to be merely a hologram. The gallery is real enough, though, and I'm grateful for the solid stone beneath my feet. "Do you want to see more?" Kyon asks me.

"I want to see everything," I reply. I do. I want to know him so that I have a better chance of surviving him. I will put up no fight yet. I have to bide my time. I need him. If I'm to be free of the Brotherhood, he's my best chance. He has as much to gain by their demise as I do. I'm just afraid that he'll see through the cracks in my heart. I have more weaknesses than I'd like to admit.

"Fulton," Kyon calls to his mentor on the ground. "Where have you put our guests?"

"They're in Beauty—garden level."

"Beauty?" I ask.

Kyon escorts me from the gallery to a long hallway that is entirely glass on one side. Sunlight falls on us and warms me. This hallway overlooks a flower garden outside. Butterflies flitter around it in droves, feasting on lush buds. "I've named all the towers in the house."

"What was the one I just left called?"

"Kingdom," he replies.

"And this one?" I ask when we reach the end of the corridor. We enter through a magnificent archway into another tower.

"This part of the house is called Foundation."

We enter at the gallery level. It looks a lot like a study. The walls of the gallery are lined with books and artifacts. Iron helmets adorned with wings as well as wicked-looking swords are on display behind glass. As I gaze over the wrought-iron railing, I find below us is another round room. The floors are stone with inlaid Nordic knot symbols. Beautiful tapestry carpets with rune symbols of green and gold cover large areas of the floor. Four sets of stairs descend to the lower level from four areas of the gallery. Spiral staircases wind upward to more levels in Foundation. The rows and rows of books and artifacts go all the way up to the pointed peak at least fifteen stories above us.

I leave Kyon's side and explore the room. Taking the stairs down, I see a study of a kind and a space that Kyon must use to tinker around with things. The first table I happen upon is covered with parts—cogs and washers and metal pieces. The inner workings of some machine is laid out in a definite pattern, as if he took a clock apart and laid it out in a road map in order to be able to put it back together. Another long table with bottles and vials and burners is laid out in the most particular way, as if an experiment had been started and abandoned, but then preserved so that he could pick it up again. I don't touch anything, treating it with the kind of respect it deserves.

"This is your study?" I ask.

"Yes. I spend much of my time here."

Only one portrait is in this room: an oil rendering of a very beautiful, petite woman. She looks like a Norse goddess. Her cerulean eyes sparkle with a secret truth that she ponders while she stares back at me. Her face is the graceful, flawless, feminine form of Kyon's. She has to be a close relation.

"Is she why you're bad?" I ask as Kyon joins me to gaze at the lovely woman frozen in repose.

"She's my mother. Her name was Farling."

"She was a priestess?"

"She was. She was also your mother's best friend. They used to say their names together—Farling and Arissa—Arissa and Farling. There's a portrait of the two of them together in a different tower."

"What happened to her?"

"My mother? She helped your mother escape Alameeda. She paid for it. They executed her for treason."

"Who did?"

"The Brotherhood—my father. He was infatuated with your mother. He wanted her for his own."

"How could Excelsior have claimed her when he had already claimed your mother?"

"He can do whatever he wants. He knows how everyone will vote because he *tells* the majority of them how they'll vote. He has always been untouchable."

"Your mother saved my mother from him?"

"She helped Arissa get out of Alameeda, but she couldn't save herself."

"Or you," I whisper to him and the portrait of the ghost who broke his heart.

"I didn't need saving. I *am* bad, Kricket, but she didn't make me bad."

"You don't have to be bad."

"I do, but I'll be worse to anyone who is bad to you. Come, let's go meet some of the Brothers." He holds his hand out to me and this time I take it.

CHAPTER 11

BEAUTY GOES DEEP

We exit through the brown leather doors, leaving Kyon's study behind. A short corridor brings us to tall, thin ivory doors. They remind me of keys on a piano. Kyon pauses before we enter the room. He turns to me, grasping my chin and making me look at him. "You'll be the most important person in the room, but if you don't demand their respect, they'll never give it to you."

"So they're normal," I reply.

"I'm always protecting you, whether you know it or not." He's not lying—at least he believes what he says. I wonder, and not for the first time, if he knows just how broken he is.

"We're on the same team for now, Kyon. I'll follow your lead. Just tell me one thing: What are they most afraid of?"

"This." He motions to both of us with his index finger. "You and I aligned and out of their control. To see us together will unsettle them."

"What if we're in love?"

"They'd be unable to look away."

"Hmm," I respond.

I wish that I'd had time to prepare for this. If I'd been given a moment, I could've launched myself into the future for a dry run. No such luck, though. I have to play this one straight and hope for the best.

My feet are heavy as I trudge into the room. It's grand in a way I'm somewhat accustomed to now that I've lived in Rafe's palace. The left side of this regal room is open to the outside by a series of white wood-framed French doors that run the length of the pastel blue room. Silken, white curtains are draped to the sides. The tranquil breeze brings with it the scent of flowers. I don't recognize them, but that aroma is lovely. They're melon-colored and grow on the vines creeping over the outside of the doorframes.

Enormous framed portraits cover the walls. They depict lovely, blond-haired, blue-eyed Etharians. The ceiling is at least two stories above our heads and painted with gorgeous Viking-like rune symbols.

There are three camps languishing in the room. On the left side of the room, by the open doors, there are a few groupings of beautiful blond women. Three of them sit at a gaming table that has a three-tier chesslike board on its marble top. Elegant stone figurines that resemble mythological creatures: dragons, griffins, winged horses, and the like, rove over the game board on their own. The women are each adorned with face candy; black lace adheres to the tall one's eyebrows, henna lines arch over the thinner one's brow, and golden chains stretch from ear to ear over the snub nose of the one with golden eyelashes.

The second camp is near the back of the room. Soft music is playing from an instrument that resembles a pianoforte. Every single inch of this priestess's eyebrows are covered with silver ring piercings. Two women accompanying the pianoforte play stringed instruments that sound like violins. Still another priestess is playing a weirdly shaped guitar that has the resonance of a mandolin.

The third camp in the room is located to the right of it. It's a group of attractive blond men who are seated on thronelike chairs. They're monsters who are wary of the shark at my side. A couple of them rise from their seats to ease their discomfort at Kyon's height advantage over them. It still doesn't help though. Kyon's the tallest one in the room . . . and the most fit . . . and if I'm being honest, he's the handsomest as well, and it kills me to think that.

It bothers me that the Brothers don't do more than glance at me. They're definitely not as afraid of me as they are of Kyon. I'm surprised to know that it bothers me that I'm the lesser of the two evils in their eyes. I want them to quake when they see me and shudder when my very name is spoken. I want them to cower in my presence. It's a bit shocking to me the depth of this emotion. Maybe it shouldn't be. They're one of the reasons that I'm here. How dare they bring me here! What right do any of them have to my life? It's mine.

Kyon leads me past the male encampment on the right without even acknowledging the Brothers' presence. He does the same with priestess gamers at the elegant card table, even though they're all watching him with road-sign eyes designed to let him know that they have no problem merging with him at any point up ahead. He doesn't seem to notice the tell-me-I'm-pretty looks he gets from them, or if he does, he's stoically ignoring them. I assess him with a side-glance. Kyon Ensin is the resident bad boy who every single one of them wants to sample. Nezra isn't alone in her adoration of him. Interesting. How can I use this to my advantage?

Kyon leads me to a small cluster of seats in front of the musicians. I notice for the first time that there's one more priestess in the room that I missed. It's Goth-girl . . . what was her name? Phlix? She's the priestess who tried to help Kyon kidnap me on the Ship of Skye—the one who can create a shadow land that hides anyone within it.

From her chair in front of the musicians, Phlix gives me a bashful smile, and then she bites her lip. Her long, blond hair is loose around her shoulders. Kohl rims her sad, blue eyes. She doesn't wear any facial adornments other than makeup. I wonder about it as I sit with a chair between us. I expect Kyon to sit next to me. Instead, he grasps my hand, putting it to his lips. "I will go speak with the Brothers. I won't be too long."

Kissing my hand, he smiles before he releases it. He turns to leave me when I say over-dramatically, "You're abandoning me, my love?" From the corner of my eye, I notice the heads of the musicians turn perceptibly in our direction.

Kyon pauses, his eyes widening briefly. He slowly turns back to me. "I'll be right over there." He points to the group of Brothers. I look in their direction with a shy smile.

Getting to my feet and invading Kyon's personal space, I use my fingertips to skim over his dark uniform sleeve. I twist a tendril of my hair around my finger and look up at him from beneath my eyelashes. "But what if I miss you?"

His eyebrows pull together a little before they go up minutely. A smile develops on his lips, but he quickly hides it from everyone. His hand touches my shoulder, slipping down my side. When it reaches my waist he pulls me closer to him. His proximity makes my heart flutter faster.

"It'll be torture to be so far away from you, but I'll be able to see you from there," he says, playing along.

"Should I give you something to remember me by?" I ask, as I trace my finger over his chest. A note of music is played off key. I pretend not to notice the cold sound of the missed bow stroke from one of the priestesses beside us.

"I think you must," Kyon replies. "I need something to cherish."

I couldn't be more afraid of what I'm about to do if I was holding a razor blade to my bare wrist. My hand rests lightly on his chest, working its way slowly up to the symbols that darken his neck. Kyon's hand slips behind my back. He presses me to him. His body has to have been carved from the mountains surrounding this place because it's granite and doesn't feel real. Leaning his face toward mine, my mouth tips up to meet his. Before our lips touch, my violet, half-lidded eyes meet his intense stare. For a second, I think I see the future in them—one with him and me and blinding stars.

I couldn't feel farther from my home than I do now.

Breathless and trembling, my lips touch his. Our feathery kiss whispers secrets to my marrow. I forget to breathe until Kyon responds with languid brushes of his lips to mine. His gentleness lulls me. *I'm safe.* My lips part; I deepen the kiss. The first stroke of his tongue is a rush of fire that cuts through me. Battle lines appear. The impact of our kiss invades my senses. I try to retreat. Kyon doesn't allow it. He draws me closer to keep me from escaping. I'm burned from my home. A chaos of emotion blossoms between us. I'm not the hunter in this game; I can hardly keep myself from becoming the prey.

The music stops; the silence is shouting around us, and still he kisses me. I've been in trouble all of my life. I've never felt it more so than now.

"Lightning has struck," one of the Brothers behind us says sourly.

A rumble of laughter comes from Kyon. I feel his smile against my lips. He moves his face away a few inches so he can see me better. The sledgehammering of my heart must be apparent to his sharp eyes. Kyon doesn't look away from me as he says, "You probably never even knew it was raining, Gannon." I look in that direction. The faces of the Brothers are bone-white and grim. I doubt any of them has heard Kyon laugh before.

Kyon presses a kiss to my temple. "I will always remember this," he murmurs against my hair. He pulls away from me and goes to the other side of the room to have conversations with the monsters who want to kill us. A part of me wants to follow him. We're supposed to be a team in this. How am I supposed to scare the hell out of them from way over here? I sink into my seat and weave my fingers together wicker-basket tight.

"He's in love with you," Phlix says from her seat beside me.

I want to laugh my head off. Kyon doesn't love me. He wouldn't know love if it stabbed him in the chest with a pink, puffy heart. I'm a means to an end to him.

"He's in love with my savagery." I feign a dreamy sigh.

"Are you still a savage?" she asks with doe-eyed innocence.

"Yes," I say. To them I undoubtedly am. That works for me. I'll play to their expectations and give them what they think they know about me.

We watch and listen as the exquisite priestesses create music that sounds like it comes from some ethereal plane of being. Every so often though, I detect a raw note, a misshapen bow stroke that is discordant from the rest. The musicians annoy me, I realize. They've spent a lifetime playing music while I've spent mine trying to survive on my own.

"Do you enjoy this melody, Kricket?" Phlix asks.

I've never heard it before in my life. "It's my very favorite," I mumble. I look over my shoulder; Kyon is watching me while one of the Brothers discusses something with him in hushed tones.

"They're Virulences," Phlix whispers, nodding toward the beautiful women playing instruments in front of us. "Trula, Greer, and Doe are designed to influence thoughts with their melodies."

"Excuse me?" I choke. My head snaps in her direction.

"They're trying to control you right now. I'm blocking them from influencing me. I've tried to block you as well, but you don't seem to need it like I do."

"What are they trying to make me do?" I wonder as I scrutinize them.

"Kill yourself," she whispers without a hint of deception. "Their music is designed to infect others. They despise you and they've been instructed to make you sick if they can't get you to kill yourself. Can't you feel the venom they're directing at you?"

"I feel nothing. You're doing a good job of protecting me."

She beams at me. I recognize her smile. It's connection. Bridget, my ex-roommate on Earth, smiled at me like that the first time I met her in juvenile detention. "You'd feel it if it was working. You wouldn't be able to keep anything in your stomach and you'd bleed from the nose and mouth."

"They're killer stereo, huh?" I mutter.

"I can't block it all. Are you sure you cannot feel it?"

I shake my head. "No. Nothing."

"Perhaps your physiology is different than ours—you're not pureblood."

"How come it doesn't seem to be hurting anyone else in this room?"

"We've all been required to build up a tolerance to it, but look there." She indicates the group of priestesses in a different cluster away from the game table. One of the priestesses is ill. Hunched over, she holds her middle as if she may be sick. Her companions are speaking to her in low, concerned tones. I can't hear what they're saying. A very tall priestess adorned with a diamond-studded headpiece signals to the Virulences playing behind me with wave of her hand. They play a different song. The sick priestess blinks a few times. Straightening, she drops her hands from her stomach before speaking as if nothing out of the ordinary has occurred.

"The Virulences may need to concentrate on a different frequency of sound in order to hurt you."

"Who ordered them to hurt me?"

With a fearful glance, she searches the room to ensure we're not being overheard. "Not here," she mutters.

"Okay."

"Do you think you'll try to escape from here?" she whispers. I don't reply. "When you do, will you take me with you?"

A small, heavy stone game piece hits the chair between us. Turning, I look in the direction of the priestesses at the game table. A blue, gemstone bird catapults from the center of the game board on its own and strikes Phlix in the shoulder. She winces at the impact, but otherwise doesn't acknowledge it. The priestess with black lace on her eyebrows giggles with delight over the prank. The lace adornment gives her catlike eyes that she uses to glare at me. I glare back.

"Who's that?" I ask.

Phlix glances quickly over her shoulder at the priestesses before turning away, saying, "Don't look at them!" She gives me a timid look. When I continue to glare unabashedly at them, she whispers quickly, "The one with the black lace cutouts is Brighton. She's telekinetic."

"How good is she at it?"

Phlix shrugs. "I think what you just saw is the best she can do. It still hurts though." She looks down at her hands that she had clutched in her lap. I size up Brighton. She's annoyed that I haven't been cowed by her death-gaze. She says something with a derogatory twist of her lips and her friends beside her both snicker. It's plain that she believes herself to be very powerful. She has no idea that she's dining at the kid's table. Giffen could eat her for breakfast with his gift.

"And the other two with Brighton?" I wonder.

"Ryker is the one with the thin dark lines on her brow."

"What can she do?"

"She can speak telepathically to animals that are of higher intelligence, such as canines, spixes, and primates. And before you ask, the last one is Ashland."

"What's Ashland's gift?" I study her. The gold chains she wears over her nose make her look regal.

"They call her a lotus. Her kiss is intoxicating. It makes the recipient forget all of his ambitions so that he worships only her."

"How long does her kiss last?" I ask out of curiosity.

"I'm told it can last a quarter of a part." *Fifteen or twenty minutes,* I assess.

Brighton glares at me again. I yawn loudly. She breaks eye contact and stares at an onyx dragon-shaped game piece. The carved beast trembles against the marble of the game board before it is flung into the air straight at me. Lifting my hand, I catch the black dragon in my palm without flinching. The sting from the impact resonates through my arm, but I never let my bored expression change. Ryker and Ashland stop smirking and glance at Brighton, who gives them a sullen look.

I hand the scaly dragon replica to Phlix. "You shouldn't let them push you around like that. You should stand up to them."

She grips the onyx figure in anger. "That's very easy for you to say when you never had to grow up with them—never had to endure their cruelty! You were lucky—raised on Earth—free of all of this." She raises her other hand to indicate the opulence of her surroundings.

"Yeah." I frown and make a whatever-you-say face. "I had it easy."

"So you will take me with you when you leave?"

"What makes you think I'm leaving?"

"I was there—I saw you fight us on the Ship of Skye. You were not about to be taken alive. You must really want to go home. I really want to go with you when you do."

"Why? It can't be just them." I gesture toward the pretty idiots over my shoulder.

"No. It's them too." She bumps her chin in the direction of the Brothers. "They have brokered a deal with a Brother named Pike."

"What kind of deal?"

"A claiming—my claiming. They want me paired to him."

"And you don't like Pike?"

"No."

"What's wrong with Pike?" I ask.

"You could ask Caramina, the last priestess they gave him, if she were still alive, but he strangled her to death . . . so I think you'll just have to guess."

"When?"

"When what?" she counters. "When did he strangle her?"

"No. When does he claim you?"

"At the end of the speck," she replies, indicating that at the end of the month, she's got a *huge* problem.

"And you want me to save you?"

"No. I want us to save each other. Kyon may love you, but you don't love him."

"How do you know?"

"Most of the time, I live in the shadow land that I'm able to create. I have to hide from these egos." She indicates the people surrounding us. "I observe others. I know fear when I see it. Kyon scares you—as well he should—he's the most frightening one in the room."

My eyes don't stray to Kyon because I know he's watching us. I can see him in the reflection of the brass instrument resting idly in front of me. I don't want him to suspect that we're discussing anything besides the other priestesses. He's aware of what's happening in this room. I think he's curious to see how it affects me and what I'll do. I'm about to enlighten him, but not just yet.

"If we go, we're going to need things," I murmur.

Phlix stops breathing for a moment. Her normally pale face becomes rosy. Cold fingers reach over and cover mine for the breath it takes to squeeze my hand, and then they slip away. "I know how to get things."

"Where do you stay?"

"Freming House."

I remember it. Kyon pointed it out to me when we flew over it. "That's not going to work out at all. We need you here."

"They'll never allow it."

"Why not?"

"Well . . . I don't know . . . it's just not done. All priestesses reside at Freming House."

"I won't."

"Are you sure?" she asks. "We're here to persuade Kyon to release you to us."

"He won't let me out of his sight."

"Then none of this will work." It's as if I just told her that her best friend died. She's crushed. She holds back tears as her clenched hand with the onyx dragon hides her mouth. We listen to the strains of the mesmerizing music. I still feel nothing from the toxic melody, and the worry it causes the group of musicians in front of me is telling. Their faces show strain.

I glance at Phlix. Her eyes are shiny with unshed tears. I exhale a breath. "All is not lost," I mutter. "Wait here." I rise from my seat.

Phlix appears startled. "Where are you going?" She rises too.

"I'm going to try to arrange a sleepover," I whisper.

"You're going to go talk to the Brothers?" she asks. "Without being summoned?"

"Yeah." I'm irritated that she thinks I need to ask them permission to speak.

I square my shoulders, feeling every eye in the room on me. As gracefully as possible, I cross the room to where Kyon is standing, leaning against the wall. I knew he was watching me, but the intensity of his stare is hard to ignore. Nearing him, I hear the Brother in front of him say, "We cannot leave here without her. He will kill us all. He won't see your hasty claiming ceremony as legitimate."

"The ceremony was legal; it was witnessed by a member of the Brotherhood. I have no intention of allowing Kricket to reside at Freming House—now or ever. She's dear to me, Ainsley. I will not allow you to ruin her. If he wants to meet her, he'll have to come to me."

"It's not about you or Excelsior, it's about the prophecy—" Ainsley stops talking when he notices my approach. His scowl is all the indication that I need to understand that I have committed some huge faux pas in his eyes by approaching them in this manner. I can't help the warmth that spreads inside me at the knowledge.

"My love," I address Kyon with pouty lips. "I was just speaking to Phlix and I have figured out exactly what this room needs. I had to rush over and tell you."

His eyes dance with amusement. "What does it need, my little savage?" He reaches over and tucks my hair behind my ear.

"A disco ball!" I smile, like it's not the tackiest suggestion one could introduce in a circle such as this.

Kyon shoots me a besotted look that makes me believe he's a much better actor than I gave him credit for. "I'll have one made for you right away as soon as you explain to me what that is."

"It's a mirrored sphere that one hangs from one's ceiling. It reflects light and makes everything shiny!" I flash my most elegant jazz hands.

Ainsley looks from Kyon to me, and then back again.

"Will it sparkle like your eyes?" he asks. I almost laugh, but I keep it in.

"Oh! That's such a good idea! Can you make it lavender, to match my eyes?" I plead like a spoiled child.

"Your eyes are more violet than lavender, and I wouldn't have it any other way," Kyon replies.

"I'd like Phlix to stay here too—to help me. She can teach me how to be a proper priestess. I need a mentor, like Fulton."

"You don't need her, Kricket," Kyon says as he takes my hand and puts it to his lips. "You have me."

I stick out my bottom lip. "I want a friend."

Our exchange is bothering Ainsley. He interrupts with a prissy huff, scolding me, "You can*not* have Phlix. She's to be Pike's newest in a matter of a few rotations."

Turning on him as if he's gravely insulted me, I growl, "But I *want* her! Spike can have her in a few rotations. What would it hurt to let me have her for such a short time?"

My assertiveness is not something that Ainsley is accustomed to or something he's ready to tolerate. "His name is *Pike!*"

"Spike, Pike," I shrug. "He can have her after I'm finished with her."

Ainsley's mouth opens and closes several times, like a fish's. "You were not sent for, Kricket," he scowls dismissively. "Your master and I are convening on a very important issue—"

I put my index finger to his mouth, cutting him off. "One moment, Ainsley. He's not my *master*. He's—" Hearing feminine laughter, I look toward the game table across the room and witness a turquoise winged-horse figurine fling off the game board and strike Phlix in the back of her head. Distracted, I murmur, "Hold that thought. I'll be right back." Ainsley's face turns red and he blusters behind me, but I ignore him.

I cross the room to the game table. Brighton, Ryker, and Ashland have their shoulders hunched as their heads lean together in some misery conspiracy. Placing my hands on the cool, marble game board, I give them each a sinister smile. The black butterfly lace of Brighton's facial adornment rises as her eyebrows do.

"Hi, I'm Kricket. We haven't formally met yet, but I've noticed that you like games."

Sitting back in her chair, Brighton gives me a smug look and says, "I'm enjoying the game I've been playing."

"I've been watching your game. It isn't funny. I think you should apologize to Phlix."

Her blue eyes shine with condescension, "I never apologize," she replies. Ryker and Ashland both giggle, enjoying their friend's disdain.

"Are you sure you don't want to reconsider? It would be a shame if you couldn't walk outta here."

Her lacey eyebrows rise together. "Are you threatening me?"

"Mmm-hmm." I nod.

Brighton's eyes narrow as she says, "You're in no position to threaten me." She flicks her hair back over her shoulder, looks at her friends, and smiles. "You won't be here long. They're taking you back to Freming House. You won't last the rotation."

"That's an interesting thing to say, since you're not clairvoyant. If you were, you might be a little bit nicer."

"I don't have to have the gift of seeing the future, because I already know yours."

"Enlighten me."

"It's only a matter of time before the Brothers kill you."

"I'm going to let you in on a little secret, Brighton." I lean near her ear and whisper, "They've already tried." Then I straighten and add, "So I'll give you one more chance to apologize to Phlix for being *such* a knob knocker."

They look at each other like I said something ludicrous. Brighton's eyes leave Ryker and Ashland's astounded faces. She concentrates on an aquamarine griffin on the game board. The feet of the iconic beast tremble and tap against the smooth surface. It lifts off the game board, heading straight for my forehead. I duck. The griffin sails over me. It strikes the large male behind me in the temple. Standing, the bearded blond Brother clutches his hand to his face as he roars in anger.

"Many pardons, Adondon," Brighton says in mortification as she holds up her hand to him and pales. "I did not intend—"

"I got this one, Don," I say to the raging Brother before I grasp the edge of the heavy marble game board, saying to Brighton, "You should've just said sorry."

A rainbow of beautiful, stone-carved creatures tumble off the checkerboard surface, clattering against the top of the wood table as I lift it up. Brighton's eyes shift to me. Her black, lacy eyebrows flap like bat wings. I swing the marble game board as hard as I can. It connects with Brighton's cheek. A tooth flies out of her mouth. She falls to the ground with a desperate moan.

I swing the game board back the other way, and it connects with Ryker on the other side of the table. Dominos don't fall this easily. Panting a little, I hoist the board over my head, intending to throw it across the table at Ashland, when it's caught in someone else's grasp. I'm lifted off my feet as an arm encircles my waist.

Kyon murmurs in my ear, "Drop it."

I don't. It's wrenched from my hand and tossed back onto the table, where it makes a tremendous noise.

"Don't get in my way," I growl at Kyon, my breathing heavy from exertion.

He turns me so that we face the room, which has gone silent except for the moans of the two priestesses on the floor. With his arm around me, Kyon holds me pinned to his body. I glare at everyone. I hate their shocked faces. They have no idea who they're dealing with, and it shows. None of them has ever had to survive a juvenile lockup.

I refrain from jerking my arms in an attempt to make Kyon release me. It won't work, so it's useless. I don't like the fact that he's been testing me ever since we entered this room, like a science experiment. He knew what would happen in here, though. His ability to read me is a bad thing.

He evaluates the priestesses writhing on the ground. "Fulton," he calls. Fulton enters the room as if he's been monitoring the situation the whole time. He has medics with him who immediately attend to Brighton and Ryker's medical issues. Once sedated, they fall silent as the medics work on them. I may have broken Brighton's jaw—it hangs at a funny angle when they quickly take her from the room. Fulton remains by the door, watching me.

Kyon's hand smooths my tussled hair as he says to the group before us, "It's as I said. Kricket is a singular alpha female. You've all

witnessed it. The beta females of the group will seek to protect her."
He gestures in Phlix's direction. "The Virulences have no outward
effect on her, because she's not someone who is at all suggestible."
His hand rises to the idle musicians, who are currently eyeballing me
with a mixture of fear and dread. "She has little fear of males." Now
he gestures toward Ainsley's direction. "She only respects an extreme
alpha male, and even then, she will constantly test his mettle. You
cannot mix her in with the general population of priestesses. She's savage. She'll eliminate all of your potential alphas, even the ones with
enhanced fighting capabilities. She'll outsmart them, outmaneuver
them, and in general, reduce them to sniveling weaklings at her feet."

"She's no good to us if she cannot be controlled, Kyon," Ainsley
says, scrutinizing me like I'm a piece of meat.

Kyon frowns. "We need extreme intelligence now more than ever
to rule Ethar. Things are changing. You're going to have to change
with them. Kricket *will* rule. She's the one—she's your empress. It's
the prophecy; it's unavoidable. And I will reign by her side."

"Your father says that she's impure. The priestess born of two
worlds and two houses cannot be allowed to govern—"

"My father," Kyon glowers, "is desperate to keep you all in line—
to maintain the status quo. The truth is Excelsior fears her, just as
he feared her mother when she slipped away from him! He knew the
prophecy. He couldn't stop it then . . . he cannot stop it now."

Fear wraps itself around the necks of everyone in the room.
They're restless. They need to run from this change Kyon is pre-
senting, or they need to make a deal with Kyon so the fear they feel
won't bite them anymore. Kyon's wolfishly strong heartbeat thumps
through my own chest as I lean against him. The arm clutching my
waist eases, allowing me to come down off my tiptoes. He bends and
inhales the scent of my hair. Primal.

From the other end of the room, Phlix's timid voice strains to be
heard. "I wish to serve our empress."

Everyone turns to look at her. She sinks to her knees, bowing her head to me. I pale when I see another priestess do the same . . . and then another, and then another. When the men begin to follow and bow down to Kyon and me, my stomach aches. I don't want to be part of this charade. "You see," Kyon breathes in my ear. "They believe, just as I do. You're the one: the daughter of our most prophetic priestess—born of two worlds and two houses—destined to be the Empress of Ethar."

The stars are no longer aligning for me; they're bleeding from the sky, turning black, and dying around me. What the people in this room don't realize is that I'm not the one. Whatever they were told in this supposed prophecy is clearly meant for someone else. Arissa had another daughter born of two worlds and two houses—one who our father protects at the expense of all else . . . of me.

Astrid.

My father and the Order of the Tempest must believe that she's destined to be the Empress of Ethar. I'm the distraction from the truth. While everyone in Alameeda and the surrounding houses focuses on me, they won't see what's really going on until it's too late. My childhood has taught me that the mark usually ends up the biggest loser in every scenario. Every time. No exceptions. The Order of the Tempest was created to protect one person. It isn't me.

I want out of this room. Out of this opulent cage. Out of this life. There's only one place left for me now. Earth. "Are we done here?" I ask Kyon.

"We'll never be done, Kricket," Kyon whispers in my ear.

He looks in Fulton's direction and says, "Phlix stays. Show her to a room in Victory. She'll be comfortable there."

"Of course," Fulton replies. He goes to Phlix and escorts her from the room.

Ainsley's head snaps up. "You cannot keep Phlix!"

Kyon lets go of me. With a bad-wolf look on his face, he approaches

Ainsley, who is still on his knees. Kyon squats down to look Ainsley in the eye. "What did you say?"

"She—" His face becomes flushed and he stutters, "Phlix belongs to . . . Pike."

"Who owns her?" Kyon asks with a dramatic arch of his eyebrow.

Ainsley searches for support in the faces of the other Brothers in the room, but none of them will lift his eyes from the floor.

"It's okay," Kyon encourages, "you can say it, Ainsley."

Ainsley casts his eyes down at to ground once more. "You. You own Phlix."

Kyon reaches out and roughly pats Ainsley's face. "Now you're getting it." Kyon rises to full height once more. Coming to me, he locks his arm with mine. "Would you like to see your new room, Kricket?" he asks. There's warmth in his stare.

I want to push him away, but I can't react without a plan. Instead, I play along, pretending to be under the influence of giants. "Let me guess—is it in the place you call Hostage?"

Kyon's smile can warm moonlight. "Your room is in Mercy." He escorts me to one of the sets of doors in the room. It's not the way we came in. These doors lead to a different corridor. We exit the tower known as Beauty, leaving the others there on their knees.

The barrel-vaulted ceilings of the hallway are carved and shaped from gray mountain stone. Windows in the silhouette of snowflakes cast light onto enormous tapestry carpets of blue and spun ivory that form an elegant path. Ancient juggernaut armor and weaponry that resembles something pillaged from some long-ago Viking ship line the walls.

As soon as the doors of Beauty close behind us, there's a tremendous noise: terror-filled screams—shattering glass and furniture. Flashes of blue sparks shine beneath the doors as I look over my shoulder at them. I try to turn around, but Kyon won't let me. He ushers me down the corridor.

"What's happening?" I gasp. The thunderous sounds turn my heartbeat stormy.

Kyon is calm. Unaffected. "They were sent to hurt you, Kricket. I cannot allow that to go unpunished. I thought you learned that at our other reception. We have to keep sending the message that everyone who aligns against us dies."

"They were submissive."

"They were complicit. I'm not going to kill them all, just enough of them to send a warning. The ones who survive will know they'll never be safe in the current regime—the regime that sent them here to die. They'll comply with the changes we make."

"Or they'll redouble their efforts against us."

Amid the drumbeat of death, Kyon shifts from the path we walk together. He shoves me up against the hard wall of the corridor. His warrior-shaped shadow engulfs me. My heart wilts. The intensity in his stare holds me prisoner. "You admit there's an us?" he asks. Darkness grows in his eyes as his hand cups my cheek and he bends nearer to me. "It's you and me, Kricket. Forever, my little savage." His lips are ragged against mine. The need in them forces me to meet his kiss with an equal amount of dream-filled midnight.

It's not you that he desires, I think. *It's the power you represent.* I turn my lips toward Kyon's ear and whisper in desperation, "I'm not the one."

"You say that as if it were true," Kyon purrs against the flesh of my neck. His voice trembles through me. I feel it everywhere.

"It is true," I reply breathlessly.

He runs his lips down my throat. His teasing kisses causes my body to react to him in ways I wish it wouldn't. "I don't believe you."

"You should."

"You are the only one. You are the true Empress of Ethar."

"It can't be me," I restate in desperation.

"Even if that were so, Kricket, which it isn't, I would kill anyone who claimed otherwise."

"Why?"

"It's simple. There's no one else for me. I've found what I want. I'll crush anyone who tries to usurp you."

The sound of weeping floats to us on the air, a lamentation that sends a chill over my skin. "Then you might have to kill everyone."

"So be it."

"Why are you so crazy?" I ask as I gently rest my forehead against his chest. "This is not the way to attain power."

"It's the only way to attain power. Every other way is disingenuous," he replies. "Everything is going to be all right, Kricket."

"For who?"

"For us. Trust me."

I don't want to argue with a violent man, so I say, "I'd like to see my room now." I lift my forehead from him. Finding his hand, I hold it. "Please take me there."

He raises my hand to his lips, kissing it. "Come then. I will show you Mercy."

CHAPTER 12
DISCOLORATION

Mercy has unobstructed views of the most beautiful aspects of Urbenoster: the grounds of Kyon's estate, the water surrounding the fortress, and the mountains in the distance. The waning sun glows red on the horizon when the gray stone walls fall away, forming a portico of archways and pillars as we walk. Cool mountain air stirs my hair. What strikes me first is that we're close to the wide river that surrounds the grounds like a moat. Elaborate sailing vessels hydroplane over the surface of the water, hardly disturbing its placid veneer.

We enter a suite of rooms. A formal sitting room adjoins the bedroom. My new bedroom is more than elegant; it's divine. Kyon trails me into it. I walk ahead of him to the doors on the far wall. They open onto a magnificent terrace overlooking the water. In the distance between the towering buildings, the snow peaks of the mountains cast grandfatherly shadows on the city as the sun retreats behind them.

"What's your next move, Kyon?" I rub my upper arms with my hands, trying to ward off the chill of the mountain air.

"Hearts and minds."

"Whose?"

"Everyone's."

"How?"

"We have to build on your little-lost-priestess-returned-home persona."

"You mean with the citizens of Alameeda?"

"I mean with all the Houses. You are seen as the priestess of the prophecy here in Alameeda. To our allies and to all the other Houses, you have been the catalyst for war. We have to make you sympathetic—the stoic leader rather than the villain. Excelsior, will start his campaign against you immediately, now that he knows unequivocally that I won't give you up to him."

"How powerful is he?" I ask.

"Not nearly as powerful as us."

"How do we make me look sympathetic?"

"We do what no one else has done. We show you to the world. We unveil the hidden priestess. We endear you to them."

"I'm not a people person."

"On the contrary, you're everything they want. I've watched you at the Rafe palace. You have an innate ability to adapt—be what they want you to be."

"Most people don't know what they want. What they want changes daily."

"You'll change with it."

"And Excelsior?"

"You'll find out his plans," Kyon replies. His arms wrap around me from behind and pull me against his solid chest. He's so warm, a balm against the cold, mountain air.

"I'll see what I can do. Let me lie down so you don't have to catch me when I leave." I try to move back inside, but Kyon doesn't release me.

"Later. You're weak."

"I'm okay."

"You're not," Kyon disagrees. He takes my hand and leads me back inside my room. Positioning me in front of an enormous full-length mirror, his hand touches my chin as he directs me to look at my reflection. Dark circles hollow my eyes. Kyon's hand skims over my skin, descending to the front of my neck. He fondles the beautiful flower on the black-ribboned choker at my throat.

My voice is shallow when I murmur, "What kind of flower is that?"

Kyon's reflection in the mirror studies me with eyes that miss nothing. "It's a copperclaw, Kricket. They're extremely rare."

His finger skims the ribbon that fastens the flower to my throat. Meteorlike fire burns beneath my skin wherever he touches me. His eyes follow his fingertips as they glide over the silken threads.

"Do you like the flower?" he asks.

"No."

"Why not?"

"I don't like flowers; they die."

"Copperclaws endure. Once they bloom, they never die."

"Never?"

"Nothing that I will ever give you will be ephemeral, Kricket." He gently nudges my hair aside. Bending to me, his lips caress my bared skin. As soft as moonlight, his mouth whisper-kisses promises of bliss. Sharp-edged desire howls through my body like a scream at midnight.

I make a small sound of pleasure and lean my back against him, closing my eyes. My knees weaken and I'm strung out and shaky from the intoxication he's offering. His hand moves to my waist, turning me around so that I face him. Opening my eyes, his blue ones are a sea on fire. "I need you, Kricket," he murmurs.

My breath catches. He kisses me. His silken tongue strokes against mine. An aching ecstasy chases through me, proof that I'm dark and broken inside. A cage closes around my heart, sealing it in glass. My heart beats against its transparent confines, knowing that when it sledgehammers hard enough, it will shatter and die from a thousand cuts.

"What do you want from me?" I ask against his lips.

"Everything."

"I can't give you that."

"Then I'll take it," he says. He kisses me again, letting me go only long enough to pull his shirt off over his head, dropping it on the floor. He's unbearably handsome.

One of his hands weaves in my hair, while another goes around my back, pulling me to him as he captures my lips again. He lifts me up in his arms and carries me with him to the bed. Sitting down on the edge of it with me on his lap, he grasps the back of my dress and pulls it apart. The buttons fly off in every direction.

I press my lips to his heart and breathe his name. "Kyon." The stone-heavy weight of it drops in ripples on his flesh, sinking against the depth of his skin until it's gone. Gently, I disengage his hands from me. His eyes are devouring as his gaze promises to make a meal of me. Rising from his lap, I back away from him, as I would from any extremely dangerous thing.

Kyon rises from the edge of the bed and slowly stalks me. I bump into the door frame behind me and adjust, backing through the doorway into the lavare. Only steps away from me, Kyon growls, realizing that I mean to escape from him. I push the button on the door frame and the door drops down from the ceiling between us. Standing there, facing the barrier, I wring my hands, terrified that he'll open it—even as my wildly beating heart presses up against its glass cage, hoping to be cut.

It becomes apparent that he's not going to break the door down. I turn around to the mirror across from the door. I can hardly look at myself. Am I Kyon's consort? And if I am, what will that do to Trey? I reach up and untie the black ribbon from my neck. Holding it for a moment, I stroke the petals of the copperclaw before abandoning it on the vanity.

Going to the shower, I turn on the water as hot as I can bear. I strip off my silver dress and get in. I don't let myself cry until water runs down my hair and covers my face. I can't even be honest about my tears to myself. I have to hide them. I rub the area of skin over my heart, trying to ease its painful ache. Then I sit down in the shower; the water pelts me as I bring my knees up to my chest and rest my chin on them. I need to see Trey. I have to figure out what to do now. My skin turns cold even under the heat of the water.

I slip outside of my physical form. The transition is finger-click fast. It's as if I inhale a breath in my shower and exhale it in New Amster. I recognize this Gothic, dust-covered entranceway I find myself in. It's the building that guards the passage to their secret city.

The sweet scent of brown sugar assails me when I ghost-move through the majestic, crumbling corridors of the outpost. Matchstick men puff on cig-a-likes, venting the fragrance into the air. It makes me shrink away from them. I associate the aroma with Defense Minister Telek. It was the last pleasure he had before I'd poisoned him . . . well, other than the threats to my life. He took great pleasure in those.

Sifting through the decadent decay of abandoned wealth, I slow when I see Trey. He's attired in a New Amster uniform, sitting alone near a broken-out window in the darkness and staring at the empty streets. They've given Trey a freston, which he has propped up on the window frame, ready to use to defend their position. If the form I have taken is my soul, then my soul aches for him.

Crouching down next to him, I grieve in a way I haven't since this has all begun, not with tears, but with discoloration. I'm a watercolor, bleeding luminosity in smearing swirls of sorrow. I've never seen him like this. Trey is hollow. Empty.

I barely hear someone else approaching. "May I sit with you?" Pan asks as he towers above us. He's little more than a shadowy silhouette in the darkness. Moonlight shines on Trey's eyes as he looks up. He gives Pan a brief nod. Pan approaches and sits down beside Trey. Leaning against the same wall, Pan offers Trey a cig-a-like. Trey shakes his head.

"You don't smoke?" Pan observes.

"No," Trey replies, refocusing his attention out the window. Streaks of light from Sinter, the larger moon, fall on his eyes, highlighting their violet brilliance.

"Kricket's mother, Arissa, made me quit when she was alive. She said it was bad for me," he says. His voice has a deep, sleepy dragon's tone to it. Holding a stylized smoker in his hand, he spins it between his fingers. "I don't smoke it. I just carry one around as a reminder."

I stare at Pan, studying all of his features. He's a hazy memory. I don't think he's aged at all, but it's been a long time. He smiles, as if remembering something, or maybe it's from the ridiculousness of him quitting smoking only to find himself in an apocalyptic situation—I'm not sure. His smile does something to me, though; it sparks a memory of the two of us on the sidewalk in Chicago. I used to like to wave at taxis as if they were a parade of floats in a carnival come to town. He used to play along, lifting me up for a better view of them.

"I was impressed by your ingenuity with the drones," Pan says to Trey.

Trey's lips show his disgust. "You like the way I can annihilate mass amounts of people with just a few keystrokes?"

"It's war," Pan says flatly. "They were toasting the demise of the House of Rafe when it happened. The House of Alameeda will level the House of Wurthem when they no longer need them. You saved many more lives by taking a few. One city. Now they'll turn their eyes to the House of Alameeda in suspicion."

"I think the cost was too high."

"Your cost?"

"Mine. Theirs," he says in desolation.

"History will show the sacrifice as just."

"Will it?" He obviously doesn't believe that.

Pan doesn't respond to that; he simply twirls the stout cylinder of the smokeless inhaler between his fingers.

"Was there something you needed?" Trey asks coldly.

"What's she like?"

"Your daughter?"

Pan nods.

"She's a loner," Trey replies. "She pays her own way. She's someone who doesn't know her place, or if she does, she doesn't abide by the rules. She'll see right through your lies. She'll steal your heart without even trying. She'll blanket you with a million whispers in the night while she holds your hand as if she's the only one who fits it right. You'll want to carry her bones inside your bones."

"So she's like her mother," Pan says softly.

"Your people say that Kricket is still alive?"

"Yes," Pan replies. He studies Trey and adds, "Don't look so guilty. You haven't done her wrong, as they say in Chicago."

"What would you call it then?" he asks bitterly.

"A little bit of circumstance, fate, manipulation."

"What about you? Do you think you've done her wrong?"

"I haven't done her right."

"Is there a difference?"

"I hope so."

"Why did you leave her alone on Earth?"

"For the same reason she left you—there was no other choice."

"You didn't have a choice?"

"Not really. Kricket has a destiny, Trey. If you get in the way of it, you'll pay . . . and pay . . . and pay."

"You talk in evasion and riddles. Come back if you ever want to have a real conversation," Trey growls. He grasps his gun and checks the setting.

"You want to know how we've come to be here? Time has conspired against us, Trey. My family has a part to play in the future. My consort was an extraordinary creature. She could see the light of future days. 'So many possible futures,' she would say. 'Where to begin?'" He laughs, but there is very little humor in it.

"Arissa saw the future like Kricket does?"

"I don't know what Kricket sees or how she sees it. She was a child when I left her. For Arissa, it was a violent explosion of atoms, tearing her away from her body, projecting her into the future."

"Sounds familiar," Trey admits. *"You still haven't answered my question, though. Why did you leave Kricket behind on Earth?"*

"Her mother told me she'd bring about the destruction of Rafe," Pan says. His fingers deftly wield the cig-a-like as if it's a baton. *"Arissa sifted through so many possible futures, looking for one where we could all be together. She could see nuances in time—the other infinite possibilities, not just the dominant markers. Can Kricket do that yet?"*

"I don't know," Trey replies. *"Are you saying that Arissa saw options in time in which things could be changed?"*

"Yes, but the problem Arissa had in changing the future was that there was so much time between her and the events that she was seeing. Trying to change time that far out is difficult. Time always tries to right itself. The changes have to be drastic if you want to affect the distant future, or it will find another course to come to the same conclusions."

"What exactly did Arissa see?"

"She saw several possible futures at war with each other—all of which were attempting to become the dominant marker—the event that happens."

"According to Arissa, what event presents itself as the dominant marker?"

"Excelsior Ensin becoming Emperor of Ethar."

"Are there other possible markers?"

"The best one we found for Rafe is one in which Astrid rules Ethar as our empress."

"Where does that leave Kricket?"

"In the middle of a war. Her future is liquid."

"What do you mean?"

"Kricket's future takes the shape of the glass you pour it in."

"I still don't get it."

"Pour her into time with a certain set of circumstances and she becomes a world ender. Give her a different set of circumstances and she shapes time in a whole other way. One thing is clear about Kricket, though: she's a catalyst. Events start and end with her. She's the person who can ensure that the worst-case scenario will happen or that it won't.

"We tried to hide her on Earth, knowing that she'd trigger the fight between the Houses on Ethar. Her keeper, Giffen, was assigned to her to prevent her from ever returning to Ethar. Giffen tracked the Alameeda who came to Earth to find Kricket. There have been several teams sent to search for us over the years even before Kyon Ensin."

"What happened to the ones who came looking for her?"

"Giffen killed them. He was tracking Kyon and his associates. He didn't realize that Rafe soldiers were also dispatched to Earth at the same time. You slipped through and he missed you."

"What would've happened had he known we were there as well?"

"He would've tracked you and killed you."

"And if he was unable to kill us, what then?"

"He would've killed Kricket before she crossed over into Ethar. That was our preemptive plan. The worst has happened, though. She slipped through, and the House of Rafe has paid the price for my inability to control the events that led Kricket here."

"You mean because you didn't kill her, this is your fault."

"If I had killed her when she was a child, Rafe would've survived."

"Do you really believe that? Do you think Excelsior Ensin would never conceive of a plot to gain power if Kricket hadn't come here?"

"Of course, we don't know. We only know that if I had been able to eliminate her, she would no longer play a role in it. Now we prepare for the events that are coming. Kricket's role in the future isn't finished. There's still a chance that we can shift the events to the best-case scenario."

"How do you propose doing that?"

"Kricket will have to get close to Excelsior Ensin."

"For what purpose?"

"Assassination."

"Kricket is not a killer!"

"Then we're all dead. Excelsior knows about the threat to his future from Arissa. She gave him the information when she was a child. He was like a nice uncle to her. She had no idea who he was until later."

"And who was he?"

"He was Arissa's creator. How much do you know about Amster?" he asks, looking around the beautiful Gothic cathedral-like building they are in.

"It's been a ruin for around a thousand floans—ever since the Black Math plague swept through most of Ethar," Trey says.

"That's right. What most people don't know is that the plague had its origin here . . . in this building. Did you know that this used to be an institute that was founded and run by Excelsior Ensin?"

"No."

"He worked extensively in genetic enhancement. He also dabbled in germ warfare."

"You're suggesting that Black Math was not an accidental mutation?"

"It wasn't. It was a well-designed plan to rid the world of masses of people while he secretly worked on an enhanced race. He and his team designed and perfected genes—powerful genes and deadly viruses. Working in conjunction with a small group of leaders, Excelsior and his extensive connections administered the plague to their own populations and held the antidote aside only for those who they deemed worthy of it. This building is the place where the virus was conceived. Here—"

Pan stands up and pulls an orb from his pocket that's no bigger than a large gumball. He touches the top of the orb. It glows golden and lifts from the center of his palm to float in the air above his head, casting soft light around them. Pan walks to a nearby pillar and uses his shirtsleeve to rub a brass plaque on the wall and wipes away the dust from it. The plaque now clearly says: ENSIN INSTITUTE.

Pan straightens and says, "The headquarters that you awoke in after you were brought here is Excelsior's ex-residence. I enjoy irony, Trey. I thought it would be fitting that the very place that spawned him would also be the place from which to stage his demise. This city was his domain. He owned it, but he grew tired of it, so he decimated it. That's who he is."

"Give me a team. I'll take Excelsior out."

"You'd have a difficult time getting close to him. Even the gifted men I have ferried out of Alameeda aren't able to get close to him. Priestesses guard him. Kricket is in a much better position to assassinate him, because she won't even have to try. He'll bring her to him."

"When?"

"Soon. Excelsior grows malcontented. He wants another New World Order with just himself at the helm. He's finished with the shared power of the Brotherhood. He's willing to seize it all from the very people who were his allies a thousand floans ago."

"Why not use germ warfare again, since it worked so well last time?" Trey asks.

"He can't risk it. Two plagues? Too many leaders who were involved in Black Math are still alive to realize the similarities in the situation. No, he needs a distraction from what he plans. Kricket is that distraction. She's the prophecy, come home to her people. He can use that to his advantage to keep the focus on her while he devises a way to take the throne from her. There's still one small problem for him, though."

"What's that?"

"Kricket is fated to kill him."

"What happens if she succeeds?"

"We'll use New Amster's military to place Astrid in control of the four remaining Houses. She's also the daughter of Arissa—she's a priestess born of two houses and two worlds, as the prophecy indicates. They'll accept her as their leader."

"Why Astrid, why not Kricket?"

"Astrid has been raised to be empress her entire life."

"Still, why not Kricket?"

"She won't survive," he says softly. He has enough decency to show regret.

"So you're saying that because I brought her here to Ethar, I killed her."

"You couldn't have known."

"Where's Kricket's mother—Arissa? I have to speak to her! I have to find a way to change the future!"

Pan shakes his head. "She's gone. She died on Earth," he says honestly.

"I don't believe you! Someone with her advanced knowledge, she'd see it coming!"

"She did see it coming! She begged me to take her life so that no one could find us."

"What?"

"Excelsior has Nezra, Arissa's first daughter. Nezra is an ingenious tracker. She would've found us eventually, when her skills advanced, like they are now. It was just a matter of time before Nezra located Arissa. Arissa wanted to protect Astrid, so she begged me to kill her. Nezra couldn't track us then because she didn't have a connection to us. Without ever having met her sisters, Nezra couldn't picture them in her mind."

"She found Kricket."

"Kricket is well-documented now. Her image is everywhere. Nezra can imagine Kricket in her mind. That's not the case with Astrid. Nezra has never seen her and she doesn't know she exists, so she'll have a hard time finding Astrid."

"I'm sorry about your consort. I didn't know."

"You don't have to be sorry. You're just like me—in love with someone who has no future. We're both trapped in an impossible situation."

"I'm not trapped. I'm keeping Kricket. I'll find her. I'll save her," he warns, but his face is one of anguish rather than determination.

"Will you? You might come to a place where you'll have to ask yourself what you're willing to sacrifice to prevent the deaths of millions of people—to protect others that you love. What would you be willing to risk in order to stop an evil dictator from gaining power and ending life as we know it? The burden of it is beyond your comprehension now. I have moments that I have to struggle to take a breath. It's why I carry this around." He holds up the smoker. "It reminds me that she wanted me to live."

Trey turns desperate. "Give me trained soldiers! I'll kill Excelsior. I swear it!"

"You're not part of this, Trey. You should get out while you still can."

"I'll never leave her alone!"

"Think about what happens if she survives."

"She becomes the empress of Ethar."

"Yes, with one of the most powerful Etharians by her side, Kyon Ensin. He'll make her his consort if he hasn't already."

"But she'll be the empress. She'll have the power to choose her destiny."

"I think that is naïve of you, Trey, but let's assume for a moment that you're correct. How do you think she'll react to New Amster?"

"She'll be threatened by you at first, but once she comes to know you—"

"We've made it a priority to keep her down. We've assured that she felt the bite of poverty; we've watched her suffer abuse, secretly hoping that someone else would destroy her so that the burden of it would be absolved from us. How do you think she'll respond to that, with all the power that she'll have?"

"You're worried that she'll want revenge?"

"Wouldn't you?"

"You're afraid of her."

"I'm practical. She's not equipped to make the decisions needed to wield the kind of power that she'd have as empress. We have to put Rafe back together. It's our duty. We have responsibilities to our civilization that she cannot fulfill."

"She's young, but she can—"

"Astrid will always be a threat to her reign. They'll constantly be pitted against one another."

"Kricket would never hurt her sister. She proved that by saving her."

"She saved herself. Giffen would have killed her had she not cooperated. If she survives Excelsior, Kricket will let you close to her, close enough for you to be able to ensure the survival of Rafe and New Amster."

"I could speak to her for sure. I can guide her—"

"Not guide her." He shakes his head. "End her. If you want Rafe to survive, you'll protect Astrid. Kricket as the empress translates to the death of our House. It will be just the four Houses."

I'm way past the point of being able to stay now. I hover near them, languishing in the dark corner, a fading memory. None of it matters anyway. If I die now or later, it's all the same. I die. No wonder no one explained the future to me—the prophecy. I have no future. No one wanted to tell me that. They want me to play my role and then get off the stage.

I let go of this time. As I leave Trey and my father, everything becomes golden and calm. For a moment, I race out on the desert plains of time in the night all alone. I'm wild and I'm free. I can be anything here, shed my skin forever—shed time forever. I search for my mother, but in the next step I take, I find that someone is holding me back. I look behind me to see Kyon forcing me to stay. The sky falls apart. I flicker like a streetlamp on the ocean of sand. The night comes up through the grains of sand to swallow me whole.

CHAPTER 13
LOVE A LIE

Kyon's mouth covers mine. He blows hard into it. His parted lips leave me as he rises up to his knees by my side. Large, rough hands seek the spot between my breasts above my sternum. I exhale the air from his lungs and inhale a gasping breath of my own. Kyon's fingers are still on me as his eyes lift to mine. I cough, struggling with the need to take in more air than my lungs can handle. I'm lightheaded and shaking. Gripping my hand, Kyon squeezes too tight. "Breathe," he demands, but it's more than that. It's a plea.

If there was a plan, he forgot it. He lifts my blue fingers to his lips, resting them there and breathing warmth over the winteriness of my flesh. I don't know what's real or what's the future anymore. I'm buried in both worlds.

"No," I murmur. I can't say more. I don't even care anymore. I don't belong in this world.

Kyon lifts me like a blanket, carrying me naked and wet from the floor of the lavare. He lays me on the bed and climbs in next to me. He holds me for a long time without speaking. I drift in and out of sleep, waving at taxis and chasing shadows of my mother. I never want to wake up. Of course, I rarely get what I want.

My eyes flutter open and I see Kyon sitting next to me, pressing a drug dispenser gun to my upper arm. He clicks it. I flinch as something burrows beneath my skin. "You don't have to do that," I begin to explain.

He scowls. "Shh!" It's a harsh sound, filled with anger. "I can't believe you would do this!" he growls, his steam-shovel jaw tensing.

"I'm—"

"If you tell me you're fine, I promise I will beat you to death," he lies. "I could kill you right now with my bare hands."

"I'm sorry," I say in a groggy voice. The drug he gave me goes to work immediately. He pulls the bedsheets up over me. I close my eyes and go back to chasing taxis.

⚶

My skin feels hot. It's no wonder, I'm half buried alive by Kyon's body pressed against mine. I inch away from him and creep over the mattress to the other side of the bed. Pulling the blanket with me, I drag it to the commodus. Once there, I see my reflection in the mirror. I look like death. Ducking my head, I look away. When I leave the bathroom, I crawl back into the bed. Cold now, I seek out Kyon's warmth. I curl myself around him, spooning him.

"Were you punishing me?" He sounds haunted.

"What?"

"Was that revenge for wanting you?"

"No," I say, thinking about how he must have found me cold and near death on the shower floor. "It had very little to do with you. It was difficult to come back."

"Why?"

"I got lost."

Kyon turns over and faces me. His hand smooths my hair away from my eyes. "What was it? What did you see?"

"Old scars ripped open," I reply in a raw voice, trying really hard not to cry. My throat aches from it. "I promise not to stay away too long again." It's not a difficult thing to promise. I won't be around long, for there aren't too many more opportunities to break it. "I have to kill Excelsior, Kyon. I need your help. Will you help me?"

"Yes," he says simply.

I'm almost crushed by gratitude. I lean forward. Pressing my lips against his, I taste his sweetness. His arms encircle me and haul me up on top of him. "Thank you," I whisper. Tears I can't hold back spill from my eyes. He becomes a thief, wiping away my tears with the back of his hand, trying to steal my sorrow from me. His fingers shift into my hair. They draw me close so that our lips meet again.

Then Kyon sits up, causing my legs to slip apart and straddle his hips. "Where did you go?"

I sniffle. "To the future. It keeps following me." I try to smile and fail miserably.

He frowns. "No. I mean where did *you* go?" He points to my heart. "You haven't come back yet. I need you to come back."

I cover my eyes with my hand. My mouth contorts in grief as I sob.

He tugs my hand away so I'm forced to look at him with tear-blinded eyes. His lips nuzzle mine with silver-lining caresses. I wrap my arms around his neck. With my wrists against the back of his head, I urge him closer as I realize how well he knows me, and how much he genuinely cares about me. He changes from my problem to my lover as he adjusts himself and pushes up into me. Our bodies connect and become one; my mouth opens and I breathe his name. A sharp thrill of pleasure causes my cells to riot.

Even swimming in sorrow, he won't let me drown. Kyon moves against me. I move with him. "You're perfect," he groans—*a lovely sound.*

I become a villain for his touch. A delirium of delicious sensations builds, intoxicating me. I can't bury the euphoria he's making me feel. Small moans and gasps hiss from between my lips as he increases his strokes and sharpens my bliss.

"Tell me you're my consort."

"No," I rasp, struggling to deny the shattering heights of passion he elicits.

He growls. I dance on the point of a blinding star with him. Our breath mingles. Wrapping my arms around his shoulders, I trace my lips over his cheek, moving them until they brush up against the shell of his ear. As I come undone, I whisper his name with the darkest part of my heart.

He's unrelenting. He sends me over the edge again and again. I disintegrate into crushing, wretched ecstasy with him. He follows me, saying my name like I've destroyed him. He lies by my side, hauling me to him once more, stroking my back as I rest my cheek against his chest. "You can run from your love for me, but know this: I will hunt you anywhere," he promises.

In the morning, I awake to the sound of the shower running in the other room. Sitting up in bed, I notice breakfast hovering on a tray next to me. Uncovering it, I smile. It's not pancakes. It's their version of quiche. My appetite has come back, so I eat everything on my plate. Just as I finish up, Kyon walks into the room with a towel draped around his narrow waist. I chew slower, my eyes following the perfect contours of his skin. He's beautiful in ways that are hard to fathom. He's symmetry. Even as he's just sinew, flesh and bone, he carries it differently than most people. Gracefully. His skin is like honey. I remember tasting it last night, sampling it. Savoring it. I swallow the last bite of quiche and blush.

"You're awake," Kyon says as he prowls around the bed, coming to my side. He leans down and gives me a thorough kiss, which makes me blush more. "How do you feel this morning?"

"I'm okay," I murmur, trying to hide my reddening cheeks from him by looking up at him through my lashes.

He touches my flushed cheek, running his thumb over it gently. "I'm glad to hear it. We have a busy rotation ahead."

"We do?" I wonder at the smile on his face. He's happy. Kyon Ensin is actually happy. I don't think I've met happy Kyon before. He's a little fascinating. "What are we doing today?"

"I want to show you the rest of the estate. Fulton will join us. He runs things for me here. I want you to become comfortable going to him for anything you need. You'll also be introduced to the rest of your security detail. You'll be able to ask Keenan about anything with regard to it."

"Like leaving the estate?" I ask with as much nonchalance as I can muster.

"Exactly."

"Will I be allowed to leave?" I ask, my heartbeat accelerating in fear for reasons I can't explain.

"Of course. There is an event planned for this evening."

"Is it a date?" I give him a sidelong look.

He flashes me an unguarded smile. It's radiant. "If you'd like."

"Are we going to see a movie?"

"Urr . . . No."

"Bowling?"

"Uh . . . Bowl—"

"Karaoke?"

Kyon leans down, his hand cupping my nape as his lips claim mine, silencing me with an exquisite kiss. I'm unprepared for the rush of desire his touch creates. When he pulls away and looks into my eyes, he says softly, "It's a victory celebration, Kricket."

"What did we win?" I ask breathlessly and with a smile.

"It's what we want to win. Hearts and minds, remember?" he says as he straightens. "We need to ensure that the public opinion remains in your favor. To do that, we need to endear you to the citizens of Alameeda."

"So . . . I should get dressed now," I say.

"You should," he agrees.

I wait for him to leave the room so that I can walk to the lavare and take a shower. He doesn't move. "Aren't you going to go get dressed?" I ask, raising my eyebrow.

He nods and says, "Mmm-hmm," but he doesn't move.

I finally get it and a small smile touches my lips. I pull the sheet back from me, rising from the bed. I brush past him, naked, and walk to the lavare. As I cross the threshold, I feel an arm wrap around my waist, then halt me and turn me around. I lean against the doorjamb as Kyon kisses me until my lips are full and tender.

"Wait," he murmurs urgently. "I just need . . ." He lifts me up and carries me back to bed with him.

❧

After we both dress for the day, he gives me the grand tour of his estate. Fulton is there to answer all my questions, which are extensive. I meet my security team in the formal gardens outside. There are a dozen of them, and I try to remember all their names. I think I have them figured out. It's important. I plan to watch them to understand their shifts and patterns. Kyon explains that they will monitor me at a distance on the estate, but I will need to schedule them for any activity that I plan to do in the city or beyond. Of course, this is for all future activities, which will be considered only after Excelsior is no longer a threat to me. Unfortunately, no one can say when that will be, not even me.

After the security team is dismissed, Kyon and I stroll arm in arm along the path near the water. "Your house is ridiculous—you know that, right?" I ask.

"I knew you would think so. That's why I took you to the island first," he replies. "Does it make you uncomfortable?"

"Yes. I will get lost and you'll never find me."

"I'll always find you," he promises. "And you'll get used to it."

"Will I?" I wonder aloud. I sound sad, even to my ears.

Kyon immediately reacts to my tone. "Why do you say it like that?"

"I don't know," I lie.

He doesn't believe me. His eyes sharpen on me and he stops walking. "What did you see last night?" he demands.

"I didn't—"

"Don't lie to me! You nearly died last night! Something kept you away. I need to know what it was. I've been waiting for you to confide in me."

"I'm not a confider," I reply. *I'm a spy, a thief, a betrayer, a loner, but never a confider.*

Kyon stares at me for a moment. He controls his anger. "You want me to hurt you, don't you? So that you have an excuse to hurt me back?—To keep your secrets. I won't give you that! I'm your partner in this! You have to trust me or we both die. My father is looking for any way to exploit our weaknesses. Let's not give him any."

"Being your partner doesn't come easily to me. You have to give me more time to adjust."

"I've given you time."

"I want more."

"What do I get in return for time?"

"My undying gratitude?" I reply, trying really hard not to make it sound sarcastic.

"Not good enough."

"How about I promise you something special—something you'll want?"

"Like what?"

I sigh. "I don't know what. I have to figure out what you like."

"I like information. I'd like to know what you saw in the future because it almost destroyed you. I need to know so I can prevent it from happening again."

"You're going to have to trust me."

"That doesn't work for me. That wasn't the first time you almost died."

"I told you: I'll handle it. I promised I wouldn't do that again."

"So you can control it?" he asks.

"I think so."

He shakes his head. "That's not a yes."

"I can't deal in absolutes. I can tell you I'm trying. This is me trying."

He growls. "This is me trying, too! I'll be in my study if you change your mind and want to talk."

"Thank you." Rising up on my tiptoes, I place a quick kiss on his cheek. It does little to fix his mood. He drops my arm and turns, walking away from me toward the house. I watch him go, unable to bring myself to stop him. I can't confide in him. Not this. I can't be responsible for the annihilation of New Amster.

I nearly wet myself when a voice near me says, "I think he's mad at you."

"Giffen," I grumble, "where are you?"

"Behind you on the bench," he replies.

I can't see him. He's invisible. "What do you want?" I bark.

"Don't be so obvious!" he barks back. "They're watching your every move!"

"I'm not the one yelling!" I whisper, walking to the bench. "Which side are you on?"

"You're about to sit on my lap," he replies, sounding amused.

I move down the bench and gingerly take a seat on it, looking out over the water. "When do I get an invisibility belt?" I ask him.

"A what?"

"An invisibility belt, like the one you're using right now. When do I get one?"

"I'm not using an invisibility anything. It's one of the abilities I inherited."

"But I saw you touch the box on your belt—when we were on the island."

"That's a battery I use to draw energy to myself, so I can speed up my atoms in order to achieve this state. Do you know how difficult it is to stay transparent? It requires energy and focus."

"So I'm not getting a belt?"

"What have you been doing since you arrived here?" he asks, ignoring my comment.

"Nothing," I reply.

"He's calling you his partner. You must be doing something right."

"Oh, that. I think I may have won him over with my savagery. He was impressed by the way I simply could *not* tolerate a couple of priestess bullies."

"Don't tell me—was it like your first day in lockup?"

It startles me to hear him say that. I forgot for a moment that he's been following me for a large part of my life. "Something like that. You know how it is: You have to stand up for yourself right away, even if you get pounded for it. It's always better than if you don't."

"Did you get pounded for it?" he asks.

"No."

"The fighter prevails."

I don't comment. I just stare out at the lovely boats that dance over the water.

"You didn't tell him about New Amster. He gave you an opening to tell him and you didn't take it. Why?"

"I hold my cards close, you must know that."

"I do know that better than anyone," he replies. "What did Kyon mean about what you saw last night? About almost dying?"

"I was monitoring the future. I let it get away from me. He had to revive me," I reply. "It upset him."

"Why would you stay away so long? You can control it. I thought we were past that when I sent you back the last time!"

He sounds upset. I can imagine his green eyes narrowing at me. "I was gathering information regarding my survival. It had nothing to do with any plan to kill Excelsior."

"Is there a plan to kill Excelsior?" he asks.

"There will be one soon. I'll let you know when I work one out. I'll come to you in New Amster."

"Make it soon. I wouldn't want you getting too used to your new consort."

"Why?"

"He's an unfriendly. He's a threat to us. You know that."

"If you want me to do this, then his death is off the table."

"You can't be serious!"

"I'm so serious."

"He's a psychopath."

"He's *my* psychopath."

"You've lost your mind!" he growls.

"You know what sugar skewers are?" I ask him.

"What?"

"Sugar skewers. Do you know what they are?"

"Of course," he retorts. "They're drops of sugar that puff out when you cook them."

"Yeah. You want to know what I noticed about them?" He doesn't say anything, so I continue, "I noticed that if you impale a piece of sugar and hold it to the fire without treating it just right, it pops, explodes, and spits all over you."

"So you're sugar now?" he asks.

"I'm an exploding mess right now, so back the hell up." I rise and start walking away from him the way I came.

"Be in touch soon with that plan, Kricket," he calls softly.

"Okay. You take care now," I reply over my shoulder.

Crossing the massive archway bridge that leads inside, I'm met by Keenan, my personal bodyguard. We haven't had much to say to each other since I've arrived. I think the fact that I tranquilized him and left him behind on the bathroom floor at our initial meeting puts a damper on things for him.

He angles the freston that he wears slung over his shoulder away from me, pointing the muzzle at the ground. "Do you require assistance?' he asks. His blue eyes watch me without expression.

"Uh, yes. I do. I'd like to see Phlix. Do you know where she is?"

"Her lodgings are in Victory. Would you like me to escort you there?"

"Oh, you know . . . that's okay . . . maybe you can just point me in the right direction?"

He frowns. "I have to follow you anyway."

"Well then, please lead the way."

He steps aside, gesturing for me to precede him down a grand corridor. Floating orbs illuminate ribbed ceilings and etched columns. It's clear when he indicates an overup concealed behind an arched doorframe that it will take me more than just a few days to figure this place out.

Once inside the elevatorlike compartment, he waves his hand over holographic buttons. The door closes. The silence in the lift is deafening. I stare at the door. He stares at the door. We stare at the door. Seconds drag by.

I mutter, "I'm sorry I had to tranquilize you—before—on the Ship of Skye. I needed to get away."

"You think you're very smart." It's not a question.

"No," I disagree. "I think sometimes I'm very desperate."

"Kyon's not the monster that everyone thinks he is."

"Yes. He is. He's just not that way to you or me."

The door opens. I leave the overup and find that we're at the top of the tower. A short corridor takes us to a copper-and-green-patina, bell-shaped door. "Is this it?" I ask. Keenan nods. I raise my hand to knock on it when it's torn open and I'm engulfed in a huge Phlix hug. Out of the corner of my eye, I see that Keenan has raised his freston, maybe with the thought that I might be in danger. I raise my hand to stay him. He lowers his weapon without Phlix ever noticing because her face is turned away from him.

"I was so worried about you," Phlix says, her cheek on my shoulder. "Are you well?"

I nod and cast my eyes upward; it helps me not to cry. I'm not used to this kind of heartfelt welcome. Phlix bounces back from me with the exuberance of a puppy and hauls me over the threshold and into a bell-shaped room with her hand in mine. Curved ceilings of tarnished green and copper bleed into ochre-colored walls. Everywhere black furniture accented with amber- and bronze-colored pillows give her sitting room an elegant-cave appearance. The sun shines through a window-wall on the far side of the room. With the glass partially open, the cool, mountain air enters in soft soughs.

"How are you?" I ask.

"I'm Pike-free at the moment, so life couldn't be better."

"Liberating?"

"To the extreme. I haven't had to hide once this rotation. It's been unreal."

"We need to talk," I whisper without looking over my shoulder at Keenan. "Privately."

She smiles brightly and links her arm with mine. "Can I show you my view of the Doedash Mountains?" She bounces with enthusiasm.

"I'd like that."

She takes me out onto the balcony, leaving Keenan in the sitting room. We're in one of the tallest towers of the estate. The graphite-colored slate roof comes down to meet the terrace. The view is incredible. The terrace runs all the way around the tower, just below the eave of the peaked roofline. A large, red, pennant-shaped flag flies atop the spire. It's a dragon emerging from a rune. Just beneath the pennant is a mounted gun. It whirls and tracks all the nearby aircraft that it detects on the other side of the dome shield covering the estate. It reminds me that we're really not as safe as I'd like to believe.

I glance into the interior of Phlix's apartment. Keenan is nearby, watching us through the glass. Taking Phlix's arm, I begin to stroll along the round track of gray stone that circles the tower. "We need more privacy. Can you shadow us?" I ask as I place my hand on the wrought-iron railing, running my palm over it as we walk. I lift my hand every time it comes upon a dragon-headed newel.

She doesn't respond for a moment, but closes her kohl-lined eyes and concentrates. Opening them, her blue eyes sparkle as she turns to smile at me. "There. We are no longer visible to anyone. We're in my shadow land. No one can hear us."

"You're sure?" I ask.

"I am."

"Good. How long can you keep this up?"

"My shadow land?" she asks.

I nod.

"The longest I've gone is a part and a half, but it left me unable to function well for an entire rotation afterward. It works best for a half a part."

An hour and a half at most—that's not as much time as I'd hoped. I lift my chin. "You said you could get things—things we need."

"I'm good at getting things. My gift of obscurity makes it ridiculously easy."

"That's perfect. We have to collect everything we need for the journey to Earth."

"So, we're still leaving," she says, her shoulders round in relief.

"Yes. We're leaving. It will be really dangerous, though. I'll be hunted. If you're with me, you'll be hunted too. If you don't think you can handle it, tell me now and I'll come up with a different plan that doesn't include you."

"I'll handle it. I want out too, maybe more than you."

"Why?" I ask.

"I've never been free. This little time I've spent here is the freest I've ever been and you seem to think it's a prison. I want to know what it's like to really be free—to answer to nothing and no one."

"I can give you that"—I lean my head to the side—"sort of. Earth has its own rules. It's not easy there either."

"Nothing worth having is easy," she replies.

"So you're in?"

"I'm in."

"Let's brainstorm then. What do we need?" I ask myself, thinking of traversing the Forest of Omnicron and all that that entails. "We need a way to travel without detection. Everyone will be looking for us."

"Every vehicle I know of has a heat signature. They're easy to track."

"Think of something that has the smallest heat signature."

She's quiet for a moment. Keenan walks out onto the terrace and looks around with mild concern. "A flipcart," Phlix murmurs. "They leave almost no trail. I can get them easily."

"Can you teach me how to ride one?"

She smiles. "You mean you haven't ridden a flipcart?"

"I know. Shocking."

"Kricket," Keenan calls out, turning in circles on the balcony, looking for me. I ignore him.

I tell Phlix, "We need food that we can carry, some medical supplies, water, one outfit—versatile—shoes that we can run in, not these torture devices." I lift my skirt hem up to show her the intricate foot-wear that makes me have to almost point my toes.

"They're so lovely, though," she says. "Are they Gurtrone?"

"I—who cares?" I reply. "We each need one of those things that Strikers use to breathe underwater." I mime shoving a breathing apparatus in my mouth. "Something that will help us survive the portal to Earth."

Her forehead furrows in concentration. "You want a tankoid?"

"If it's the thing you put in your mouth that's attached to a small cylinder that lets you breathe underwater, then yes, I want a tankoid."

"Okay. That might be hard to get, though."

"See what you can do," I tell her. I may be an okay swimmer now, but I know my limits. Having oxygen in the massive current that will drag us through a wormhole to Earth ups our likelihood of survival, and unlike the Cavars, I have no qualms about using Etharian technology here or on Earth.

"We'll need rock climbing equipment."

She shakes her head. "Not if we have flipcarts. They levitate. They can take us straight up."

I rub my forehead. "Cavars are *insane*! You know that, right?" Then I say to myself, "Rappelling cliffs that they can just use a flip-cart to descend! I am so *over* it!"

Keenan runs past us in a panic, yelling, "Kricket!" He disappears around the bend in the balcony.

I point at Phlix. "You need inoculations. You've never been exposed to the kind of diseases that are on Earth. I can't have you dying on me."

"I'll get what I need. It's going to cost, though, and take some time."

"How much time?"

"I don't know," she says. "I need to develop a contact among the security team. They seem to have the greatest access in and out of here."

"Do you need money?" I ask.

"Yes. I have none."

"Will people barter for things?" I ask.

"Maybe."

"There's so much stuff here that probably won't be missed for a while, if ever. I'll give you some things that look valuable. Work on getting your vaccines first. We don't leave until you get vaccinated, okay?"

"Okay. I'll let you know," Phlix agrees. We both pause for a moment and look out over the grounds. "We're really doing this."

"Yes," I say. "Just you and me."

"You're not planning on anyone else joining us?"

"No," I reply softly. "It'll be just us."

"I don't even know what it'll be like not having someone decide every aspect of my future," she says.

"It will be epic," I reply and find that I really mean it. I hear Keenan's pounding feet coming from around the bend of the balcony again. "You can unshadow us now."

"Done," she breathes.

Keenan rounds the balcony at a sprint. He slows when he sees us turn to face him. "I was looking for you," he pants.

I manage to look confused. "Did you need something?" I ask.

"Kyon asked me to remind you of your date this evening. He thinks you should return to your room to dress for it."

"Thanks, Keenan," I say. "Maybe you can show me the way there?"

"Of course."

Turning to Phlix, I ask, "Do you need anything from me before I go?"

"Yes," she smiles defiantly. "Can you say good-bye to Pike for me if you happen to see him?"

It's in this moment that I know that we'll be friends for as long as we draw breath. "It would be my pleasure," I reply.

"Thank you, Kricket," she says. We walk to the door of her apartment, and she hugs me farewell at the threshold.

The trip back to my room is uneventful. When we arrive, Keenan precedes me into the suite. He checks around, and I'm surprised to find that Kyon isn't there. For some reason I thought he would be. Keenan leaves, and I consult Oscil on what I should wear. I change, and when I'm attired in a soft coral-colored dress, I brush my hair and leave it loose. After waiting for more than an hour for Kyon, I decide not to hang out in my room any longer. I leave and go exploring. Walking the garden level, I slip outside and follow the path along the house. I like this perspective, looking through the glass at what's inside.

Dusk begins to settle on the grounds. Soft lighting coming from one of the rooms along the walkway draws my attention. I see a flickering fire on the far wall facing me. Above it, two crossed swords burn bright with reflected firelight on their steel edges. I touch the handle of a glass door and it opens without me turning it. Kyon is in a large emerald-colored chair by the fire, its gleaming covered buttons make it somehow regal.

I traverse the rune-embroidered carpet. The plank floor creaks as I step on a loose board. The warmth of the lazy fire dances over my skin, drawing me closer to it. I come up to Kyon, but he doesn't look at me. His hand loosely clutches something. A small, glass hoof sticks out from his fist. I don't say a word but perch on the matching green chair adjacent to his and watch him. He's completely oblivious to my presence. It's as if he's not here himself.

I test my theory. First, I rise from my seat and go to his. Then I run my fingertips softly down his dark blue shirtsleeve. The fabric is warm beneath my touch. Kyon doesn't blink; the firelight burns a reflection in his eyes. The dry heat caresses my skin as I slip between Kyon's knees and stand directly in front of him. My shadow falls over his eyes. No reaction. He stares ahead as if I'm not here. Reaching out, I touch his cheek and course the back of my knuckles over it. I realize that I can kill him with my bare hands right now, because for whatever reason, he can't stop me.

Lowering myself onto his lap, I curl up and rest my forehead against the cogs of time interlocking a path on his tattooed throat. My eyes fall on the object protruding from his fist. Grasping his hand, I try to ease it open. I can't. I wait instead.

I know the instant Kyon returns. Electricity runs through me. He inhabits his skin with a gentle buildup of steps. He's nothing if not control. His muscles tighten. He turns his cheek in confusion; it bumps lightly against the top of my head. I feel him working out the fact that I'm sitting on his lap. His arms bow away from me at first, but then they drift back, wrapping around me. His lips find the top of my head again. He kisses me, breathing against my hair.

My fingertips skim over his closed hand. I gently pry his fingers apart. Sharp points poke my skin. Warm, smooth glass weighs heavy in my hand as I take the object from him. I lift it up. In my open palm is a crystal spix, exactly like the one I'd rescued from Charisma's collection of Crystal Clear Moments. The inanimate equine sparkles in the firelight.

"So you're like me?" I ask him. "A genetically engineered freak?"

"I like to think of myself as exceptional."

I gather a few strands of his hair in my hand. Using the sharp edge of the crystal spix's horns, I cut his hair. The severed pieces shrivel to ashes while new hair regrows in an instant. I blow the ash from my palm. It floats toward the glowing logs.

"He doesn't know, does he?" I ask.

"I never would've survived if Excelsior knew."

"How did you keep your gifts a secret from him?" I ask.

"My mother shielded me at first. When I inherited her gift, I was able to do it for myself."

"What was your mother's gift?" I ask.

"She could influence others to believe any lie. It made your mother her instant friend. Farling couldn't lie to Arissa effectively. Which forced my mother to respect yours."

My fingers close around the crystal spix and I draw it close to my heart. "You lie to me without me knowing, don't you?"

"Sometimes."

"How do you make me believe you?"

"I'm stronger than you. I've been doing it longer."

I think about something he said to me. It was at our first dinner at the Palace in Rafe. "You once told me that you weren't like me—that you weren't born with the gifts that I was given."

"It's only half a lie. I have different gifts than you. I had to see if you knew that I was special," he says. "I influenced you then to believe I was telling you the truth. If I hadn't, I ran the risk of you exposing me to everyone in the room. It was a risk I was unwilling to take."

I feel betrayed. "You knew I was a soothsayer even before I caught Em Nark in his lies."

"I did. Your mother told my mother you'd have the gift. It was a secret she only shared with me when she made me promise to find you. Arissa had said she would gift it to her strongest daughter. She said it would help her to rule Ethar."

"Is it fun for you? Lying to me?"

"Sometimes. But, lately you see through them. It's frustrating. It was so much easier when you didn't know me."

"Do I know you, Kyon?" I ask.

"More than anyone ever has."

"Are you lying to me now?"

"I've never loved another like I love you, Kricket."

"I don't believe you."

"You know it's true."

"How do I know?"

"I'm there—in the future you project into—if there's danger, I'm there to defend you. I've hung my happiness on what we could be. I won't kill you to keep my secret. That's not something I'd normally let go. Only one other person knows it."

"Fulton?" I ask.

"Yes. It's against the law here for me to exist. If anyone should find out about me, I could be executed. I would have no protection under the law."

"Tell me what else you can do."

"I can read things—objects—things someone has held. Objects carry memories."

"Like my spix?"

"Yes."

"And you can, what? See these memories?"

"I can walk through them. This spix was in your pocket when I brought you to the island. It's a curious object. It whispers secrets to me."

"What kind of secrets?"

"Your secrets," he murmurs. "It used to belong to Charisma Sandersault. It was given to her when she won a Biequine competition. She shot every target with near perfect accuracy . . . all while mounted on a spix. Her memories of it are clear. Concise. Unguarded. Probably like her. But she gave it to you because you asked her to."

"Did it share other memories?"

"It did. But the ones of you are murky and shrouded. You're very guarded."

"Do you plan to share them with me?" I ask.

"I don't. No."

"Why not?"

"They're memories filled with fear of me. I'd rather make new ones with you." He lowers his mouth to mine. His lips are coaxing as he kisses me. "I don't want you to be afraid of me."

"I believe you once told me that you were okay with me fearing you as long as I obeyed you."

"You've changed me. I want to be the favorite taste that touches your lips." His tongue caresses mine; the sharp pleasure of it cuts through me. It steals my breath. "I want to be what you yearn for every moment of every rotation."

"I still can't trust you," I reply with a whispery caress as my lips just brush his. "You're an open wound. All you care about is revenge."

"You're wrong," he insists softly, his blue eyes seeking mine. "I want to understand you—your buzz, your sting, the nectar on your unbroken wings." He runs his hand over me and I am honey. "You're the empress in my dreams."

His words cause an ache deep within me. It's an insatiable hum of piercing hunger, which only heightens when his lips descend to mine again. His hands cup my bottom as he lifts me up and takes me to the table meticulously laid out with brass cogs and winding gears from another object he's taken apart. He slides his hand over the menagerie of metal, wiping it off the table and onto the ground. The broken pieces make garish sounds as they object to being discarded. He perches me on the edge of the wooden surface, touching me as if he knows what my body needs . . . and he does.

I don't know which of us is the beguiled and which is the muse. "I adore you," he whispers. I put my hand on his chest, trying to hold him still, trying to catch my breath from the relentlessness of our attraction. He grumbles, "What are you so afraid to lose, Kricket? Tell me you love me too."

"What do you think will happen if I do?" I ask, knowing that I have no future here with him. I have no future at all.

"You'll stay with me forever." His intensity makes it sound like a demand. I try to repress the thrill I feel at the sound of it. I hate that I want to mean something to him.

He reaches out to undress me; his finger glides under the strap of my dress. It slips off my shoulder. His mouth teases my skin where it had rested. Closing my eyes, I lean into him. "You *will* stay with me forever," he repeats. I want him to save me, but that's like asking poison not to kill me.

"I won't," I reply.

I try to make myself appear cold and pale, but he kisses me again, coloring me in. His hands inch up my thighs, pushing the length of my dress up, exposing flesh as he goes. I set the spix aside and cover his hands with mine. My hunted heart beats like cornered prey. He frees his hands, undoes his belt, and then his trousers fall away. Gripping my legs behind my knees, he jerks me forward, spreading them apart. "I'm the truth you've been searching for, Kricket."

"You're a liar, Kyon," I say against his lips as he makes love to me. Deep down, however, I fear that I've come to love a lie.

CHAPTER 14
THE WORLD ENDER

The lonely dragon has found that he has a heart, and it beats within me. Kyon holds my hand in the hawk-shaped Hallafast as we approach our destination. His thumb rubbing over my knuckles, he stares at our clasped hands as if they're the most fascinating things he's ever beheld. Lifting my hand to his lips, he kisses it. I blush and have to look away from him so I can think.

I stare out the window. Our aircraft is surrounded by Kyon's extensive security detail. We weave between wickedly tall buildings that disappear into the darkened sky above us. "Where are we going?"

"There is a public celebration taking place in the main center of the city known as the Sylvan Square."

"What are we going to do there?" I ask.

Kyon shrugs. "Whatever it is they do there. I've never been here among common people."

"'Common people'?" I try not to roll my eyes.

"Non–decision makers."

"I think they're just called people, Kyon."

"I know the *people* stroll the avenues, frequent shops, buy desserts—dance."

"Dance?" I ask, raising my eyebrows. "Does Kyon Ensin dance?"

"With the right partner."

The Hallafast sets down on a landing pad on the ground. Kyon doesn't get up immediately. I glance at him in question. He let's go of my hand and reaches into his pocket, pulling out the copperclaw I'd left in the lavare. He straightens the black ribbon that holds the fiery flower. "Will you wear this?" he asks without looking at me.

"Yes," I reply.

His eyes lift to mine. The brightest smile I've ever seen from him transforms his face from handsome to striking. "Thank you."

I lift my hair for him and brush it aside so that he can tie it around my throat. When he's finished I feel his warm lips caress the nape of my neck. "What are you doing to me, Kricket?" he breathes against my skin, turning my insides to fire, like a dragon, infusing me with heat.

"We should go if we're going to do this," I tell him.

He leans away from me, and I drop my hair back into place. When I turn back to him, he takes my wrist in his hand and applies a gel-like sticker to it. I recognize it for what it is: a locator. "Just in case we should become separated, I can find you faster," he explains.

It reminds me of the one I wore for Trey, and it makes me feel like a huge traitor. *Is Kyon really my consort? Did I just agree to that when I let him put his flower around my throat once more?*

I don't have time to think about it, because Kyon takes my hand and escorts me from the Hallafast. As we descend the stairs, Kyon puts a small, round bead into his ear. It's a communicator. He presses it and a microphone snakes out to hover by his lips. "Oscil, take the Hallafast to the hoverpad. I'll call for it when we're ready to depart." He touches the earpiece again and the microphone retracts, recoiling into his ear. We reach the bottom; the stairs to the ship retract and the door closes. The aircraft lifts off straight into the air and disappears from sight.

I shiver, chilled to be out in the mountain air. I feel exposed. I haven't been in a public place in so long that it feels threatening. "Are you cold?" Kyon asks.

"I forgot my wrap," I reply, gazing at the crowded street fair ahead of us. There are hundreds, maybe thousands of people wandering everywhere between the tall buildings and hovering vender carts. This place makes the Taste of Chicago, the largest annual outdoor food event in that city, look like a neighborhood block party.

"Here." He takes off his navy jacket and drapes it over me. His arm goes around my shoulders. We walk through the crowd of people; they fill in around us when we reach one of the grassy avenues. No one seems to be paying any attention to us. I glance at Kyon, who's watching the crowd. I pull up short, trying to avoid a rowdy pack of men who are running through the crowd and jostling each other. Kyon scowls at them, ready to take the nearest one of them by the throat, but I quickly lay my hand on him. "Relax," I order. "I'm fine."

"He touched you!" Kyon retorts with barely suppressed rage. "No one is allowed to touch you."

"It was unintentional—we're here to fit in—don't beat anybody up! You. Must. Chill. Do you know what that means?"

He looks at me in exasperation. "I never know what you're trying to say. I have no idea what being cold brings to this situation."

For all the stress we're under, his words make me smile a little. I place my arm around his waist. "Walk with me." As we stroll, I marvel at the carnival-like atmosphere around me. Everyone is celebrating the victory over Skye. It makes me shiver. Do they know what they've done? Do they understand that people are being slaughtered? Would they care if they knew?

I don't get much farther before I start to attract attention. The first person to notice me gasps when I walk next to her. She holds her hand to her mouth, and then she turns to the man next to her and says behind her hand, "It's Kricket and Kyon Ensin!" She nudges him until he turns and gazes at me. Recognition shines in his eyes. I smile at them as we continue down the crowded street.

"They know me? Us?" I ask, looking up at Kyon's face.

Kyon nods, glancing over his shoulder at the couple that is now openly gawking at us. "You've been major news. The Brothers have been talking about you ever since you arrived on Ethar. They've given news conferences. The media here, which is controlled mostly by the Brotherhood, has reported that you have been a hostage in Rafe all this time and were being forced into an engagement to Manus."

Their propaganda has truth to it. I was never allowed to leave the palace in the Isle of Skye. Manus had attempted to force me into becoming his consort before the Alameeda attacked us. Us. Us? Was there ever a moment when I was one of them, or was I only fooling myself? My own father doesn't even want me. Did they use me? My heart squeezes tight as I think of Trey. No, that was real. Everything else may have been a lie, but the way I felt about him was true. I loved him and he loved me.

It's over now, though. I know that. I have to let him go or I'll crush him. I have no future. He isn't made of stone, like me.

I glance behind us to find that we're attracting a crowd. People are beginning to follow us. "Welcome home, Kricket!" a girl calls to me, waving her hand like she knows me. I smile back, seeing delight on her face at my response. She's absolutely radiant.

Kyon leans near me. "They've never been this close to a priestess before."

"Really?"

"It's unheard of. You're to be protected at all times from all possible threats."

"That's no way to live," I reply.

We walk farther on. Kyon stops at a vendor who has the most beautiful wraps in colorful displays from his hovering caravan. "Would you like one?" he asks.

Reaching out, I smooth my hand over a soft ivory-colored one that feels like cashmere. "This is lovely," I say to the vendor. He smiles shyly at me.

"We'll take this one," Kyon says. He holds his hand to a scanner. A bright light flashes over it. When he removes his hand, he gently takes his jacket from my shoulders, replacing it with the ivory-colored wrap.

"Thank you," I say.

Something is wrong with me. I never would've allowed anyone to give me something without feeling indebted or feeling the need to somehow repay him. I'm surprised that I don't feel that way now. I just feel grateful.

As I puzzle over it, several round, one-eyed camera-bots come upon us. Shaped like white, hovering basketballs, they circle us blinking, clicking and filming our every move. I see myself reflected on the side of building surrounding the thoroughfare. It's like Time Square's Jumbotron, but on a much larger scale—my image encompasses every side of every building I can see. I exhale deeply. Smile fading, my heart is a frantic drumbeat in my chest.

"Welcome home, Kricket!" someone in the crowd calls to me. I force another smile. I resume walking, but faster.

"How does it feel to be home?" Someone else calls out. I'm nervous. This is bad for me. Everyone will see this—not just the Alameeda. Whatever I say now could be used by Excelsior to damn me as a traitor. Everything can be spun. Innocent words can be made to appear sinister. The same goes for my answers in Rafe and New Amster. What I say now could make me a traitor there as well. They'd have even more reason to kill me, not that they need it.

"I—I miss Earth," I stammer. My enormous images reflect my confusion. I appear fragile, probably because I am.

The crowd begins to murmur. Kyon gathers me closer to him. "My consort has only just arrived home. We must all make her feel welcome."

Another ripple of discussion passes through the crowd. Within moments, the low rumble of voices becomes full-on shouts of my name accompanied by applause and whistling. The cheers become louder and more boisterous. People extend their hands to me as I pass, touching me as if I'm some kind of celebrity or cult leader. It becomes harder to walk more than a few steps without having to nod and smile at all the well wishes coming at me from everywhere.

"Are you ready to go?' Kyon asks in my ear. "I can call the ship. We can be back home shortly."

"No," I reply, hearing music up ahead. "We're not running. Anyway, you promised me a dance."

"I did?"

"Yeah, you did," I say with a smile. I pull him along to where the music is playing in a lighted pavilion. When we reach the place where people are turning around the floor, I tug on Kyon's hands to get him to come with me. People are gathered in a circle around the dancers, clapping and singing along to the music. It's not something I've ever heard before. If I had to liken it to anything, it'd maybe be a modern version of polka. I join in the clapping. It makes me giggle because if they came to Earth, some of them might find the dancing criminally vulgar. "Do you know how to do the dance they're doing?" I ask.

"Yes," he says as if he's admitting to a crime.

"Why do you say it like that?" I ask, continuing to clap.

"I was in that club where you worked on Earth. I saw what passes as dancing there. This must be very provincial."

"You must think I'm very judgmental," I say. "I actually think that if more people spent their time dancing, we'd all be better off. Any form of dancing, especially if it's with someone they love."

He takes off his jacket and takes my wrap from me, tossing them in a pile of castoffs behind us. His large hand swallows mine. He brings me out onto the floor. The music changes to an elegant composition. It sounds postclassical with a haunting pianoforte minimally adorned with electronica beats. With one hand in mine, and the other on my hip, he turns me around the pavilion like we were always made to be here. As I spin with him, I wonder which direction Earth is. Does it matter? What if I allow myself to be lost here in the moment with him?

I let go of everything around me and live on borrowed time. I act as if it's my last night alive. Who wants to live forever anyway? Laughing, I try to catch my breath while Kyon whirls me in an intricate move.

Fireworks go off, booming and rumbling loudly, the sounds reverberating in my chest. It startles me until the flash and sparkle of colorful light shines on Kyon's hair, turning it from red, to rose, and then to silver in strobing patterns. Everyone stops dancing to watch the explosions rain down. Watching the fire spread across the sky, I promise myself that I'll get back the upper hand.

Kyon turns to me with fire in his eyes. Our time is limited. We'll go our separate ways soon. If all goes well, I'll never see him again. How was I to guess that that thought would hurt me like it does?

My head begins to ache, like something is hammering on it. I rub my temples to try and ease the pain. All of a sudden, I'm overwhelmingly nauseous. Kyon touches my arm. "Are you ill?" he asks.

"I don't know . . . I'm—" I drop my hands from my head and notice a blue laser dot on my chest. I look up, following the direction of it. I see Nezra next to an Alameeda soldier in a Striker uniform. His freston is leveled at me. Before I can react, Kyon grasps me and turns me around. He growls when the blue laser flash of ammunition pierces his arm and passes through the meat of it. It doesn't stop him from pushing me to the ground and drawing his harbinger from his side holster. He turns back around and begins to fire at the Alameeda Strikers who are aligned outside the tent.

Somewhere behind us, Kyon's security team swarms in, creating a barrier between the Strikers and us. I'm lifted off the ground by

Kyon's arm around my waist. He places me in front of him as he ushers me away from the fighting. I stumble into a crowd of panicking people. I don't know where to go. Kyon moves me toward a round circle of light. The spotlight slowly shrinks over the ground ahead of us. People are scrambling to get out of its harsh glare.

Looking up, I realize that it's Kyon's Hallafast. It lands in front of us and the stairs descend from it like liquid pouring down. I'm urged up the stairway and into the aircraft. Kyon follows me in and closes the door. He pulls me to his chest, kissing me hard. His good hand is on me, running over me as if he's assessing my state of being. I kiss him back. His kiss becomes gentler when he slowly realizes I'm not hurt. "You're okay," he says with relief.

"You're not. You've been shot." I indicate his arm.

He glances at it and then looks back at me. "It's not bad," he says, as if his wound is inconsequential. "You see my knife in my shoulder holster?"

I nod.

"Take it out and cut my hair."

I do as he says. Grasping the short handle of the knife, I walk around the back of him. Rising up on my tiptoes, I capture his hair at his nape. I don't have the strength that he has, so I can't just cut his hair off in one swipe. I have to saw through his hair. It can't feel good, but as I do, shiny new hair grows out from his scalp. I feel foolish for never having suspected his secret. While we were on Earth, I'd watched as Luther had shot him, and yet he hadn't been killed. He also hadn't died from the knife wound I gave him.

When I'm finished cutting his hair, I walk back in front of him and hand him his knife. He rolls his shoulder, testing its healing. It already looks better, but not by much. His skin is less bubbly and crisp in some places. "Your sister is a psycho," Kyon snarls. "She brought Verka with her." He stuffs his knife back into the holster.

"Who's Verka?" I ask, my eyes going to his upper arm where the skin is scalded and burned away. The charred flesh is becoming smoother. It still smells as gruesome as it looks.

"Verka is a cooler. Her gift is blocking other priestesses from using their gifts."

"My headache?" I ask.

He nods. "She blocked you from seeing them coming."

"I had no warning," I admit.

"Nezra has crossed the line! She tried to kill you!"

"She's in love with you. She warned me to stay away."

"I didn't give you a choice," he says. The skin on his injured arm is starting to peel and flake. It's not weeping anymore. It's gross but it's also fascinating. "If I didn't promise to take care of her, I'd kill her right now."

"Who did you promise?" I ask.

"Our mothers," he growls. "I'm sending you home. You'll be safe. I'll send an escort with you. I'll join you after I sort out this mess."

"What? You can't go back out there!"

"It's Nezra," he says in a derogatory way. "She's already done her worst. She'll be horrified that she hurt me."

"You're worried about her?" I ask.

"No. She should be worried about what I'm going to do to her."

"What are you going to do to her?"

"Something dire." He clenches his fists and stalks toward the door of the Hallafast.

"Wait!" I call. "Let me see if it's safe! I'll go into the future and look—"

He turns in my direction and shakes his head. "That won't work. You're going to be cool for a while."

"What do you mean?"

Amy A. Bartol

"Verka blocked you. I have to cleanse her from your system. I have something that will help at home. I'll see to it when I get there." He turns to leave again.

"Wait!" I call again. "You can't just go out there blind. Anyone can be out there."

He pauses, and then a smile forms on his lips. "Are you worried about me?"

My mouth drops open. I begin to bluster, "No! Of course not! That's so stupid!"

Kyon crosses back to me and takes me in his arms, kissing me as if he has caught my soul. "You're full of surprises, Kricket. I'll see you when I return home." He lets go of me. Using his communicator, he tells Keenan to report to the ship.

I lean down and tear the hem of my dress away, making a long strip of silky fabric.

"What are you doing?" Kyon asks.

"I'm protecting your secret. Everyone saw you get shot. No one needs to know that you heal fast." I walk to him and gently press the scrap of my dress to his upper arm, tying it loosely around it.

"You're protecting me?" he asks as if dumbstruck.

"I'm protecting *me*. The only person standing in the way of Excelsior tearing me apart at this moment is you."

"Admit it—you have feelings for me."

"You're my partner. It's temporary. Don't read into it."

He leans down and whispers close to my ear, "I'm your lover, at the very least." Behind him, Keenan boards the airship with several other members of my security team. Kyon reaches out and cups my cheek, making me look into his eyes. "I'll be home soon and we'll continue this conversation." He gives me a quick kiss, and then turns and disappears back into the night.

The Hallafast ascends at a stomach-dropping rate, and we fly back to Kyon's estate. Touching down inside one of the many inner courtyards of the snowflake-shaped castle, I disembark with Keenan by my side. As we walk to the door that leads into the Mercy tower, Oscil halts us in our tracks. I'm startled as its fem-bot voice announces, "Security breach, south perimeter. Security breach—"

Keenan growls. "Protect the priestess," he says to the other security team members. They form a circle around me. "Back to the Hallafast," he orders me, making me turn around. Just as I do, every soldier of my security team collapses to the ground as if they're mechanical toys and someone has turned them off. Then I'm struck by dizziness. I sway on my feet. Ahead of me, New Amster soldiers swarm over the courtyard. Among them, I recognize Giffen and another dusty-blond, long-haired soldier. He has a look of concentration on his face as he raises his hand out in my direction. As he brings his hand down in front of me, it's lights out for me. I lose all ability to function and drop to the ground like a stone.

⚜

Aboard Kyon's Hallafast, I open my eyes, staring up at the ceiling as someone strokes my hair. "She's waking up," Jax says beside me.

Confusion and disorientation make me feel nauseous. I start to retch. I try to sit up, but someone has me on their lap, so instead, I lean over.

"What's wrong with her?" Jax barks at someone behind me.

"Jaden is an arterial contortionist."

"What's that?" Jax demands as he hands me a small bag and I vomit into it.

"Jaden has perfected the ability of contorting the arterial vein to cease the flow of blood in the neck. It momentarily cuts off the flow of blood to his victim's brain, rendering them unconscious. A side effect of what he does is usually dizziness and vomiting when the victim regains consciousness."

When I'm done throwing up, Jax takes the bag from me and hands me a handkerchief. I wipe my mouth. "Jaden is a total knob knocker," I growl.

Jax takes the handkerchief from me and gives me a small square piece of paper. He pushes it toward my mouth, saying, "It's mint-flavored antinausea medication. Take it and you'll feel better." Trusting him, I put it in my mouth. It dissolves instantly.

From across the room, I hear Giffen say, "We need that plan you promised us, Kricket. Excelsior is still drawing breath, and it's making us angry. People are dying."

A warm hand touches my clammy skin, smoothing my hair back from my face. I look up and blink a few times, seeing Trey looking back at me with a pained expression. My head is in his lap and I'm stretched out on a long divan in the common area of the aircraft. "Can we talk to her alone, without you?" Trey asks as he looks in Giffen's direction. "I want an opportunity to explain things to her in a way she can understand," he adds, like I'm some kind of halfwit.

I glance around me. There are a lot of New Amster soldiers on the ship. They're all staring at me with their burning matchstick eyes.

"You have a quarter of a part, then we're out of here."

"All right," Trey says.

Giffen frowns at me as he and his men leave the ship. I realize when they're gone that Wayra is here as well. He's just staring at me as if I'm a favorite pet that he has to put down. His look makes goose bumps break out on my skin. I try to sit up on my own, but I end up needing Trey's help. I hold my head in my hands as I rest my elbows against my knees.

"Please tell me one of you can fly this airship. I can, but I've only done it once," I mumble, before lifting my head and trying to see through my double vision. "If we can make it to the Forest of O, we can be at the reservoir to Earth in a matter of a day or two—maybe we can fly all the way there this time. Once on Earth, we can make arrangements to smuggle out my friend Phlix and your families—"

Wayra moves from the wall and starts to pace, as if he can't stand to be still a moment longer, "Aww, she's breaking my heart, Trey! Make her understand why we're here before she rips the rest of my guts out!"

Trey reaches out and takes my hand. "Kricket, we can't take you to Earth just yet."

"Oh. Is it too far?" I ask, rubbing my forehead. "Are we going to New Amster then?"

"We can't take you to New Amster, either. With Nezra's ability to track you, it's too dangerous to them to have you there."

"Okay, then where are we going?" I ask.

"We're not going anywhere yet," he says gently. "We need a plan from you to wipe out the Brotherhood and their leader, Excelsior Ensin. They've ordered their troops to attack the remaining bases in Rafe. Cavars are holding their own at the moment, but Comantre Syndics have been monopolized by attacks on their own soil by Wurthem and Peney. Alameeda Strikers are pursuing the citizens of Rafe into the annexed area. They've located our base camps in the Forest of O and are systematically attacking them there as well. If we don't act soon, there will be nothing left of Rafe to defend."

I remove my hands from my face to look at him. "You know what'll happen to me if I give New Amster a plan to destroy Excelsior and the Brotherhood, right?"

Trey reaches over and gently tucks my hair behind my ear. "We'll have a team in place to help you execute your mission," he says reassuringly, but he has doubt—huge doubt.

"My mission?" I ask. Even though I know what he's been told by my father, I want to hear the words from him.

"I'll be there for you, in whatever scenario you come up with, to defend you, Kricket." He believes what he says for the most part, although his answer shows that he has grave reservations as to whether that's right.

"I was there, Trey," I say quietly, "when my father spoke to you at the Ensin Institute and told you about his expectations of me." Trey frowns and I continue: "Pan told you that when I do this, the moment I kill Excelsior, I'm as good as dead too. New Amster wants Astrid as empress. They don't want me."

"They don't want Kyon. We'll be there to kill him so that he's no longer part of the equation. You just have to do your part and this is over," Trey says naïvely.

"You're wrong. Kyon's not the problem. I am. My father and New Amster are afraid of me. They think I'll want revenge against them for abandoning me on Earth."

"They'll see reason. And if they don't, maybe Earth *is* the option. Maybe letting you return there is all they need to allow you to live."

I shake my head. "Pan is known as a ruthless strategist. He understands that as long as I live, I'll always be a threat to Astrid. Someone powerful need only find me on Earth and return me to Ethar for this to happen all over again. I threaten her reign. The only way that ends is if I'm dead."

Wayra stops pacing and says, "Kricket would make a stronger leader than Astrid. You've met her, Trey. Astrid's smart, but she doesn't have the kind of heart needed to make the brutal decisions it takes to rule."

"See?" I say to Trey. "The debate begins already, and with it comes a new war—sister against sister. Pan won't allow that. He loves Astrid too much to see that happen. So if I don't leave Ethar soon, I never will."

"He's your father."

"He left me for dead a long time ago."

"You could abdicate to your sister."

"Really? Could I? Because that's worked so well for me before when I've refused to do something. I was almost Manus's consort, not because I wanted to be, but because he wasn't going to let me refuse. How hard is it for you to envision a scenario like that happening again?"

"If you leave Ethar without helping us, then everyone we love dies," he retorts with anguish in his eyes. "My brother, Charisma, my family will all be wiped out! This war began because of what we did, Kricket! We have a duty to save our people from the destruction we brought to them!" He knows what he's asking me, but since he and I are responsible for this, he sees the sacrifice as justified: my life and maybe his for the lives of Rafe. "I'm asking you to do this for me."

"So be it," I say softly. "I'll get you your plan on one condition."

"Anything," he replies.

"Promise me you'll protect Kyon after I kill Excelsior."

Wayra growls, "Giffen's right—you *are* insane."

"I'm not crazy, Wayra." I glance at his face and see his disgust. "Kyon wants what you want. He's Excelsior's son, but they're bitter enemies. Kyon has been hunting me all this time for the same reason you are now: so that I'll kill Excelsior. He's not the person driving this war; he has been trying to protect me because he swore to my mother that he would. He thinks I'm supposed to be the empress of Ethar. He doesn't know about Astrid."

"Have you slept with him?" Trey demands with mounting anger.

My face snaps back in Trey's direction. "Are you kidding me right now? What difference does it make?"

"Have you?" he insists.

"Yes," I whisper.

His reaction is violent; he reaches for my throat and tears the ribbon choker from my neck. He crushes the copperclaw in his fist before throwing it onto the floor. "You were mine!"

"Tell me not to do this and I'll be yours still."

"I can't do that," he says wretchedly.

"You're so bad for me, Trey," I reply, shaking my head. "Your Boy Scout bullshit is bad for me. You brought me here to Ethar! I begged you not to, but you wouldn't listen to me! You promised to protect me and you couldn't. I saved your life from Giffen, so you don't get to judge me for how I chose to survive losing you."

"I've never felt more sorry for finding you than I do in this moment."

"I'm a world ender, Trey. You should be sorry."

"I promise to protect your consort Kyon," Trey says like I cut his heart out. "When do we get that plan to kill Excelsior?"

"I'll start on it tonight. When I have something, I'll come to Giffen in New Amster, like I already said I would. You can tell him that. He'll know what I mean."

Trey gets up from the divan, making it clear that he can't wait to get away from me. He walks to the door of the aircraft and doesn't look back. Wayra doesn't know what to say to me. So he doesn't say anything, he just follows Trey out. Jax is slower, his shoulders rounded. "I'm sorry . . . for my part in all this, Kricket. If any of us had known what would happen when this started, things would've been different. If it means anything to you, I'd like you to know that I think you're the bravest Etharian I've ever met." He turns to leave.

"It means something to me, Jax," I say in a choked voice. "Can I ask you for a favor?"

"Yes."

"Will you tell Trey and Wayra, after this is all over, that I did love them?"

"They know."

I nod because I can't speak right now without crying. Jax leaves and Giffen reboards the aircraft. "Your guards will come to soon.

Darken the Stars

Our nepenthe, Sanham, has wiped their memories of tonight. You can explain what happened to them any way you want to, but you can't mention New Amster or us."

"Is that it?" I ask. I can't look him in the eye. I just have to get through the next couple of minutes and then I can fall apart.

"That's it, fighter," Giffen answers.

"Why do you call me that?"

"Because I've never lost anything betting on you." I watch as he has my unconscious security team brought back into the aircraft and spread out on the floor.

227

CHAPTER 15
HIGH KINGS

Keenan groans next to me, vomiting on the floor of the Hallafast as he becomes conscious. He sits up and looks around in confusion. When he sees me sitting numbly on the sofa, he rises and stumbles to my side. "Are you okay?" he asks with concern, trying to regain his composure.

I'm close to tears, but I reel them in. "You of all people should never ask me that question," I reply.

He looks at me suspiciously. "What happened? Did you do this?"

I shake my head and raise my shaky hand to my brow. I don't have to pretend to be scared. I am scared.

He helps me up from my seat. The other guards are beginning to regain consciousness as well. All of a sudden, it's a pukefest inside the cabin of the Hallafast as my bodyguards suffer the same kind of nausea I had endured upon waking. Keenan ushers me to the door and helps me descend the stairs. "You should go see if anyone needs your help inside," I tell him. "I'm okay."

"I should stay with you," he objects. "Do you want me to take you to your room?"

"No, I won't be able to sleep. I'd like to go to Kyon's study and wait for him to return."

"Are you sure?" he asks. "Maybe I should take you to the medical facility instead. You look like you're going to fall down."

"I'd rather go to the study. There's a sofa there. I can rest on it if I need to."

He doesn't argue with me further, and takes me to Kyon's study. Once there, he orders Oscil to stoke the fire and makes me sit in the emerald chair Kyon had been sitting in earlier. "I'm going to call Fulton. I want him to examine you to make sure you're okay." Before I can object, he says, "Oscil, summon Fulton to Foundation, garden level."

Oscil replies, "Fulton Coalfax has been summoned. He indicates arrival in two fleats."

Fulton enters the room with a serene look on his face. His eyes go from Keenan to me, and he immediately comes to my side. Kneeling down, he looks in my watery eyes. "Oscil, send a visor," he commands. He lifts my wrist and holds his fingers to it. "Did you have a trying evening, darling?" he asks me. I nod my head, choking back tears.

Fulton takes my hand and holds it. He looks up at Keenan, who is hovering near us. "What happened?"

"Plenty."

"Where's Kyon?" he asks. I watch the firelight shine in the silver streaks of Fulton's blond hair.

"He sent us home. Nezra crashed their outing. He's dealing with her. We had a problem upon arrival here."

His brow furls. "What sort of problem?"

"The Hallafast malfunctioned and the landing was a bit unstable," Keenan replies.

Fulton turns his attention back to me while Keenan retrieves the visor that Oscil sent to the room in a hovering pod. He hands the body scanner to Fulton. I allow Fulton to put the sunglasseslike contraption on my eyes, knowing that it will take all my vital signs and display them on the surface of the glasses.

"The blood flow to Kricket's brain was momentarily interrupted, but it seems to be satisfactory now. There's no sign of clotting or blockage. It's all very curious. Did something happen to the cabin pressure in the descent?" Fulton asks.

"Possibly," Keenan replies.

"Submit the Hallafast to maintenance immediately. I want them to go over every aspect of it. When they're finished with their evaluation, I want it to remain out of service."

"It will be done," Keenan replies.

"Keenan, go see to yourself. You look as if you're about to collapse. I'll sit with Kricket until Kyon returns."

Keenan hesitates. "She's my responsibility."

"She's safe here. I'll see to it. Have another team double the patrols outside if you're worried. Otherwise, get some rest."

Keenan debates it for a second and then he nods. To me he says, "Kricket, have Oscil locate me if you need me."

"I will," I agree.

Keenan drags himself from the room and Fulton gets to his feet and walks over to a wall near the fireplace. "Drink?" he asks. Touching a panel, a bar opens up for him. Shelves of different sizes and shaped bottles make him look like salesman pushing his elixirs. "Would you like a Winslet?"

"I don't drink," I reply.

"That's why I offered you a Winslet; it's mild. You should have one."

"Okay," I reply. I realize I really don't care if he were offering me poison. It really doesn't matter anymore.

He's a little surprised that I've agreed. He runs his fingers over the holographic menu. An ice-frosted flute emerges from the countertop. He grips the long stem in one hand and a fat tumbler of amber-colored liquid in his other, bringing the icy one to me. He sits in the emerald-colored seat next to mine.

After he settles in and the fire and alcohol have had a chance to mellow us both, I glance at him. "Tell me about Excelsior," I say, as Fulton takes a sip of his drink. He nearly chokes on it.

"My, you're direct," he says with amusement.

I don't reply. Sipping my drink, I find that it's a dry cranberry-flavored sparkling wine. It's good.

"Why do you want to talk about my ex-employer?"

I toy with the stem of my flute. "Because everyone here who knows about the prophecy thinks I'm going to kill him." Fulton's glass hovers near his lips as he studies me. "Even Excelsior is laboring under that impression. I'd like to know some things about him before I murder him. It's one of those quirks I have."

"Excelsior Ensin, Excelsior Ensin . . . where to begin . . . Ah! I can say without hesitation that I know of no other person more deserving of a horrifyingly painful death than Excelsior Ensin. What else would you like to know about him?"

"What does he do if he wins?"

"What do you mean?"

"I mean walk me through it. You're Excelsior Ensin. You've managed to slaughter your son, Kyon, and your daughter-in-law, Kricket. There's no longer any threat to your reign. What do you do?"

"If I'm Excelsior Ensin?" he asks for clarity. I nod. He thinks for a moment and then he says, "I assassinate the rest of the Brothers. They're in my way. I then begin to stage assaults against the leaders of the other Houses. I find ways to crush and rout them from power."

"What do you do to establish yourself as the leader of Alameeda, before you take on the other leaders of the remaining Houses?"

He thinks for a moment. "Excelsior is one for pageantry. He'll probably throw himself a coronation."

"What? Like with crowns and stuff?" I ask.

Fulton laughs, delighted by that. "Exactly like with crowns and stuff—maybe even a scepter." He smirks. "He'll be the emperor.

He'll need a symbol of power. A crown would be fitting. The Ensin family is supposedly descended from the ancient kings. It's something that Excelsior bragged about often—or at least it was when I was in his employ. He has made several pilgrimages to their perch at Diadem Rock. It's a stone circle high upon the Cliffs of Mogotrevo."

"I'm familiar with Diadem Rock," I reply, remembering the stone circle where Kyon met Giffen for our hostage exchange.

"Excelsior might be smart enough to model himself after one of the ancient kings—play on the supposed lineage."

"Do you have anything written down about these ancient kings?" I ask.

"Yes." He lifts his hands to the sheer cliff face of books that reaches in tiers up to the towering ceiling above us. "You are among kings," he says dramatically. "Kyon has a collection of their artifacts here that is the envy of any museum. I believe the only reason he collects them is so that his father won't get them."

"I'm not the only one with daddy issues then," I mumble.

"What was that?" Fulton asks as he lazily lifts his glass to his lips once more and takes another sip.

"I was wondering what you think Excelsior would do if Kyon and I had a coronation of our own."

He pauses. "You're a dangerous woman."

"Do you really think so?"

"I really do," he says.

"You say the sweetest things, Fulton. Maybe we should try on some of the crowns—the more ancient, the better."

"You'd look nice in a tiara," he replies. He sees my face light up. "Oh . . . you were serious?"

I nod emphatically.

"Shall we have another drink and make a production of it?"

"I insist," I say, holding out my empty glass to him.

ॐ✧ॐ

Two hours later, Kyon bursts into the study at a run, his feet pound on the plank floor. "Kricket!" he calls, searching for me.

"Shh!" Placing the book that I was reading aside, I uncross my legs on the floor. Crawling forward on my hands and knees, I poke my head through the wrought-iron railing four levels above his position on the garden level. "You'll wake up Fulton!"

"What?" he asks, sounding a little less panicked than he did a moment ago. "I was just told that the trift you were in crash-landed in the courtyard. Are you okay?" I hear him jogging up the spiral stairs on the side of the room.

"It was nothing a little Winslet couldn't fix," I reply. Or a lot—I haven't stopped drinking it. Fulton and I had decided just to bring the bottles up here. I'm a little wrecked at the moment. I scoot back to my spot on the floor, leaning up against a glass display cabinet. I try to find my place again in the tome I was reading, as I balance the thick book on my lap. Next to me, Fulton snores. He's on the floor too, with his back against a bookcase and his chin on his chest. An ancient bronze crown leans at a jaunty angle on his head.

Reaching our level, Kyon pauses when he sees me with one of his ancestor's thick metal crowns on my head. "What are you doing?" he asks.

"Reading," I murmur.

"What did you do to Fulton?" he asks.

"I just had a few drinks with him and we tried on some crowns."

"You know he's over three thousand years old, right?"

"Really?" I ask.

Kyon nods.

"Huh." I stick out my bottom lip. "He looks good." As Kyon crouches down next to me, looking me over, I add, "I'm—"

"—fine," we say in unison.

Kyon frowns. "Yes, that's your mantra," he says.

"Here." I lift up another crown from the ones I've collected on the floor. "I picked this one out for you. I think it suits you." I place the crown on his head. He looks like an ancient Viking warrior. I blink a couple of times, because it's actually a little startling. "I was right. It looks good."

"Why are you picking out crowns?" he asks.

"I don't know. I just am." It's true. I don't know, but there's something here. Something that will give me an edge against Excelsior, I can feel it in my bones, in my blood.

Kyon reaches over and touches Fulton's leg. Shaking it gently, he wakes his mentor.

Fulton yawns, "Ah, you're back."

"Yes. Thank you for staying with Kricket for me."

"It was a very amusing endeavor," Fulton replies. He takes the crown from his head and places it on the floor by the others I have surrounding me. "Thank you for the interesting evening, Kricket," he says with a smile.

I lean over and kiss his cheek. "Thank you for your help. I think I may owe you my life."

Fulton looks at Kyon. "She's perfect for you. Try not to ruin it. Excuse me while I retire for the evening."

Kyon doesn't say a word, but helps Fulton get to his feet.

"Good night," I say absently with my nose back in the book.

Fulton leaves us, and I lift my eyes to Kyon's again. They're dark and brooding. "How's your arm?" I ask.

"Healed." He flexes his hand, showing me that he has no discomfort.

"How's my half sister?"

"Broken. I don't want to discuss her. Chandrum is dealing with her and her mess."

He reaches for me and plucks me off the ground, hoisting me over his shoulder. I have to use my hand to hold the crown on my head. I drop the book I was reading. "What are you doing?" I ask in outrage. "I was in the middle of something!"

"You're about to be in the middle of something else." We leave Foundation and take a few turns in corridors I haven't yet been in. We enter a dark room in which soft lighting turns the space to elegant shadows. It's a massive bedroom. I don't see much of it before I'm set on my feet.

Kyon reaches for the straps on my dress and unfastens them. The silky, coral fabric slips from me and pools on the floor. He peels his shirt off. I'm not surprised to see that his skin is flawless once more. It makes me shiver, though, knowing we have both been genetically manipulated. He takes the crown from his head and sets it aside on the table by the bed. I reach up to remove the thick, heavy circlet of gold from my head, but I pause when he says, "Leave it on."

Kyon pulls me into his bed and rolls me on top of him. His hands touch my breasts, running over my skin to rest on my hips. I look down at him. "Tell me you love me," he whispers as he moves inside me.

"Never," I whisper back, but I find myself slipping away from never and freefalling toward always.

❧

I awake from the nightmare I was having, finding Kyon asleep next to me. My heart crashes against my chest in fear. In my dream, I'd been lying in a field of wild znous. The intoxicating smell of their poisonous petals was as strong as the velvety softness of the flowers that closed in around me.

I pull back the blankets covering me and hop out of bed. I run to the attached lavare. Finding Kyon's robe, I wrap it around me. It's ridiculously big, but I don't care. As I exit the lavare, I say, "Oscil!"

"Requirement," Oscil responds immediately.

"Take me to Fulton," I demand. Tightening the belt of the robe.

An orb of light appears before me. "Please follow the light and I will guide you to Fulton Coalfax. Shall I advise him that you are on your way to him?"

"Yes."

The orb of light begins to float away from me. I follow it. "Kricket?" Kyon mumbles sleepily from bed. "What are you doing?"

"Be right back," I say over my shoulder. "Faster, Oscil." The orb of light takes off at a pace that has me running to keep up with it. Holding on to the end of the robe so I won't trip over it, I nearly wipe out on a loose rug as it skids out from under my bare feet when I round a corner to another corridor. From somewhere behind me, I hear Kyon growl my name as he follows me.

The orb of light passes through a closed door and I stop in front of it and pound on it with my fist. A startled Fulton opens his door. Panting, I say, "Can you have a special crown made for me?" I rest my hand against the doorjamb, leaning over and pinching my side.

"A special—"

"One that I design? And I want a party. A coronation. Can you arrange that for me?" I ask. Kyon creeps up on me from behind. I glance at him over my shoulder. "Hello," I say, "I'm just working out a—" I notice that he's naked.

Fulton tries to hide the confusion from his face when I look back at him. "Kricket," he says placatingly, "you can have anything you want. If that's a party or a crown, I'd be happy to arrange it for you."

"Thank you," I exhale the word like it's my last breath. "Okay. Sorry. You can go back to sleep now." I straighten up and start to move back down the hallway. Fulton stops me and says, "Next time you can just hologram with me."

"Yeah? Okay," I say. "Good night."

Kyon comes up next to me. "Are you going to tell me what that's all about?" he asks.

"Yes. I need your help to design a crown. Do you think you're up for it?"

"I'm up for a lot of things," he replies. "Start explaining."

CHAPTER 16
WINSLET AND WHISPERS

Sitting on top of Kyon's worktable in his study, I pore over his sketches for the crown. He's so talented it's scary. I just had to tell him what I wanted last night and he stayed up all night working on it. "What do you think Excelsior and the Brotherhood will do when they hear that we're planning a coronation?" I ask Kyon.

He hunches over his worktable, testing a spring latch he's designing. "They will accuse us of treason."

"That's perfect. What will happen after that?" I ask.

"They'll try to arrest us. Why don't you project into the future and tell me if this all works out so I can decide whether or not to keep going here?"

"I can't. Your friend coolered me last night—Vilma—"

"Her name is Verka," he corrects me. "I'll fix you in a few moments, as soon as I'm done here."

"I don't need to see the future. This will work."

"How do you know?" he asks.

"I know because I met your dad's gigantic ego. It's almost as big as yours," I tease him.

"I'm nothing like him," Kyon replies, as if I hurt his feelings.

"I know that," I say contritely. "I'm sorry."

"You're forgiven," he says.

"Am I?" I ask.

"Always."

"How fast can we get this done? We need to leak word of the crowns and the coronation soon."

"I'll have it done within the next couple of rotations."

"Good. I have to go plan the party with Fulton. Everything has to look legit."

"The coronation will be legit," he says with a frown.

"It will be," I agree. "I have to go." I jump down from my perch and start to walk to the door, but Kyon pulls me back.

Turning me to face him, he plants a kiss on my lips. "Did you forget something?" he asks. He lets go of me.

"No, I don't—" He shoots me with something that looks and feels a lot like a Taser. Electricity courses through my body and I immediately lose my ability to stand upright. Luckily, Kyon catches me in his arms and holds me against his chest while I twitch.

"I just burned the Verka out of you. How do you feel?" he asks in my ear.

"Not good," I whisper when I regain the ability to speak. I rest my cheek against his chest.

"Should I have warned you first?" He strokes my hair.

"I don't know," I reply honestly, "maybe."

"It should stop stinging in a moment."

"Should I do you next?" I growl, as feeling returns to my arms and legs once more. It's enough so I can stand again on my own.

"I shot myself last night after I sent you home."

"Pity," I groan. "Yes. Definitely warn me next time."

"Or I could kill her so it never happens again," he replies.

"Table that suggestion. We'll revisit it when I'm feeling less angry. I will see you later." I drag my feet for a few steps before they lose their numbness. Leaving the study, I locate Fulton with Oscil's help. He's in the tower known as Glory. This tower is for entertaining guests. It has a ballroom that ascends fifteen levels like the tiers on a wedding cake.

"Do you like this space?" Fulton asks.

"It's very lovely," I say.

"Do you like it for the coronation?"

"No," I reply absently, gazing around. "I was thinking that something more public would be better. I don't want people here. I want our home to remain private. Is there somewhere else that would suit?"

We go over several options for locations. "I think it should be here," I say, admiring the hologram image in front of me of very beautiful floral gardens.

"The Botanical Gardens?" Fulton asks.

"Yes."

"But it's very hard to defend such a wide-open place."

"It won't be necessary to defend it. By the time the ceremony begins, there won't be any resistance to the coronation. Trust me."

He looks confused. "Do you want any special type of arrangements at the event?" he asks, going down his list.

"Flowers, you mean?"

"Mmm," he nods.

"I want znous—as many as you can get."

He laughs. "You do know that those are poisonous, don't you?"

"I think I heard that. I still want them."

"Then you shall have them."

"Is there a bar in here?" I ask him.

"Yes. He shows me the bar, which is better stocked than the one in Kyon's study. I take two bottles of Winslet from it, one in each hand.

"Can I have these? I want to have a couple of drinks with Phlix."

"You can have anything you want, Kricket. This is your house."

"Thanks. If it's okay with you, I'd like to finish the planning later."

"It's okay with me," he replies with a smile.

Leaving the ballroom, I have Oscil guide me to Phlix. She's outside, walking along the riverside. When I reach her, I extend a bottle of Winslet out to her. "Care for a drink?" I ask.

"You mean alcohol?" she asks, looking stunned that I would offer it to her.

"Yes. I mean really freaking expensive alcohol."

I pull out the bottle's gold-ball stopper and hand her the emerald-green bottle. "Here taste it."

She takes it from me and sips. "That is delicious," she says before taking another sip.

"Yeah, it's good. You know what else is good? It's worth five thousand Alameeda Gipsons. That's insane money."

"I can get vaccinated with that kind of money!" she says.

"Do you have a contact?" I ask.

"I think so. Can you get me more bottles like this?"

"I can take requests, but do it as fast as possible. We're running out of time."

"I understand." She hands me the open bottle and I take a sip of it, savoring the flavor. We walk along, looking at boats. "Are you going to miss this?" she asks.

"No," I say immediately, but I don't know if that's true. "I won't miss being scared all the time."

"Will we ever not be scared all the time?" she asks.

"I hope so."

"I'm glad that I'll have you." She links her arm with mine.

"Me too."

"Do you think you can shadow us?" I ask.

"No problem," she says.

She closes her eyes and concentrates. "We're invisible to others now." She winks at me.

"Fantastic. Come with me. I want to show you something."

I lead her around the outside of the house to the gigantic doors where I first entered the estate. "This is Kingdom. Have you been in here yet?" I ask.

She shakes her head. "We were brought in through an interior courtyard."

I show her inside. It's just as I remember it, a creepy art gallery of portals. I take her over to the one of Naren Falls. We watch the falling water hit the pool of blue water, sending up spray everywhere. The dead body of the soldier isn't visible anymore. Maybe some big beast dragged it off and made a meal of it. I don't know, but I'm glad I don't have to see his corpse.

"You can feel the mist on your face when you're not in your secret bubble," I say. "It's a portal."

"Cease speaking!" she says in disbelief. "Who made this?"

"Kyon."

Her eyes get wider as she says again, "Cease speaking!"

"It's true," I reply. "Watch this." I wind back my hand and throw the round, gold bottle stopper at the portal. It lands on the lawn and it half-rolls, half-hops on the turf, because the sphere is now caved in. "It's sort of brutal on anything that passes through it though." I take a sip of the Winslet, then pass it to her.

She takes a long draught before staring straight ahead at the falls. "That's in the annexed area, isn't it?"

"Yes. It. Is." I feel her nudge me with the bottle. I claim it for another drink.

"How dangerous is the portal?" she asks. I glance at her. She looks at me, and then at the Winslet bottle.

I wind my arm back and throw the open bottle into the portal. After the emerald-colored glass crosses the frame, it implodes, shattering and spewing sparkling wine all over the lawn in front of Naren Falls. Birds on the branches of the trees inside the frame take flight.

"Well, that's not good," she admits.

"No. It. Isn't."

"I liked that wine."

"It was good, right?" I say.

"Mmm."

"So we'll have to find another way there, unless you can think of a way we can get through this without imploding."

"I'll work on it."

"I'll look for another mode of transport. How are our flipcarts coming?"

"I asked Fulton for a couple. I told him that I wanted to teach you how to ride one, because you expressed an interest in learning."

"Really? What did he say?"

"He said the flipcarts will be here sometime after zenith."

"I like Fulton."

"Yes," she agrees. "He has a beautiful aura."

"It's nearly after zenith now. Should we go get our ride on?"

"I don't know what that means," she says.

"Let's go see if the flipcarts are here and stash the other bottle of Winslet."

"Let's," she agrees.

CHAPTER 17
PART OF THE PARADE

Leaving Phlix behind in her tower room in Victory, I return to my room in Mercy. I wander onto the balcony. Resting my chin against the railing, I look out at the river. The surface is without waves; the boats glide over the water without disturbing it, as if it's solid and not liquid. My flesh tingles with an eerie feeling. The river has its eyes on me, watching. The still surface feels unnatural. There's something in the river's depth that wasn't there before. My skin grows cold, and I have the overwhelming urge to shed my bones—to project into the future.

Stumbling into my bedroom, my timing is off and I don't make it to my bed. My cheek hits the soft carpet and it rattles my head. Something attempts to keep me here even as I slip away. I blink and see the outline of Nezra, who crouches down on the carpet by me to smile as my vision fades. The curl of wintry breath passes through my parted lips.

I leave my body, but Nezra's heavy gravity holds me just above it. She fights me, trying not to let me go. "Kricket," she says in a singsong voice, "I can't wait to see you burn for what you've stolen from me!"

I bury her in the night as the stars rip me away and I drift in time. I follow the events as they happen in the future. Strikers arrive to take me to Freming House, the gilded cage where they keep their priestesses hostage. It's not all they do there. It's a lab, as well—a testing ground for more new genetic mutations. It's a house of horrors. The things they'll do to me border on the depraved. I can't stay and watch it very long—it's too brutal, and I'll get the chance to experience it firsthand soon enough.

I turn in time and shift to another destination, one that I've promised to go to with a plan for Excelsior's death. I have that plan now; it's just unfortunate that I won't survive to see it come to fruition. At least I get to die knowing he'll follow me soon.

Touching down outside the crumbling governor's mansion in New Amster, I find Giffen and Pan speaking together in low voices by the giant sentinel statues that preside over the manor. Giffen feels my presence immediately when I near him. He looks in my direction. He pushes his energy toward me, and I become a golden silhouette of billowing stardust and light walking out of the night. I keep my attention on Giffen, ignoring the man who was only my father for a brief time. There's nothing really to say to him, anyway. He walked away.

"You'd better have a plan, like we discussed, Kricket, or bad things are going to happen to—"

"I do," I interrupt. "We're creating a Trojan horse for Excelsior. It's something that he won't be able to resist. He'll be dead in two days."

"What is this Trojan horse?" Giffen asks.

"I'd rather not say. It'll ruin the surprise, and I don't really think I can trust you to keep a secret."

"If he's not dead by then, we'll turn your Rafe friends' families over to the Alameeda."

"Is that what you told Trey?"

"He didn't tell you?" Pan asks beside me.

"No. He never told me about your threat. He just asked me to do it for him—for his family."

"And you agreed?" Pan asks, like what I've said doesn't compute.

I ignore him. He gets nothing more from me. Instead, I say to Giffen, "Will you tell Trey something for me?"

"Depends on what it is." Giffen replies honestly.

"Tell him that I said I never loved him, that I was just using him."
I turn to leave, but then I think of something and add, "Oh, and don't forget to watch the show, Giffen. You earned it."

"What show?" he calls as I fade to go back in time.

"My execution."

I slam back into my body in a rush. The frigidity of it lets me know I stayed away just enough to feel like I'm dead, but not to actually *be* dead. It occurs to me that being dead is the preferable choice in this situation, now that I know what will happen to me. The bad part would be that if I die here, there might be no vengeance against Excelsior and that's all I have left.

"Oscil!" I pant, when I return to my body. "Oscil!" I call for the automated intelligence that is always available, but I get no response. I knew there wouldn't be, but for some reason I had to try.

I struggle to get up from my floor. When I did this moments ago, in the future, I moved as fast as my numb legs would carry me to the balcony. But because I just lived it, I know without looking that the river outside is solid in several places. Strikers run over the surface of it with frestons strapped to them. A handful of Strikers are on the side of the house. They're rising on clear disks that act as lifts, bringing them up toward my balcony.

Instead of having them arrest me out there on the balcony, I turn and run to the lavare. Moving to the counter, I splay my hand over it. Toiletries of every type rise from the surface. Selecting a fat, sticky lip liner, I write on the mirror:

Kyon—
Stay away. Nothing you can do. They'll kill you. I've got this.
Finish my crown for me.
—Kricket

It's a lie. I don't really have this. They're going to eviscerate me in the most painful way possible, but there's really no reason for Kyon to die too. It would only serve to give Excelsior more pleasure, and I really don't think that's fair. I just need Kyon to get the crown to Excelsior. He can do that without dying. And a part of me very much wants him to live so that he can have the kind of vengeance he's dreamed about his entire life. It frightens me that I want that too.

A sound at the door makes me turn around. It's the Striker with the pirate smile. He sends a chill straight to my heart as he says, "Your father, Excelsior, is expecting you."

"Thank you, Ceecil," I reply, using his name just to freak him out. It works. He collars me with a restraint and has me on my knees as he pushes the button and chokes me until I see spots. I drop the fat lip liner.

"What is this gibberish you've scribbled on your mirror, eh?" he asks.

"It's a secret message to my consort. It says that I'll kill Excelsior and see him soon and to make sure he has my empress crown ready for me when I get back."

"Does it really say that?" he asks, and I realize that he can't read English.

"It actually really does. I'm going to kill my father-in-law." That earns me another push from his button, but this time I don't just see spots—everything goes black.

⊰❦⊱

My throat aches as I attempt to swallow. I open my eyes. Soft sheets slide beneath my fingertips instead of sterile, course fabric. Lifting my head from my pillow, I try to figure out where I am. I'm alone in a small but elegant bedroom. I've never seen it before. This is a new experience! I've never been in this room in my life or at any time in the future!

I shiver because I know I'm no longer on the same predictable path of time as I once was. I'm experiencing a new set of events. I've changed the future by at least a small degree. Last time, the Strikers brought me to Freming House. I had been conscious. Another very notable difference from this time versus last time is that I'm not having my ovaries removed in an operating room. This is a much better path so far.

I try to move my arm from the bed and find that it's strapped to a railing. I lay my hand back down on the sheet. It's a relief that I'm still wearing my own clothes, but it looks as if I've been in them for days. I'm rumpled and messy.

The door swings open and a technician enters the room. I recognize him. He's one of the laboratory staff who had helped perform the procedure to remove my reproductive organs in the alternate time line. Before, he made several sullen complaints about the sloppiness of the other technician. It angered him that his colleague had messed up while creating a new batch with the eggs they had harvested, and it was left to him to exterminate several male offspring as a result.

I blink a couple of times while the technician adjusts the vial strapped to my arm. "Dobrey," I murmur his name. My voice is thick, like I've been asleep for a while. He flinches hearing it, immediately moving away from me. "I'm sorry. I didn't mean to frighten you." He reaches for a tranquilizer gun, his hand shaking a little. "I have a plan! You'll never have to kill another batch!"

He pauses. His blue eyes squint at me. "What are you talking about?" he asks.

"I know you're being forced to do what you do. I know that the moment you stop doing it, you die. If Excelsior is made the emperor of Ethar, you'll be made to kill on a scale that no one has seen before. You know what I'm talking about, don't you?" I whisper.

"It's that virus they're working on in the lab next to ours, isn't it?" he asks in a whisper so we're not overheard.

I don't really know what he's talking about now, but I pretend that I do. "It is," I tell him. "If you untie me and help me get out of here, I promise to get rid of Excelsior."

He straightens, like I've said something completely ridiculous. My mark isn't falling for it. I try again. He picks up a syringe gun full of clear liquid. "Forget that I said anything. Letting me go will get you in trouble," I say, as if I care what happens to him. "You should just do whatever you came here to do. What did you come here to do?" I need to know what they're planning in order to formulate a plan.

"Excelsior ordered me to administer RU7 to you."

"What's RU7?"

He holds up the syringe gun of clear fluid, "It's an interrogation drug."

"What does it do?" I ask.

"It makes you see the stars," he says. "And tell the truth."

"He's going to make me tell him the truth?" I ask.

"Among other things," Dobrey admits. He takes a step toward me.

I hurry and ask, "How long have I been here?"

"I don't know. A couple of rotations I guess."

"Why have I been asleep so long?" I cringe, wondering if they took out my organs and then healed me.

"They've been preoccupied. They've been fighting with your consort, Kyon Ensin."

"Fighting how?" I ask.

"Fighting for their lives," Dobrey admits. "He's been killing off all the Brothers not present in the compound. We're all on lock-down."

"Why am I still alive?" I ask. In the future, I would've already been executed.

"Well, you probably won't be soon. Excelsior has promised to send Kyon your head if he doesn't submit to the Brotherhood at your trial."

"When is my trial?" I ask. This is new. He never put me on trial in the future. Have I managed to change things just by writing a note to Kyon on the mirror? The problem is that I don't know if I've changed anything for the better, although, it probably can't be much worse than before. Maybe.

"Your trial is this rotation."

"Will my trial be public?" I ask.

He shakes his head vehemently. "No. Never. No one is allowed into the chamber with the Brothers. It's secret. They have their rituals in there."

"But that's not fair! They can do anything they want and no one will know about it."

"I think that's the point. If it's any consolation, your execution will be public."

I know he's right. I've already been to one of my executions in the future. I don't think I want to be at this one, too.

"Aren't you curious to see what goes on in there?" I ask. "There has to be a way that I can record it for you."

"Why would I want to get involved in that? It's none of my business!"

"If there's one thing I know about men like Excelsior, it's that they like to talk. He's going to say a lot more interesting things to me than I'm going to say to him at my trial—things that will make people mad, Dobrey. If you could somehow leak my trial, I doubt you'll have to show up for work on Fitzmartin or kill anyone else you don't want to ever again."

He looks around, making sure that we're not being overheard. "There could be a way. A small, oral camera could work," he murmurs timidly. "We use them to study the digestive tracks of the priestesses. They swallow them. But I could maybe put one on you somewhere. Make it look like a button or something. They may not check you once they prepare you here."

I know I can't push him. He's skittish. If I push too hard, he'll fold. "It's your call," I whisper. "I just don't want to see things get worse for you when it'd be so easy to change them. And I'm dead anyway, so I have nothing to lose."

Another attendant enters the room and makes Dobrey jump. "You haven't given her the RU7 yet?" he scolds; his blue eyes are so light as to be almost milky. "Gimme the gun and go check on the other one."

"I have this one, Mieko," Dobrey whines.

"Do it now!" Mieko retorts. "I'm tired of your insubordination! You're going on my report. I'll personally see you demoted to full-time extermination! Do you hear me? Now go!"

Dobrey hurries out of the room, and Mieko wastes no time pushing RU7 into my arm.

"Who's in the other room?" I ask while the drug burns a raw path through my vein.

But Mieko is all business. He sets the gun aside and leaves me tied to the bed.

A galaxy of stars floods my vision as I look around me. Colors and shapes shift and drift in and out of focus. My head lolls on my chest as someone takes off my restraints, lifts me up, and strips off my clothing. I have a hazy notion that I'm being bathed and attired in something tight and torture inducing, like the dresses I've seen Nezra and some of the other priestesses wear. My hair is roughly done up in intricate braids. Finally the metal collar is tested again and matching metal arm restraints are added to my ensemble at my wrists.

Dobrey leans over me and says something. It sounds the same as if he were speaking to me underwater. He presses something into the stiff fabric of my dress. It pokes my skin, a pinprick. Then, he's gone. I stare at the lights on the ceiling again.

Bland-faced men lift me from my bed and place me into a black coffin-shaped transport pod hovering nearby. The lid closes. My blurry eyes look up through the pod's window at the white lights on the ceiling. The pod moves slowly down a hall.

Dizzy, I strain to focus. Every person who passes stares down at me through the glass, and I come to think of myself as being a part of some black parade. The hoverpod pauses. A soldier opens the lid of the pod. He runs his hands over me as he gazes at my breasts, which push up from the cinched-too-tight corset. I want to push him away when he touches them, but nothing about me works right. I try to concentrate on his face, but I don't recognize it so I quickly lose interest in him. He closes the lid to the pod and waves his hand and I move on.

The hoverpod enters a round-shaped room. Above me, there are tiers of seated Brothers, all shrouded in darkness as they gaze down upon me in my black bullet-shaped coffin. The hoverpod stops. The lid opens. I shift from the interior of the pod as the liner lifts me out by an extension arm and deposits me on a black tufted chaise lounge in the center of their horseless carousel.

Above my head hovers the turning hologram of the brilliant blue star, the symbol of the Alameeda Brotherhood. Beside me on a black table rest the two crowns that I had Kyon design for me. They're his and hers. I smile at them. They're so lovely. He did well.

"Kricket," a voice resonates in the room. It sounds like Kyon's. I'm disappointed when I lift my chin to see it's not him. It's Excelsior. He has an easy stride as he walks toward me; he owns the room, and he knows it. When he nears me, he goes down on a half-bended knee, so he can look me in the eyes. His are a colder blue than his son's—a soulless blue.

He's dressed in a dark military uniform with a holographic Star of Destiny on each of his pointed lapels. "Do you know where you are?" he asks me.

I look around. "I'm in a snake pit." A titter of male laughter rises from the theater-in-the-round.

"You're in the Universe Chamber in the House of Alameeda." He snaps his fingers. A hovering pod comes within reach of his fingertips. Lifting a cauterizing implement from it, it's clear by his easy glance that he's well acquainted with all of the hideous tools on it.

"It still looks like a snake pit."

Excelsior lifts a small device and presses a button on it. The metal cuffs on my wrists lift from my sides and slap against the metal T-shaped poles on either side of the chaise lounge by my ears. I try to yank them down, but it's too powerful.

He shows the long-handled, silver device to me before he presses the glowing trident to the pale skin of my right forearm. The smell of my skin burning is almost as painful as the claws of fire that run down my flesh. The pain is accompanied by a canyon-sized rush of terror that fills my chest. When he lifts it from me, I have a glowing, red wolf scratch.

"That should wake you up a bit," he whispers near my ear. I bite my lip because it's beginning to tremble and it's really important that I not show him the depth of my fear. "You're going to have to tell me when you've had enough. I have a tendency to go too far sometimes."

I don't shy from him; instead I force myself to laugh as I pant. "Does that usually scare all the little girls you torture?" Inside though, I know I'm not going to be able to keep this act up for very long. He has a dead heart. It barely beats. I recognize the look in his eyes; he can spin heartache into any color he chooses.

Above us, no one makes a sound. He replaces the silver cauterizer on the tray and picks up a razor blade. Its surgical sharpness gleams in the small spotlight we're under. He plays with it as he attaches it to a short-handled grip. Taking his time is meant to increase my panic.

"Do you know why you're here?" he asks me.

"I'm here to kill you."

Hisses of "Treason" come from several places and heights on the tiers.

"Why would you want to kill me, Kricket? I'm your creator. Your Maker."

"There are so many reasons to kill you, Excelsior. The fact that you think you're my creator is just one of them."

"I'm also the one who saved you from him," Excelsior says. He presses another button on his device. A hole opens up in the floor near us and a tank rises up from it. Inside, Manus, the Rafe regent, sways in the water of the medical stasis tank. His skin is blue-veined and translucent. Paper-thin pieces of it hang from him and float in the water. Gone is the dark, rich color of his hair. It's now bone-white and has shed in large patches. Curled in a fetal position, his gnarled hands warp, as if his bones have become waterlogged and bent. Whatever his medical tank is supposed to be doing for him, it stopped doing it a long time ago. He belongs in some horror-filled sideshow act, a dreadful curiosity to strike fear into chill seekers.

Excelsior prowls toward Manus. "I sent the Strikers to liberate you from his plan to mate with you. My creation!" He says the words as if he's disgusted by the very thought. He lifts the device in his hand again, and it gives off a stark, piercing noise that cracks the tank. Water squirts from between the cracks until it shatters the glass and spills Manus out onto the ebony floor. The stench that rises into the air makes me throw up in my mouth. The water quickly drains away into the hole in the floor, but it still reeks of decomposition and death.

Attendants are called in; they pick up pieces of Manus as his flesh falls off his bones. The mess of him is quickly discarded into a hatch in the floor and the water vacuumed up by sucker-bots. Attendants bring in water. Tall glasses are poured for each Brother in the theater seats above us. All the while Excelsior watches me with his killer-come-to-call stare.

When the attendants leave the room, he asks, "Do you know why you're really here, Kricket?"

He wants to tell me, so I let him. "Why am I really here, Excelsior?"

"It was the only way I could get all the Brothers in one room together. They came to see you. I knew that they would. They were hoping you'd kill me so they could be rid of me."

Choking noises sound from above us. One Brother stands up, holding his throat, and coughs up blood as he topples over the railing and falls into the snake pit with us. More gurgling and vomiting sounds cause chaos in the room. Brothers begin to succumb as blood pours out of their orifices. I look back at Excelsior, who is watching me with keen interest.

"You poisoned them!"

"When znou axicote is found to be the cause of their deaths, everyone will assume it was you who murdered them. I was impressed when I heard you'd poisoned the Rafe defense minister with it. It showed real brilliance and an unflinching desire to survive. You're the kind of genetic anomaly I strive to achieve in all my work."

"You say 'nature,' I say 'nurture.' I wasn't bred to do it. I was raised to do it," I reply, denying him any credit for the way I am.

"If only my son had turned out to be more like you. He's been an insufferable failure," Excelsior growls as he pushes another button on his device. In the floor, another hole opens up. Out of it rises a T-shaped metal whipping post. Kyon is manacled to it by his wrists. His unconscious body hangs listlessly, held erect by the magnetized irons on his wrists that stick to the top portion of the pole. He looks barely alive. Bare-chested, he's riddled with cuts and stab wounds. Blood has turned his bruised flesh red.

Inside, my heart feels like it is dying. I search for any sign from Kyon to indicate that he might still be alive. I need him to be alive. My throat aches with anger and unshed tears.

"He must love you, Kricket."

Pain rips through my chest. "Why do you say that?" My voice comes out raspy.

"When he found out that I had you, he offered himself to me in exchange for you. He said you'd go back to Earth and never bother me again. He said I could have your crowns, the ones you planned to use to steal my rightful throne from me."

"I *will* steal it from you!" I say with feigned righteous indignation. "I was meant to be the empress—to wear the crown of the high kings from which I descended. You will bow to me!" Inwardly I cringe. *That sounded so fake! Did I overdo the delusional priestess role?*

Excelsior's vicious eyes narrow at me and I think he sees right through me. "I'm the one who is descended from the high kings! You will all be made to bend to me!" He walks to the beautiful crowns, which lie gleaming on a bed of soft black velvet, and picks up the smaller circlet of heavy gold. It's not delicate, but solid and substantial, a crown that an ancient king would wear—one that a conquering hero would create. He tosses it aside. It clangs on the ebony floor, making my heart beat achingly in my chest.

He's not going to fall for it! I despair. I want to cry.

He lifts the other crown in his hand, testing the weight of it. It's the same style as the first one, only this one is bigger. "You'll never be able to kill me, Kricket. I've lived for thousands of floans. I have brought down whole nations of people. You're just a rabid dog to me—an experiment gone wrong. It will be nothing for me to end you."

I laugh. "I've already killed you, Excelsior. You just don't know it yet. You'll never wear that crown!" I fake a smile.

His hand curls tighter around the golden trophy. He raises the shiny circlet to his head. "You mean this crown?" he asks.

My smug smile fades.

Excelsior rests the golden crown on his head, pushing it down for a better fit. The spring-loaded trigger that Kyon designed trips. Four sharp prongs jut out from inside the crown, impaling Excelsior's skull. His shrill screams race through me, adding to my fear and fascination. Blood oozes from the sides of his temples just as turbine boring worms pour from the hollowed out wells in the golden chaplet. They burrow into his brain, their twisting, wiggling bodies squirming to cut through his bone. Higher-pitched, agonizing caterwauls wrench from his lips as he falls to his knees beside me, knocking his hovering cart of torture implements on the floor and scattering them. The scene is unbearably gruesome. I shy away as the worms devour his eyes.

His screaming stops and the only sound left in the room is my hacking breaths. My whole body is shaking. I open my eyes and try to stand, but my arms are still shackled and stuck to the poles beside my seat. I look around for the remote that Excelsior used earlier. I spot it on the ground beside his head. The worms are squiggling in and out of his cranium, their shiny, rippling white flesh turning rosy from the blood they've consumed. I try not to look at them as I rise up as far as I can and point my toe, sliding the remote closer to me with my foot. I use my pointed high heel to press several buttons. Kyon's manacles release, and he drops to the ground with a loud thud. I cringe, knowing that probably hurt him more. I point my toe at another button on the remote. My hand slips down from a pole. I tap the same button again and my other hand slips down as well.

Rising to my feet, I bypass Excelsior's corpse and run to Kyon. His skin is cold. I look behind me seeing torture devices strung out on the floor. Finding the razor blade, I clutch it and crawl back to Kyon's side. His blond hair is pulled back in a ponytail at the crown of his head. I gather what I can and lop off huge chunks of it. It regrows, the shorn-off pieces shriveling and melting away as I cut. I wait for a second to see if he'll regain consciousness. He doesn't. I put my ear against his chest. I can hear shallow beats. That's all I need to get me moving again.

I stand and run to the hovering coffin in the corner that brought me into the room. I touch it, and it moves with me like a baby duckling following its mother. I guide it to Kyon and push it to the ground. I don't know how to operate the extension arm, so instead, I push and shove Kyon with all of my might, rolling him over and over until I force him into the transporter. Sweating and panting, I place my hand on top of the coffin, closing the lid.

I guide the black transporter to the door, which I open. My plan is to bully and intimidate my way out of here. With that in mind, I square my shoulders and almost run straight into Dobrey. He puts his finger to his lips, reaching out and plucking something off the bodice of my dress. He shows me the little disk before dropping it on the ground and crushing it with his heel.

"You did it!" he breathes, as if in awe of me.

"What did I do?" I ask.

"You brought down the Brotherhood! Everyone in Alameeda saw it. The entire world will see it by nightfall!"

"You recorded it!" I exclaim.

He nods vehemently. "I fed it live stream to the hologram network. They aired it in real time. There is a crowd forming outside as we speak! They're attacking the Strikers, demanding the release of their empress!"

"We have to get out of here. My consort is wounded. I have to get him help! Will you help me?" I ask. My knees are shaking so hard that I don't think I'll be able to keep standing if I don't move.

"I have a trift. I can sneak you out of here."

"I'll pay you back. I swear it."

He sheds his black lab coat and hands it to me. "Put this on." His scrawny hands touch the lid of Kyon's transporter. "It's this way,"

Darken the Stars

he says. "The Strikers and everyone else are watching the crowds at the front of the building. We'll head to the hangar."

"Do you have a code to get this collar off me?' I ask as we traverse an empty corridor.

He shakes his head no. I try not to worry about it. Instead, I help guide the transporter, running ahead to open up doors. There are a few guards posted at the entrance to the hangar. Dobrey hides me around the corner in an empty exam room while he rushes over to the guards. "There are people breaking into corridor three two five! They have sanctumizers!" He points away from me, before wringing his hands. The guards all run in the direction he indicated.

I don't wait for him to get me. I push Kyon's hoverpod out into the corridor again and we hurry into the hangar. He takes me to almost the last spot in the garage. We stop at a ship that looks like a huge milk carton. "What is this?" I ask.

"It's my trift!" he growls, while opening the hatch and loading Kyon into it. "What does it look like?"

"I've just never seen one that looks like this."

"Like what?" he asks, sounding offended.

"Like this amazing," I reply.

He closes the hatch. "She's superfast. I just had the engine modified. Guess what I used for my starter code?" he asks rhetorically because he tells me, "It's Dobrey's Domain. That's catchy, right?"

"Cryptic," I reply.

"She's my—"

Dobrey's head explodes. I make a noise that's close to a scream. Dobrey's headless body crumbles to the ground. The guards Dobrey distracted earlier run toward me with their guns raised. Reacting out of terror, I hunch over and dive into the open doorway of the ugly trift.

I locate the door button and press it. The door closes. I scan the control panel. It looks almost nothing like any of Kyon's trifts.

259

This one is a simple manual transmission. I enter Dobrey's starter code and the trift lifts off the ground, hovering. Directing the craft straight up, I angle it so that the guards can't shoot me as I wheel it in the direction of the distant mountains.

Knowing which way to go is not a problem. All I have to do is find the center of Urbenoster and I'll find Kyon's house. I slip into traffic, hiding among the pack. As I pass among the buildings, I see Newsreel playing on the sides of them all. My face is everywhere, along with Excelsior's. They play over and over the turbine worms chewing through his skull. I begin to shake again. My skin grows clammy.

I locate the river and follow it. Approaching the house, I head right for it. A wailing sound erupts in the cabin. It feels as if it stabs me. I try to turn it off, but it continues its incessant noise. Someone's voice breaks through a speaker in the cockpit of the vehicle. "White Sestin four five two four two, abort from your current course or you will be shot down."

I press the blinking button on the control panel. "This is Kricket! Can you hear me?"

"Kricket Ensin?" the voice asks.

"Yes! It's me! I need your help! Please! I need to land and I don't know how!"

"Do you want us to bring you in on auto?" the voice asks.

"You can do that?" I ask.

"Affirmative. I just have to lock on to you. Would you like me to do that?"

"Yes! Do that! Please do that!"

"I am locked on. Where would you like to touch down?" he asks.

"Close to the house. I need medical assistance. I need Fulton!"

"He will be notified. I will bring you in near Victory."

"Thank you," I reply. I want to fall apart now as I let go of the controls and the ship flies on its own.

Landing in an interior courtyard. I scramble out of my seat. The hatch opens when I press a button by the frame. Exiting, I find Fulton waiting for me. I run to him and fall into his arms. I hug him as if he was a beloved parent. Hot tears burn my eyes. "Kyon needs your help," I cry against his chest.

"You brought Kyon back with you?" he asks incredulously.

I nod. Pulling away, I look up into his eyes. "Excelsior hurt him. I don't know how badly. Will you fix him?" I know I sound childish. I can't help it though. I grip his wrist, ready to wring his agreement out of him.

"I will help him," Fulton assures me. He gently removes my hand and directs men to unload Kyon from the back of the trift.

They take him to a surgery that has all of the trappings of a real medical facility. Men that I've never met before puzzle over his injuries. Some of the wounds are healing faster than they can account for. He has suffered an intense amount of damage to some of his organs—all but his heart. It was untouched. When they finish cauterizing his wounds, they bandage him and give him sedatives. He won't be able to wake up for a while.

I order everyone out except for Fulton. "Do you have scissors?" I ask him.

He produces them from his pocket. He's way ahead of me. Going to the bed, he cuts Kyon's hair again. A rush of blood flushes his cheeks. "You have to take him back to the island, Fulton."

"We can leave within the hour. I will have everything arranged."

"I can't go with you," I reply.

"What do you mean? I believe the city will be unsafe for you for the near future."

I'm confused about what to say—what to tell him. "I'm going to be hunted, Fulton. If I go to the island with you, they'll kill both Kyon and me. His only chance is if we split up. They'll follow me. That will give him time to recover."

"Who are they?"

"There are other males like Kyon who survived Excelsior. They'll be fighting for their own supremacy soon. I will be seen as in the way of that. I will have to run."

"We can protect you on the island—"

"Think about it, Fulton! A bunch of angry men with abilities just like Kyon's will have an ax to grind with me. I have a sister. They follow her. I threaten her reign. It's a fight I can't win."

"What will you do?" he asks.

"I plan to travel," I say evasively.

"He's going to be impossible to live with when he wakes and finds you gone."

"Just as long as he wakes up," I say.

"You love him."

"Don't be silly, Fulton. He's a ruthless killer."

"He's *your* ruthless killer."

"I'm giving him back," I reply.

"He'll never let you."

"I gave him what he wanted most. Maybe he can be happy with that."

"Which was?" he asks.

"Revenge."

"I don't think that was what he wanted most." He stands. "I will take him to the island within the part. I make no promises for what he'll do when he recovers."

"The Tempest will be too busy for a while hunting me and establishing their government to care too much about him. But be careful. They're dangerous."

"You're speaking about Kyon Ensin. I fear for these other men and for your sister."

"Don't. They're really not worth your time."

"You are, though," he replies. "You're worth it."

I have to bite my bottom lip to keep it from trembling. "I have to go too, before they find me." I stand and give him a very brief hug before I turn and run from the room.

I don't stop running until I make it to Phlix's room. Pounding on the door until she answers it, I fall into her arms when she opens them to me. "I thought you were dead," she says as she rests her cheek against my head.

"Me too," I whisper.

"I watched it all—everything. Your crowns worked!"

I ignore her and say, "We have to go now."

"Are you sure?" she asks. Her trepidation is clearly etched on her face. "I think that all the Brothers are dead. We don't have to run—"

"We're in more danger now than we ever were."

"Danger? From who?"

"I have another sister. Her name is Astrid. She wants to be empress. She has males who she saved who are our genetically enhanced brothers—they have our abilities—and they want revenge. I will explain everything later, but we have to leave right now before they arrive."

"I am ready. Shall I get the gear?"

"Yes," I reply.

She goes to her closet and I shed the black lab coat. I don't feel like I have time to change. I will have to do it when we get to the trift I plan to use to take us to the basin near the Forest of Omnicron. If all goes well, we won't need any of this gear, but I can't rely on it. So many things can go wrong.

Phlix hands me one of the two backpacks and a flipcart. The backpacks have special straps on the outside of them that hold the flipcarts secure. When the backpacks are on, we look like snowboarders heading to the mountains.

Leaving her room, we enter the overup and take it down to the garden level. Exiting the lift, we walk toward Kyon's study. I slow when I near the fire snapping in the grate. Someone is seated in the green chair, sipping on a fat tumbler of amber liquid. I drop my backpack, because it will slow me down when I run.

"Greetings, Kricket. Your father was proud of you. You killed Excelsior just as he always knew you would."

"Yeah? Well, tell him I said he's welcome. And tell him good-bye for me."

"Good-bye? You think you're leaving us?" he asks, setting down his drink. His golden dreadlocks shine brightly in the glow of the fire. "But I'm here to take you to see him. I just have to kill your consort first. Where have you hidden Kyon, Kricket? I'm very tired and I don't feel like playing your games now."

Slowly, I inch away from him. I look toward the stairs and the only thought in my mind is making it to them. I look around for Phlix, but she's nowhere in sight. She's hidden herself away in the shadow land. I envy her that ability.

In front of me, Giffen stands. He growls as he says, "I'll ask you once again. Where is Kyon Ensin?"

CHAPTER 18
HALF AWAKE AND ALMOST DEAD

Giffen lifts me up off my feet telepathically and pulls me into his waiting arms. I lose my breath when I hit his chest hard. "You didn't think we were going to just let you leave, did you? You're too dangerous for that."

"What are you going to do to me?" I ask.

"There's a place in the annexed area that I have set up for you. It's actually very beautiful. You'll be comfortable there. Your sister can visit you."

"And you can all keep an eye on me?"

"It's the compromise that I worked out to keep you alive. Otherwise, you're dead."

"So I'll be a prisoner for the rest of my life?"

"It's better than being dead."

"You can let go of me now. I'm not going to run. I know it's pointless."

He sets me on my feet. From behind him, Phlix says, "I have another option for you, Kricket." Electricity pulses out of the Taser-like gun that she presses into his side. He convulses and flops on the ground fish-out-of-water style. "You can come with me to Earth like we planned."

"Phlix!" I'm almost too surprised to move.

"No one is making us their prisoners again," she says. "I will hurt them all if they try."

I grab Phlix's hand. "Let's go. That shock doesn't last long."

Phlix tugs back on my hand, saying, "Wait! We have to get our packs!" We put them on, and then run up the stairs to the balcony level of Foundation. We scurry through countless corridors to the tower called Kingdom. We take the tree pillar elevators down to the garden level of the creepy art gallery. "All we have to do is make it to the Hallafast in the topiary maze outside. It's not very far," I whisper. Clutching her hand, I lead the way to the giant doors. I open one and pause. Outside, the courtyard glows with fire. The Hallafast that we need to make our escape is a raging ball of orange light and choking black smoke. My heart crashes in my chest.

I sink to my knees on the ground. "I'm dead. I'm so dead."

"What's wrong?" Phlix asks. She looks past me to the aircraft. Her soft gasp is a crushing weight on me. She pulls the door closed, slamming it. She looks around us.

"We're not giving up," she says, squaring her shoulders. "We're leaving."

She tugs on my upper arm and pulls me up. We scramble back toward the pillars, and Giffen suddenly appears at the top of the gallery. He looks pissed.

"Shadow land!" I yell.

Phlix pulls us into her secret world. She grasps my hand and we back up from Giffen as he descends the pillar onto the garden level with us. "He can probably sense us, Phlix. He's creepy like that," I whisper.

Giffen picks up a chair telepathically and spins it around as if it's caught in a tornado. It whirls around the room, coming so close to us that we both have to drop on the floor to avoid it. "We have to go," Phlix whimpers, grasping my hand.

"I know!"

We both back up, coming up against the Naren Falls landscape. We turn around and stare at the dark, canvaslike opening that now has a view of the two Etharian moons visible in the night sky. "We have to try," Phlix whispers.

"Are you sure?" I ask.

"It's worth the risk. On the count of two," Phlix breathes. "One—"

"—two!" we say in unison. With our hands clasped, I scrunch my eyes as I jump with Phlix into the portal.

I feel the impact of the grassy lawn beneath me. My hand is torn away from Phlix's. I roll away and I lay on the ground, looking up at Inium and Sinter in the sky. I spit out the dirt in my mouth.

"Phlix," I call, not seeing her anywhere.

"Here," she calls back.

"Where," I scream, panicking. I wiggle out of my backpack getting to my feet. I don't even see a shadow of her anywhere.

She suddenly appears a few yards away still attached to her backpack. "Sorry. You rolled out of my shadow land," she explains.

I rush to her and hug her. "Holy shit! You did it! Your shadow saved us!" I laugh and start jumping up and down with her in my arms. She squeezes me back, jumping up and down too.

"We did it! We did it!" she squeals. I don't know when we stop jumping and stand there crying in each other's arms, but I eventually wipe my eyes on my sleeve and pull away from her.

"We have to go."

"Put on the terrain outfit," she orders. "It's made from that same fabric as the camouflage blankets you asked me to get." As I locate them among my gear, she adds, "You can change the setting on the clothing. See, just press these buttons and it can make different patterns." She demonstrates the settings. "The camouflage setting is probably the best here. I packed you terrain shoes, and night-vision glasses."

We change quickly. I braid my hair while Phlix locates the compass. With our night-vision glasses, we pore over the laminated terrain map. "We can't waste time. We have to get as far away from here tonight as possible. They're going to figure out where we're going."

Phlix goes to my backpack and pulls out a dark cap. "Here, wear this. Your hair is like a beacon," she says. "And don't worry so much. We have me. I can hide us."

"You can hide us for about a part and a half," I reply.

"That is plenty of time to lose anyone."

Not Cavars, I think, but I don't say it out loud.

We mount up on our flipcarts, and I lead the way through a path that takes us by incredible views of the valley below. I try not to think about the fact that New Amster is down there somewhere in the darkness. I hope for our sakes that they're not thinking about us either.

Riding a flipcart is fairly easy under normal circumstances: flat terrain, few tree branches to slap me in the face, and the agility that comes with not having a thirty-pound backpack. Now, though, we have to make frequent stops to rest, stretch our backs, rehydrate, and check our course. Just before dawn, the two of us are so tired that we can hardly stay on our flipcarts.

"We have to find a safe place to sleep," I say. "Keep your eyes open for a cave or something that will hide us from aircraft."

Not long after, Phlix spots a fallen tree. It's one of those enormous trees that a city bus could drive through easily without hitting traffic on the other side. The tree has fallen against a rock formation, forming a lean-to of sorts. "What do you think?" she asks wearily.

"I say yes. I say hang up a camouflage blanket over this branch and it is lights out."

We place our gear against the rock and spread out a blanket. We drape our remaining blanket over a low branch before we climb inside and pull the blanket over the opening to conceal our presence. Phlix rummages in her backpack, then she tosses me a protein bar.

It tastes exactly like the ones I ate before when I journeyed here with Trey, except now it doesn't just taste like cat poop. It tastes like cat poop and freedom. I eat every bite without complaint.

"Do you want me to take the first watch?" she asks like she might die if she has to stay awake a second longer.

"No. We both sleep."

"Isn't that dangerous?" she asks.

"We're either caught or we're not—dead or we're not. We don't have any weapons and your shadow land only works if you're awake to use it, so . . . we don't have to worry about it."

"Okay." She yawns. "You make dying in my sleep not sound so bad."

"There are worse things, huh?"

ॐ

I awake to a deep, rumbling growl close to our tree fort. It makes every hair on my body stand on end. I don't move other than the widening of my eyes. I stare at Phlix. She heard it too, if the look of terror in her blue eyes is any indication. Something big snuffles around the base of the fallen tree only meters from us. Phlix's hand finds mine when the beast outside howls so loud it shakes dry, dead needles from the branches above our heads. Something heavy crashes against the other side of the tree trunk. The ground shakes. Phlix squeaks, scrunching her eyes tight. Frozen, not knowing if it's better to stay or better to leave, I wait, holding my breath.

Silence.

Phlix breathes, "Is it—"

"Shh." I listen some more.

I sit up, leaning back against the rock. Phlix moves next to me. A darkening pool is seeping beneath the tree by my feet. I pull the blanket away from it. "What is it," Phlix whispers.

"I don't know," I reply. On my knees, I crawl near the oozing dark patch. Touching my finger to it, it comes away red. Cringing, I rub my finger in the dirt, trying to get the blood off. I join Phlix again. "It's blood," I say near her ear.

"Blood" Blood from what?" she asks.

"I have no idea," I reply. "Stay here and I'll go look."

"I'm coming with you," she whispers, clutching my hand so that I don't leave her behind.

We creep out of our tree fort. I pick up a medium-sized stone, and grip it tight, ready to throw it at anything that moves. It's growing dark, but it's not quite there yet. We have to walk around the tree's massive roots in order to see what's on the other side. With cautious steps, I lead us there. I press my back to the tree's uprooted base. Holding my breath, I peak around the side. My heart hammers in my chest and I pull myself back, flattening against it again.

"What is it?" Phlix asks urgently.

"Hovercar-sized wolf with horrifying fangs."

"What's it doing?"

I peek around the tree again. It hasn't moved. "It's either sleeping or it's dead." I take a deep breath and sneak around the end of the tree. Walking slowly near the beast, I can't see any breathing. The head comes into view. It has several recurve arrows sticking out of its face. I straighten immediately, turning around and glancing at the tree line behind me. Nothing moves, but I know we're being watched.

Hurrying back to Phlix, I grasp her elbow and urge her back to our fort. "Cavars are watching us. They killed that thing. Let's get our packs and move."

"How do you know Cavars killed it?"

"They used recurves," I growl. "No one else uses those."

"Why would they help us?" she asks.

"Maybe they want the pleasure of tracking us and killing us."

"Like sport?" she asks.

"I don't think we should hang around and find out." We grab our backpacks and consult our map quickly. Hopping on our flip-carts, we leave as soundlessly as possible. We travel without incident for the next few hours, traversing fields by surfing waves of flowers.

When we stop for a water break, I pull my flask from my backpack and take a sip. There's not much left. We'll have to find more soon. Phlix makes a frustrated sound next to me. She's pulling all the contents from her backpack out. When it's empty, she glances at me with fear in her eyes. "I think I left my water flask where we slept last night." I extend my flask to her. She takes it and sips from it. "We're going to need more water soon," she says guiltily.

"Then we look for some on the way. Does the map show where we might find some?" I ask.

She shakes her head. "It just shows the basin where we depart Ethar. That's still at least two rotations away if we don't increase our pace."

"Then let's increase our pace," I reply. "There has to be some somewhere."

At the next stop, we waste valuable time looking for water, but come up empty. It worries me. Maybe we can just push through this without water, I think. Then I look at Phlix, whose normally pale face is flushed and sweaty, and I worry that she won't be able to handle it. She's not used to this much exertion. I hand her what's left in my flask and insist that she drink it.

Morning comes, and I find myself licking the dew from leaves to ease my dry throat. Searching for shelter to rest during daylight, we find a niche in a rock formation. It's only large enough to fit the backpacks and the two of us. We place our flipcarts on the ground inside and lay on top of them, using our backpacks as pillows. Phlix has several muscle cramps during the day that keep her awake. As soon as night falls, we emerge from our hiding place, gathering our stuff together quickly.

"What's that?" Phlix asks, pointing at a shiny metal object on a nearby stump. Walking to it, she reaches out her hand for it.

"Don't touch it," I warn her.

"But it's my flask! And it's full of water!"

"Leave it," I bark.

"Where did it come from?"

"Them," I say, grabbing her hand and pulling it back from the flask. I look for some kind of trap, but I can't see one. It doesn't matter. The water itself could be contaminated.

"Them? Who are they?"

"I don't know, but they aren't us, so let's go." Right before we get on our flipcarts, I hear the hum of airships. Phlix glances up at the same time I do.

I tug on her arm to pull her back toward the hole, when she says, "Wait!" She closes her eyes and concentrates. "We're shadows, Kricket. They can't see us," she promises.

I wait. Two formations of hawk-like ships pass over us slowly, searching the area. One of the ships I recognize because I've been in it before. It's Giffen's ship. He's looking for us. "That airship there"— I point to Giffen's ship—"belongs to the guy you electrocuted in Kyon's home."

"Do you think he's still angry?" she asks with a weary smile.

"He's sort of a grudge holder."

"That's unfortunate. He's a bit on the handsome side."

"He is," I agree.

We quit speaking when the ship in question dives toward us abruptly. My heart claws at my chest to get out. The ship hovers near us, as if it's checking us out. I hold my breath, not that it will help, but I have no control over it. Just as abruptly as it descended, it ascends, climbing back to rejoin its formation. When it disappears from sight, Phlix sits down and wraps her arms around her knees. "I thought they saw us for a second."

I crouch down next to her. "Me too."

Using her gift has clearly drained her energy even more. "We should go," she says.

We travel half the night without resting. We stop when the trees get denser and it takes more effort to weave between them. It's actually good news, because the aircraft that we heard earlier will have a harder time finding us with this much vegetation. I leave Phlix to rest by our backpacks while I scout around for water. She's listless and has a hard time concentrating on anything I say to her.

"Did you find anything?" she asks with her eyes closed when I walk back to her.

"No," I reply.

"Okay," she says and gets to her feet. "We should be there soon. I can make it."

"We'll make it," I say confidently, but I may be lying.

I repack the backpacks, taking the heaviest items from Phlix and putting them in my pack. I lead the way, checking the compass and the map frequently. We come upon a small hill, and just as I crest the top of it, I spot Phlix's flask in the middle of the path we've been following. My flipcart flies over it. I don't stop. Glancing behind me, I notice that Phlix sees the flask too, but she ignores it as well and we keep going.

Stopping at a big tree, I wait for Phlix to catch up. When she does, she dismounts from her flipcart and sits down with her backpack still on. She leans it against the tree and closes her eyes. I shrug off my backpack and put it next to her. "I'll go look for water," I whisper.

"They're watching us, aren't they? Taunting us."

"Yeah," I reply.

"It doesn't matter. Even this is better than Pike."

"We're going to make it. I promise."

"Kricket," Jax says from somewhere behind me. I straighten and turn to see him walking slowly toward me. In his hand, he carries

Phlix's flask of water. "I think you dropped this." He cautiously moves forward.

"What is it?" I ask.

"Its just water. That's all," he replies honestly.

He stops a few feet away and stretches the bottle toward me. I look around between the trees, but I don't see anyone else with him, not that I thought I would. The only time I'll see them is when they want me to see them. I take the flask from Jax and back away from him. Moving to Phlix, I unstop it and hold it out to her. "It's okay," I say. "Its just water."

"You're sure?" she asks.

"Yes. He isn't lying," I tell her.

Phlix takes the flask from my hand and takes a sip and then another. She hands it to me. I shake my head, saying, "I'm okay. You drink it."

"You need some too," she urges.

"Maybe later," I reply and straighten.

"Your friend is right, Kricket. You should drink some water," Jax says worriedly. "You haven't been eating either. You're going to be sick. Do you need food too?"

"No. I don't need anything. Are you almost finished, Phlix? We have to go." I start to walk to where I left my flipcart, but Trey emerges from behind the tree next to me. He grabs me by the throat and pushes me up against a nearby tree. In his hand he holds a bottle of water.

Scowling at me, he says through clenched teeth, "Drink this!" His jaw is so ridged I'm surprised he can speak at all.

I wasn't aware of just how betrayed I feel until this moment. I know it's wrong to blame him for doing the right thing—for doing what he had to do to save everyone and everything he loves . . . everyone but me. I think I'm the most hurt by the fact that I'm not like him. I would've chosen him over everything else. The whole world could've burned down and I would've pulled him from the wreckage of it.

"No. I don't want anything from you, Trey."

His violet eyes narrow as his hand lets go of my neck and he clasps my chin, squeezing it so that my mouth opens. He tilts my head back and pours water between my lips, making me swallow large gulps of it. I choke a little, coughing and gasping, but otherwise he isn't hurting me.

By the time the bottle of water is empty, the front of my shirt is wet and I'm livid. Tossing the empty bottle aside, Trey shifts his hand back to my throat and holds me steady against the tree. His violet eyes never leave mine as we try to kill each other with drop-dead stares.

Then Trey holds his hand out to Jax, "Hand me a protein bar," he demands.

"Sir . . . I think she's capable of—"

Trey's scowl deepens as he growls, "Hand. Me. A. Protein. Bar!"

Jax follows orders and places one in his hand. Trey tears off the wrapper with his teeth and holds the protein bar up to my lips. I clamp my mouth shut, but he forces a bite into my mouth. I turn my face away from him and spit it out onto the ground.

Dropping the protein bar, Trey winds back his fist. I cringe, steeling myself for the hit. Instead, he punches the trunk of the tree by my head. His fist comes away bloody again and again, but he doesn't stop. "Jax," I whisper. Trey continues to hold me by my neck as he pounds the tree with his fist. "Jax!" I yell. "Give me a protein bar."

Trey's bloody knuckles rest against the bark of the tree. I feel Jax place the protein bar in the palm of my hand. Bringing it to my lips, I take a bite, chewing it. I almost choke on it because of the lump in my throat, but I manage to get it down. I eat the whole thing in three bites. Trey lets go of my neck. He leans forward and rests his forehead against mine. I don't move; I just close my eyes and breathe for a moment. Then I put my hands on his chest and push him away from me. I don't meet his eyes. I can't. Instead, I duck away from him and look at Phlix. She's on her feet, staring at me with fear in her eyes.

"Are you ready to go?" I ask her in a broken voice. She nods. I turn and gather up my backpack, hitching it onto my shoulders. Then I mount my flipcart and take off in the direction of the basin. When I look back over my shoulder, the only person I see behind me is Phlix.

We travel all the rest of the night through the Forest of Omnicron at a faster pace than before. According to the map, we will make it to the water containing the portal to Earth just before dawn.

As we rest for the last push to the mountain that forms the basin, Phlix asks, "How will we know where to enter the water?"

"I don't know," I admit. "I was sort of unconscious when Trey dragged me out of it last time."

"Trey? You mean that enormous Cavar back there who made you eat that protein bar is the person who brought you here?"

"Yes," I reply.

"He's in love with you."

"No. He isn't."

"Yes, he is."

"He's too good for me. I never would've made him happy."

"He would've been happy the rest of his life with you," she replies quietly. "He will live a lonely existence without you. I only hope he's gracious in defeat."

"What do you mean?"

"He doesn't strike me as someone who ever allows himself to lose."

"Believe me, Trey will figure out soon that he dodged a bullet."

"He's a soldier. He lives for bullets."

"Please drop it, Phlix," I beg. My voice is raw. It feels like I swallowed chunks of glass.

She reaches out and strokes my hair. "He'll wait for the day he can say that you're his again. You don't have to fret about it now. It's the reason neither of you said good-bye to each other back there. It's not over."

We travel through the last part of the Forest of O on foot, carrying our flipcarts on our backs. From the cover of the trees, we see the water. It's amazing in the darkness. The surface is black in every area except where the portal resides. In that place, it's as if sunshine rises to the surface.

We make our final preparations. Finding the tankoids that will allow us to breathe for a time underwater, we set them aside to carry them to the water's edge. I find the small box that I'd asked Phlix to pack for me, the one gift-wrapped with a pink bow. I set that aside too. Phlix raises her eyebrows. She must not have peeked inside. I knew she wouldn't. Everything else that we no longer need gets abandoned in a pile there. Taking turns, we use strong tape to fasten our flipcarts and backpacks more securely to us. Then we fasten rope around that to make sure our gear stays with us, no matter what.

Howls call out in the moonlight. My flesh erupts in goose bumps and my back bows in fear. It's unbearably real; this feeling that we still might not make it. I step out of the trees, my knees shaking, exposed on the smooth rocks to the cool breeze coming off the mountain peak. I'm as desolate as a prayer in the wind.

Phlix takes my hand and squeezes it. It makes me feel a little less unholy and unwanted. "I've shadowed us," she says, "but know that once we reach the water, the ripples will reveal us to whoever watches."

We both walk hunched over to the illuminated path at the water's edge. Letting go of her hand, I find a large rock there and leave my pink-bowed box on it. Phlix doesn't comment. She puts the tankoid in her mouth and sets her nose clamp, preparing to enter the water. I do the same.

Nodding to her, I try to wade into the water in a way that causes the fewest ripples. It's colder than I remember. I'm not sure if I begin to quake from fear or from the frigid temperature. Either way, it numbs me to the terror we face as huge spotlights shine down on us from above. Hovering airships, the kind that New Amster soldiers use, descend from far above us. I prepare to dive beneath the water when a ship sets down on the bank near us and the maw of it opens up. Matchstick men emerge like roaches.

From the far bank, I hear an agonizingly beautiful voice yell, "Baw-da-baw!" Blue laser fire comes from the far bank, near the sandy dunes and tall reeds, scattering New Amster soldiers along the shore as they scurry away for cover. Treading water for a moment, I watch the Cavars pin down the men sent to kill me.

Phlix touches my arm and nods. I nod back. We both stop treading water and submerge into the glowing abyss. The unendurable need for oxygen is not present this time around; the tankoid takes care of it. I'm able to swim without my lungs being turned to fire. The current becomes stronger the deeper I dive, pulling me into the bright light. My skin ripples as the pressure increases. It tears at my golden-blond hair, which streams behind me. I can't see Phlix. I pray that she's still with me. I need her probably more than she needs me.

The riptide of the portal slows and the glow begins to dim. My skin is snowy white as I make for the watery hilltop speckled with underwater stars. The current becomes almost nonexistent. It lets go of me. I struggle and tumble in the cold pool as the heavy pack on my back weighs me down. Fighting to reach the bank I can see ahead, my breathing becomes shallower, because the small tank of oxygen is running low. I almost weep when my feet scrape the incline of the bank, and I stand with my head above the water. I trip forward, wading until I fall to my knees and crawl the rest of the way through the black volcanic sand to the lip of the pool. I rip the tankoid from my mouth, taking my first breath on Earth in so many months.

Beside me, Phlix spits out her tankoid, coughing and wheezing as she collapses with her cheek in the sand. We stare at each other, panting and gasping and in shock. I reach out and take her numb hand in mine. I know we have to move soon so that we don't become hypothermic, but I can't seem to make myself do it just yet.

Phlix's voice reverberates in the cave, bouncing off the dripping stalactites that threaten us from the rock above. "Your friends saved us."

I nod because I can't speak. I can't talk about it now or I'll never make it. I'll just lay here for the rest of my life with a dead heart. She seems to sense that I'm close to tears.

Instead she asks, "What was in the box?"

"A letter to my sister and a warning not to follow us."

"Do you think it will work?" she asks.

"I hope so, but we won't take any chances. We'll have to hide. We can't go to Chicago. We have to start over."

"Where would you like to do that?" Phlix asks.

"Have you ever been to college?"

"I've never been anywhere."

Rising to my feet even though I'd rather not, I help Phlix up. We unwrap each other from ropes and tape. Unfastening our flipcarts, we carry the boards out of the glowing chamber, away from the pool. We put on our night-vision glasses once more, and it's easier than I expect to find my way to the bottom of the cliff wall; I merely have to follow the footprints on the ground.

Phlix shows me the holographic buttons to press to change the mode and make the flipcart elevate straight up. Hers rises faster than mine. As I rise past the rock, I remember almost dying in this spot. When I'm almost to the top, I don't know why, but I look down into the darkness and shout out, "Baw-da-baw!" The sound echoes.

Then I'm at the summit, where Phlix is already waiting for me. We shift our flipcarts back to hover mode and surf our way through the rest of the cave. The night sky greets us as we emerge from the dark mouth of the cavern.

Phlix lets out a deep gasp as she sees the moon for the first time. It's autumn and the moon glows orange, hanging low in the sky. We pause for a moment, staring at it. "They call that a harvest moon," I say, as my damp hair stirs in the warm fall breeze. "It's not always like that."

"Where is the other moon?" she asks.

"There's only one moon," I reply.

"That rips my heart out. It must get so lonely," she murmurs.

"It's not alone. It has the world."

EPILOGUE

Dear Astrid,

If you're reading this letter, then you know that I've chosen to leave Ethar and live out my life under different stars. I promise to stay far from you, beneath Earth's darker skies. It's my hope to become a vapor trail, fading from your world and from your mind.

Memories of you are the most desolate aspect of all of this for me, because I know that I once loved you. I'm certain of it. Whenever I try to remember you, it's as if I'm looking into the sun. I see glimpses of the little girl you once were, but it begins to hurt my eyes and it fades and I'm forced to look away. What I think I know is you're the well and I'm the hollow. You're the tree with roots and I'm the swallow. I hope you don't think I never loved you because I did. I spent my life looking for you—for Astrid.

I don't want to be a star, caged by the night. I won't be hung up in the sky for others to decide how high I can soar. No one gets to do that but me. I can't be someone's possession. I won't be owned. My heart has grown fiercer; I want wildflowers without worms. I want love, but on my own terms.

With all of my reasons to go, a few make me want to stay. I will miss dancing in caves. I will miss sleeping in graves. I will miss days filled with honey. I will miss Wayra because he's funny. I will miss seas bright with stars. I will miss hovercars. I will miss my Crystal

Clear Moment. I will miss a love that I had chosen. I will miss betting on asses. I will miss puke and rally clashes. I will miss ships in the sky. I will miss my lover who lies.

For all those things, as well as for the affection I feel in my heart for the people whose lives had become hopelessly intertwined with mine, I tried to ensure that each of you received what you wanted most. You, Astrid, will be empress. Pan will rebuild Ethar. Giffen will get to live out his days at home instead of on Earth. Jax will have Rafe back, and Wayra will too. Trey will have his family, and Kyon has had his revenge.

No, I don't regret coming to Ethar.

I fell in love . . . maybe even twice.

Along with this letter, I have left a gift for you—a token of my affection. The street vendors in Urbenoster began selling these little, plastic toy tiaras upon my return to Alameeda. I have a hazy memory of owning something similar to this one when I was about five. I don't recall if you had one as well, but I'm betting that you did. You're the empress now, and I accept your sovereignty over Ethar. You will probably make a better ruler than I ever would. However, should you send your people to Earth to harm me, I'll find a way to make your crown as worthless as this one you find here.

Farewell to you and your royal throne.

Hugs and kisses, I'm going home.

Your sister,

Kricket

Acknowledgments

God, all things are possible through You. Thank you for Your infinite blessings and for allowing me to do what I love: write.

To my readers and bloggers: Thank you! The outpouring of love that I receive from all of you is mind-blowing. Your generosity toward me is humbling. You make me want to write a thousand books.

Tom Bartol, you're my best friend. I cannot imagine my world without you in it. I love you.

Max and Jack Bartol, I count myself as the most fortunate person in the world to have you both in my life. Thank you for knowing when to let me write and when to rescue me from my computer.

Mom, thank you for your constant love and support.

Jason Kirk, thank you for challenging me and inspiring me to grow as a writer. I'm grateful.

Ben Smith, you're a superstar! Thank you for your time and for your hard work marketing this project. It means the world to me.

Britt Rogers, you're such a lovely person. Thank you for your support at 47North.

Tamar Rydzinski, one of the best days of my life was when you agreed to be my agent. Thank you for always having my back.

To my lovely friends: Georgia Cates, Shelly Crane, Samantha Young, Rachel Higginson, Angeline Kace, Lila Felix, thank you all for your unwavering support.

Michelle Leighton, I love you! Your heart could warm moonlight.

Glossary

Abersuctonal: an antidote for znou axicote poisoning.

Alameeda: one of the five clan-houses of Ethar. An ally of Wurthem. Ruling body is the Alameeda Brotherhood. A member of the Alameeda House.

Alameeda Striker: a member of an elite body of troops trained to serve the Alameeda Brotherhood.

Amster Rushes: an ancient city where skeletal remains of skyscrapers are located near the border of Comantre in the no-man's-land restricted/protected area of Ethar.

baw-da-baw: a war cry used by Cavars in the Rafian military—means "hoorah."

Biequine: a competition wherein a rider takes a spix through a course of obstacles and shoots targets for both points and the best time.

Black Math: a virus that decimated the population of Ethar approximately a thousand years ago.

Brigadet: a member of the Rafian military police on the Ship of Skye.

Cavar: a member of an elite body of troops trained to serve on land and sea; a member of the Rafian military of Ethar, similar to Earth's Marine.

click: approximately one kilometer.

Comantre: one of the five clan-houses of Ethar. An ally of Rafe. A member of the Comantre House.

commodus: a bathroom.

copperclaw: the exotic flower symbolically used in the weddinglike commitment ceremony in which a Brother of the Brotherhood weds his consort priestess.

Crystal Clear Moments: small, crystal-like figurines that animate when put into a star chamber gravity field.

Em: an honorific denoting an ambassador.

Ethar: a planet in a dimension similar to Earth's.

EVS819: Etharian Virtual Strain 891. The gene or genetic mutation that allows for extrasensory gifts.

Etharian: a native of Ethar.

Fitzforest: Thursday.

Fitzlutzer: Monday.

Fitzmartin: Wednesday.

Fitzover: Sunday.

Fitzsetter: Tuesday.

Fitzsumptner: Saturday.

Fitzwinter: Friday.

fleat: one minute.

flester: one week.

flipcart: a hovercraft skateboard.

floan: a unit of time similar to one year.

Forest of Omnicron: also known as *the Forest of O*; a wilderness in the restricted/annexed area of Ethar.

freston: the tricked-out, riflelike black gun.

fritzer: a type of card game.

Gurtrone: an Etharian shoe designer.

Hallafast: a fast airship that resembles a hawk.

hovercar: also known as a *skiff*; a car capable of flying. It is propelled by forced air and does not have wheels.

Inium: the smallest of Ethar's moons. It is blue in color.

Isle of Skye: the city where the Regent's palace and the corrective court are located. It's the legal center of the House of Rafe.

kafcan: a beverage that is similar in every way to dark-roast coffee.

Kalafin: capital city of the House of Wurthem.

knob knocker: an Etharian curse word.

Loch of Cerulean: the tropical island where Kyon's estate is located in Alameeda territory. A body of water on Ethar. The political seat of the Alameeda Brother, reminiscent of a fiefdom.

Oxfortshire: a town in Wurthem where Em Sam lives.

overup: an elevator that moves up, down, sideways, and slantways.

part: an Etharian hour.

Peney: one of the five clan-houses of Ethar. This House has always remained neutral in wartime. A member of the Peney House.

Rafe: one of the five clan-houses of Ethar. An ally of Comantre. A member of the Rafe House.

Rafian: a citizen of Rafe.

recurve: a crossbow.

Riker Pak: an Alameeda jet pack.

sanctumizer: a small flash grenade. A nonlethal explosive device used to temporarily disorient an enemy's senses.

Ship of Skye: a floating military fortress owned and operated by the House of Rafe and their Skye Council.

skiff: also known as a *hovercar*, a hovering car capable of flying. It is propelled by forced air and does not have wheels.

slipshield: a clear sticker resembling the symbol on a USB port that can be used as a locator.

soothsayer: a priestess who has the ability to know through intuition if someone is lying.

speck: an Etharian month.

spix: a horse with wicked-sharp horns behind its ears (plural is *spixes*).

squelch tracker: a heat-seeking, automated bomb that can be programmed to assassinate a target.

Striker: a member of an elite body of troops trained to serve the Alameeda Brotherhood.

Sylvan Square: a part of the city of Urbenoster, where Kyon and Kricket attend a street fair.

Syndic: a member of the Comantre military.

tankoid: a small breathing apparatus containing oxygen used for underwater respiration.

Terraglide: an oval-shaped aircraft.

Triclone: Pan Hollowell's Cavar unit.

trift: a smaller jet that looks like a Stealth Fighter.

Urbenoster: Capital city of House Alameeda.

venish: venisonlike meat pie.

visor: a medical device, also known as *grandma goggles* or an *ostioscope*, that fits over the eyes like glasses and used to perform a full-body scan. It checks vitals: synapse firing, dendrite chemical composition, reuptake rates.

White Sestin: Dobrey's trift.

Wurthem: one of the five clan-houses of Ethar. An ally of Alameeda. A member of the Wurthem House.

zenith: noon.

znou: a dangerous flower known to be teeming with turbine worms. It grows in the restricted area of Ethar. The petals are poisonous if ingested, causing the erosion of organs. The plural is *znous*.

znou axicote: poison from the znou flower.

About the Author

Photo © 2013 Georgia Cates

Amy A. Bartol is the award-winning and bestselling author of the Kricket Series (*Under Different Stars* and *Sea of Stars*) and the Premonition Series: *Inescapable, Intuition, Indebted, Incendiary*, and *Iniquity*. She lives in Michigan with her husband and their two sons. Visit her at her website: www.amyabartol.com.